D1715716

A NIGHT TO REMEMBER

"I'm willing to forget that you're a mystery man as long as I know this isn't an unexpected amusement for you."

Don't think that, Caroline, not even for a moment," Sinclair said. "When I came out on the terrace tonight, my mind was full of plans for retribution and revenge, but as soon as I saw you, all that seemed to fade."

Slowly his hands came up to clasp her shoulders, and even in the dim light Caro could feel his eyes smoldering as he looked at her. A response began to form deep inside her, spreading like lacy tendrils through her veins.

"If I were any sort of gentleman, we wouldn't be here right now," he said, all the while pulling her closer.

Caro's arms encircled his neck. "As far as I'm concerned, you're a perfect gentleman."

"What wonderful flattery." His mouth brushed lightly against hers. "And for that there's only one reward. . . ."

Remembrances

Eleanora Brownleigh

PINNACLE BOOKS
WINDSOR PUBLISHING CORP.

PINNACLE BOOKS

are published by

Windsor Publishing Corp.
475 Park Avenue South
New York, NY 10016

First printing: May, 1988

Printed in the United States of America

Sweet are the uses of adversity.
Which, like the toad, ugly and venomous,
Wears yet a precious jewel in its head;
And this our life, exempt from public haunt,
Finds tongues in trees, books in the running brooks,
Sermons in stones, and good in every thing.

William Shakespeare
As you Like It, Act II, Scene I

Chapter 1

The wig was a perfect fit. Shortly after the invitation had come, Caroline Worth had gone to a highly regarded theatrical wigmaker with her drawings, and now she was wearing the perfect results. Unfortunately, it was all too clear that her carefully thought-out costume wasn't appreciated by many of the other female guests.

It's as if these idiots have never heard of a Manchu princess before, she thought, keeping back her laughter as she accepted a glass of champagne from

7

a tray held by a polite footman. What a pretentious crowd. Well, Caroline, you wanted to come, so you'd better make the best of it. All I can hope is that the midnight buffet will be worthy of this place.

The Linden Trees—like its equally lofty predecessors, Meadowbrook, Shinnecock Hills, and Garden City Golf—was a country club whose members were influential and wealthy New Yorkers. It offered them a perfectly laid-out golf course and a large clubhouse with every modern convenience. Tonight the main floor reception rooms were decorated for the holiday season with rich swags of evergreen and Della Robbia wreaths, and in the ballroom, quite near to where Caroline stood, was the tree, a large douglas fir with gold and silver *papier-mâché* ornaments hanging from its branches.

There was such a holiday atmosphere here that Caroline almost forgot her feeling of being out of place . . . almost. The whispers she was sure she was supposed to hear reached her ears and reminded her just where she was.

"Well, of all the costumes to choose! Just who do you think she is?"

"Oh, I don't know. I heard someone say she's just back from China."

There was the sound of a definite sniff. "*That's* obvious, my dear. Why else come as a Chinese unless you've lived there?"

And to think that for this I left Cove House, Caroline thought, sipping her champagne so that she didn't give away her true thoughts and laugh at the two young women, their hoopskirts swaying and

8

1860s-style dresses rustling as they walked past her. If they're going to insult me, they can at least learn the difference between Chinese and Manchu. What bores.

"Now, Caro, the champagne can't be that bad. Your expression is positively grim!"

"Actually, the champagne *is* rather good," Caroline told Richard and Megan North. She had come to the costume ball with the Norths, and now she noted that Dick, wearing his father's 1865 Union Army dress uniform, and Megan, in an 1834 dress of cream taffeta with lace ornaments that her Charleston grandmother had worn to a St. Cecilia ball, were two of the most attractively costumed guests in the club. "It's only some of the people we have to drink it with that bother me."

"Most of them are rather . . . overdone," Megan agreed after a moment's consideration. "Most of these costumes should be worn at a private party on Fifth Avenue, not at a Long Island country club."

"You mean something like the Bradley-Martin ball," Caro suggested wickedly, referring to an overly elaborate costume ball of several years before. It had had such repercussions in a time of financial panic that the party-givers had had to leave the country and take up residence in England. "It's all the same crew, or maybe I've been away too long."

"Or possibly a dance would help," Dick suggested. "Shall we?"

"No, I think a Strauss waltz belongs to a happily married couple," she returned, and gave them one of her few genuine smiles of the evening. "I'm going out to the terrace to get some air."

"It's freezing out tonight!"

"Oh, Meggie, it's not that bad, and I'm not going to wander over the grounds."

"Well, don't stay out there too long—you don't want to miss the buffet. There's always the chance that it will be good."

"Don't we all hope." With characteristic ease, she placed her champagne glass on the nearest surface, and after a final word with the Norths, began to walk across the ballroom, threading her way past the richly costumed men and women. She passed a woman representing the Empress Theodora, another gowned as a Venetian lady of the eighteenth century in orange brocade and black velvet and topped with a powdered wig, and a lady trying for an imitation of Elizabeth I, but with a countenance that strongly suggested Mary Tudor. Among the men she saw a Doge of Venice, a Roman general, and a Regency dandy, none of whom did any more justice to their costumes than the women did.

But all these people look *normal* to each other, she realized, neatly avoiding a young woman about her own age who was resplendent in a gown of the richest pale-pink taffeta with scalloped edges, rose-ribbon bows, and silver lace ruffles that Marie Antoinette would have panted to own. And I'm the one who looks odd, she thought.

But if she seemed oddly costumed to her fellow guests, it was a difference Caro reveled in. Her wig copied to perfection the style of a highborn Manchu

10

lady in a wing-like arrangement on top of her head, and her robe of peacock-blue brocade embroidered in gold, with wide, loose sleeves, fell below her knees, contrasting with wide black satin trousers and black satin pumps with court heels. Whether it was the wig, her kohl-rimmed eyes drawn to give her a slightly Oriental look, or the idea that part of her costume consisted of trousers, as she approached the series of French doors that opened out along the length of her terrace, all eyes were on her. In a gathering that was largely overdressed and over-bejeweled, Caroline Worth was an attraction in herself.

Caro shivered slightly as she stepped outside, but the cold air was a welcome counterpoint to the stuffiness inside, and she walked along the stone path, away from the ballroom and the sound of the orchestra playing yet another Strauss waltz. This was definitely not the gala pre-Christmas gathering she had expected.

I've been away from New York too long, she thought, leaning against the stone balustrade. The people here tonight—except for Dick and Megan—aren't my friends, so there's no reason why I should feel displaced or annoyed. This isn't the first awful party I've been to, and it won't be the last, but it's a bad sign when the buffet sounds like the best part of the night.

It had been more than a year since she had left the Orient, but Caro felt a sharp pang of longing for China, for the homes in Peking and Shanghai and Hong Kong tht she'd shared with her father and stepmother, and for the enchantment of living in a country that was a never-ending mystery. But that part of her life was a closed chapter now, Caro reminded herself, and her passing chill had nothing to do with the cold night. They had left New York for China in June 1893, and now it was December 1901; eight-and-a-half years in the Far East, and then the past year in Hawaii, in a beautiful white house on Diamond Head, where she and her stepmother had settled in to spend their year of mourning for Garrison Worth.

It hadn't been hard for Caroline and Vanessa to decide to come back to New York. No matter what their wanderings in a part of the world whose mildest description was exotic, this was home. Strange to think that only ten weeks earlier the Pacific Mail Line's *Manchuria* had taken them from Honolulu to San Francisco, and within a week after arriving in California, they were back east, settled in a suite at the Waldorf-Astoria.

The miracle of modern transportation, she thought, listening to the music behind her and staring into the darkness ahead. Somewhere out there was a golf course, and the Long Island Sound; inside, men and women were dancing and drinking champagne and having, she supposed, a wonderful time. And I'm out here, sorry I came, distracted, and all alone. . . .

" 'Lawn as white as driven snow, cypress black e'er was snow,' " a quiet, well-bred male voice said behind her. "Very appropriate, don't you think, Allie?"

Caro swung quickly around. The man standing

12

not three feet from her, wearing superbly tailored white-tie and tails, a black silk mask covering the upper half of his face, was definitely not a guest here tonight. She was sure of that. At twenty-six, with nearly ten years behind her of followers and callers and beaux and even one almost lover, she knew how to come to a party and scan it for interesting, intelligent, and available men. And this man—whoever he was and whatever he looked like under that mask—hadn't been in the ballroom earlier.

"I couldn't agree with you more—and my name isn't Allie," she told him, and even in the shadows she saw a flash of surprise pass quickly over his eyes.

"Please forgive my mistake," he replied immediately. "When I first saw you, I thought you were someone I knew a long time ago. It was the light, or rather the lack of it; and the lady I assumed I was seeing again would select a costume like yours," he explained. Even with his formal tone and highwayman's mask, Caro thought this stranger rather appealing.

"As long as you've mentioned *A Winter's Tale*, perhaps I should say 'Sure this robe of mine does change my disposition.'"

"Does it? Change you, I mean."

"Not at all, and it's completely lost on the people inside. Except for the friends I came with, no one can tell the difference between Manchu and Chinese."

"A Manchu lady never has bound feet," he said, and came to stand beside her.

"You have just saved my evening," Caro responded.

"Anything for a beautiful lady," the stranger answered with a gallant bow, and Caro wondered what he looked like in full light and without the mask. "You must be new to this part of the country," he added.

"I hate to be a disappointment so early, but I'm a born and bred New Yorker, albeit one who has been absent for several years."

"And you've been in China. But I won't make the mistake of saying your father went there to make his fortune."

"A perceptive man is always appreciated. Just before you made yourself known, I was thinking that all those years in the Orient, and the last year in Hawaii, went by so quickly," she told him. "Right after my father died, the days dragged on endlessly, but as soon as my stepmother and I landed in San Francisco it all started to go again, and this time like a steam locomotive. I still don't think I've adjusted."

"I know that feeling all too well," he said, and for a minute they shared a companionable silence. "I hate to tell you this, but a part of that isolation never goes away, and you always feel that you've lost something that can't be recaptured, that you'll never really belong again."

For just a moment, Caro felt she had a passing glimpse into this man's complicated feelings, and she was suddenly sure that although he might be an uninvited guest, he was not here because he wanted to be at a highly social event.

"You must have had a great many unhappy experiences to say that," she replied as gently as she could.

"It's all very complicated, very much along the line of 'Though I am native here and to the manor born.'"

"Does quoting *Hamlet* mean that you don't have an invitation?"

"I have to remember that fooling an astute lady is out of the question."

"Oh, I wouldn't say you were trying to fool me. I think the correct word would be evade—"

Slowly, very slowly, he began to smile. "Would it help if I told you that I'm here on a secret and very important mission?"

"Well, I didn't think you came to show off your costume." Her eyes had long since adjusted to the darkness, and with the diffused light coming from the ballroom, she not only liked what she could see, but enjoyed his company. "Can you tell me if you've had any success, or are you still trying to corner your quarry?"

Even in the half-darkness, she could see the startled look in his eyes, and she was sure that under the concealing mask his features were overlaid with surprise.

"How did you know?" he asked, a rough edge to his well-bred voice.

"You're not some society sponger," Caro replied, not at all intimidated by the sudden change in his voice. "You also don't want to be here any more than I do, so it stands to reason that you would want to get your meeting started as quickly as possible."

"Then you don't know who I am?"

"Have you considered taking off your mask?"

"That wouldn't be the wisest thing I could do."

"Ah, I see. You keep it on to intimidate your opponent."

"I doubt it—he's a tough old bird. Or so I thought. No, I'd rather keep it on to intrigue certain ladies."

Caro laughed. "I just bet."

"Are you intrigued? Isn't meeting me like this something for you and your girlfriends to giggle over?"

"You don't know my girlfriends. But I am interested," Caro told him. I'm enjoying this, she thought. But why does he think I should know him? "I'm glad that's over."

"Excuse me?"

"The latest Strauss waltz," she explained. "They've played so many tonight I'm starting to think that the musicians come from Vienna."

"Well, if the next selection isn't straight from the Vienna Woods, may I have the dance?"

The question was so thoroughly unexpected that it seemed to fall between them like a star from the sky.

Caro took a deep breath in an effort to quiet her suddenly pounding heart. "I can hardly call you a calculating man," she said after a minute's silence.

"In fact, it seems your request is more like a slip of the tongue, and from what I can see in this light, you seem surprised at what came out of your mouth."

"Are you going to let me off the hook?"

"Guess again."

"Going in that ballroom on my arm and dancing with me is not going to enhance your reputation."

"Oh, *please*. Can't you come up with something more interesting than *that*?"

"I mean it."

"I'm sure you do."

"This isn't funny."

"Not to you," Caro said, her patience wearing thin. Apparent good looks and breeding could carry a man only so far. "But would you care to tell me in specific terms why I'd be in such social danger if I'm seen with you?"

"Because I'm Sinclair Poole."

Chapter Two

For a second Caroline simply looked at him, a feeling of exasperation settling over her.

"Am I supposed to recoil in horror, faint, or run far away from you?" she inquired with a slight edge to her voice.

"I'm the most notorious man in New York."

"That's what they *all* say."

Quite suddenly, at age thirty-two, Sinclair Poole felt as untried and stymied as he had on his first day at Miss Viola Wolff's dancing class. All he had wanted was a few minutes of fresh, cold air to banish the after effects of his meeting. Ten minutes to give the man he had come to see time to pull himself together, and then it would be back to the card room to collect the letter he had spent six years seeking. The conspiracy that had destroyed his father and enriched a small group of men almost beyond belief was going to be exposed, but his delightful thoughts of revenge long delayed had abruptly ended when he'd seen a Manchu princess leaning against the stone railing of the terrace. For a moment, from his place in the shadows, he thought she was someone else, but almost at the same time that he realized his mistake, he was talking to her. His elation at having the hour of his retribution almost at hand faded as he slowly accepted the fact that he'd rather be with the woman whose name he still didn't know.

"I thought you should know that," he offered finally, some primal instinct warning him that this was not a woman to whom he should use the word *protect* in any way, shape, or form.

"I appreciate your interest, and as long as we're introducing ourselves, I'm Caroline Worth," she said, allowing a suitable interval to pass.

"I never thought I'd meet anyone like you tonight, but I'm suddenly very glad I have," he told her with an almost boyish grin that in no way reduced his sophisticated demeanor. "And for the record, I most certainly *do* want to dance with you—as long as it's not Strauss."

"That sounds perfectly reasonable to me. Shall we go into the ballroom?" Caro asked, tucking an arm through his. "Or am I really keeping you from your business appointment?"

Sinclair took a deep breath, and the crisp December air was all but lost due to the fragrant cloud of Guerlain's Jicky that surrounded Caro. "Business can always wait. But be prepared for when we walk in. Your friends are going to have a very decided reaction."

"Oh, I have a lot of friends," she told him, "and only two of them are here tonight."

When they first entered through the French doors, no one in the ballroom seemed to notice them. It was almost time for the buffet supper, and the guests who'd wandered off to other parts of the clubhouse began to return as the orchestra played the opening notes of John Philip Sousa's "Jewel of the Ocean Waltz." Sinclair and Caroline were among the first couples on the highly polished dance floor, and they had their first look at each other in full light—or, at as much as they could see, considering their disguises.

Caro was tall, over five-eight, and with her court-heeled shoes she was on eye level with Sin—a situation she found most enjoyable. Despite the black mask that obscured his face from forehead to nose, she could see he had rich brown hair, amber eyes, a sensitive-looking upper lip, a mouth that seemed not to smile very often, and a chin that showed that whatever else he might be, he was nobody's fool.

Not bad for a discovery in the dark, she thought as they twirled around the floor in a series of complicated steps in time to the lively music. On the other hand, leave it to me to find a man who sounds like he's living his very own mystery novel.

More than a few of the other men present had—wisely, in Caro's opinion—eschewed fancy costumes for white-tie—aided by identity-concealing masks—and at first Sin was all but indistinguishable from at least half a dozen other men of similar age and build. But as he had warned Caro, he lived under such a cloud that his presence could literally be sensed. For her part, Caro had often been to functions where one guest or other wasn't up to some great unwritten mark, but it had never been like this; the looks, the headturning, and the hissing comments had an edge of pure spite to them.

"Look! It's him."

"No . . . yes. I don't believe it. How dare he!"

"Do you remember. . . ?"

"How could anyone forget?"

"We have to do something about this. . . ."

"Do you suppose he has an invitation?"

"Don't be silly. He's crashed our lovely costume ball and ruined it!"

At that last comment, loudly whispered by a much-too-stout lady arrayed in a rich Louis XIV lavender satin gown, Sin and Caro could barely contain their laughter. "I told you so," he whispered to her.

"So what—this is the most fun I've had in ages. You seem to forget that I'm not a member of this club, either," Caro returned as they continued to dance, attracting even more looks than comments, with expressions that ranged from the curious to the outraged. "What is it exactly that you're so guilty of?"

"Nothing I could be put in jail for."

"A social indiscretion, then, such as refusing to marry a very suitable but highly boring young lady?"

"Actually, she refused to marry me," he replied, and from the look that appeared in his eyes, Caro saw at once that he was telling the truth. "Actually, there's also something far more serious than that, and when the dance is over, I have to leave."

"I don't mind going back out to the terrace, as long as it's with you," she responded. For a night that had been going badly, she now seemed to be caught up in a definite act of intrigue and was determined to enjoy every moment of it. "I'll go back in when the buffet opens, and you can go back to your business meeting."

"If you hadn't reminded me just now, I honestly might have forgotten that someone is waiting for me in one of the card rooms."

"I wish I could say that I'm sorry," Caro told him as they swirled out of the center of the dance floor and toward the edge of the dancing couples.

"And I'm glad I was so unsuccessful at convincing you that you shouldn't dance with me," Sin said, and a new sight appeared in his amber eyes. "Caro—"

Whatever he meant to say was cut off as the final notes of the waltz were played, and as they walked across the floor and out the doors, his conversation went in another direction. "No one is going to stop talking about us for the next week," Sin said. "But I'm not going to ask if you mind."

"Do you?" Caro threw back at him.

"Why did you come here tonight?" he asked unexpectedly. "This is not exactly your sort of crowd."

"My stepmother and I are spending the holidays out at Cove House, and when the invitation arrived, I thought it would be fun to go to a Long Island country club party. It appears it's quite a bit less than I expected—and a lot more. And you?''

"I take it you're not asking me why I came,'' Sin inquired softly.

"I think we can go a little beyond that.'' Caro found herself wishing that they were free of their costumes and disguises and were any place but here. "I'm even willing to forget that you're a mystery man as long as I know that this isn't an unexpected amusement for you.''

"Don't think that, Caroline, not even for a moment,'' he said, a new and richer tone to his voice. "When I came out to the terrace tonight, my mind was full of plans for retribution and revenge, but as soon as we started talking, all those plans seemed to fade.''

"As long as I wasn't imagining that there's magic between us—'' Caro began, but before she could go any further, another couple stepped through the French doors, disrupting their privacy. "So much for no one coming after us,'' she murmured.

"As long as they're not carrying tar and feathers, I'm willing to share our trysting spot with them,'' Sin whispered back as they walked the length of the terrace, stopping only when they reached their original meeting spot. "And as for there being magic between us—''

Slowly his hands came up to clasp her shoulders, and even in the dim light Caro could feel his eyes smoldering as they looked at her. A response began to form deep inside her and then spread like lacy tendrils through her veins. The instinct on which she so heavily depended told her that Sinclair Poole was not the sort of man who played silly flirting games. From the moment they spoke, she had been far more direct with him than she would have been with any other man. Quite logically she knew her actions hadn't been based on the natural attraction provided by a mystery man whom she might never see again, but rather on a rare feeling of mutual trust.

"If I were any sort of gentleman, we wouldn't be here right now," he said at last, all the while pulling her closer into his embrace.

Caro's arms encircled his neck. "As far as I'm concerned, you're a perfect gentleman."

"What wonderful flattery." Sin's mouth brushed lightly against hers. "And for that there's only one reward."

Why was one man's kiss so different from another's? It was as much a theory as a question, and one that Caro had considered on more than one occasion. It really had nothing to do with looks, since she knew some stunning men who didn't make the basic requirements at all, and some diamond-in-the-rough sorts who knew all the tricks. But Sinclair was different and, for her, the best—not that she wouldn't want to have lots of confirmation, she decided, the cold of the night driven away by the warmth of his body and the pressure of his mouth against hers. It seemed that every fiber of her being was affected by the kiss they shared.

"I know you have to see someone here," Caro said after an endless pause, resting her head on Sin's shoulder. "But do you have to make a dash for it as soon as it's over?"

"I thought I'd have to, but now I'm not sure," he said, and surprised himself even further by his next words. "I have my carriage waiting for me, but I might be persuaded to follow you back to Cove House."

Caro laughed and kissed him again. "Am I on the right track?" she whispered in his ear.

"Very much so . . . I may even take my mask off."

"I think that would be a good idea," she returned in a level voice, but her thoughts were already racing ahead, imagining their arrival at Cove House, introducing him to Vanessa, seeing him without his mask. "Shall we have our second kiss without your mask coming between us?"

"Our third kiss," he promised, pulling her closer. "When this meeting is over, when I have the letter that will clear my father's name, when I've done what I set out to do. . . ."

The second kiss was more demanding than the first, but it also held more promise. It was the realization of a man and a woman, each of whom had been through difficult times, that they were nearing a new beginning. But they were on very fragile ground, ground that had been watered over the years with tears of fury and frustration, and it gave way beneath them with the sound of a single gunshot.

Instantly, they pulled apart from each other, and as women screamed and men shouted, they looked at each other in shock and surprise. At the other end of the terrace, the other couple disappeared inside, and through the open French doors the rising babble of voices was growing louder by the second.

But Sin didn't have to listen to them for a clue to what had happened. He knew what the gunshot meant the moment he heard it, and horror seeped through every inch of him as a male voice shouted, "Davis Moreton's dead! He's shot himself!"

"Damn, damn it all," Sin swore, anger replacing horror. "I had him in the palm of my hand, and now I've lost it all!"

"Sin *Sinclair!*" Caro grabbed his shoulders. "What is it, what are you talking about?"

"There's no time to tell you, but plenty of others are going to be more than happy to do it for me. Please don't believe them if they tell you I drove him to this.'

"No, I'd never do that, but can't you tell me—"

"No, I can't stay. They'll want a scapegoat, and I'll be it!"

Caro's heart pounded raggedly and her mind was full of questions, but the one she was determined not to ask was "Will I see you again?" Her intense pride would rather she be romanced and abandoned than have to inquire about his true feelings. But something else was far more important now. Sin had been on the verge of revealing his mystery to her; now that door had been slammed, and there was only time for her to decide if she trusted him.

Yes, she thought, and knew what she had to do.

"Go on," she told him. "I'll handle everything here. Is your carriage far off?"

"No, just very well hidden. Caro—"

"It's all right. I *do* understand."

"I'll explain it all to you soon, I promise," he said, and almost allowed himself the luxury of kissing her again. " 'Now I will believe that there are unicorns,' " Sin quoted, and he went over the balustrade, disappearing into the darkness, swallowed up by the night almost as if he hadn't been on the terrace at all.

Chapter Three

Sinclair Poole hit the ground running. With the speed and skill that had made him such a stellar athlete during his student days at Columbia University, he covered the dark and icy ground that surrounded The Linden Trees. The sprawling mansion-sized clubhouse with lights blazing from every window served as his guide to the spot off the long gravel driveway where the closed brougham was waiting for him.

There wasn't the slightest chance that the Woodbury Police would arrive in less than twenty minutes, by which time he wanted to be well on his way back to New York. He slowed his pace slightly—the last thing he wanted was to take a flop on the icy, winter-hard terrain. He'd had enough surprises for one night.

"Mr. Poole, please don't run like that—it's dangerous in the country at this time of year," George Kelly said. He stepped out of the shadows formed by the large, leafless trees and the brougham, his professional boxer's body made even more bulky by the long, heavy overcoat he wore. A fashionable bowler was tipped forward over his forehead, but the gaily-striped muffler wrapped around his throat in no way reflected his mood; if anything, George was more apprehensive than the man whose bodyguard he was. "It hasn't gone well," he said flatly, making a statement, not a question. "Did Moreton back out on you at the last minute?"

"You might say that," Sin responded, pulling off his mask as George, with the skill of a trained valet, put the velvet-collared Chesterfield he'd left behind over his shoulders. "Davis Moreton's dead—he shot himself."

"He committed suicide in front of you?" George's voice was openly shocked.

"No, and I don't know all the details. With this crowd, I wasn't going to have a glass of champagne while I waited for the police," he said, opening the door of the brougham. Let's get out of here before the police come. With my luck, the police chief here has a hankering to see his name in the New York papers."

"Sean, see to the horses. It's time we got out of here, so be quick about it!" George instructed his young cousin, who began to pull the heavy plaid blankets from the patiently waiting horses. He trusted Sean, but George still waited until they were inside the tan velvet interior of the brougham before speaking again. "You know that if someone saw you—or even thought they did—you'd have to talk to the police.''

''And I'll tell them anything they want to know— on my own territory,'' Sin replied with his usual coolness as he wrapped one of the fur-lined lap robes around him. Suddenly he was tired and chilled to the bone, and the nagging pain in his right side was worse after his exertion. ''I came so damn close I can't believe it,'' he said, and gave George the details of his meeting with Davis Moreton. ''And now I'm back where I started.''

''Why did you leave him alone for so long?'' George insisted.

''He was very upset, and asked me as one gentleman to another to please give him a few minutes. And I fell for it.''

''If you'll forgive my saying so, Mr. Poole, from the way you describe it, it seems to me that you gave Moreton more than a few minutes.''

''I did the right thing by going out to the terrace. I just didn't expect to meet someone I could have an interesting conversation with.''

George didn't need a theater program to tell him what had happened. ''I hope she's pretty.''

For the first time since his hasty escape, Sin smiled. ''For a moment, I thought she was someone else, but we got past that—talked, had a dance, and, yes, George, she is very pretty.'

. ''I should have known.'' George's voice was distinctly good-natured. ''And I won't even inquire if you danced with this lady on the privacy of the terrace.''

"Since I screwed up everything else tonight, why should I have been careful about that? No, don't answer."

The brougham was on the road now, and since Sean was a steady and proven hand with the horses—when he wasn't going on about those new motorcars—George allowed himself the luxury of leaning back against the seat and relaxing just a little bit. He didn't like how Sinclair looked, not at all. But then, as the Bard of Avon had written in *Othello,* what wound did ever heal but by degrees? George Kelly, once a professional boxer and now Sinclair Poole's personal bodyguard, knew Shakespeare inside out and always had an appropriate quote handy, but now his mind was occupied by another question, one he knew would be asked and debated in countless other situations. He knew what drove Sinclair and recognized it as a righteous cause motivated by love and the need for truth and justice. But as that quest came closer and closer to being accomplished, all he could wonder about was that when his employer got his revenge, what would he do with it?

"Have I been asleep long, George?"

"Twenty minutes or so, Mr. Poole. We're on the main road now."

"I'm glad to hear that." Sinclair stirred uncomfortably and ran a hand through his thick, closely cut hair. "Now to figure out where I go from here."

" 'Yield not thy neck to fortune's neck, but let

thy dauntless mind still ride in triumph over all mischance,' " George advised.

"Yes, but look what happened to Hamlet," Sin pointed out. "If only I had gotten that letter. . . ." His voice trailed off, aware that if he continued to dwell on his loss it would eventually begin to obstruct everything else he had to do. "I hope Caro isn't having a hard time with the Linden Trees crowd."

"She's not one of them?"

"She's better."

"I didn't doubt that for a minute, but was it quite the gentlemanly thing to do, leaving a young lady to face those wolves?" George asked with a faint hint of disapproval.

"Miss Caroline Worth may have just returned from the Orient, but she is most definitely not just off the boat."

"I'm very relieved to hear that," George returned, and paused for a moment. "We should be in Garden City soon. I have a friend who keeps a rather good roadhouse near there, and he'll have something hot for us to eat. What say you to a piece of beef and mustard?"

" 'Ah, good Grumio, we're a good way from Padua.' " Sinclair managed a slight smile. "I'm not very hungry, but a stop sounds like a good idea."

"We won't stay too long. We don't want the police dropping in on us in the middle of the roast beef, and Gregori's probably chewing the wallpaper by now—he was more nervous than you were about tonight."

"Greg will be fine," Sin said, referring to Gregori Vestovich, who was his secretary and had a background that was all but completely shrouded in mystery. "I won't call him from Garden City, though. At this time of night you can never be sure that a bored operator isn't going to listen in."

George agreed, and both men lapsed into silence, each absorbed in his own thoughts. The older man was replaying every detail that had gone into tonight's meeting, and he assumed Sin was doing the same, but for once the perceptive, Shakespeare-quoting bodyguard was quite wrong.

Despite his problems of the past six years—and quite possibly because of them—Sinclair had never had any difficulty when it came to attracting women. He was equally appealing to them no matter what their station, and although most of is assignations had to be carried out with a high degree of privacy, his choices certainly weren't limited. But whenever he dwelled on a particular woman, only two could totally occupy his thoughts—the woman who would have stood by him and the one who used him . . . until tonight.

Caroline Worth, he thought. *Caro.* What did we get ourselves into, and what have I left you to face? Of course, if I had to take a bet on anyone coming out on top, it's you.

Slowly, almost as if he were reading it in a very intricately plotted and paced novel, it began to dawn on Sin that for all of his behaving like a high-society highwayman, complete with identity-concealing mask, he had been reminded of his humanity and his vulnerability in a very special way. The thought of revenge had formed such a core in the center of his being that all else revolved aroung it, and that quest was the prime mover of his life, or so he thought. But now Caroline had seemingly cut through all of that. To vindicate his father was still paramount, but other things were crowding in on him, reminding him that life was meant to be multifaceted.

And one more thing, besides.

Sinclair was long used to being able to steal the hearts of interested women with ease, but now for the first time, he had not only collected a heart that he could treasure more than any other, but he had left his own behind in return.

Chapter Four

Caroline surveyed the ballroom, feelings of distaste and contempt mingling within her as she saw the pandemonium taking place. A man had just committed suicide, and most of the people in their rich assortment of costumes were acting as if Davis Moreton had pulled the trigger with the sole purpose of deliberately ruining their lovely gathering.

So far, no one had noticed her return, and she made her way through the chattering throng to where Dick and Megan were waiting beside the Christmas tree, trying hard not to attract any of the other gossiping, speculating guests.

"That was some few minutes on the terrace," Dick remarked. "I take it you and Sinclair hit it off?"

"Do you know him? I mean really, not just to gossip about?"

"I know him to speak to—if he wants to speak, that is—but as for knowing him—"

"Oh, Dick, don't be cryptic!" Megan exclaimed. "Not after all that's happened tonight. It's a long and terribly complicated tale," she told Caro, "and the details will have to wait until we get back to Cove House."

"I can be patient. I hate to find anything amusing in a suicide, but it looks as if the curtain is about to go up," she said. A stout, balding man whom she had been introduced to earlier as Palmer Harris, the president of the Linden Trees, mounted the steps to the musicians' dais, and in a stentorian voice that would have done credit to the best Washington politician, requested silence and everyone's attention.

"My friends, a terrible tragedy has taken place here tonight. One of our charter members, a dear friend and great gentleman, Davis Moreton, is dead. Unfortunately, there are some questions about the manner of his demise and the police have been summoned. At the request of the Woodbury police chief, I must request that none of you leave, but to make our wait easier, I suggest that we enjoy the buffet set up in the dining room and raise our glasses in a toast to our dear, departed friend."

"Well, so much for sneaking out of here early," Dick said. "Shall we get something to eat, ladies?"

In Caroline's unvoiced opinion, the club dining room, nearly as large as the ballroom, lacked only heraldic flags hanging from the exposed oak beams to resemble the great hall of an old English country house. The tables, set for four and eight, were weighed down with heavy damask tablecloths. On each was a centerpiece consisting of a silver bowl of red carnations surrounded by small lamps with red-silk shades with crystal beaded fringe. Heavy silver place settings and water goblets and champagne glasses of fine crystal with deep gold borders complemented the service. Royal Doulton buffet plates of white, gold, and cobalt blue were stacked on a serving table near the buffet that at first glance seemed to stretch on forever.

Apparently even the assumed suicide of a highly regarded member of the club wasn't enough to dim the appetites of the guests, Caro observed. They took their plates and joined the rapidly growing line for the supper everyone had thought would be filled with such holiday cheer and celebrating. If nothing else, this was as good a chance as any to see if it was true that food could soothe and sustain one in the middle of a crisis.

Oysters were in full season, and first they were presented with an abundance of Chincoteagues on beds of crushed ice in large copper trays. Next there were a succulent turkey, roast beef, and a Smithfield ham waiting to be sliced by white-toqued chefs and then garnished with candied sweet potatoes and creamed celerey au gratin. If that didn't appeal, there were a series of copper chafing dishes filled with chicken à la king, lobster Newburg, and beef Stroganoff with rice. There was an endive salad with a choice of Russian dressing or chutney sauce, and finally there were the desserts: a maçedoine of fruit to be topped with whipped cream, marron parfaits, chocolate mousse, lemon snow, and, appropriate for the season, a lavish cake topped with slivered almonds.

"How can these people eat like this?" Caro whispered to the Norths as they took possession of an empty table near the doors. She had considered each dish carefully and now had a very small serving of lobster Newburg, a large serving of salad, and a stemmed crystal dish of lemon snow. Unhappily, compared to the laden plates of most of the other guests, her selections looked like subsistence rations. "A man—supposedly their devoted friend—shot himself; we're all waiting for the police; and they're stuffing themselves like it's Thanksgiving Day all over again!"

"People do get hungry when they dance," Dick pointed out mildly, signaling for a waiting footman to fill their glasses with champagne. He looked at his plate of oysters with obvious relish. "Also, my dear Caro, never underestimate the drawing power of a free meal!"

Despite her misgivings, Caro couldn't help laughing. Over the next few minutes, the three friends discussed the latest books—always a favorite topic since Dick was an important editor at Doubleday, Page—and the Osborne, a justifiably famous New York apartment building where the Norths made their home and where Caroline and Vanessa had recently taken up residence.

"We've done quite a bit of decorating already, and hope to get it finished by the middle of January," she offered. "We're looking forward to having a home of our own again, but every so often we wish we had something from our Peking house.''

''Did the Boxers take it all?'' Meg asked.

''No, the house was too neatly cleaned out for a crowd to have carried it all off, and we had it from very good sources that the mob that broke in were definitely *not* Boxers, although they probably had their protection.'' Caro moved her fork over and between the endive leaves, spreading the Russian dressing more evenly. ''At any rate, it's all gone now, and we can't waste our time hoping we'll find it again.''

''You can always use that excuse to contact Sinclair again,'' Megan pointed out as they ate.

''What help would that be of to me?''

''I thought you knew, that he must have told you—''

''Told me what?''

Megan glanced at her husband, who was happily eating his oysters and clearly not about to become involved. ''Sinclair's a dealer in Orientalia, and very successful at it, too.''

''Well, sometime soon I hope we can talk about the Orient together,'' Caro responded, deciding that this was the safest comment to make.

''Just hope that you won't have to make that conversation on visitor's day,'' Dick remarked, his handsome face serious.

Caro, in the act of lifting a bite of lemon snow to her mouth, returned the spoon to the dessert dish. A cold tremor ran through her as she remembered Sin saying that he had to leave before he became a very convenient scapegoat. "How can a man be arrested for another man's suicide?" she asked, keeping her voice level.

"Caro, you know that when a man of Davis Moreton's prominence kills himself, there's a terrible stigma slapped on both the deceased and his family," Dick said in a quiet voice, and Caro recalled that before pursuing a career in publishing, Dick had studied law. "The first instinct of the family—the most natural instinct—is to deny it and if at all possible, assign the blame to someone else."

The cold feeling in the pit of Caroline's stomach was joined by a swift rush of concern for Sinclair: he had been right to leave, but was he also right to think that they would try to pin it on him?

"You do know that if Sinclair needs an alibi, I'm it—and there was another couple on the terrace with us."

"Did they see the two of you together?"

"Yes."

There was a brief pause as waiters arrived to pour fresh champagne into their glasses and deliver small silver baskets filled with chocolate bonbons, glacé nuts, and cherries iced in frosting. Caro felt herself growing more nervous as each second passed, and the basic answer to all the questions rising up to plague her was still missing.

"What did Sinclair do to have him treated like this?" she asked in the lowest possible voice. "Why would these people go so far as to want to pin on him a crime he didn't commit?"

No one has done that yet, and as for what he

did—'' Dick looked to Megan, then back to Caro. "He defended and believed in his father when just about no one else did—and that's all I can tell you for now."

And it was almost enough. The upper strata of New York society was ruthless in the way it treated those who broke the rules. But would it go so far as to use Sinclair as a scapegoat? Not if I can help it, she thought.

"Caro, are you sure you want to bring your name into this?" Megan asked, her rich blue eyes filled with concern. "You've been away from New York for a long time, and without meaning to, you could make things very difficult for yourself."

"If I had to choose, guess who'd I'd pick to stand beside?" she asked, trying to keep the acid out of her voice. "I told Sinclair that I understood and I trusted him. In my book, that doesn't mean saying I never saw him before in my life!"

"I wasn't suggesting you do such a thing!" Megan replied, aghast. "Just that you could be discreet—"

Megan's softly pitched voice with its slight South Carolina accent faded as the commotion outside the dining room announced that the police had finally arrived. There were the sounds of doors slamming, of male voices asking Mrs. Chandler to please be calm, and then, cutting through all the others, a woman's clear, sharp tones voicing an opinion that was anything but calm or discreet.

"—and I'm telling you that my father *did not* kill himself!"

"Poor Cynthia," a woman at the next table remarked to them, her eyes bright from too much champagne and the anticipation of a really juicy scandal. "Why, she just fainted away when her father . . . well, you know. I understand she's been in the ladies' lounge since it happened. And poor Davis's death means Cynthia and Curtis will have to cancel their Valentine's Day ball. Such a pity, since they are the most romantic couple. . . ."

Caro longed to tell the other woman to shut up, that her stupid prattling was making her miss what was being said at the other side of the carved oak doors. The position of the doors blocked her view, but she could hear Harris Palmer trying to offer soothing sympathy, while anonther man—probably the police chief—tried to ask questions. Cynthia listened to no one as she pressed her point of view, whic grew sharper and more insistent.

"I keep telling you, if you want some answers to why my father is dead, find Sinclair Poole and ask him!"

Cynthia Moreton Chandler's disembodied voice carried through the dining room with the clarity of a church bell on a cold winter morning. Immediately a buzz of voices began to rise, the food and champagne forgotten as the need to gossip, to slander, to lie and fling mud asserted itself.

"Do you suppose. . . ?"

"Well, he *was* here without an invitation—"

"But to murder—"

"Be quiet!"

"The police have to know—"

44

"We have to help Cynthia in her hour of need. . . ."

"Lucky thing that she never—"

"Oh, what a scandal—"

"Nursing a grudge for years—"

"It must have turned his mind—"

"We have to do the right thing—"

Why, this is nothing but a society lynch mob, Caro thought, horrified. Give them another ten minutes and they'll be ready to convict Sinclair right here. Well, they won't, not as long as I can do something.

"I'm going out there before she hands them a rope," Caro said, getting to her feet. "I was with him when it happened, and it's about time the police heard that."

To her surprise, Megan offered no objection, and Dick smiled as he stood up. "Yell if you need a couple of character witnesses," he offered.

Dick's gesture was for courage, and Caro decided this was a case where she could use every bit. Who knows what this Cynthia Moreton Chandler is like, she thought, and a moment later realized she should have known all along.

It was the young woman in the Marie Antionette get-up, except that now the careful illusion of perfection was ruined with the removal of her elaborate powdered wig. The sight of the other woman's coal-black hair tumbling in thick, rich waves to her shoulders reminded Caro that her own costume was fully in place, but the reminder that no one was quite what they seemed tonight was only momentary, and her full attention was fixed on the tableau taking place in the corridor.

Harris Palmer and a ramrod-straight man who was immediately indentifiable as a police official, even though he was wearing a dark business suit, were trying without success to soothe the determined woman. Both men were so intent on trying to quiet Cynthia Chandler that for the moment, Caroline, even with her height and looks and striking costume, was completely ignored.

". . . .there was a man in the game room with my father, Mr. Hathaway. I'm telling you I heard *two* voices, and one of them was probably Sinclair," Cynthia stated, her voice empathic but minus any sort of hysteria. "I heard them shouting at each other, and then, just as I began to walk back to the ballroom, I heard the gunshot that killed my father. Now why don't you stop wasting my time with these stupid questions and go find Sinclair Poole. He's the one you want!"

Chapter Five

"No, he is not."

The instant she spoke, her voice calm and clear, Caro's status as the unnoticed, unacknowledged fourth party vanished, and three pairs of eyes regarded her with varying degrees of anger, suspicion, and surprise. She looked back at them, her calm and steady gaze informing them that she wasn't the sort who was easily intimidated. She had spent all her life surrounded by money and influence and power and knew far too well that sometimes the truth had nothing to do with winning, but right now it was the only tack to take.

"Are you a memeber of this club?" Palmer Harris inquired, the first to recover.

"And would membership have something to do with the veracity of my statement?" Caro responded in her coolest voice.

"No, no, no," the Linden Trees president assured her quickly. "I asked merely because I didn't recognize you, and since there seems to be a problem with an uninvited guest here tonight. . . . '' His voice trailed off, a clear sign that he wasn't sure how much he could safely say, and Caro recognized her first advantage.

"My name is Caroline Worth, and although I'm not a member, I certainly do have an invitation. I'm visiting William and Adele Seligman at Cove House, and I believe the club's governing committee contacted all members to ascertain if they would be having house guests so they could be added to tonight's guest list." Caro's voice was deliberate in its slight disinterest. "And now that we have this matter settled, may I tell you why sending out a search party for Sinclair Poole would be a waste of time and energy for the Woodbury Police?"

Palmer Harris, stout and fiftyish, with years of good living behind him and little experience in the sordid, looked nonplussed. "Chief Hathaway, I think it would be a good idea if you took it from here," he told the man standing beside him.

"Yes, and perhaps you should escort this lady back to the dining room, or better yet, off the club's premises," Cynthia interposed coldly. "And perhaps now, Palmer, you'll agree that club dances should be exclusively for club members. !"

For a woman whose father had just died, Cynthia looked altogether too calm, Caro observed silently. It was only her mussed hair and the whiteness of her face beneath her maquillage that proved she had had some reaction to the incident. But now it was obvious that her main objective was to have her way, and she didn't mind using her power to get it.

Faced with two strong-willed women, both men looked as if they were about to waffle, to go with the safe and easy and socially acceptable way. At least three of the four people standing in the wide corridor would have preferred everything be made right as quickly as possible, and two of the four wanted to push the entire ugly matter under the carpet, but the interests of justice, after a few uncertain moments, finally won out.

"Miss Worth, would I be correct in saying that you believe Mrs. Chandler is lying?" Wilber Hathaway had retired from the Philadelphia police force in order to take over the position of police chief in this quiet Long Island community, and he knew he had to tread carefully when dealing with what might very well be a society crime. "This is a very serious charge."

"So is everything Mrs. Chandler is saying," Caro responded, keeping a tight grip on her temper. "And I don't mean to imply that she's lying—there very well may have been another person in the room with her father—I'm only stating that it couldn't have been Sinclair Poole."

The police chief gave her another considering look, and Caro silently speculated that in his eyes, compared to Cynthia's rig, her costume made her less trustworthy. With my luck, he's a bungler, or worse, wants to make himself look good in front of all the club people. Well, whatever he is, I have to play my part out, be cool and collected and try to stare him down. . . .

"Mr. Harris—ladies—I believe we should retire to someplace more private before we continue this conversation," Chief Hathaway said finally, his response startling the three people he was addressing, each for an entirely different reason. "I have to take statements, and I don't care to do it standing out here."

"Now, really!" Cynthia's dark eyes flashed in anger. "I've given you all the information you need. Are you going to pay attention to this—this—*unknown?*"

"I thought that in this club there were no unknowns," the older man replied with deliberate mildness. "And please believe me, Mrs. Chandler, you don't want to be standing here in a few minutes."

Caro had wondered where the rest of the police were and why Cynthia's husband wasn't with her, and belatedly she realized that the men so conspicuous by their absence were in the game room and that they would be ready to bring the body out in a short time.

"Mr. Harris, where is the best place for us to go?" If Cynthia was trying to have things her way by a show of demand and influence, possibly she could swing things in the other direction by showing the police chief her ability to think quickly and decisively. "It should be someplace that's comfortable, but not too near the dining room or ballroom."

"Ah . . . well, yes. You're quite right, Miss . . .

Worth. That would be the ladies' sitting room. It's quite spacious and very restful—quite the best of all possible spots. . . . ''

God, he sounds like a real estate agent, Caro thought as they all went upstairs, Mr. Harris continuing his monologue on the decoration of the Linden Trees. While the police chief had risen in her estimation, the club president was looking more and more like a man who would go in whatever direction the breeze was blowing.

But she had to concede he was right about the suitability of the room. Admittedly, it was all a little too fussy for her taste, what with rich green carpet and the floral wallpaper with big pink cabbage roses splashed against a pale green background. The same pattern was repeated in the curtains and in the chintz covering the assortment of sofas and chairs, but however overdone it was, there was privacy and they could talk without all the guests listening in.

"Mr. Harris, will you do me a great favor?" Chief Hathaway asked. "I'd appreciate it if you went back downstairs and found Officers Barton and Morrow. Have them make sure no one leaves until I give the say-so. My assistants will ask the preliminary quesitons and let me know if I should speak to anyone else."

Palmer Harris left, no doubt glad to remove himself from this difficult atmosphere, and Wilbur Hathaway motioned to Caro and Cynthia, who, while not glaring at each other, were definitely eying each other with nervous distrust.

The police chief coughed softly. "If you ladies will

sit down, we can settle this matter as quickly as possible.''

"You're certainly not going to listen to her!" Cynthia protested, and Caro, with an exclamation of annoyance, sat down in a corner of one of the sofas and crossed her legs in a heavy swish of satin.

"I'm the police chief in the service of this community, and I'll listen to anyone with a plausible story when it's a case like this," he responded, allowing himself a brief glance at Caro's narrow ankles. The sight of a woman in trousers, even as part of a costume and cut full enough almost to be mistaken for a skirt, was definitely intriguing, he decided, sitting down at one of the writing desks. He took a notebook from his jacket and uncapped his fountain pen. "Shall we begin our discussion, Miss Worth?"

Caro gave him a considering look. "I was under the impression that this was going to be my official statement."

"Possibly, dear, Chief Hathaway wants to make this as *un*official as possible—so you won't be in an embarrassing position when you have to change your story," Cynthia suggested. She sat down opposite Caro, the wide pink paniers of her gown spreading out over the flower-patterned sofa cushions.

"That's very nice of the police chief, but if anyone has to change their story, it won't be me . . . *dear*."

Wilbur Hathaway rapped his knuckles on the bleached wood surface of the writing table. This perfumed, feminine atmosphere that hinted of power and money was unfamiliar to him, but what truly disturbed him were the two women seated there. They were sleek, rare beings—and pure danger. Both of them would risk almost anything, and only one of them was telling the truth.

"Are you ready to begin asking me questions, Chief Hathaway?" Caro asked, her voice warming.

"We may as well begin. The way it stands now, I have Mrs. Chandler insisting that Sinclair Poole was in the game room with her father at the time of his death, while you insist he was with you in another part of the club."

"Yes, that's exactly how it is."

"Well, this is a difficult situation, as you can well imagine. Both Mr. and Mrs. Chandler have provided me with a great deal of information about Sinclair Poole. I imagine you have quite a different story to tell me."

"Yes, I do, beginning with the fact that we were together on the terrace when we heard the gunshot."

"Can you describe Mr. Poole?"

"He was wearing a mask, so any description beyond height and eye and hair color is pure conjecture."

"Are you going to believe what she's saying?" Cynthia interjected in a newly composed voice. "It's more likely Miss Worth arrived with her friend, and he left her behind to cover up for him!"

"Mrs. Chandler, I'm sorry for your loss, but please allow me to do my job, and, Miss Worth, kindly answer fully any questions I put to you."

"I came in here with every intention of doing so, but I think I've already given sufficient proof that I was invited to be here tonight. I want to give a statement, not answer pointless questions."

Caroline knew she was caught in a potentially dangerous situation. If Chief Hathaway turned out to be the sort of man who liked his women helpless, there would definitely be a problem since Cynthia was more than sharp enough to play on her new role as the victim's distressed daughter; her earlier insistence would give way to tears and the police officer's sympathy would go to her. But one game being played tonight is too many, she reminded herself. I'm not going to add to it.

For an endless minute, the man's expression didn't change. "When did you first meet Sinclair Poole?" he asked at last, and at his words, some of Caro's apprehensions lessened.

"I never met Sinclair Poole before tonight. But I don't know any of the reasons as to why nearly everyone considers him to be some sort of untouchable, someone to be avoided at all costs but at the same time remain perfect fodder for gossipmongers," Caro said, purposely keeping her voice quite conversational. "We met quite by accident, talked about a few things, and he mentioned that he was here for a business meeting." She hesitated for a moment. "Mr. Poole also mentioned that the man he had come to the Linden Trees to see was upset, and he had come out to the terrace in order to give him a few minutes of privacy."

"And that person was Davis Moreton." It was a statement, not a question.

"I really couldn't say, Chief Hathaway. Mr. Poole never mentioned a name."

"So all you and Mr. Poole did on the terrace was talk?"

"No, we decided we would like to have a dance, and we went into the ballroom."

"And you had no compunctions about having a dance with a man who was not only a member of this club, but who was here without an invitation as well?"

Caro took a deep breath and bit back her comment that she'd rather have one dance with Sinclair than have her dance card filled with the names of every so-called "available" male members of this club. "Chief Hathaway, I've just returned to New York after several years in China. Now, in the Orient, when one invites another to his club, his friend is encouraged to enjoy the facilities of the club, even if there's a large party taking place that he normally wouldn't have been included in." As far as Caro knew, this wasn't even remotely true, but she was willing to take the chance the chief didn't know that. "Naturally, I assumed the same courtesy held true here."

"Well, that's quite understandable," Chief Hathaway responded. "I'm sure there will be a number of other guests willing to confirm Mr. Poole's presence on the dance floor."

"That's a certainty," she said. "It's what else they might say that concerns me."

"What they might say," Cynthia interposed coolly, "is that there's no proof other than your word—and you *are* a stranger to our group—that Sinclair was on the terrace when my father . . . when my father. . . . " Her voice broke and she raised a dainty, lace-edged handkerchief to her eyes.

What an act, Caro thought. In another minute she'll be calling herself a poor, helpless orphan.

"Miss Worth, did anyone here see you and Mr. Poole on the terrace at the time of . . . of this unfortunate incident?"

"Yes."

"Do you know who they are?"

"No. Perhaps you could ask one of your officers to inquire among the guests as to which couple was on the terrace when the . . . incident happened?"

"Miss Worth, that's a plausible enough suggestion for me to look into this myself," he said, slowly rising to his feet. "I won't be long."

"Poor Chief Hathaway, I really think he expects that someone is going to be big and brave and say they saw you and Sinclair on the terrace," Cynthia said as soon as they were alone together. "Isn't it funny how even a tough old police officer can have illusions of someone coming forward and telling the truth?"

"It will be even funnier if—oh, let me say *when*—someone does," Caro returned evenly, and for a moment the women regarded each other.

"It's too bad that you seem to have a predilection for picking the wrong men," Cynthia continued silkily. "You and I might have been friends."

"I think that I'll be much happier if we stay—as you so charmingly put it—strangers. And I might remind you that you know nothing at all about my taste in men."

"If you're defending Sinclair, then I have a good idea."

"I should have known that you had a past with him," Caro said, not taking her eyes off the other woman's face. "Did he stop seeing you because he was never sure which face you'd be wearing?"

"Perhaps I found a better prospect."

"I'm sure you did—some people always have better prospects."

"Things just seem to fall that way, don't they? Tell me, whose word do you think the police are going to take—that of a devoted daughter, or that of a woman no one really knows, who comes to a costume ball as a Chinese princess, stands on the sidelines all night making nasty little comments to her only friends in the room, and then allows a man no one will receive to dance with her and then take her out on the terrace for who only knows what?"

Well, she certainly isn't stupid, Caro thought, but the only comment she allowed herself was, "One never knows—that's what makes everything so exciting."

There were times Caro made comments that went over with all the popularity of an invasion of ants at a picnic. It was the penalty of having what her stepmother called "a slightly too witty tongue," but now she knew the sweet delight of having said the right thing at the right time. Almost as soon as the words were out of her mouth, she heard male voices in the hallway, voices that grew louder and more contentious as they came closer to the ladies' sitting room. She didn't dare look at Cynthia. There was such a thing as too much triumph, particularly since one voice could clearly be heard saying that no one was going to tell him what to say—ever.

The young man who filled the doorway had all the dark, sleek good looks of a professional actor, an appearance that was enhanced by his costume of a Mississippi riverboat gambler and the utterly intractable expression on his face. In fact, he might have made Caro's list of "availables" except for two reasons: first, he was clearly a few years younger than she, and second, when she had first noticed him, he appeared to be very interested in another female guest.

He was also the male half of the other couple on the terrace.

Chief Hathaway was next in the room, looking slightly out-of-breath, as if he had run up the stairs in order to be first in the room. "Well, we seem to have an interesting development here," he said, trying to regain control of the situation. "This is Drake Sloane from California."

"From Los Angeles, Pasadena, and San Diego, to be specific," Drake said. "In southern California, we tend to mvoe around quite a bit."

'And I'm sure that makes you a paragon witness," Cynthia remarked, regarding him with suspicion.

"Mrs. Chandler, I must remind you that although this investigation isn't being conducted in the usual manner, certain formalities need to be observed," Chief Hathaway warned. "I've already had to place your husband under the guard of two of my officers. Please don't make me remove you from this room."

"Oh, let her stay," Drake said, flopping down next to Caro on the sofa and giving her a conspirator's smile. "Before Chief Hathaway appeared on the scene, Curtis Chandler was busy trying to strong-arm me into seeing things his way—with certain prizes for my cooperation thrown in, of course. We may as well let one member of the family see that it doesn't work."

"I have to compliment you on your timing," she whispered to him. "We were just discussing the possible outcome of Chief Hathaway's investigation."

"I should have spoken up right away and gone out to see the police when you did, except my future in-laws were a little over-cautious. Nan and I talked them around, though, and they do believe in justice. Have you had a rough time here?"

"Let's just say no one was offering me interesting prizes if I didn't tell my story."

"That's how these things usually go, but we'll make it right," Drake said, his voice growing serious.

"Mrs. Chandler, Mr. Sloane has been kind enough to offer testimony that he and his fiancée, Nancy Hull, were on the terrace along with Miss Worth and Mr. Poole, when they heard the gunshot that killed your father." Wilbur Hathaway was in the process of having to accept that this situation was all but out of his control, and the best he could manage was to conclude this very irregular meeting as quickly as possible. "Perhaps you would care to reconsider your statement that Mr. Poole was in the game room?"

"But Chief Hathaway, I never said it was definitely Sinclair Poole, only that it was probably him." Cynthia's voice was both silky and careful. "It was quite a logical assumption on my part. Mr. Poole has nursed an unreasonable grudge against my father for years, he came here tonight to see him, and the conclusion I reached was a natural one. If you have proof that it's wrong, no real harm has been done."

"Well, I think accusing a man of a crime he didn't commit in a place where there are people more than delighted to agree with you is doing harm with quite a bit of malicious intent!" Caro exclaimed hotly. "Do you think you can get away with everything, that you have no responsibilities?"

"I have a responsibility to find out what happened to my father, Miss Worth."

"By indiscriminately pinning it on another man because of some grudge?"

"My, but you do believe in truth and justice. That only happens in flukes like this one."

"Yeah, it just goes to show you how neatly things can be arranged when you have a husband who can dangle business deals and club memberships in return for silence," Drake remarked, venom dripping from his voice.

"Would you care to explain that remark, Mr. Sloane?" Chief Hathaway asked. "You seem to be describing a somewhat illegal activity."

"The last time I heard, it was called obstruction of justice," Caro couldn't resist putting in.

"Mr. Sloane?"

"I'd say Miss Worth knows what she's talking about. But if you insist on specifics, one of the Chandlers' helpful friends heard me say that I was on the terrace with Sinclair Poole, and rushed over to inform Curtis, who then came to my table and said he could make it worth my while to have a memory lapse."

"Would you care to explain that further?"

"Mr. Chandler is well aware of my family's extensive real estate holdings in California, and he made certain suggestions about our combining forces and the profits we could reap. And then he dropped what he thought would be magic words—Shinnecock Hills, Union League, Garden City Golf."

"Chief Hathaway, I'm sure Mr. Sloane has completely misunderstood what my husband said to him." Cynthia stood up, looking rather like a large, crushed rose in need of a vase of water. "Now, I'm perfectly willing to admit I made a mistake and Sinclair Poole was not in the game room with my father. Why don't we forget everything else?"

"That sounds reasonable," the older man agreed, not looking at either Caro or Drake. "Why don't we all go downstairs? I want to give the word that the other guests can leave—"

While Caro and Drake looked at each other in

61

cynical silence, Cynthia seemed to glide out of the room.

"Such an anticlimatic ending for so dramatic a night," she sighed. "But thank you for coming up here. I thought it was going to be my word against Cynthia's."

"I know it must have been hard for you, and all you can be sure of now is that even though the police aren't on our side, they're honest enough not to go after an innocent man."

Drake's quiet words cut through some of Caro's bitterness. That Cynthia could glibly put a man's freedom in danger, accuse him of all but being party to a premeditated crime, and then, faced with proof that her lies wouldn't hold up, say that she had only *thought* it was Poole's voice she heard galled her so terribly that she had a sour taste in her mouth. None of it—except for being able to prove that Sin had been with her—was fair. But when she considered the end result, that was really the only thing that counted.

But one question was still unanswered.

"Where's Chief Hathaway?" she asked Drake. "Carrying Cynthia's train?"

"Something like that. Let's see if we can find him."

They located the police officer in the hallway, studiously writing something down in his notebook. He looked up when the scent of Caro's perfume reached him, a slight expression of annoyance forming on his features, as if he already knew their purpose in seeking him out.

"May I help you, Miss Worth? Mr. Sloane?"

"Actually it's more in the nature of a question that only you can answer, and I'm sure Mr. Sloane would like to know the answer as much as I do," Caro said directly. "Tell us, was it suicide or was it murder?"

"Miss Worth, your work is done here this evening, and that's a question you needn't—"

"I think it's an excellent question," Drake put in, catching sight of Caro's expression. "And for all Miss Worth's gone through tonight, she certainly deserves an answer."

Chief Hathaway took a long minute before answering. "Quite truthfully, it could be either one."

"But I always thought that there were sure indications—"

"Usually, but not in this case. The angle of the entry wound and the fact that Mr. Moreton was ambidextrous could indicate either that he took his own life or that it was foul play."

"But surely there were fingerprints—"

"That procedure, Miss Worth, is still quite experimental, and in any case, it's for a big-city police department to follow through on. No, I'm afraid that here in Woodbury we work by ordinary and conventional means."

"But there will be some sort of inquest?" Caro persisted.

"Yes, but you probably won't be called to testify. Your statement should be sufficient."

"I'm not concerned about that."

"What we both want to find out is the probability

that the inquiry will rule that Davis Moreton died by his own hand," Drake said, his voice as incisive as Caro's. "I mean, if the coroner thinks it might be foul play, are you all going to play spin-the-bottle and come after Sinclair Poole?"

The chief's scathing look said it all. "Despite any misgivings you and Miss Worth may have, Mr. Sloane, your friend Mr. Poole is no longer a suspect."

"We're very glad to hear that, but for the record, Mr. Poole isn't my friend. In fact, we've never met." Drake's dark gaze was fixed on Chief Hathaway, almost daring him to ask why he had put himself in this position when so many others would have taken an easier route. "But after all we've been through tonight, we don't want to go home with any loose threads hanging."

"We'll want to ask Mr. Poole a few questions, no more than any other guest here tonight was asked. Now, if you're quite finished. . . ."

The chief went down the stairs with the swiftness and grace of a much younger man, and Caro followed his progress, leaning over the handrail and looking down at the main foyer to see him promptly buttonholed by Palmer Harris. With Drake standing beside her, she watched as Cynthia, swathed in a floor-length, hooded sable cloak and accompanied by a tall and aggressively handsome man who had to be Curtis Chandler, shook hands with the two older men before sweeping out the front door and into the black winter night.

"What a performance," Drake muttered.

"And I thought it was going to be so dull and dreary here tonight!" Caro remarked, and couldn't help laughing. "We'd better go back downstairs. My friends and your fiancée are probably very concerned about us."

"Not to mention their having to stand up to a lot of questions and comments for what we've done."

"I'm so glad you're not the sort of man to give in when various club memberships—as well as several money-making schemes—are waved under your nose," Caro said as they began to go down the stairs. "I don't doubt that my word would have held up in the end, but you prevented some long and probably ugly scenes."

"Oh, it wasn't anything," Drake said, sounding very much like a modest and justice-minded cowboy (who also happened to own half the state and a railroad as well) out of some romantic novel. "Curtis Chandler doesn't seem to be a stupid man, but he thinks that because I'm from California—*Southern* California—it's akin to being just off the boat. Besides," he went on, the humor growing in his voice, "in my part of the country we're very well known for being more than willing to believe in causes that almost no one else will touch!"

Chapter Six

"There were times tonight I didn't think we'd ever get back here!" was the first thing Caro said as she hugged her stepmother. She turned over her evening cape of black velvet warmly lined in mink to the waiting butler. On arrival at Cove House, Vanessa and their hosts, William and Adele Seligman, were waiting for them in the entry rotunda that was dominated by a Lalique glass table with a large vase holding an arrangement of pink and white Maiden's Blush roses. "You won't believe what happened in the middle of what had to be the world's dullest costume party!

"Unfortunately, we have a very good idea of why you all are so late," Bill said, a grim expression on his usually pleasant face. "Davis Moreton commited suicide."

"How did you hear?" Dick asked as he handed over his topcoat to the butler.

"One of the chefs at the club is a cousin of one of

our maids, and he called us. I imagine there was quite a rout there."

"Oh, Bill, don't keep them here," Adele injected. A superb hostess, she began to lead them out of the entry foyer. "I have an idea that this is going to be a very long story, and the library is where we belong."

"And we were waiting there for you until we heard the carriage in the driveway," Bill added. "Does anyone want anything special?"

"A hairbrush," Caro said. "I can't stand this wig another minute"

"Sackett, please ask Muriel to bring Miss Caroline's hairbrush," Bill told his patient, correct English butler, then ushered them all into the main hall. "Never let it be said that our guests don't have their wishes fulfilled as soon as possible."

There was something so special about being a welcome and wanted guest, Caro thought as they went toward the library, past a yellow-and-cream drawing room, a dining room with beige silk chinoiserie wallpaper and Georgian crystal chandeliers, the blue salon, and the Chinese salon. In contrast to those at Linden Trees, no one here ever gave any indication that some guests were more equal than others.

Built in 1895 to replace the original family estate in White Plains that predated the Revolution, this seventy-eight-acre property on Long Island's North Shore included sweeping lawns, perfectly kept gardens and grounds, its own dairy, greenhouse, tennis and squash courts, a brick carriage house with circular turrets, and a wood-framed beach house. The interior of the four-story, eighty-five room house included a state suite, an indoor swimming pool, a billiard room, and a Turkish bath and was one of the largest private homes on what was rapidly becoming known as the "Gold Coast."

In the library the rich, hand-finished walnut paneling gleamed and a custom-designed Axminster carpet of dark green woven with yellow leaves set off the splendid yet comfortable furniture which included several fine dark red leather chesterfields. On the shelves were books that ranged from first editions to the latest bestsellers, and stretched out on one of the sofas was an elegant young woman in a Callot Soeurs dinner dress of pleated rose crêpe de chine with insertions of ecru lace. As the group of six closed the double doors behind them, she put down her copy of *Lord Alingham, Bankrupt,* and smiled at her friends.

"Well, if it isn't the empress and her court! If I'd known the dull old Linden Trees could put on such a show, I wouldn't have turned down their invitation!" Alicia Leslie Turner remarked emphatically.

"Alix, everyone knows that if there's one thing you hate more than pompous people, it's costume parties," Caro returned, sinking into a comfortable wing chair. "If some fortune teller had told you exactly what was going to happen tonight, you still wouldn't have gone. Oh, I've been waiting hours to do this," she went on, pulling off the expensive costume wig. Her hairpins followed next, and her hair, the exact hue of roasted chestnuts, fell in waves to just above her shoulders. "I think I got the police chief to listen to me by looking so exotic he couldn't ignore me.''

"You have to tell us absolutely everything," Vanessa said as she sat down. She was wearing a Worth end-of-mourning dinner dress of black figured net over silver-grey satin, but the restrained colors couldn't dim the glow of her luxuriant dark-red hair or cast a shadow on her elegant face. "What you've just told us sounds suspiciously like the middle— start from the very beginning.''

"Sit back everyone; this is going to be better than Mary Roberts Rinehart," Dick said wryly.

"Surely not that bad?" Adele questioned as she sat down, her Paquin dinner dress of royal-blue silk whispering expensively.

"Worse." Megan's voice was firm. "We were almost ready to leave before the . . . incident. "Wait until you hear about the buffet—''

"Start with when you first arrived." Alix put her book aside and sat up straight, her rose satin evening pumps making contact with the carpet. "I bet that in spite of the fancy costumes it was the tackiest crowd imaginable.''

"You don't know the half of it," Caro responded, accepting her hairbrush from Muriel. "Excuse me for doing this here," she said, applying several quick brushstrokes to her hair, restoring it to some sore of order. "I swear, this is my last costume party!''

It had finally begun to snow, but in the spacious library it was snug and comforting, and it made the events of a few hours before seem somewhat remote . . . all of it except for meeting Sinclair, Caro decided as she and Megan and Dick took turns relating the events of the night.

Their friendly audience listened with almost spell-bound intensity. What had begun as just another holiday season gala had ended in one man's sui-cide—unless it just possibly was murder.

It was only when she mentioned the name Sinclair Poole that the atmosphere changed.

"What an interesting name," Vanessa said.

"I'll have to tell Cliff this first thing tomorrow," Bill remarked, referring to his eldest son.

"Sinclaire must have had a very good reason to risk letting that crowd see him again," Adele offered.

But Alix's reaction was the most interesting of all. From the top of her shining brown hair, wound into a very fashionable Gibson knot, to the pointed tips of her handmade satin shoes, she didn't seem to be either moving or breathing, and her face now had a haughty look, one that she donned like a mask when she wanted to hide her deepest thoughts.

"I hope you didn't make the mistake of thinking that Cynthia is either stupid or silly," she offered with slashing accuracy. Alix was a doctor, and at times her observations bore a great similarity to medical diagnoses. "She's one sharp lady, the kind who can teach a few tricks to J. P. Morgan and John W. Gates, if either were the sort who listened to advice from women."

"I'm afraid I learned that truth the hard way," Caro admitted, and described her confrontation with Mrs. Chandler. "But what I want to know is why nearly everyone there was so virulently opposed to

71

Sinclair. Dick told me it had something to do with defending his father when no one else would. There must have been a terrible scandal.''

Bill and Adele exchanged significant looks. ''Are you sure you don't know anything about Stanford Poole and the big Wall Street investment scandal of 1895? he asked.

''All I can say is that obviously it didn't stand the trip to Peking too well.''

''It is possible that Garrison knew about it,'' Vanessa put in quietly. ''He received Wall Street reports on a regular basis, and if he did know, the only reason he didn't share it with us was that talking about it might have disturbed him too much.''

''That wouldn't surprise me at all,'' Bill replied. ''Garrison was always a fair and careful man— something you can't say about too many other people . . . particularly the ones who like nothing better than when a conservative and cautious and conscientious financier is caught doing something very illegal—such as offering shares in a company that doesn't exist.''

''What?'' For a long moment, Caro could register only a feeling of deep shock and surprise. ''Somehow what you've just told us doesn't sound right— almost if it were all a put-up job—a house of cards designed to fall.''

''That's what we always thought, not that it made any difference. It was all too carefully orchestrated— the house of cards, as you said—but it was all too tightly done up for anyone to be able to prove otherwise, and, unhappily, Stanford compounded his own problems by not engaging either private detectives or a first-class criminal lawyer.''

"I don't think another lawyer would have helped,'' Dick pointed out. "The year 1895 was not a good one for a financial scandal.''

"It's only in the past few days that I've started to realize that we've missed being away,'' Caro said. "And we can't even brag about being in the middle of the Boxer's siege of Peking, since we were in Japan when it happened! And when we did hear about politics and scandals and society goings-on and the latest financial panics, it didn't seem very real because it was all half a world away.''

"With some of the things that have gone on in the past five or six years, no one would have blamed you for wanting to stay in a paradise like Hawaii,'' Adele said in a soft but knowing voice.

"Hawaii *is* very beautiful, but it has its own problems and, unhappily, it can get very boring there,'' Vanessa related.

"Let's save that for another time,'' Megan said. "Right now I think it would be better if we discussed the Pooles, and what happened to them.''

"I couldn't agree more. I heard a lot of gossip and rumors and half-started tales tonight, and now I'd like to hear the truth,'' Caro said.

It had all started in the first weeks of 1895, Bill told them as all attention turned to him. The banker's panic which had begun in early 1893 and then turned into a full-scale gold crisis, had finally begun to abate, although the monetary scars left by the endless months of bank and business failures would

73

take a long time to heal. It was about this time that Stanford Poole had made available to investors an offering of shares in something called the Great Northwest Lumber Company.

The financial community's immediate reaction was to consider it as yet another jewel in the Poole diadem, which already included a very profitable railroad line serving several Western states and an equally lucrative shipping line that called at every important port between Southern California and Alaska. Stanford Poole had always played fair with his investors, he'd always showed a profit; and he'd always paid his substantial dividends on time, so when the first rumors began that the Great Northwest Lumber Company was only so much paper there was as much disbelief as concern.

If it had happened on Wall Street in the 1880s, it was unlikely that there would have been such a thorough investigation. But the newspapers were improving and expanding their financial coverage, and publications like the *Wall Street Journal*, the *Chicago Journal of Commerce*, the *Philadelphia Financial Journal*, and the *Boston News Bureau* were growing in readership and importance as they forged ahead in their efforts to keep readers advised of the latest news from the nation's stock markets and ever-changing businesses. Therefore, the urge to expose a scam that was cheating men and women out of millions of dollars was too great to resist, particularly when there were so many facts right at hand.

It was one of America's unwritten laws that the rich and powerful do not go to the executioner. But occasionally, since justice in the United States is more evenly applied than in other nations, such men do go to trial, which is exactly what happened to Stanford. And as each revelation was made, proving beyond a shadow of a doubt that the Great Northwest Lumber Company did not exist, each day's court session became more and more like a circus. It was, everyone agreed, the scandal of the year, and possibly of the decade, and there was only one verdict the jury could deliver. . . .

Except that they never had the chance to decide.

While the jury was engaged in its deliberations, Stanford Poole's overtaxed heart simply gave out. The defendant was dead, but his son was still available and defending his father's reputation, insisting to anyone who would listen that it had been a frame. And then there was the matter of all the people who had invested. . . .

"Sinclair paid back every penny to the investors," Bill concluded quietly, his eyes sad. 'The only one who refused the money—or most of it—was a fellow named George Kelly who used to be a professional boxer. Sinclair hired him as his bodyguard."

"I suppose he needed one," Caro said, trying to absorb everything she'd just heard. "Talk about finding out who your friends are."

"It didn't matter to him that not everyone thought he was a wild young man who deserved all his misfortune," Adele added. "Sinclair cut himself off from those of us who did want to help him."

No wonder he isolated himself; he must have felt

he'd suffered a terrible betrayal, Caro thought, aware than unless she wanted to give away far too much, it would be better if she sidestepped this particular topic.

"Meg and Dick told me he imports Oriental objects," she said finally. "How did he get into that business?"

"It was the only one of his father's enterprises he didn't liquidate—that and an old town house on Prince Street, just off the Bowery. When all the dust settled he moved downtown," Bill finsihed.

"Is he terribly bitter?" Alix asked, speaking for the first time.

"No, he was utterly charming, funny, and a very good dancer," Caro said, both her suspicions and her curiosity aroused by her friends' question.

"I don't have to ask about his dancing, it's his attitude I'm interested in."

"And did you do a lot of dancing with Sinclair back before all those terrible things happened to him?" she asked, suddenly sure who Sinclair had mistaken her for the moment they met on the terrace.

"You might say that," Alix said as she stood up and collected her book. "There was a time when I thought I was going to marry him."

Chapter Seven

"That was some exit line," Caro told Alix as they went down the corridor toward their rooms.

"I'm rather good at them," Alix returned, unperturbed. "You should have heard what I told a stuffy young surgeon who wanted to give me the honor of marrying him!"

"I imagine you told him in clear and certain terms that you had no intention of living—where, in Boston?"

"Actually, it was Cleveland."

"Then good riddance to him."

"My feelings exactly. But I wonder who'll turn up next?"

Laughing, their arms around each other's waists, the two girlhood friends went into Caro's room. Decorated with splendid but understated French furniture, it was one of the series of rooms most favored by female guests. All pink and cream with touches of silver, it featured a white lacquer four-poster bed swathed in yards of pale rose-pink satin. The attractive low chests and writing table were of pale beechwood, and the delicate loveseat was covered in a pink and silver brocade.

"Look at this wig," Caro said, her disgut obvious as she tossed it on the nearest chair. "I spent a fortune on it, and now I don't care if I ever see it again."

"That's very understandable, but please don't throw it away," Alix replied as she sat down in a chair upholstered in a pink-and-white-striped silk. "The Henry Street Settlement could use if for the next Columbus Day costume parade."

"Fine, I'll contribute the wig and the rest of my costume to boot," Caro replied, kicking off her shoes and stretching out on the Frette linen-covered bed, her head and neck supported by a profusion of pillows. "Let someone else enjoy the experience."

"Getting dressed up in disguise is fun only when you're under twenty-one and it's for a Halloween party," Alix agreed. "But then, if you'd played noble tonight and stayed home, you wouldn't have met Sinclair."

"And a lot of good that may do me."

"You're not going to let him slip away that easily, are you?" She leveled an intense look. "I hope you're not worried about what the Linden Trees crowd and all their pals will think."

"Absolutely not! But it may eventually occur to him that if I hadn't been there, he'd have been able to conclude his business before Davis Moreton shot himself. He might have even been able to prevent it."

"Knowing how the Moretons—father and daughter—treated Sin, I doubt if he'd have gone through any strenuous measures to save that man's life. There's also the possibility that Davis could have used that gun of his on Sin."

"I hadn't thought of that." For a moment, Caro concentrated on a vase filled with pink and white tulips. "Alix, I know we haven't seen each other in years, and we certainly haven't written much, but we were very good friends once—"

"From the day you started Brearley, and I was a year ahead of you." Alix smiled. "Do you want to know how I became so involved with Sin."

"Is that what you call him?"

"It's what nearly everyone has called him at one time or other, and in a funny way it's rather appropriate. Shall I tell you all about it now?"

"Is there any answer besides yes?"

"No, but I don't want you to think that you're hearing a story from a jilted fiancée. Sin and I were never formally engaged—or even informally, for that matter. I was a lot younger and took a lot of things for granted that I wouldn't now."

"No man has ever fooled you, Alix, and if he had, you wouldn't have any kind or tender feelings left for him the way you do Sinclair."

"I couldn't hate Sinclair if I tried," she said in a tone of voice that made Caro's suspicions even more concrete.

"Did Sinclair ever call you Allie?"

"He's the only one I ever let do that. It's either Alix or Alicia or Miss Turner. Why do you ask?"

"Because when he saw me on the terrace he called me Allie. My back was to him and he realized his mistake as soon as I turned around—" Caro stopped, aware that she was explaining too much, something she almost never did.

"It's nice to know I'm remembered," Alix remarked quietly. "I wasn't too sure."

"Do you ever think about what it might have been like if you'd married him?"

"Not in the last few years. In the end, it never pays to look back, and I have too much to look forward to. But I don't mind a recollection or two."

"Was Sinclair very rich?"

"Wildly, extravagantly, impossibly so. Everything his father touched seemed to mint money, and it goes without saying that Stanford Poole started out with a great deal. But he was also a man of great social and family responsibilities, and he raised his son with a lot more restraints and far less leeway than most young men of his group."

"What a Calvinistic-sounding approach."

"No, not really. Please take my word for it that they lived very well indeed. But there was also a bond, an understanding between father and son that went beyond most relationships of that sort. Sinclair would do almost anything his father asked of him, and for a very long time, Stanford trusted his son with his most secret business dealings, let him attend meetings at practically the same time he put on his first pair of long trousers."

"It sounds like an ideal father–son relationship. But something like that usually doesn't work forever."

"I should hope not; it's a highly limiting way to live." For a moment Alix stroked the soft skin at the base of her throat. "Sin thought he would be made his father's private secretary ten minutes after graduating from Columbia. But his father sent him off for a long summer in Europe, and when he got back and was ready to start work, someone else was settled into that position. Sin was given a sort of window-dressing job, not the sort of thing he'd been expecting at all, and when his father suggested he enjoy himself, he did—and with quite a vengeance."

"Is that one of the reasons why the Linden Tree crowd can't stand him? I imagine he never tried to be overly polite when he couldn't stand the people he was talking to."

"Yes, and because he was very rich and his father had so much power and influence, they had to take his behavior. Fortunately it was only a phase, a short rebellion, and by the time he started paying attention to me during the summer of 1893, that was pretty much over."

"Or you reformed him," Caro pointed out, and both women laughed.

"If I had a choice in the matter, I'd rather do it the other way: uncover the vital side of an otherwise quiet man and enjoy the results rather than be the tamer of a wild man."

81

"I never thought of it that way. It sounds like it might have its advantages."

"Well, finding out is an entirely different thing. But to get back to Sin. . . . I won't bore you with all the social details of our courtship, except to say that I was sure he was going to ask and I knew I'd say yes. But other things happened. My grandfather died in May, and my parents were killed in November," Alix told her. She took a moment to regain her composure. "I was profoundly affected by both events, but not too overcome to notice Sin hadn't been to see me since his first condolence call. At first I thought he simply didn't want to intrude on my grief, but I learned a very hard lesson when his engagement to Cynthia Moreton was announced."

"That bitch! I knew she had some tie to Sinclair. You should have heard her tell me about her so-called 'better prospects.' "

"I can just imagine. Curtis Chandler may be some women's version of a dream come true—if you like the caveman sort, that is."

"I caught a glimpse of him. He *is* rather aggressive-looking."

"He's a good dancer, but in his single days he had the habit of looking at every woman as if she had a price tag hanging from her wrist instead of a dance card."

"Oh, yes. He and Cynthia are like a pair of vampires with their teeth sunk in each other's throats. If one pulls out the other bleeds to death."

"It figures. But where did that leave Sinclair—except holding the bag?"

"At least he didn't look or act overly heartbroken, and I'm going to be presumptive enough to say that he really would have preferred to have been engaged to me."

"Do you think his father pushed him to Cynthia?"

"Yes, and that would make perfect sense if all this business about Davis Moreton being at the head of a conspiracy to destroy Stanford is true. Can you think of a better way to reel in your catch and deflect all suspicion by suggesting that your families cement a business alliance with a wedding?"

"From the little he was able to tell me and everything I heard tonight, Sinclair must be desperate to clear his father's name."

"I'd say obsessed is more like it."

"Obsessed men don't dance," Caro observed. "Whatever he's after, he was sure of success tonight. He even said something about coming back here and seeing everyone again."

"Well, *that* would have been interesting! He must have really found something out about the Consortium, men Sin swears banded together to destroy his father. I believe him, and so do a few other people, but it was all so long ago, and as for proving it—" Alix shrugged.

"It's too bad he didn't get engaged to you," Caro said, not a bit of envy seeping into her words. "That may have been his only mistake."

"I thought so too at the time. I would have stood by him no matter what," Alix said. That explanation was needless; her loyalty to those who'd earned

83

it was an accepted fact, but now she had picked up on something else, something she had noticed while Bill had held them spellbound with the story behind the story. So Caro was attracted to Sin, and quite possibly he to her. Sin had never been a dabbler with either a woman's affection or her emotions. He was as straight as a die; it was one of the qualities that had drawn her to him, and in her experience it was a trait far too few men either had or knew what to do with. "If things had worked out differently between us, I wouldn't have acted out of defiance or to somehow keep him in the social fold, but out of real and true affection and caring and respect," she explained, careful not to use the word "love." "Eight years ago, I thought he was the closest I was going to come to having the grand passion of my life. It seems that I'm still looking for that man."

"You can't possibly be worried about not getting married."

"No, the size of my bank account assures me that acquiring a husband isn't going to be much of a problem at all. It's only finding the right man that makes it all so complicated," Alix replied, and stood up. "I think we've talked long enough, and I have a train to catch tomorrow."

"I thought you were staying here through the holidays."

"So did I, but there's some pressing family business in New York that won't go through unless they have my signature, and it has to be done in person. As long as I'm there, I can decide what I want to wear to Alice Roosevelt's coming-out ball. Will you be going down to Washington?''

''I wasn't invited,'' Caro responded as she swung her legs to the floor and stood up. ''And I wish I could say I cared.''

''I'm trying to figure out why I said yes. Oh, well—'' The two friends embraced. ''I'll be back the day after tomorrow. Do you need any last-minute presents from the stores?''

''No, I'm happy to say that I have a large suitcase with me that is brimming with Oriental goodies.''

''It sounds intriguing. Look, if you want to talk about Sinclair, I'll be here for you. If he was willing to come back here tonight, he can't be as antisocial as everyone says, and if there's a chance of your seeing him socially, it never hurts to have a few extra hints.''

In her bedroom across the corridor, all pale blue and silver with touches of cream, pale furnishings and crystal vases filled with white tulips, Alix got ready for bed.

In a house well supplied with servants, it would have been the easiest thing to ring for a maid, but it was late, and she was experienced in taking care of herself. Most of all, she wanted to be alone with her thoughts. Weary as she now was, Alix was quite familiar with her sleep pattern and knew that as soon as she slipped between the cool, expensive, hand-made Italian sheets her slumber—with rare exception—would be dream-plagued and largely unrestful.

But I'm used to that; it's Sinclair Poole who's going to give me problems, she thought, turning off the bathroom light and crossing the Aubusson rug to the bed draped in blue chiffon lined in thin white silk. I could have sought him out if I wanted to, and kept him a part of my life until he either accepted me or told me there was nothing for us, but my pride was hurt because he picked Cynthia over me.

And possibly there was something else that kept me from fishing around for a reason to see him again, she thought with brutal honesty. I didn't love Sinclair the way I felt I should.

If, in his worst hour, he had answered the letter she sent him and indicated in any way that he cared, she would have gone to him and stayed by his side. She knew he had received the letter—her cousin Philip Leslie had gone to see him and had told her he put it in his hand, and Philip would never lie to her—but there had never been a reply, and for seven years she had kept her distance.

And there was a good chance that the reason this distance between them had remained unchallenged was that each knew he wasn't right for the other, that some essential component was missing.

Alix, who sometimes thought she could have almost any man she wanted, had avoided marriage. She was convinced that the great love of her life was waiting somewhere for her; the worst possible thing that could happen was to be married to another man when the right one walked into her life. She would never marry simply to have companionship, or a more lavish household, or a family; her essentially private, though not solitary, personality rebelled at what was to her something she considered only a few steps above an arranged marriage. But every so often she realized that all the looking and meeting and traveling, not to mention all the dinners and receptions and balls, were not quite the marital hunting grounds that others assumed them to be.

Alix had a special weakness for Frette linen, so at least her fitful sleep was quite comfortable, and as she dozed and woke and drifted back to sleep, her mind spun busily along. As always, there were too many memories of the past and speculations about the future, but here on Long Island, in the snug security of Cove House and the affection of her friends, she felt some sense of sustenance through the long and difficult night.

In Austria, however, it was already morning, and at that moment, the man she would meet in May and marry at the end of July was walking through the stable yard at Schloss Langau, on his way to breakfast with his host, Baron Albert Rothschild. The schloss and its surrounding buildings were glistening from a fresh blanket of snow that made everything take on a picture-postcard perfection, but the reserved, erudite, and often witty Englishman scarcely noticed any of this natural beauty, since he was thoroughly occupied with his thoughts. This was one of those days when he would willingly give his entire art collection for the chance to share his life with a woman who would love him and not count his fortune or care about his place in London society.

If Alix could have known that the man she wanted was truly out there and that in four months they would meet on a somewhat slippery marble staircase, she would have undoubtedly slept a great deal better. But when she awoke for the second time in less than two hours, she took a deep breath and made a promise to herself.

I want to see Sinclair again, she thought, but only to establish a friendship—not a romance. We've denied each other that, and we can't go back . . . but no matter how hard I try to avoid or deny it, he is a loose thread in my life, and I have to tie it off before I can truly go on.

Caro frequently dreamt about China. The Worths' travels around that vast and mysterious country were more extensive than those of most Western visitors, and the results remained imprinted on her memory.

Occasionally she dreamt about Tientsin, where beautiful rugs were woven, but where the river froze from November to the end of February; or Soochow, that center of silk weaving and embroidery, where there were willow-lined canals and the loveliest gardens that had been cultivated since the eleventh century. She rarely dreamt about Russian-influenced Harbin in the north, or the very commercial city of Canton in the south; and only when her night fantasies took a dramatic turn did they center on the mountain city of Chungking, on the promotory where the swirling waters of the Yangtze and Jialing Rivers meet near the Red Silk Mountain; or of Nanking, so old and so close to the Yangstze and the peaks of the Purple Mountains; or of dreamy and distant Hangchow, with its pagodas and temples and pavilions surrounded by weeping willows and cypresses and the almost unspeakable beauty of West Lake.

Much more frequent were remembrances of bustling Hong Kong, and Shanghai, that cosmopolitan, commercial, international city with its vast foreign population, the Bund, and the seaport that was never quiet.

And then there was Peking.

Sometimes her dreams of the beloved city that they had made the center of their lives were so vivid, so strong that she would wake up and swear that she had felt and seen the fine dust that blows in from the Gobi Desert on the other side of the Great Wall.

Peking, that city of squares upon squares and walls within walls. Peking, the city of 700,000, the capital of the Chinese Empire, with its five cities divided by history and tradition as much as by the walls and gates, each keeping the other out; Peking, the enigma that was China.

The Worths had made their home in the Legation Quarter, where almost all the foreigners settled themselves. Here was a very European atmosphere, clean and quiet, with Legation Street as the main thoroughfare. Here, too, were the hotels, the spacious houses, the shops and clubs—China made ever so faintly understandable.

And sometimes she dreamed about the Forbidden City, where the Imperial Palace was open to very few. To most of the citizens of Peking, both native and foreign, all that they ever saw of it was the roofs of the palaces and temples overtopping the walls, their imperial yellow impressively vivid even on the darkest of days, but in June 1896, the Worths, under the protection of a high official who acted as their guide, presented themselves at the Gate of Celestial Peace.

In that early morning hour, they were shown through a park planted with fig trees to the Temple of the Imperial Ancestors before proceeding to the Gate of Majesty. A short time later they were at the Noonday Gate, the entrance proper to the Forbidden City. From then on, as far as the eye could see, a series of halls stretched northward, separated by courts and monumental gateways, all of which led, finally, to the Winter Palace, with its garden and lakes providing a vista of unbroken serenity.

Those few precious hours in the spot that was hidden away from most of the world had imprinted itself on Caroline's memory, and when she dreamt of it, the colors remained vivid and she could almost feel again the soft spring breeze as it moved through the trees. But tonight, half a world away, on a frigid winter night, her dreams weren't about the sights and sounds and colors of China.

Tonight she dreamed about a man whose face was concealed under a black satin mask, a man who was on a special mission. No matter how close he seemed to her, she knew with the comprehension that only comes in dreams that he was single-minded in his pursuit of the truth, but that his emotions were not closed off to other, more tender and intimate feelings. The dream was long and fragmented and confusing, but when she awoke, Caro knew she had been dreaming about Sinclair Poole; and as she returned to full wakefulness she wondered if, back in New York City, he was dreaming about her.

Chapter Eight

"Well, darling, which do you think it should be?" Vanessa asked as she and Caro sat together on the sofa, studying two paintings that were set up on display easels. "That nice man from Durand-Ruel will be by tomorrow morning, and we want to have an answer for him."

"I think we should start his week in a nice way and take both of them" Caro responded, feasting on the Sisley of an apple orchard in full bloom, and the Pissaro landscape depicting the countryside of southern France. "I love them both, and we certainly have the wall space."

"And they are a remarkable investment."

"Oh, I agree . . . in fact, the value of any Sisley has gone up so much since the artist died that I may want this particular painting as my wedding present. My husband—assuming I ever find one—should have the proper appreciation for a wife who brings an Impressionist painting with her that's not only beautiful, but appreciates better than some stocks!''

"That sounds like a good plan, and when you get married, the Sisley will be yours—provided that now we get all our invitations and social plans in order," Vanessa said, indicating with a graceful sweep of her richly jeweled hand the neat stacks of letters and engraved Bristol cards they had been sorting through before they'd turned their attentions to the paintings.

It was Sunday night, January 12th, four days since Caroline and Vanessa had moved from their suite at the Waldorf-Astoria to their ten-room apartment in the Osborne, the painters and plasterers and floor refinishers having completed their assigned tasks quite a bit ahead of schedule.

The Osborne, located at Fifty-seventh Street and Seventh Avenue, diagonally across from Carnegie Hall, was, seventeen years after its completion, a leader in the ever-growing assortment of Manhattan apartment buildings. Like the Dakota up on Central Park West at Seventy-second Street, the Osborne had been hotly debated as an outlandish structure built in a neighborhood where decent people would nevr consider living, but the critics had failed to take into account Manhattan's inevitable move uptown. Now, in less than twenty years, both buildings were certain to be considered landmarks as the new century progressed and would probably be there, when, in ninety-eight years, the century turned again.

Of course, there were drawbacks to the eleven-story Osborne, the main one being the rather hulking Renaissance-Palace style. The lobby, however, was incredibly ornate, with matched marbles, the best mosaics, and perfectly spaced arches, all accented with gold. Caroline and Vanessa had been taken with the seventh-floor apartment they'd seen on their second day in New York. The rooms were in perfect condition, but the existing height-of-Victoriana woodwork and details were not to their taste at all, and before leaving for Long Island, they left exact instructions for the changes they wanted.

The contents of the house in Peking might be gone, quite possibly forever, but they still had selected treasures from the Shanghai and Hong Kong residences, as well as the contents of the Gramercy Park house that had been in storage since they'd left for China. Now, even on a winter's night, in the drawing room with the newly installed eighteenth-century French paneling, the impression was one of light and welcome. It was free of useless clutter, dark carpets, heavy curtains, and dreary furniture—the hallmark of decor in far too many homes.

The Osborne's dark parquet floors had been polished to a rich gleam before the Bessarabian carpet of ivory, rose, black and gold had been rolled out and the furniture moved in. Two great puffy sofas and a love seat were covered in heavy ivory silk and contrasted with the Louis XIV fauteuils with needlepoint backs and seats. Regency chairs were upholstered in watered silk and a small pistacho-silk footstool was tucked under one of the Venetian tables just for fun. Until they decided on exactly which paintings they wanted to hang in the drawing room, the paneled walls were bare, but the windows were graced by rose taffeta curtains lined in ivory silk. The only distinctly Oriental touches were the white satin-shaded lamps with jade bases and a collection of small celadon objects arranged on the marble mantle.

"Do you have the same feeling I do—that at the first party we give, some well-meaning person will come up to us, give us extravagant compliments on the apartment, and then say that it looks as if we were never in the Orient?" Caro asked in a voice touched by both amusement and cynicism.

"Oh, my dear, I'm not only expecting that reaction, I'm dreading it," Vanessa returned. "The more proper people are, the more they're eager to see the inside of an opium den."

"I'd love to have our presentation rug and my painting of the nine little Pekes again, but if we're going to astound some people with this apartment, I'll be prefectly happy."

Vanessa smiled and slit open one of the last sealed envelopes with her ivory-handled silver letter opener. "Oh, this is fun. The Fowler Gallery on Fourth Avenue is having a special private exhibition of Orientalia prior to auction," she said, showing Caro the engraved card. "Shall we go?"

"Yes, let's. We probably won't want to bid, but it should be fun to see what they have," Caro said, and marked down Tuesday afternoon at one in the appointment book open on the low rosewood coffee table in front of them. "And before we sort through the invitations, why don't we decide on what show to build our theatre party around?''

New York was enjoying an abundance of hits in what was going to be the 1901–1902 theatre season. Caroline and Vanessa had already seen *The Messenger Boy* before it closed on January 4th at Daly's Theatre, as well as its replacement, *Frocks and Frills*. They had applauded the great Maud Adams in *Quality Street* at the Knickerbocker Theatre and had laughed heartily at its successor, *The Toreador,* a London Gaiety Theatre musical farce. *Under Southern Skies,* with Grace George, was sold out too far in advance for them to consider it for their theatre party, and *The Duchess,* starring Anna Held, had already been selected by Philip and Kezia Leslie for their theatre party at the end of February.

''It looks like our best bet is *D'Arcy Of The Guards,*'' Vanessa said, studying *Theatre Magazine.* ''I'm going to rely on my old friendship with Henry Miller and have him save fourteen seats for us. Five couples, you and some handsome young man, and me with some appropriate dull blanket!''

''That'll be the day.'' Caro laughed and regarded her stepmother, elegant in a Callot Soeurs dinner dress of white, black, and gray dotted silk chiffon over ivory satin and trimmed with black Chantilly lace and pink satin ribbon, with obvious admiration and affection. ''I not only don't see you with some boring old man, I think it would be an insult to Daddy's memory. He wouldn't want you to be bored to tears.''

"Well, we've both shared enough tears in the past year."

"I had a long talk with Thea Harper, and she said it's too bad her father's away on an expedition—he's on his way to either Hawaii or the Amazon, I can't remember which. She said it would be fun to introduce the two of you, and I agreed with her."

"Matchmaking already?"

"Well, why not?"

"Then, it wouldn't bother you terribly if by and by I find myself a nice widower and we have a pleasant friendship together?"

"The only thing I'd really and truly mind is if you decided you wanted to go back to London. I don't think I'd be very happy living there on a permanent basis."

"On reflection, neither would I. If I *had* enjoyed it, perhaps I wouldn't have been so eager to come to New York twelve years ago." Vanessa was quiet for a moment. "But never mind me. We still have to decide which wildly handsome and terribly well-off man we should invite for you. Any ideas, darling?"

"One or two. What would you say to Sinclair Poole?" Caro had been trying to find an opportune moment to mention Sin's name since they'd begun to discuss their theatre party. "He seems to fit both requirements, and a little thing like not being received shouldn't matter too much," she went on jauntily. "And it would be a nice way to thank him for the roses."

"You can't be sure he sent them, though."

On Saturday afternoon, a messenger had delivered a dozen dark-red American Beauty roses with the longest stems Caro had ever seen. There was no card, but she was certain from the moment she untied the ribbon and opened the box that they had come from Sinclair, for two good reasons. The first was that she hadn't really met any eligible men since her return to New York; the second was reputation of the florist. Among her set, the accepted shops for ordering in-and out-of-season blooms were Thorley's, Wadley and Smythe, the Fernery, and the Fifth Avenue Florist. Her roses had come from Max Schling's shop. The place that billed itself as "the telegraph florist of New York" was patronized by out-of-towners sending flowers to friends in the city, well-off theatrical people, and nouveau-riche tourists—it was just the place for someone who knew he would have less than first-class service at a society florist.

"He sent them. I rang Schling's, and they said the man who sent my roses paid cash and didn't give his name, but the description sounded very much like Sinclair."

"When you met him, most of his face was hidden by a mask."

"Oh, you don't have to remind me!"

"Still, the flowers are a good sign—it shows he has style. But the question remains, do you think he'd accept?"

"All it's going to take to find out is a stamp."

Vanessa nodded but made no move to add Sin-

99

clair's name to the guest list. "Are you very interested in him, darling?"

"I think I could be—and it isn't just some sort of a crush," she said. "I'm not intrigued with him because he has all the markings of a mystery man, or because he supposedly has an impossible personality."

"What makes you say something like that?" Vanessa questioned, surprised.

"Oh, it's just a theory of mine, based on everything we heard at Cove House. I think Sinclair has divorced himself from society almost more than he's been cut. There are still people who care about him. If he'd stayed with them when the tragedy with his father happened, he'd have had a social base to work from, and that, gradually, would have widened into other circles—ones where he could keep a close eye on his father's enemies."

"Yes, that's all very true, but sometimes even highly intelligent men don't take the right and easy course in life," Vanessa responded with great seriousness. "For whatever reason, they prefer to follow a far more complicated pattern. You have to admit that doing it this way must make him feel much more true to himself."

"And I admire him for the way he's done everything, from paying back the people who invested in the nonexistent company to building his import firm, and most of all for believing in has father. But he was also very willing to come to Cove House if everything had worked out differently," Caro said. "I think we should send him an invitation."

"Done, but we will have to keep a name in reserve in case he refuses—which he may very well do."

"I know, but it's the best way I can think of to let him know that I haven't changed my mind about him. When a man's been betrayed once, he's always going to hold on to the feelings that act generated."

"I believe I missed something," Vanessa said slowly. "Who betrayed Sinclair?"

"Cynthia Moreton-Chandler," Caro said, and told her stepmother about her and Alix's suspicions about the woman who had once been Sinclair's fiancée.

"What a dreadful woman she sounds like. Unhappily, some men can't get past that kind of hurt no matter how hard they try."

Vanessa's words sent a wave of apprehension through Caro. The line between love and hate was so thin that at times it wasn't there at all, and the only ray of hope she could come up with was that Alix had been right: the engagement between Sinclair and Cynthia had been based on meeting parental needs—to please their fathers, although each had an entirely different ulterior motive. In fact, if indeed he were in love with someone all this time, she would much rather have it be Alix. Even though it could make her life just as miserable, there was some satisfaction in knowing that your competition was your equal.

"I think I should send him something," she said at last, "just to thank him for the flowers. A book would be about right, and since I could use a break from all our social arrangements, why don't we go into the library?" Caro rose to her feet, her Lucile dinner dress of pale blue charmeuse dotted with steel beads and insets of pointe de Venise lace over chiffon and satin letting out an expensive whisper. "I'd like your advice in the matter."

"Well, don't send him a romance."

"Oh, funny."

The library was the only room that gave away the secret that Vanessa and Caroline weren't completely settled in their new home. As in the rest of the rooms, the heavy dark paneling had been removed, but here the walls and bookshelves were painted a soft hunter green. A fine needlepoint rug of gold, burgundy, dark green and ivory contrasted with the dark green leather chesterfields and deep armchairs upholstered in paisley silk, and paisley silk throw pillows were scattered around to make the atmosphere even more welcoming. But the packing crates pushed into corners and numerous packages from Brentano's and Scribner's on the tables and the half-filled shelves proved they still had quite a bit of arranging to do.

"Do you think Sinclair would like Lafcadio Hearn's *Glimpses of Unfamiliar Japan?*" Caro asked, considering the books on one of the shelves.

"I'm sure he'd appreciate it, but it's become such a classic since it was published eight years ago that he may have read it already."

"You're probably right, but I do want to send him a book with an Oriental theme," Caro said, and turned to a nearby table. "I know there's something in the latest Brentano's delivery. . . . Here it is," she said triumphantly, holding up an elegantly embossed volume. "*Mythical Japan.* I'll wrap it up in the morning, write a note, and send it downtown with a messenger."

"How do you know where he lives?"

"Sinclair may be out of the *Social Register,* but he doesn't seem to have anything against being listed in the New York Telephone Directory. I just happened to be glancing through it a few weeks ago and came across his name," she added, not seeing where it was necessary to add that she had consulted the telephone listings while they were still at Cove House. "All things considered, I think the invitation should be sent separately."

"I wouldn't have it any other way. I've always said that good and interesting men are very hard to find, and sometimes a woman has to do what isn't considered to be good form."

Caro regarded Vanessa with true affection. 'I have an idea that if Sinclair accepts our invitation, we may engender quite a bit of attention of the wrong sort. Are you sure it won't matter to you? If I remember correctly, certain segments of New York Society just don't appreciate eccentricity."

"I think we'll manage to get by."

"Then this will be my last word on the subject. It's hard to tell why a man and a woman are attracted to each other, but I felt something all the time we were together. There isn't a woman alive who can make a man feel something he doesn't want to, but I owe it to myself to find out if there's really

103

the possibility of an attraction between us or if I was simply caught up in the excitement of meeting a 'mystery man,' '' she explained. ''Besides, when Sinclair does clear his father's name, he won't be isolated any longer. Eventually, some woman is going to decide he's more than worth the effort to go after—and I don't see any reason at all why it shouldn't be me!''

Caro reclined in bed, her head resting against a pile of pillows, as she read *The Last Word*. Having delivered her final statement about Sinclair Poole— as well as anything else even faintly romantic—she and Vanessa had sorted through all their invitations, decided on their replies, and finished the plans for their own theatre party, so that now, shortly before midnight, she was more than comfortably tucked up in bed, reading a new novel.

Or trying to.

She was a voracious reader, but tonight her mind was on other matters, and she slipped a bookmark between the pages and closed the volume, nestling into the pillows. Ever since her return to New York, she had had difficulty falling asleep at night. Since the problem hadn't plagued her at Cove House, Caro had decided that it had been their suite at the Waldorf, ornately overdecorated by Arnold Constable, right down to the gold Steinway piano in the sitting room, that caused her uneasy repose.

With that in mind, she had decorated her bedroom in soft shades of blue, ivory, and touches of gold. Her large bed was draped in ivory silk studded with faux pearls, and the same fabric was at the windows. The room as designed to be cool and relaxing, right down to the Childe Hassam landscape and the small, pretty pastel paintings on the walls, but as yet, none of it seemed to be working.

Some of it, she supposed as she tucked a small pillow under her neck, had to do with being in a city that, unlike some of its citizens, never went to sleep. And that, she knew, wasn't what she had remembered at all. There was something almost embarrassing about a native New Yorker feeling uncomfortable in her own city.

During the day I'm fine, running from one place to another, and the evenings aren't bad, not when I have all those parties to go to, but it's late at night that gets to me every time, she thought, twisting a silk ribbon, one of several that ornamented her Lucile nightgown of ice-blue satin.

It would have been nice—not to mention romantic—to think that her problems with sleep were tied up with her attraction to Sinclair. But since this was life and not a romantic novel, Caro had to admit that while the masked man she'd met on the terrace and danced with and kissed and then been rudely torn away from most certainly *did* have a special place in her heart, he was not keeping her up nights. It was being back in New York, where she now felt she didn't quite belong, but which, for all intents and purposes, was her home.

I feel so unconnected, she thought with a rush of

sudden and unexpected desolation. And I can't tell Vanessa any of this.

Caro often thought that she was as close to her stepmother as she had been to her real mother; in fact, she had known Vanessa for a longer period of time. She called her Mummy, and confided in her, and they shared sorrow and joy, but she couldn't tell her about this feeling of unfamiliarity that clung to her like a silk dress on a hot and humid day. Even onetime close friends felt a bit like strangers, and she couldn't lose the feeling that among the social circles they traveled in, it was best to tread very carefully.

And New York City itself had changed so much.

Of course it was impossible to expect that this, the most intriguing of all metropolises, would stay the same, but the changes that had taken place between June 1893, when they left for China, and November 1901, when she and Vanessa stepped off the Twentieth Century, were almost too much to absorb in such a short time. Caro began to understand why some people who visited New York for the first time loathed it instantly, vowed never to return, and badmouthed it at every possible opportunity.

It encompassed so much, and it was almost beyond belief that one island could hold it all.

The Waldorf-Astoria was considered the city's premier luxury hotel, but it was also a sure bet that it wouldn't occupy that lofty position alone for much longer; Delmonico's and Sherry's vied with each other to attract the most fashionable diners and the most top-drawer parties and receptions in the elegant private rooms; and an amazing array of millionaires' mansions filled Fifth Avenue from the Fifties to the Metropolitan Museum of Art. The area was once considered almost too distant for museumgoers even to visit, much less as a site on which to build a house. And then there were the skyscrapers, those buildings that only nine years earlier had been topics of heated debate but were now an accepted architectural style.

It was all change without end, and Caro was anything but against progress; but her life for so long had been lived in a culture that was ancient and unchanging that now she had trouble adjusting.

Would it have been better to spend the last year in San Francisco? she wondered. It might have been easier to get used to a faster pace there than in Hawaii. Of course, the ultimate irony was that in the Orient, the Worths had been considered perfect examples of progressive, fast-thinking, and decisive Westerners.

Some days she felt as if the rush and push of the city were about to overhwelm her, that there was no chance to focus on one thing before something equally interesting and compelling clamored for her attention. Yet New York would always work its own strange alchemy over her, and she really wouldn't want to be anywhere else right now.

Where else could I have met Sinclair Poole? she asked herself, and slowly began to smile.

Here was the irrefutable fact about New York . . . anything could happen here, and no matter how unconnected she felt, how lifted up from one place and

107

set down in another—she had to be ready to move with the moment. Not only that, but she had to know when it was wrong as much as when it was right. She had seen it far too often in China—girls getting engaged to young men because the glamour of the moment made them lose touch with what lay beyond the moment and past the façade.

Caro opened her book again and centered her attention on the printed page. Somehow, probably when she least expected it, she would have the opportunity to see Sinclair again, and with any luck she—no, they—would begin to put their first meeting into some sort of perspective. And quite possibly that night, instead of being an unexpected interlude, would prove to be the first strands in a leitmotif that they would weave together.

Chapter Nine

On the voyage from Honolulu to San Francisco, the Worth women had decided that when it came to furnishing their home in New York City, and in order to put their period of mourning behind them, they would not try to recreate the decor of their homes in China. Any Oriental touches, they agreed, would be no more than what any other serious collector might display. But such a decision did not in any way preclude their examining the treasures of the Far East, and today, Tuesday afternoon, January 14th, they were looking forward to the exhibition prior to auction at the Fowler Galleries.

They had spent the morning most engrossingly at Thurn's, the premier shop for the newest and best Paris imports, viewing the latest selections; enjoyed an extremely pleasant lunch at Sherry's, increasingly the most fashionable restaurant in New York; and now the brougham delivered them to Fourth

Avenue and Twentieth Street and the great gilded doors of the Fowler Art and Auction Galleries.

In just three short years, the Fowler family would celebrate its fiftieth anniversary in offering superb and authenticated antiques, paintings, and objets d'art with an accent on the fine arts of the Orient. They had changed quite a bit since the day the first enterprising Fowler had taken a shop near Union Square in order to sell a large shipment of Chinese Export Porcelain that a Yankee Trader cousin had brought back from Nanking. Now there was a solemn-faced doorman to usher the clients in, but a member of the family was never very far away, particularly when a top-drawer, by-invitation-only crowd was expected.

"Mrs. Worth, Miss Worth, welcome to our gallery!" Jay Fowler, a jaunty young man in his late twenties who Caro remembered from dancing school, appeared in the reception room featuring a blue-and-white dragon-motif carpet, laquered tables, and brocade-covered settees. "My grandfather is going to be so upset that he wasn't here to greet both of you himself, but he had a luncheon appointment at Delmonico's, and that can go on for some time!"

"We finished lunch early and decided to come directly here," Caro replied pleasantly. Arrayed for the clear, cold winter day in a Lucile dress of navy wool trimmed with inset panels of embroidered ivory wool and ivory lace edged in yellow thread, she easily captured Jay's attention. "Do you have to keep us away from the exhibition area until two, or can we get an early preview?''

''That's really why we came a bit early,'' Vanessa added, looking at Jay through the light veiling that ornamented her baum marten toque and set off her Doucet afternoon costume of dove-gray wool flecked with white and trimmed with off-white silk piping. ''We know everything you have to offer is of the finest quality.''

''Thank you, Mrs. Worth. I'll be pleased to show you and Miss Worth upstairs and give you a guided tour of the exhibition room. You're the earliest arrivals,'' Jay told them with almost puppy-dog eagerness. ''Now don't worry about your wraps, leave them right here. ''I know that you'll appreciate what we have here, and we are accepting sealed bids in advance—''

The first floor of Fowler's was divided into reception rooms and salesrooms, each decorated to represent a particular style of antique furnishings. Every item was for sale, but the Belgian tapestries hung along the staircase wall were for admiration. ''You'll see that we've made major changes since the last time you were here,' Jay said as he escorted them upstairs. ''About two years ago, my father decided to remodel the second floor, and now we have a room to conduct the auction in and another for exhibition,'' he told them proudly. ''We have a series of movable screens so either room can be made larger or smaller, depending on what we need.''

They reached the top of the stairs, and Jay took them down a carpeted hallway toward one set in a series of sliding carved-oak doors. "Last night, my father told me about one rug—a masterpiece, really—that he's certain is going to impress you," he said, sliding open the doors and then stepping aside so Caro and Vanessa could precede him.

For a moment, both women stood transfixed. In a room easily twenty feet long, with walls painted an unobtrusive pale gray and elaborately framed mirrors that reflected everything, were what had to be as many treasures of the Orient as had ever been collected in an auction house at one time.

"We've tried to divide the rugs and furnishings and porcelains by dynasty and period," Jay informed them, puzzled by their silence.

"So I see," Vanessa murmured, her usual British sang-froid apparently having deserted her. "Caro, look at the rug—"

There was an undefinable atmosphere in the room now; it had enveloped Caro the moment the great doors slid open and they saw the vast display of riches. Now she felt as if ice water were trickling slowly through her veins. A combination of horror and disbelief seemed to storm her as she dragged her fascinated gaze away from the rug to survey the rest of the room.

"*Ours,*" she whispered at last, in a voice she didn't quite recognize as her own.

"All of it ours." Vanessa's voice echoed her incredulity.

Still unbelieving, Caro crossed the shining parquet floor to where a vast Chinese presentation rug was displayed on a specially constructed stand so that

112

its full beauty was visible. Stopping before it, she ran an expert hand lightly over the background of antique ivory and the porcelain-blue border, and looked at the flowers and medallions: Gobelin-blue and cloud-pink, rich salmon and soft sage green, and dashes of pure Chinese yellow. Confident that it was really here again and not likely to disappear, Caro relaxed just a bit, but to be sure, she lifted a corner of the rug and checked it for a small mark woven in the back that confirmed it as theirs.

"Darling—" Vanessa's voice, with that single endearment carrying so much expectation, sounded with the clarity of a bell. "Darling, is it really ours?"

It was as if a spell had been broken.

"Oh, yes. *Yes!*" Caro exchanged looks with her stepmother and then studied the room again, this time with a clearly investigative glance. "And so are the celedon cachepots," she said a minute later, gesturing at a nearby table. "And my Pekes—" Placed before one of the many windows was an easel displaying a narrowly framed watercolor, painted in the late 1700s and depicting nine happy Pekingese puppies frolicking in a garden.

"Mrs. Worth, Miss Worth, I don't quite understand—" Jay managed to get out, comprehending what was happening all too well. If his suspicions were true, he thought, shuddering, it could be the juiciest scandal ever to rock the closed little world of New York's antique dealers and auction houses. "If there is something I can help you with. . . ."

Vanessa held off all comment until Caro was by her side again, well aware that the physical sight of a united front was quite powerful in a situation like this. 'I'm afraid we're on the verge of quite a serious problem,'' she said at last. ''It seems that most of what you have in this room belongs to my step-daughter and myself; it was all stolen from our house in Peking during the Boxer Rebellion.''

The color ebbed swiftly from Jay Fowler's face. ''But this was all purchased through a highly repu-table dealer in Orientalia. Of course, if it's just a question of the rug and the cachepots—'' He stopped to draw a deep breath, and Caro spoke quickly.

''I wish we could say it was only those,'' she said, her heart racing. ''During the Rebellion, the entire contents of our Peking house was taken, cleaned out, it all vanished. We never expected to see any of it again, and now—''

Jay seemed to grow paler. ''Surely you're not suggesting that everything here is. . . .is yours?''

''No, so far I don't see any of our jade, or any of the furniture.''

''But this is my husband's T'ang Dynasty horse,'' Vanessa said as she examined an equestrian figure with a green-gold exterior. ''I recognize it by the dent in one of the hooves.''

With Jay looking on, both women began to move around the large room, shaking their heads at some items and touching others with great tenderness. To-gether they found several carved tables, a pair of cloisonné elephants from the Qianlong Period, a large celadon saucer with an incised decoration of a lotus flower, a quartet of 19th-century famille noire beluster vases, two cabinets full of blue and white

114

porcelain dishes and vases, a two-hundred-piece set of Rose Medallion china, and finally, after numerous other items had been either identified or rejected, Caro's 18th-century Chinese writing table with intricate hand decorations.

For a house as large as the one they had occupied on a cul-de-sac off Legation Street, it wasn't very much, but for an exhibition room in an auction house, it was quite a bit. Both Caro and Vanessa knew that Fowler's, with its sterling reputation, wouldn't dream of selling as much as a teacup when ownership was in doubt. But that didn't mean that the next half-hour or so was going to be either easy or pleasant for any of them.

"We realize that this is a distressing moment for both of you," Jay said finally, employing the polite royal "we," a certain sign that this was not going to be easy. "But you'll understand that we need more than your word in this matter."

"We have bills of sale," Caro assured him. "We also have some family photographs in which the rug and several other pieces show quite clearly."

"It will take a few days to gather everything together," Vanessa added. "But in the meantime, I'm going to have to request that this exhibition be canceled."

"That's a perfectly reasonable request on your part, Mrs. Worth, and as much as I hate to say this. . . ." Jay's voice trailed off for a moment. "Before I discuss this with my father and grandfather, I need a bit more concrete proof than a special mark on the back of a rug or a dent in a hoof," he concluded, and felt quite pleased with himself. Distraught women with outlandish claims were not unknown; one had to proceed with the greatest of care.

"Would some old letters do?" Caro asked. "A few days after the desk was purchased, I discovered quite by accident that it had a secret compartment. Since it was in my room, I never mentioned it to either my father or my stepmother; even though I never had any reason or need to hide anything from them, I rather liked the idea of having this secret spot. Every woman should have a secret place for her love letters," she concluded, forcing herself to look directly at him." If you want to come over to the desk, I'll show you which panel to move—"

"Well, I've never seen anything like this before!" Jay exclaimed a minute later when the appropriate panel moved back and a drawer sprung out.

"I couldn't be sure these were still here," Caro said, taking out a thick sheaf of letters tied up with a green satin ribbon. "In fact, I was hoping that knowing about the drawer and how to open it would have sufficed, but as you can see, they are all addressed to me, and there is no way I could have planted them there beforehand."

"I have to speak with my grandfather," Jay said after one look at the envelopes. "He should be back from lunch by now."

"And I would like to go with you," Vanessa said, apparently fully recovered from her shock at seeing some of their Peking belongings again, and at the revelation of the secret drawer. "There isn't any time to waste."

"Particularly with so little time before the other invited guests arrive," Caro added, looking at the oval face of the velvet-banded gold watch at her wrist. "I'm not presuming to tell you your business, but shouldn't the staff be alerted to inform everyone that this afternoon's exhibition is—" She hesitated for a tactful moment. "—not going to take place?"

Caro remained behind in the exhibition room while Vanessa and Jay went off on their appointed tasks. She had decided that the discussion her step-mother was going to have with Horace Fowler was best conducted in as much privacy as possible, and she certainly didn't want to trail along with Jay while he dealt with the other guests who must already be arriving.

Caro's shock over all this had not completely subsided. It was a clear indication that even more was going to happen—events like this weren't single incidents—but for the moment, all she wanted was to spend a few minutes alone among the dear possessions she thought had been lost forever. Holding onto the letters—they wouldn't fit into her handbag and she certainly wasn't going to put them back in the writing table—she walked across the floor to the rug on display, content simply to look at and touch it, and slowly she began to realize that her feeling of being disconnected, of being someplace that she was supposed to know but couldn't seem to find herself in had changed. It wasn't gone, but the worst of it had subsided.

Finding all of this again, she thought, was in its own way as shockingly unexpected as the gunshot that had announced Davis Moreton's suicide. And it was a suicide; Caro was sure of it. If there had been the slightest chance that the Chandler-Moreton group could have pinned the whole ugly incident on Sinclair, they would have done so as soon as they left the Linden Trees, and the newspapers would have been full of their accusations.

For the first few days following the incident, Caro had approached the morning papers with heart-racing trepidation, but the only reports carried had been the ususal ones—the short article stating that Davis Moreton had died suddenly at a Long Island country club; the longer, highly laudatory and clearly family-written obituary in the *Times;* and the notice of the time and place of the service. Quite obviously, the Reverend Doctor Morgan at Heavenly Rest wouldn't conduct a funeral service about which the question of suicide was being openly discussed in the papers.

She was pondering Sinclair's narrow escape when Jay returned, his usual composure firmly restored, carrying two crystal flutes filled with champagne.

"Bollinger '98," he said as she accepted a glass. "Not exactly saki or plum wine, but we didn't think anyone would complain. As it is, one of us in this room does have a cause for celebration."

Caro smiled. "Is it all settled?"

"Just about. Oh, Grandfather's pretty shocked, but the proof that some of this belongs to you and your stepmother is all but irrefutable."

"I know you don't have to tell me this, but how did you acquire these treasures? One dealer, or a series of them?"

"Only one, and as far as I know, despite a murky past, he's always been completely honest and reputable. I wouldn't be surprised if Grandfather decided to refrain from doing any further business with Sinclair Poole."

Caro knew who he was talking about before Jay finished his first sentence. Well, I wanted a way to contact him again, but I didn't expect anything like this, she thought. Now I have to make sure that Sinclair's having avoided being implicated in Davis Moreton's death wasn't just a prelude to his being called a dealer in stolen goods.

"I certainly hope you're not going to take any action against him," Caro said at last, deliberately keeping her voice pitched at a level of calmness she didn't feel.

"Well, *I* wouldn't, but I don't know about Grandfather—he's a real stickler for propriety. Never let the slightest smudge of doubt touch the name of Fowler, and all that. He may want to make a fuss just to show up how pure we are."

"How unfair. Good dealers in Orientalia are difficult to find," she went on swiftly, covering herself. If for one moment Jay suspected she had an ulterior motive. . . .The gossiping that went on in the world of art galleries, auction houses, and antique dealers was unbelievable. One slip on her part and the fact that she knew Sin would be all over New York before she even had a plan worked out about how best

119

to arrange to see him again. "Can't you dissuade him?"

"I can see you don't know a thing about Sinclair Poole," Jay said, his voice changing from that of the reserved dealer to one of conspirator imparting some absolutely thrilling information. "Why, Caroline—may I call you Caroline. . . . ?"

"Of course, I was just going to ask you to," she said, hoping he'd get to the point of his story—which she already knew but had to pretend she was hearing for the first time. "Tell me, does this story refer in some way to all of the missing items we found?"

"Well, not exactly," he told her, "but about seven years ago he was involved in a horrible scandal . . . just ask anyone. Sinclair didn't have anything to do with selling all those fake shares, but he's never stopped insisting his father was the victim of some sort of conspiracy. But his reputation as a dealer is absolutely spotless."

"Shouldn't that count for more than anything else?" Caro hated the sweet, conciliatory note she forced into her voice. It wasn't her at all, but for the moment she had to play it as if she were hearing all this for the first time. Now, if ony she could get the conversation past the basic point that everyone seemed to get stuck on. What had happened in 1895 didn't matter, but right now did. "I mean, you do sound as if you and Mr. Poole got on well, and respect each other on business matters. I imagine you even have lunch together occasionally."

"I've gone to his club once or twice. Dad thinks

120

it's good business practise, but Grandfather would have a fit if he knew.''

"Mr. Poole has a club?" she questioned, drawing him out.

"It's a place for people who have businesses on the Bowery, and he has quite a good cook, a Chinese named Wong, who can whip up just about anything.''

All of this was very interesting, but it wasn't much of help, Caro decided. There had to be something else, some bit of information that would tell her more about Sinclair.

"I suppose that for a man who had to change his life so completely, he doesn't do anything the way other, more . . . conventional New Yorkers do?" she fished carefully.

"You'd be surprised. Do you know I got to know Sinclair Poole? At the Thursday morning Communion Service at the Church of the Transfiguration,'' Jay said with such satisfaction that it was immediately clear he felt he was imparting some bit of news that he was certain no one else knew. "I guess he still likes to think of himself as a good Episcopalian, even if it *is* the Actors' Church.''

Then why do you go there, Caro thought nastily, refraining from asking that loaded question. "I think that sounds very nice," she said at last, and meant every word. "Rather traditional, in fact.''

"Oh, it is that. But it makes me wonder if he goes to services to—'' Jay lowered his voice to a conspirator's whisper even though there wasn't anyone around to overhear him. "—to *make up* for some-

121

thing. Maybe he is inventing all those stories about someone deliberately arranging his father's downfall. . . . ''

Caro recoiled instinctively. "We don't know that either version is correct."

Jay smiled indulgently. "I love how women always want to be fair. It's such an admirable trait."

"Don't patronize me," Caro said shortly, watching as his smile faded. She could hear Vanessa's voice in the hallway outside, together with a deeper one that was probably old Mr. Fowler. "It's not at all good for business," she went on, patting her rug again with a fond touch. "Too bad this will have to go into storage."

"Fowler's will be happy to store it for you both—and at a very nominal charge, provided you use us when you decide to sell it."

"Thank you, but I doubt we'll need either of those services," Caro answered with a sweetness she certainly didn't feel. "And now I have my own theory as to why Sinclair Poole goes to the Little Church Around the Corner," she went on. To gather the strength to deal with all the auction houses and antique salons who are waiting around for him to do something dishonest!"

"What happened to us this afternoon was a sign."

"Oh, Mummy—"

"No, darling, it most definitely is a sign for us," Vanessa insisted as the brougham took them back uptown. "We've tried to smother our years in China

122

because of our grief. Your father wouldn't have wanted us to do that."

"Of course not, and I wasn't scoffing at you, but we don't have to bring the supernatural into this," Caro said, patting her stepmother's hand.

"Well, I'm not talking about ghosties and ghoulies—nothing like that at all—it's just that we shouldn't deny ourselves certain things that we like or believe in."

Caro began to smile. "Such as?"

"Before I left Mr. Fowler's office, I rang home and told Mrs. Cavendish to forget about whatever I told her to make for dinner." Patrick and Flora Cavendish had previously worked as houseman and cook for the director of Barclay's Bank in Hong Kong, and Caro and Vanessa had been able to persuade them to resign their positions in favor of coming to work for them in America. "I said that instead she was to fix her famous lemon chicken."

"Well, I'm certainly not going to complain about that!"

"And now we have to find a pet shop, one that can order black fish for us."

"Feng shui," Caro said, referring to the Chinese art of placement of objects to create an environment conducive to health and good fortune. "I've wanted to do it in the apartment."

"Why didn't you say something before this?"

"Because I've been feeling so disconnected from everything—not living in the Orient any more, but not really a part of New York yet, either. I was afraid you would think that by our using *feng shui* I was trying to hang onto something familiar.''

''Oh, this is so funny,'' Vanessa said, but tears appeared in her eyes. ''I've been wanting to say the same thing to you, but I couldn't. Just now, I really had to take the plunge and hope you wouldn't think I'm the one who's clinging to the past!''

''For two women who've never had the slightest difficulty expressing themselves, we decided to be reticent about the wrong things!'' Caro exclaimed as they embraced. ''When we get home, I'll go through the telephone directory to find out where we can get exotic fish.''

There was a lot to discuss, but as they talked, Caro's mind was on another directory listing, and what she would do with it after she made a list of the pet shops. Once that task was completed, she would ring the Church of the Transfiguration and find out what time their Thursday morning service started.

That should be easy enough, she thought as Lawton turned the brougham uptown on Fifth Avenue. The hard part is going to be deciding if I want to follow thorugh with my plan. It's possible he sent those flowers hoping I wouldn't be able to find out he sent them. No, that doesn't sound right, any more than it sounds right that he deals in stolen merchandise. Well, this isn't going to be easy, but then, I don't think anything involving a good man ever is.

Chapter Ten

The Church of the Transfiguration, much better known as the Little Church Around the Corner, had received its unusual sobriquet in December 1870, when the noted actor Joseph Jefferson tried to arrange a funeral service for his friend and fellow thespian George Holland. He was informed by the Reverend William Tufnell Sabine, Rector at the Church of the Atonement, that his parish didn't bury theatricals, but that the "little church around the corner" might be willing to oblige.

It did conduct the service. From that day on it was known as both the Actor's Church and as "the Little Church Around the Corner" to such an extent that it was hardly ever referred to by its proper name.

Although no secret marriages or marriages between divorced people were performed here, the Transfiguration provided a house of worship for those who, for one reason or other, shied away from the more "fashionable" Episcopalian churches, and its regular Thursday morning service drew working actors who had been up all night following Wednesday's two performances as well as regular parishoners (some of them highly regarded pillars of the New York community) and area businesspeople. It began promptly at eight, making Caro a good five minutes late.

An early riser, she had left the Osborne in plenty of time to get to One East Twenty-ninth Street, but traffic had been heavy and not even her skilled driver could maneuver deftly through the congested streets. Instructing him to wait, she crossed the sidewalk, and went past the wrought-iron fence, which enclosed a garden with handsomely laid-out shrubs, hedges, and flower beds, all presided over by large old elm trees. Clearly at other times of the year it was a very pleasant place: at the height of winter it was cold and bare and gave greater emphasis to the church's fourteenth-century Gothic architecture.

Caro walked through the tile-roofed lych-gate, a structure seen often in English church gardens but rarely in the United States, and soon found herself approaching the double doors, her heartbeat quickening with apprehension.

So much for my plan to meet Sinclair before the service starts, she thought, standing in the vestibule. But it may be better this way—a man can feel strange about something as simple as attending services when it doesn't seem to mesh with his personality . . . meeting him afterwards is easier, less pointed.

And if by some chance he were a serious communicant, there was no need to upset him by letting him find out too quickly that unless it were a wedding or a funeral, she didn't go to church, Caro added silently as she hesitated, uncertain about disturbing the minister by walking in late.

The furnace was working very well, and Caro pulled off her cashmere-lined leather gloves before unbuttoning her Lucile coat of black wool trimmed with black velvet to reveal a Callot Soeurs suit of burgundy wool broadcloth ornamented with dark red velvet and black soutache and worn with a black satin blouse. Quickly she slipped off her coat and decided that as long as she was late, the best she could do was to familiarize herself with her surroundings. There was a great deal to be admired in the handsome chestnut and oak woodwork, but gradually her attentive gaze took in the Visitors' Book. Set open on the writing shelf, it invited all newcomers to inscribe their names.

Unable to resist, Caro entered her name and address before approaching the entrance to the nave and quietly slipping into an empty back pew.

For a few mintues Caro sat quietly, her attention fixed on the chancel where the Reverend Dr. George Clarke Houghton, nephew of the first rector, was conducting the service, listening as she would in a theatre; but gradually she let her gaze wander over the handsome interior, admiring the fine stained-glass windows before she tried to pick out one particular figure. It certainly couldn't be any harder to identify a man by the back of his head than to try to imagine what he looked like without a domino mask.

It was a typically cold January morning, and the number of worshippers was correspondingly small. Thanks to heavy winter clothes, nearly all the men had a uniform look, but Caro knew that someone like Sinclair Poole was incapable of blending into a background, and when her gaze settled on one masculine figure seated on the right side of the nave, quite near the front, a jolt of certainty ran through her. Her heart began to beat faster and a warmth quite apart from that provided by the central heating spread through her veins.

And now that you've found him, Caro, what do you intend to do about it? she asked herself, well aware that if given half a chance, she just might opt for slipping out of the church as quietly as she'd arrived. Suppose he saw her and ignored her, or worse, thought she was chasing him? Should she have telephoned, and, acting dignified and detached, asked for an appointment to discuss why he had sold Fowler's stolen merchandise—her belongings, to be specific?

Oh, no—I'd never say *that*, she thought. It sounds like something Cynthia would do.

The thought of the imperious Mrs. Chandler led quite naturally to thoughts of Alix . . . two women, each of them strong and demanding and knowing exactly what she wanted.

Just like I am.

Both of them part of Sin's life at a crucial time.

Just like I am.

And both of them remaining unresolved chapters in his life.

The way I won't be.

Her determination as she pondered the similarities between herself and the two women who figured so importantly in Sin's life disturbed Caro. Intelligence and determination were considered terrible detriments to any woman, and while she'd never played either helpless or stupid in order to win approbation, she had almost deliberately lost contact with her sense of purpose, her ability to follow through in a situation and get the job done. Despite her witty-tinged-with-acid ability to indentify bores, boors, and freeloaders of every stripe, her usually refined manner fooled not only others, but herself as well. With fresh insight, she realized that one of the reasons she probably disliked Cynthia with such intensity was that she recognized some of that woman's traits in herself. True, she would never lie for her own gain or profit or to implicate an innocent person in a criminal act, but still. . . .

Startled, Caro realized that the service was nearly over and that Communion was about to be offered. Blinking herself to attention, she watched as the first group of communicants made their way to the altar rail, and couldn't help but smile when she saw the man she was certain was Sinclair Poole rise. There was something more than slightly familiar about his sleek profile and catlike grace, she decided, not taking her eyes off him.

If she wanted to leave, now was the perfect time,

but she overcame that first instinct to flee out of the sheer curiosity to find out what would happen next.

Sin walked up the aisle with the certainty of one who knew the feeling that someone was watching him only too well. His amber eyes scanned the back pews—he had long ago learned to spot the odd ones on sight—but he didn't see anyone who fit that description, only a woman wearing clothes that clearly announced that their place of origin was Paris, topped off by an elegant sable toque. She was looking directly at him, but there was neither coyness nor resentment in her eyes, and then it all fell into place for him.

He stopped beside the back pew. "Good Morning, Miss Worth."

Caro rose gracefully to her feet. "Hello, Mr. Poole," she returned.

"Do you attend regularly here?"

"No."

"Are you thinking of doing so?"

"I'm afraid that's not too likely."

"I see," he said; belatedly, he did. "Then I can safely say that it's me and not this historic spot that drew you here."

Caro smiled. "That's just about it. There's something important we need to discuss."

If this was a new line, Sin decided, he liked it, but with the congregation returning up the aisle at steady intervals, they couldn't remain standing where they were. By mutual consent, they walked out of the church and through the garden without exchanging a word, but on the sidewalk they paused.

"I'm completely at your disposal, Miss Worth."

"Anyone who can select roses like the ones you sent me can call me Caroline, or Caro, if you prefer. And that's my brougham waiting near the corner. If it suits you, we can talk there."

"It doesn't seem as if I have another choice," Sin answered, not ready to admit that he really didn't want one. He had always disliked wishy-washy women and now it was far too late for him to decide he would like it better if Caro looked at him with appealing eyes and asked him to decide the best place for them to talk. "Do you have a chaperone waiting?"

Caro caught the look in his eyes. "Do you really expect me to believe that you actually mean what you just said?"

"Even after all these years, I still seem to have the habit of following form, even if I couldn't care less about substance."

"I feel a sudden sense of recognition," Caro responded, a mixture of relief and adjustment settling up on her. She wouldn't relax just yet, but at least her heartbeat was back to a normal level. "And since we both agree, shall we get out of the wind?"

"Do you suppose things will get easier when automobiles eventually take over?"

"I haven't the vaguest, but I can't wait to find out," she said as they settled into the brougham. "One thing, though, before I take up a very serious topic. You *did* send me those stunning roses?"

"So much for Max Schling's people being able to keep a secret."

"But they did, sort of. The salesman you placed the order with didn't tell me your name, just what you looked like. Which," Caro went on, starting to smile, "wasn't completely conclusive since you weren't wearing a black satin mask in the florist's!"

Snug and relatively comfortable in the brougham, the aroma of leather mingling with the scent of Jicky, Sin felt some deep coil of tension loosen inside him. "I thought you had black hair."

"Only through the expertise of Van Horne Costumes and Wigs."

"Are you going to tell me what happened after I left the Linden Trees?"

"Didn't Chief Hathaway give you a detailed description of the ensuing events when he came to question you?"

"He barely stayed long enough to take off his hat and coat and have a cup of coffee. His visit gave new meaing to the expression 'dropping in for a moment.' Of course, when I read all the reports about Davis' funeral, it all fell into place," Sin finished wryly.

"If it all weren't so horrific, it might actually be funny—which brings me to the reason why I had to see you today," Caro said, finding the best way to proceed. She was enjoying their one-line exchanges—an easy ability to make conversation was a good sign—but at this moment it didn't matter very much. "This is not the simplest thing to tell you about."

"If this is as serious as your face indicates, I'd much rather hear it from you than through gossip,"

Sin said as apprehension spread its narrow tentacles through him. "Unhappily, something tells me that this has nothing to do with what happened at the Linden Trees."

Although Caro could always flirt with the best of them, at this moment that was shoved out of her ken. Without embroidery or dramatics, she told Sin about the events of Tuesday afternoon.

For his part, Sin listened to every word, enthralled. Her voice, low and compelling, would have held him captive had she been talking about flower arranging or croquet or any number of things that also held no interest for him, but now it also helped keep his growing dismay under control.

Stolen merchandise, he thought—just what I need in my life now.

"I know from my family's own business dealings that items can pass through any number of hands before the transaction that brings them to a gallery or auction house takes place, and any one of those dealings can be illegal. However, I don't believe for a minute that *your* actions in handling the objects that turned out to belong to us was illegal."

"You don't?" Sin asked. "I have to admit I feel as indecently relieved as a schoolboy. When you began to tell me about the surprise you found at Fowler's, I thought I had walked into a denouncement."

"Do I look like that hasty a judge of character?"

"From where I'm sitting, you don't look as if you're hasty about anything. Neither am I, but I suppose Jay Fowler told you in no uncertain terms

133

that I verge on being a very shady character?'' he said.

''He went to great pains to tell me how fair he wanted to be about you, how he's been a guest at your club, all about what a wonderful chef you have.''

''All very important details.''

''Incidentally, what kind of club do you run?''

''It's really more of a gathering spot for area businessmen as opposed to a club in the uptown sense of the word. Did you think I was running a refuge for heirs to auction galleries whose taste in ladies is definitely less than proper?'' he finished with a smile, leaving no doubt as to whom he was referring.

Caro laughed. ''And here I thought that Jay had no interest in ladies. There's a certain delivery to his speech—''

''If that were so, his father and grandfather would kill him and hide his body in one of those Oriental cabinets with a secret compartment,'' Sin said before dissolving into laughter. ''No, I have a say that when Jay pays attention to a member of the chorus, that person definitely wears skirts. Unfortunately, it's an easy assumption to make about someone, and more often than not, it turns out to be wrong. I know; I was convinced I had a man dead to rights on that count, and he wasn't that way at all.''

Caro instantly read the look that appeared on his face. ''That person had something to do with your father's downfall, didn't he?''

''Quite a bit, and this is the first time I even alluded to it outside of my own circle,'' Sin said quietly, his voice heavy with feeling as his eyes searched her face. "Somehow I think you know how it feels not to be able to speak to another person about some great matter."

For a second Caro didn't breathe. "Yes, that's exactly what I've been through at various times, either because I couldn't relate emotionally or intellectually to the other person, or because it's someone I care for very much about and telling her what's bothering me would hurt her greatly."

The bond she'd felt forming between them on the terrace was there again, Caro thought. Through some deep level of understanding, he had trusted her enough to confide in her, and even though that confidence was couched in the vaguest of terms, it was still something to be both respected and treasured.

For a long minute, they sat side by side, looking at each other, not needing to exchange words; there was nothing wrong with the silence between them. Perhaps it was because of the small space the brougham's interior provided, but Caro had never felt more aware of the possibilities that could exist for them.

"We can't stay here forever—much to my regret," Sin said at last as a gust of wind whipped down the street, rattling everything in its path. "But since we still have so much to discuss, may I take you to lunch?"

The sentence was out before Sin could exercise his usual expert control, making sure that not one unnecessary word came out of his mouth. He not only wanted to take Caroline Worth to lunch: he wanted to take her to the Waldorf or the Café Martin, a showy place where they would be noticed and where she would be sure to make every other woman look either frumpy or tawdry.

"I'm going to say yes before you change your mind," Caro said lightly, "but if you *do* want to back out, I'll probably understand."

"I was thinking how much I'd like to take you to a very grand and expensive restaruant, but just now the cost would still be too high—and I'm not referring to my ability to pay the bill. Do you like Italian food?"

"I'm a firm believer in the legend that says Marco Polo was responsible for bringing pasta to Italy."

"Then I'll meet you at Roversi's on Twenty-seventh Street at noon."

"Good, that gives me plenty of time to keep my business appointment."

"Busines appointment?"

"Oh, how sweet—you think I'm a lady of leisure. Will it disillusion you that my stepmother and I run the silk importing business my father established? Today I have to see the silk buyer at Altman's," she explained, and motioned toward the leather portfolio resting on the opposite seat.

"I'm sure he'll place a very generous order, and I'll look forward to hearing all about it," Sin said as he collected his hat and got out of the brougham.

Caro looked out the window at Sinclair standing on the sidewalk. They smiled at each other and she opened the panel and extended a hand. "Take care of yourself until I see you again."

'Why do you say that?'' he asked, a slow smile lighting up his serious features.

"Because right now you look like you might want to go slay a dragon—or a Wall Street banker, whichever is more convenient.''

"For you . . . anything.'' Sinclair raised his hat and saluted her. " 'Now I will believe that there are unicorns.' ''

Located between Eighth and Twenty-third Streets, bounded on the east by Broadway and on the west by Sixth Avenue, was New York City's famed "Ladies Mile.'' Contained on these streets were magnificent structures with cast-iron and marble facades devoted to selling the best and most luxurious of goods. Brooks Brothers had settled in at Broadway and Twenty-second Street, providing a decidedly masculine touch, but despite that presence and the fact that many of the stores had departments both for the outfitting of male customers and the furnishing of one's home, this part of the city was largely reserved for the woman shopper.

The profusion of high-quality emporiums had begun in the late 1870s, and now, in the second year of the new century, John Wanamaker's carried on with its Philadelphia-bred traditions; Siegel-Cooper's showed off with a columned entrance, and, just inside, a reproduction of "Republic,'' the famous fountain that had graced the 1893 Chicago World's Fair; and Best & Company boasted of its superior children's department, known as the Lilliputian Bazaar. Bonwit Teller devoted itself to fine women's clothes; and Altman's, McCreery's, Stern's, Arnold Constable, and Lord & Taylor all vied with each other in attracting that affluent group of shoppers know as "the carriage trade."

Caro, like all her friends, was a devoted shopper, and it made no difference at all whether the shop was a small and inconspicuous place in Shanghai that offered the finest jade or a major American department store. It was more than shopping, merely going to buy something; this was being part of a living theatre in which the show was never the same.

And on this Thursday morning, as Lawton drew the Worth brougham to a halt in front of Benjamin Altman's "Palace of Trade" at 295 Sixth Avenue, she was certain that no actress waiting for the curtain to rise on what would be the hit of the season could feel the same sense of energy, purpose, and anticipation that she did upon entering the six-story cast-iron building.

Inside, all was ornate perfection. Each floor was open around a central rotunda that topped by a stained-glass dome. There was the quick whisper of bullet-shaped brass carriers holding sales receipts and money as they traveled their pneumatic path along pipelines from various departments to the central cashiers' office and back again. The softly persuasive voices of the salespeople mingled with those of the customers, whose tones ranged from uncertain to imperious. But Caro crossed the white marble floor toward the elevator without paying too much attention either to other people or the counters offering a wide selection of fine merchandise. At this moment she wasn't a shopper looking for the latest bauble or bagatelle; she was a businesswoman with an appointment, and until it was concluded, even thoughts about her impending lunch with Sinclair Poole would have to wait.

The silk buyer, a dignified and reserved man who looked and acted a good ten years older than he was, was clearly torn between his desire to keep buying fabric from Worth Silk Importers and his reluctance to have to deal with the daughter of the founder. To be sure, he welcomed Caro into his office with a great show of warmth, but he surveyed each sample with the intensity of Sherlock Holmes examining a vital piece of evidence, and asked a series of questions that no one would ask unless he was trying to trip the other person up.

For her part, Caro was in no mood to charm. She could pour on the sugar with the best of them, but she rebelled against acting like that in any way except a social situation—and now particularly it seemed a cheap way to behave, considering the naturalness of her conversation with Sin.

"I suppose our deliveries will be received as regularly as they were when your late father was at the helm." Mr. Morris said, making it very clear that he was thinking exactly the opposite. "We serve a very discriminating clientele, and when we promise to have the finest China silks to offer, we want them on our shelves."

"Of course you do," Caro responded, putting away her samples and deciding the best tack to take was to deliberately misunderstand what he was saying. "I understand completely your concern that you won't be able to get your full quota of silk. Orders have never been higher and the silk buyers at the City of Paris in San Francisco, the Broadway in Los Angeles, and Marshall Field's in Chicago have great trust in us. Their orders are very extensive."

"I'm sure that's very gratifying for your order books, and of course we do wish to continue our association with your family firm," Mr. Morris said rather stiffly.

"I can't tell you how glad I am to hear that." Caro rose and gathered up her belongings. "My stepmother and I have been discussing limiting the stores we deal with to one in each major city—Filene's in Boston, Woodward and Lothrop in Washington, Wanamaker's in Philadelphia—I think you have the general idea. Our merchandise does merit this sort of exclusivity, don't you think?"

"Well, of course. . . .of course, there's never been as much as a single complaint."

"I'm so glad to hear that, particularly since, if we carry through with this project, we haven't decided on a New York store. Wanamaker's will probably feel that they have some claim, but—"

"But you wouldn't *not* consider Altman's!" Mr. Morris interjected quickly.

"I can assure you that in all discussions my stepmother and I have about this project, Altman's will have equal consideration with every other fine department store. In the meantime, I do have other appointments, and you have my card, so you know where to call when you're ready to order—''

Caro allowed Mr. Morris to show her to the door but managed to dissuade him from escorting her out of the store, and once she was away from the silk buyer's dour presence, her straight face dissolved into a smile. Normally she would have let the buyer show her out of the store and to her brougham, but before she left Altman's there was one more stop to make.

Altman's furniture department, which included the necessary accessories of rugs and lamps and antique bibelots, was so highly thought of that it ran a close second to W & J Sloane's, whose entire business was based on furnishings for the home for those of the carriage trade. A shopper would have to be truly fussy not to find at least half-a-dozen items of interest, and Caro was no exception. No one could walk across the floor or around the rotunda without stopping to admire the displays. However, today she didn't have enough time to browse, and her gaze swept over the selling floor until it settled on a young woman her own age in a Paquin dress of castor-brown French broadcloth, trimmed with black and gold cord, giving an attentive group instructions about arranging Hepplewhite so that it caught the customer's eye.

Caro waited until Thea Harper was finished before signaling to her friend. ''I was worried I might have missed you,'' she said as they exchanged a quick two-cheek kiss. ''I stayed longer than I expected with Mr. Morris.''

"He does know his silk, but what an old sour-puss," Thea responded as they sat down on a love-seat. "He simply hates to deal with women, so I expect you spent most of your time giving him a song-and-dance routine."

"One that's good enough for a musical comedy." Thea worked for Benjamin Altman, helping the art collector keep track of his purchases, but since she also had an eye for arranging, she was often called on to speak on such matters to those employed on the furniture floor, and she knew most of the foibles of the store buyers. "I suppose he thinks Vanessa and I are simply incapable of carrying on the business." Caro laughed. "He'd probably faint if he ever found out that the silk importing business is just one of the many we're running. In any case, I decided to tell him that we were considering limiting our sales to the best stores in each major city, but we hadn't quite settled on which New York store best fit in with our plan."

"You're not really going to do something like that?"

"Never—it would ruin our system of distribution. But Mr. Morris hasn't figured that out yet."

"And he won't. Right now, he's probably just worried about explaining his gaffe to Mr. Altman. That's a serious enough situation to make him forget all about the Cellini cup he's buying."

"I *hate* having to do things like that, but when it comes down to being treated properly, certain formalities go straight out the window."

"Isn't it fun to put stuffy men in their places?" Thea asked with a knowing look.

"I'm not sure I get as much enjoyment out of it as you and Alix do."

"Well, that's just because you're back from the Orient, where everyone is reserved and polite. After a few more weeks, you'll be nasty right up there with the rest of us."

"Thank you, I think."

"By some chance, are you free for lunch?"

"By no chance, I'm afraid. We'll do it another day, go to Sherry's and drink champagne and have a wonderful gossip," Caro promised. Floating around in her mind was the thought that she might ask, in a very discreet way, of course, what her friend knew about Sinclair from a business standpoint, but that would mean confiding more than she was ready to, and some things were better left unsaid. "By the way, has anyone told you lately what a great touch you have in arranging furniture?"

"Oh, one or two people," Thea smiled, keeping her own secrets. "Who knows, if I'm lucky there may be something of a career in it for me."

At Roversi's on Twenty-seventh Street, Papa Roversi, thanks to Sinclair's highly accurate description, identified Caro as soon as she walked into the homey, welcoming restaurant. He greeted her warmly and then led her past tables bright with red-and-white checked tablecloths to a quiet table in the rear, banked by potted palms, where Sinclair sat waiting for her.

"The bread is just out of the oven and the chianti is from Papa's private stock," he said by way of greeting as he got to his feet, gesturing at the long loaf of bread snugly wrapped in a napkin and the wine bottle encased in woven straw. "I hope you're hungry."

"I'm absolutely famished," she replied as they took their seats. "It's been a very busy morning."

"Did you charm the silk buyer with your voice, astound him with your beauty, and leave him speechless with your superb grasp of the silk business?" Sin asked, filling their glasses with wine.

"Oh, what lovely flattery to have along with lunch," Caro said, breaking off a good-sized chunk of bread and spreading butter across its surface. "Unhappily, all Mr. Morris cared about was that the company is now being run by two women."

"What an unappreciative man," Sin said as they touched glasses. "I hope you put him in his place."

"Something like that." Briefly, she told him about her meeting at Altman's, and the story she'd been forced to invent.

"So you made it up out of whole cloth."

"Oh, you're *not* a punster!"

"Sorry, I couldn't resist. If I were the buyer, I'd place an order for a hundred bolts of every sample available."

"That's a much better compliment than the ones I'm used to hearing," she said as a beaming waiter

144

arrived at their table and placed steaming bowls of hearty minestrone in front of them.

"I hope you don't mind that I ordered for us?"

"Not . . . not at all," Caro amended quickly. She certainly couldn't say "not this time" because they might not be together again. How did she know what impulse had led him to tender this invitation? For all she knew, he was regretting it even now and was simply putting a good face on everything.

"Is something wrong with the soup?"

"No, it's absolutely scrumptious," she said, looking at him over the rim of her wineglass. "I was hoping you weren't having second thoughts about this invitation."

"Why would I?"

Well, you've really walked into a corner this time, she thought, and took a sip of chianti to give herself a moment to gather her thoughts. "Because I don't think you make a decision or say one word without thinking it through and examining it from every possible angle," she said at last. "And you're asking me to lunch seemed to come on the spur of the moment."

"Do you mind that my invitation was so spontaneous?"

"Mind? I'm almost beside myself from the compliment."

For a second, two messages warred inside Sin. The first, which came from his head, told him to look for duplicity in her words; and the second, which came from a heart he had long ago hardened against romantic fancies, sent him another message entirely. The conflict was unfamiliar, but only one reaction could win, and he began to smile in a way he rarely did any more.

"I love the book you sent me," he said warmly. "It reminds me of the books I loved as a boy. I could never read enough ancient tales about castles and knights and beautiful women menaced by dragons."

"I don't think there's anything like mythology to spark the imagination," she said, finishing her soup. "Were you ever in the Far East?"

"Once, for a year, about eighteen years ago. My father wanted to establish some new trade agreements with China and Japan."

"That means you saw the Orient when there were relatively few outsiders there—primitive by our standards, but with its beauty still unspoiled and untouched."

"Then you were always aware of only being a visitor there?"

"Of course. My father was adamant about our treating everything and everyone with respect and never forgetting that we were guests in a country with a vastly different culture."

The next course was hot antipasto, featuring tender shrimp and delicately seasoned eggplant in a blanket of red sauce, and while they ate this fragrant and spicy speciality, Sin and Caro discussed their impressions and remembrances of China and Japan. The portions were generous, giving them ample time to discuss Canton versus Hong Kong versus Yokohama and Tokyo. While they traded impressions of the beautiful city of Kyoto, Caro felt as if the other

146

diners in Roversi's didn't exist, and that the bond between them was growing deeper and stronger.

"What led you to setting yourself up as a dealer in Orientalia—besides the obvious?" she asked, dabbing her bread in the sauce.

"Well, it wasn't my father's rousing success in the China Trade," he said, smiling. "It didn't fail, but there wasn't an overabundance of money flowing in, either. I guess if you won't touch contraband, income can be limited. But it was a steady income, which is the main reason why I held onto it. Then there was the matter of the jade trees."

Anyone familiar with the art of the Orient knew that the jade tree represented the ultimate skill of the craftsman. Usually a foot high, the carved tree was ornamented with quartz or topaz berries, leaves of jade, and blossoms of crystal pink or smoky crystal. In the finest jade shops of Shanghai and Peking, Caro knew, the proprietors would hide the best of their selection of trees whenever foreign customers were in the shop, bringing them forward only if the client—usually a woman—proved herself "a woman of face," the shopkeepers' way of referring to a lady of knowledge and good taste.

"They're strictly for the connoisseurs' taste," she observed. "Everyone oohs and aahs over them at first, but there's no long-lasting interest or appreciation—at least in the American market."

"Still, I had six of them turn up unexpectedly along with another shipment. The papers were in order, and much later I found out that the representative we dealt with in Hong Kong had included them with a regular shipment of procelain because he thought my father would enjoy them. Of course, he had no way of knowing that in the time it took to get from China to New York, my father died.''

Caro saw the look that appeared in his eyes. There was a starkness there undimmed by the passage of years, years that had apparently healed little or nothing.

''I hope you kept one for yourself,'' she said as gently as she could, realizing that the only way she could comfort him was not to ask the wrong sort of question. ''And sold the others for a vast profit.''

''I did keep one for myself, but I sold it last year for a sum of money that almost made me blush. The other five went to dealers in Boston and Philadelphia. I couldn't go back to dealing in the stock market just then, and quite by accident, I had the way to bring in a good source of income. I thought Orientalia was a limited market, but in the last few years it's turned into quite a gold mine.''

''I sometimes think that's the way things should be—finding out almost by accident how successful a particular project can be,'' Caro said, and paused while their waiter whisked away the remains of the antipasto, replacing it with plates heaped with ravoli draped in tomato sauce and garnished with freshly grated Parmesan cheese. ''It's not that I think there's anything wrong with being successful at making money. It's the cold-blooded going after it with eyes narrowed and nostrils flaring that bothers me.''

''That sounds like quite a few people I knew at

one time or other." Sin laughed, surprising himself at his reaction. "But I promise you that I never go into a business speculation with greed in my eyes."

"Such an attitude would defeat your whole purpose, wouldn't it?" she asked, then bit her lower lip as dismay filled her. "Please forgive me . . . I didn't mean. . . ."

"I'm not insulted—or angry." Sin's voice was gentle. "In fact, you're very much like another woman I knew a long time ago."

"I don't think Alix Turner would like being referred to as someone you knew a long time ago," she said, looking at him through her lashes, gauging his reaction as he registered her words.

"I should have known you were friends," was all he said, his face not giving a thing away.

"These things happen."

Quite unexpectedly, Sin began to smile. "Have I been an interesting topic of conversation?"

"I don't think we know each other well enough for me to tell you what Alix and I discussed at Cove House."

"Would it be safe for me to say that she expanded and elucidated on whatever else you heard about me?"

"It was just boudoir talk."

"Why does that news send a chill down my spine?" Sin questioned in a tone of voice that could almost be called whimsical. "I suppose you and Alix are good friends from your days at Brearley?"

"Yes and no." The time for this slightly flirting conversation was over. "I was a year behind her, but we always had a lot in common, or so I thought—until the day I told her I was going to China with my father and stepmother instead of going to college. Alix is very definite about women getting a university education—so am I, for that matter, but you know all about the lure of the Orient—and we had a hot disagreement. We're still putting our friendship back together."

"Then you don't think that some friendships are irreparably damaged by time and circumstance?"

"Only if the friend is someone whom, deep down, you don't like anymore. But if that friendship is based on true understanding and shared interests— not to mention mutual affection and regard—it can usually be restored."

"I sometimes wonder, when all this is over, when I've cleared my father's name, if I will every trust another man outside my own circle again," Sin said, poking his fork at his pasta as if suddenly discontented with it. "No, let me amend that," he continued. "I should have said *easily* trust."

"That does sound less cynical, although you probably have good cause to be distrustful about nearly everyone who crosses your path."

Slowly, and with no little surprise, Sin began to realize that the usual feeling of bitterness he had grown so accustomed to, while not dissipated, was noticably lessened in its intensity. He was perfectly content to stay in Caro's company, looking into her eyes as she sipped the rich chianti, breathing in her perfume, and, in short, behaving like a lovestruck collegiate.

Now *that* was the very last reaction he was supposed to have, he thought. His life was plotted out to center around one goal, and while he had never spurned the attractions of beautiful and desirable women, his emotional reactions were isolated incidents, not destined to go very deep or continue for very long. Or so he had assumed. And all because he'd stepped out onto the terrace to get some air.

And that almost makes me sound as if I'd been a welcomed guest at the Linden Trees, he thought, knowing that it would be a long time before the mental picture of Davis Moreton, white-faced, ill, and almost overcome, would fade from his memory. But it still doesn't change the outcome of that night, and I still don't know what I'm going to do about Caro.

Well, not exactly. He was almost sure what he wanted to do about Caroline Worth, but she wasn't the sort of woman who was ready, willing, and eager for a short-lived affair, and he couldn't offer her a normal courtship to be followed by a proposal of marriage.

Not yet.

Possibly not ever.

"Is having lunch with me such a terrible strain on your standards?" Caro asked finally, unable to bear either his silence or the look of conflict in his eyes.

"I feel like the proverbial moth to the flame," Sin replied shamefacedly, appaled at his lapse into silence and at the thoughts she couldn't possibly guess. Or could she?

"Do you know how risqué that makes me feel?" she asked, perplexed and angry at the same time. "Do you think of me as playing some sort of siren song to tempt you, the upright man dedicated to a high ideal, to forget your mission? If that's the case, I'll leave you to your fantasy and go on about my business."

Caro's words came straight from her heart, but her great exit line was ruined by the sight of both their waiter and Papa Roversi approaching their table. It was patently obvious that she couldn't walk out now without embarrassing herself and humiliating Sin, and she stayed in her seat, forcing a look of interest on her face.

"Everything is delicious," she assured both men, deliberately not looking at Sin.

"But next time you promise to give Papa Roversi advance word that you're coming, and I will prepare my special lobster fra diablo and zuppa inglese for dessert," he said, bestowing a beaming smile on the couple. "But for today we have cannolli. Guido will take care of everything, but let me know if there is anything else you need."

Sin and Caro remained silent as their completed entrée was removed and replaced by plates holding the cylindrical pastries filled with sweet creamed cheese studded with candied fruit and chocolate bits, together with cups of hot espresso and a bottle of anisette.

"I really should be eating crow," Sin said when

Guido had departed. "Or is it humble pie? My knowledge of clichés tends to get scrambled when I have to face the fact that I'm acting like a prig."

"Not quite *that* bad." Caro sunk her fork into the cannolli, speared a small portion, and began to enjoy its sweet deliciousness. "Except that I'm not quite sure what I can say to you."

"Oh, say whatever you want to," Sin said after a moment's consideration. "I have the hide of a buffalo by now."

"I hope so." Caro gave him a level look. "By some horrible chance, are you confusing me with Cynthia Moreton-Chandler?"

"Only if I were congenitally stupid or deranged. You're nothing alike."

Caro gave him a sidelong glance. "All women with their own money have similarities, some of them not very nice."

"But I'm still not blurring the lines that separate the two of you. It's simply that I'm not in a position to behave toward you in the way you were brought up to expect."

"I see." Caro's voice was deliberately neutral. "You didn't seem to think like that on the Linden Trees terrace or in the ballroom."

Her words deliberately conjured up the time they'd spent together a few weeks before, a dance and a kiss that no matter how hard he tried to tell himself otherwise meant far more to him than a few stolen moments. "I was so sure that night was going to end differently," he told her honestly. "And I don't think I've thanked you properly yet for saving me from being accused of either murdering Davis or somehow forcing him to do the deed himself. You said that you could handle everything, and you did it beyond anything I could ever have expected, yet I don't seem to behave properly toward you." Sin reached across the table to cover her free hand with his. "I'm sorry if I made you feel like a character in a risqué novel."

"Well, just for the record, I *love* risqué novels. My favorite book a few years ago was *The Diary of an Idle Woman in Constantinople.*"

"Then why did you say. . . ?"

"Because there's good risqué and bad risqué."

"Are you going to elaborate?"

"No, I think I've told you enough feminine secrets for one day. What I really should have said is that you asked me to lunch out of a sense of duty—either that, or you hate to eat alone," she added in an attempt to soften her words.

"I always thought that Italian food was meant to be shared," he said with a smile that very few people saw any more. "Whether one is twirling spaghetti or wiping up red sauce with a chunk of crusty bread, it all tastes better in good company. But the drawback to that is that the better the company, the easier it is to let down one's guard."

"If that's a compliment, thank you." Caro arched her neck like a swan and tried to peer between the fronds of the potted palms that discreetly shielded their part of the restaurant from the rest of the room. She also noted that although the restaurant was doing a brisk luncheon business, the tables closest to theirs were empty, an effect that gave them all the privacy a couple could want. "Are we going to leave by the back way?" she inquired lightly.

"That's one way you won't run the risk of being seen with me."

"And the other?"

"We'll have Guido bring us more pastry and espresso, and we'll sip anisette and talk," Sin said with the assurance of one born to making such decisions. "By the time we've gotten to know each other better, the restaurant will be empty again and we can walk out through the front door like any other boring and respectable patrons."

"That's what I mean about feeling risqué. I'm not sure if you're protecting me from you or vice versa."

"Do you realize," Sin said as he poured anisette into small crystal glasses, "that according to all the rules of what a proper unmarried lady does, you shouldn't be having lunch alone with me, even if I were the most staid and upright bachelor in Manhattan?"

Caro laughed softly. "You wouldn't be staid and upright if someone offered you a million dollars. And since this is the beginning of a new century, why don't you think of me as one of the new breed of woman who can look out for herself?"

"I wouln't dream of answering that in any way but the affirmative," Sin said, silently deciding that at some point he had crossed over the boundary line that separated him from his old life. He was now in some vast and uncharted territory, walking a twisting road that had a mysterious end—and as long as he could be near Caroline Worth, all the inherent dangers didn't matter.

"Are you very much interested in what American importers are bringing in from the Orient?" he questioned.

"As long as it's legitimate business dealings and not plunder for the fun of it. I have to tell you, though, that my special interests are in the field of fabrics, wallpaper, and rugs. If you want to have an in-depth, expert discussion about porcelain, you'll have to talk with my stepmother."

"I'll keep that in mind for future reference, but for right now, would you care to come to my office on Monday, spend the day, and see all the latest offerings that my Far East contacts have sent me?"

This is a test, Caro thought; it has to be. Despite his assurances to the contrary, he was trying to get rid of her, and he'd found a way that when beyond insults or obnoxious behavior.

Sin's office was also his home; it was located on Prince Street, off the Bowery. The Bowery was a spot that no respectable woman was supposed to know anything about, much less be invited to visit. Whether or not there was any duplicity or hidden motive in his invitation was a matter open to question. But right now there was only one answer she could consider giving.

"Next Monday will be fine. My calendar is clear, and I'll look forward to joining you then."

Chapter Eleven

On Monday morning, Sinclair Poole awoke in the bedroom of his townhouse on Prince Street off the Bowery to the sound of the milkman from the Walker Gordon Dairy—the best in the city—making his early-morning delivery of milk, cream, and eggs. This was obviously not the milkman's most favored stop along his otherwise fashionable route, close as it was to the Bowery and the Third Avenue Elevated, and he vented his annoyance by rattling the bottles, no doubt imagining that he was disturbing everyone asleep inside. Of course, he had no way of knowing that the residents of this house were all early risers who kept hours that would make him look like a man of leisure.

Sin heard the wagon move off, its load no doubt quite a bit lighter, considering their usual substantial delivery, and he turned over, his gaze falling immediately on *Mythical Japan*. He had placed it on one of the bedside tables, fully aware that it would probably be the first thing he saw in the morning and the last thing before he fell asleep at night. The richly bound volume had arrived last Monday afternoon, and upon opening it, he immediately forgot about such unimportant things as stock market fluctuations, bond market vagueries and commodity upsets; and he had all but memorized the note, written in blue-black ink on cream-colored Dempsey & Carroll stationery and engraved with her initials.

Dear Sinclair—(he remembered)

Simply saying thank you for such beautiful roses isn't enough. The grower who managed to coax the roses into growing such long stems and big petaled and fragrantly perfumed blooms certainly deserves a prize. In case I've made some horrible mistake and you're not the gentleman who used Max Schling's as his intermediary to get the American Beauty roses to me, I apologize, and the enclosed book is still for you. Hopefully, it will go with your interests in Orientalia.

Best wishes,
Caroline Worth

His first thought on reading the note had been that whatever else she might be, Caroline Worth obviously wasn't the sort of woman who liked mystery gifts. Either that, he realized at once, or else she was perceptive enough to know he sent them without launching a full-scale investigation.

She certainly hadn't had to hire a private detective to find him, he thought, remembering his surprise when he'd first caught sight of her in the back pew at the Little Church Around the Corner. All the information she needed had been handed to her by Jay Fowler, a man who could never resist telling tales out of school; he had to remember to thank him. He didn't mind silently admitting that he'd been impressed with how she'd handled the problem of her missing furniture turning up at Fowler's. It was obvious that she cared, that it had affected her deeply, but there was none of the possession hysteria that many women displayed. So far, Caroline appeared to be discreet and reserved, but not secretive; chic and elegant, but not about to fall victim to outlandish whims of fashion; and warm and sensitive, without ever falling into the trap of cloying sentimentality. He couldn't wait to see her again.

He smiled and wondered if Caroline, a fellow dealer in Orientalia, lived as he did. The only items representative of the Far East in his bedroom—except for the book *Mythical Japan*—were a pair of Japanese bonsai plants in terra cotta planters that ornamented the marble mantlepiece, an exotic touch in an room otherwise given over to the French art of the *toile de Jouy*, the cotten–linen fabric where little scenes were printed in red, green, black, brown, or blue on a cream-colored background. Sinclair had decided to use toiles not as a counterpoint to all the Oriental merchandise he dealt with, but because it seemed to fit in so perfectly with the townhouse, which had been built in the 1840s in the graceful Federalist style.

The blue-and-cream toile, with a pattern representing the first elevation of a hydrogen-filled balloon, not only covered the walls, but was repeated in the curtains and used as upholstery for the six-foot sofa in front of the fireplace. A few fruitwood bergéres in heavy blue silk, several gleaming fruit-wood tables and chests, and a leather-topped writing table completed the decor. This quiet retreat still managed to make a definite statement about the iconoclast who occupied it.

And it was quite unlike the mansion on Fifth Avenue he'd grown up in, with room after room filled with substantial, dreary antiques, thick velvet curtains, and certified Old Masters. Now, nearly seven years after he'd walked out of that house for the last time, leaving behind an empty shell picked clean with the help of the auctioneer's gavel, he wondered how he and his father had managed to live happily and normally in such an atmosphere. No doubt about it, he thought, the bond between them had been strong enough to sustain the sometimes all-too-fragile father–son relationship. But the more he remembered his old home, the more certain he was that the rich and ponderous residence they'd shared had been a presage to the string of events that had, in only a few short months, changed everything so they'd never be the same again.

Some nine years earlier, when Stanford Poole advised his son it was time to start considering what young lady he would eventually make his bride, the selection was small. The attributes of someone who'd make a suitable wife to one of New York's wealthiest and best-connected young men were woefully lacking in the current crop of New York girls between the ages of eighteen and twenty-one. Even the two at the top of Stanford's list, Alicia Turner and Cynthia Moreton, had strikes against them. The former was allowed an alarming amount of independence by her parents; the latter had a streak of self-centeredness that wouldn't do in the event she found herself in charge of the boards of the leading charities.

"I won't see you betrothed to some woman who's going to remind you every so often what an honor it was to have married her," Stanford remarked. "Your mother and I had eleven splendidly happy years together, and I'm sure that if she were alive today, we would still feel the same way about each other."

"Is that why you've never remarried?" Sin asked, making that inquiry for the first time. "You certainly can't be unaware of the number of attractive widows throwing themselves in your path."

"No, I'm not unaware of either the ladies or their attractions, but you lost your mother at a tender age, and I felt that if I remarried—either to a woman who already had children, or to someone whom I might have a family with—you would eventually feel that your place had somehow become secondary in my life."

"I never thought of it that way," Sin replied, and decided wisely not to say that he had always wanted younger siblings. His father's statement made him regret his actions after he'd been passed over as

Stanford's private secretary and that stuffed shirt Avery Dutton had been hired instead. His father always wanted the best for him, and if he thought it was time he turned his attention to finding a bride . . . well, he had to get married eventually. "Is there a time limit on this?"

"I suppose that your friends tell you that you're funny. No, and the names aren't carved in stone either. I want you to have a happy marriage. An actress is fine for amusement, and you're a popular young bachelor, but you have to consider settling down within a few years."

"And when I do that, will I become your private secretary the way I should have been two years ago?" Sin knew he was risking opening an old wound, but this particular hurt had never healed, and it smarted every day in the offices of Poole Enterprises whenever he came into contact with Avery's smarmy presence. "It galls me every time I look at Dutton," he said, his voice far more revealing than he intended. "There's something underhanded about him, and for the life of me, I don't know why you can't see it!"

"You have to remember, Sinclair, that not every young man has your connections and influence, not to mention good luck with the ladies," Stanford said in a soothing voice that only served to further annoy his son. "And Avery has been invaluable to me. The amount of work he puts in is more than commendable."

"And was there something—or someone—who told you I wouldn't do my share of work? You trained me to do that. Being made your secretary was going to be a great moment in my life, and then you pulled the rug out from under me. First you send me off to Europe and when I get back, Avery's in the office I should have with the title that belongs to me!''

''My dear boy—'' Stanford's gray eyes regarded his son with affection and forbearance. ''In a few years there's going to be such expansion and growth that you're going to have more work than you know what to do with. And as for that summer in Europe—you and Cliff cut quite a swath for yourselves.''

''We certainly did,'' Sin replied with a wide smile. ''Two rich, twenty-one-year-old bachelors having a swell time for themselves. And when I got back to New York, since I didn't have any demanding tasks at work, I just kept carrying on.''

''Well, the worst of that is pretty much over for you, just as I always knew it would be. You know what's right, Sinclair—I've never doubted that for a moment. Now, what do you know about the northwest?''

''That when it's not snowing it's raining.''

Stanford laughed. ''It's also a fine source for lumber. On Friday, Avery—Sin, don't make faces like a petulant schoolboy—brought a new company to my attention. A venture for us. . ...''

When Sinclair had returned from his long summer in Europe to find the position he had long thought would be his in Poole Enterprises and was instead handed a consolation prize that was little more than an attractive office and an all-but-empty title, he decided to enjoy life as only a wealthy young New York bachelor can. Within six months he had a reputation as a ladies' man that other men had taken years to develop. His florist bills nearly equaled those he ran up at Tiffany's, but if others were shocked, the recipients of his largesse were supremely pleased and showed him how much with great skill and passion. But by the time his period of rebellion—about two years from start to finish—was over, he had not only managed to collect any number of feminine hearts, but more dangerously, quite a few enemies as well.

These were mostly dowagers and hidebound gentlemen whose important functions he had scorned. Worse, he'd let it be known that he wasn't at all honored or interested in being included in their select groups. He'd ignored the men in the clubs and on the golf links. Oddly enough, his father had taken his son's rebellious attitude with a grain of salt and not a little amusement; all of this was perfectly natural and to be expected in a vital and highly intelligent young man who had just completed his education and hadn't found his place in the world yet, Stanford told his concerned friends. In a few years the novelty of being rude—and the attention of chorus girls—would begin to wane, and it was much better he got it out of his system at twenty-one rather than forty-one.

As much as he hated to admit it, Sinclair slowly began to agree with his father's assessment. Unlike far too many of his friends, he had not grown up so starved of parental affection that he had to look for it constantly and permanently in the arms of actresses and very high-priced ladies of the evening. The strict yet very loving way he'd been raised set his high standards and his ideals and he wouldn't abandon them for long. He was still frustrated at work—the duties he was given made him feel like a glorified office boy—but with is father's new assurances that this was only a temporary situation that would soon change in his favor, his resentment began to recede.

And so, Sin began to consider the dozen or so suitable girls his father had listed. Almost immediately he decided ten of them wouldn't even do for consideration. Some were too dull, others too plain, and a few were simply unlikeable. The two that remained were Alix Turner and Cynthia Moreton, and he knew that deciding between those two women would not be easy.

Cynthia was so beautiful that she could literally stop conversation in a crowded room by merely gracing it with her presence, but she did have the displeasing habit of preening, of expecting all attention and conversation to be directed to and centered on her or on the things she was interested in. Alix, on the other hand, didn't have people standing on chairs to look at her; but it never failed that less than ten minutes after her arrival anywhere, she was surrounded by men jostling each other to write their names on her dance card. But as exquisitely dressed as she was, she never went to any lengths to obscure either her intelligence or her opinions. Then 1893 turned into 1894, and it was Alicia Turner to whom he was drawn; some fourteen months after that first conversation with his father, he went to him with the information that he was prepared to ask Alix to be his wife.

"I know Alix would make you an excellent wife," Stanford said after some hesitation, "but have you really given Cynthia fair consideration?"

"Only enough to know that I don't think we could be happy for very long," Sin replied, surprised at his father's reaction. "I wouldn't go so far as to say she's devious or dishonest, but when we're talking I never feel that I have any contact with *her*, what she's really like."

"That's a very astute observation, but it shouldn't turn you premanently against her," Stanford said slowly. "More than regard and affection have to be taken into consideration when people like us consider marriage."

People like us, people with more money than they can count, Sin thought with apprehension. "You don't want me to marry Alix," he stated flatly, wanting to get directly to the point without all the discussion his father had ready to bring up.

"No, I'm only suggesting that you might have to postpone your plans to propose," Stanford said, and went on to explain that Davis Moreton wanted in on the continuing project of the Great Northwest Lumber Company. That wouldn't do at all, but Davis had let on that Cynthia was very fond of Sinclair and wouldn't play silly games if a marriage proposal were offered. "Goodness knows, you young people

166

get yourselves engaged and disengaged at such a rate these days you'd think Tiffany's rings were made of glass instead of diamonds," he finished. "You certainly don't have to marry the girl if you don't want to, but—"

But if it were humanly possible, Sin wouldn't disobey or disappoint his father. Besides, from the viewpoint of an appreciative male, Cynthia was neither ugly nor stupid. And so, with great skill, so that neither woman would take special notice of being ignored or paid attention to, Sin shifted his courtship from one to the other. Alix would understand, he told himself. Of course, when his engagement to Cynthia was ultimately dissolved, he'd have to do a bit of groveling, of admitting what a terrible mistake he'd made, but what woman wouldn't enjoy that? It was a small price to pay if he could keep that bloodsucker Moreton away from his father.

But there was no easy way to know that they were the victims rather than the masters of the game. It was all too good, too easy, and they fell headlong into it without a second glance.

In early January 1895, the first reports began to appear in the financial pages that the Great Northwest Lumber Company, whose shares were being handled exclusively by Stanford Poole, did not exist in any way, shape, or form. At first it caused only a ripple in the business community; the very idea that such a respected financier could be a swindler was beyond comprehension. But there were further disclosures, and what had first been dismissed as idle rumor became cold, hard fact.

What began as a small annoyance turned into a nightmare. The world of Wall Street and high finance appeared to be populated by high-minded conservatives with only their investors' profits—and the subsequent growth of America—in mind. By the late 1890's, this was largely a matter of illusion. In reality, there were very few controls on the Stock Exchange, and the number of crises and panics in the years following the Civil War proved that beyond any doubt. It didn't mean, however, that those who stole, swindled, and cheated with seeming impunity were above the law; they simply had to commit a misdeed so vast that it couldn't be brushed under the rug and ignored. And what was being viewed as Stanford Poole's enormous dereliction of duty demanded immediate action by the district attorney's office.

It was, everyone agreed, going to be the best scandal since the days of Boss Tweed.

And the trial, when it began, seemed to break all the bounds of restraint and decency; New York had been all too respectable lately, and this was far too good to let pass. For Sinclair, raised in an atmosphere of restraint and culture with only the usual bachelor-about-town amusements, this was like being thrust into a maelstrom. It was all a nightmare, he thought repeatedly, but even in the worst dream, one eventually wakes up. This, however, despite the stange trail of events that had led in a straight line from an innocuous four-line mention in the financial page of the *Sun* to the packed courtroom overflowing with reporters and spectators, was all too horribly real.

Shortly after the trial began, while his father was having a discussion with his lawyer—a man Sin thought was woefully inadequate to defend anyone facing serious criminal charges—he left the courtroom and took himself on a tour of the Criminal Court Building. This part of lower Manhattan was almost completely unfamiliar to him, and now Sin wandered along hallways, exploring the complicated building as a March snowstorm blanketed the city, curious and even interested in his surroundings until he found himself at the entrance to a covered passageway that extended to the building across the street.

"What is this?" he asked the guard, outfitted in the uniform of New York's Finest, replete with nightstick and pistol.

"Why, that's the walkway to the Tombs," the man explained, gesturing toward the other side, a malicious gleam appearing in his pale eyes. "It's how we take the prisoners back to the city jail after trial. It's where we're going to take your father after he's been convicted, Mr. Poole, and he's going to sit in a cell until they transport him up to Sing-Sing, where he's going to spend the next ten or twenty years sitting in another cell!"

Sin recoiled instinctively from the picture the guard's voice conjured up. The dreamlike feeling that had surrounded his life for the past few months vanished instantly and was replaced by a steady, seeping, all-consuming horror. His father was going to be convicted. It didn't matter that the case still had weeks to run; the decision had already been made, and all the protestations, all the statements Stanford Poole made weren't going to count for anything.

"My father never did any of the things he's charged with," he said at last, his feelings burning through all the layers of amazement and uncertainty and confusion that had been threatening to smother him. "He's never hurt another person in his life, and all of this is a pack of lies made up by a group of men who want to see him ruined and in disgrace!"

"Mr. Poole, if you were a lawyer, your father'd be found not guilty in ten minutes," the guard said, his hostility fading. "But it still doesn't give back the money to the people who invested in that lumber company, particularly those who can ill afford such a loss."

"Anyone who invested money in the lumber company will be paid back even if we have to sell everything to do it," Sin promised, and he was aware of his words ringing back in his ears, of being at that very moment etched in stone on some great list of unbreakable commitments. "No one is going to be reduced to penury because they invested in that— that—" His voice trailed off, unable to utter the words "Great Northwest Lumber Company."

"I don't understand," the guard pressed. "You seem like a pretty smart young man, nothing like all those newspaper stories make you out to be. Why didn't you notice that something was wrong with that company?''

"I would have if I'd ever seen any of the paperwork," Sin replied, and reality dawned. He had been kept away from anything to do with the lumber business from the very beginning, except for what his father had told him. He knew precious little about the true workings of this false company. "I was never brought in on the investment agreement. I only know what I read in the papers," he finished, giving the old saying an entirely new meaning.

"I guess you could take it as a compliment," the older man replied. "Someone thought this out real well—to keep you away from all this. And if it wasn't to protect you, it was because you were too smart to be taken in and no one was willing to run the risk that you wouldn't buy what they were trying to sell your father."

Sin went back to the courtroom to sit and watch and listen through that day and the next and all the days that followed. His father had been set up, framed, not because he was stupid, but because like so many other wealthy, successful men, he let things slip ever so slightly out of his grasp. And because someone—either working alone or with a group—wanted him ruined.

But did they also want Stanford convicted? he asked himself over and over again as the trial stretched on and winter began slowly to give way to spring. If he remembered a previous New York scandal correctly, Jim Fisk had served only four years in Sing-Sing for shooting Ned Stokes; his father probably wouldn't get off so lightly . . . if indeed he were in any condition to serve the sentence imposed on him.

For all those weeks, he watched as his father turned into an old man who could only rally for short periods and spent the rest of his time sunk in a silent reverie, and Sin slowly took charge of whatever remained of their life and business. Most of their employees had left shortly after the trial had begun, resigning because they knew that to stay on, even if their employer was cleared of all charges, would stop their careers cold. Most of their servants were let go for the same reason; to stay with the Pooles would make them all but unemployable in any first-class household. His father's office manager, Martin Lyle, who had grown old working for the Pooles, stayed doggedly on, as did Sin's old nemesis, Avery Dutton, and there was no question as to which man he trusted. On Sin's instructions, Martin came to the office every day, not so much to oversee what little work remained, but to make sure that Avery Dutton had no access to the files which were now kept securely locked. There might well be a clue in them, but studying their contents would have to wait until the end of the trial.

He never left his father's side in those months, offering him his love and support, his heart aching for the once competent and strong and wise man who faded daily under the strain of the legal proceedings. Sin now had no social life; in fact, he scarcely felt a pang of regret when Cynthia returned the impressive engagement ring he'd given her. The only real regret he'd felt at the letters that arrived from Meadowbrook and Shinnecock Hills on Long Island, from the New York Athletic Club, the Metropolitan Club, the New York Yacht Club, the Union, the Union League, and that bastion to which only descendants of the best old Manhattan families belonged, the St. Nicholas Club—all of them asking for the resignations of Stanford and Sinclair Poole so that father and son wouldn't have to suffer the indignity of being struck from the membership rolls.

Sin never showed the leters to his father—he was in no condition to read them—but he did save them. If this nightmare ever came to an end and if he were invited to join an "exclusive" club again, he wanted these letters at hand to remind him that that particular folly was one he could never afford to indulge in again.

He didn't want to leave his father's side for as much as a day, but back in November, before the debacle had begun to spread its dark and bitter stain over his life, he had promised his best friend Clifford Seligman that he would be the best man when Cliff married Julia Newstadt in Philadelphia in late spring. As the trial began to reach its apex in April, Sin naturally assumed that because of the social scandal his name would bring to any event, he was out of the wedding party. But he hadn't counted on Cliff's almost furious loyalty—no one was going to tell him who was better suited to be his best man— and his father's insistence that he not miss the event. Focusing on his son with an intensity Sin hadn't seen in months, he told him that he must go and show the flag, prove that the unfortunate events of the past weeks hadn't made them cowards.

So Sin packed his bags (his valet had long since departed for greener fields at one of the many mansions belonging to the Vanderbilts), embarked on the two-hour train ride to Philadelphia, and found that traveling to another city really didn't change anything. No one snubbed or ignored him either during the prewedding festivities or during the reception itself, but he was addressed in those frigidly polite tones that immediately lets the recipient know that he is being tolerated on sufferance, that not to exchange greetings with him at these happy events would be a sign of poor breeding and worse manners, but that he wasn't to expect anything more than these few crumbs of social intercourse.

All that he could be sure of, Sin decided when it was all over, was that as much as they liked to hold themselves on another, higher level, Rittenhouse Square wasn't all that different from Fifth Avenue, and even if the two sets weren't highly interconnected, their circles did touch and speak and exchange information—meaning that there was no refuge for him there—or in any other East Coast city, for that matter.

If he were going to suffer along with his father, he thought during the return trip, he might as well tough it out in New York City.

He returned to find that his father's case had gone to the jury, and all that remained was to find out how long they'd take to find the defendant guilty, and what kind of sentence the judge would impose.

Sin could already imagine the headlines—they were probably set in type right this minute—and all the reporters would have to do to complete their stories was fill in the blanks.

The jury was out a full day, and on the second day, as they were preparing to leave for court, Stanford Poole collapsed, his heart simply unable to bear any more strain.

Sin held his father in his arms, willing to give anything if only he could impart some of his own strength to his parent, all too aware that the doctor who was being summoned would never arrive in time, and some small part of him whispered a notice he could neither ignore nor accept—that this was the only way his father could cheat all of those who hated him enough to do this and those who were so twisted that they fed and enjoyed the pain and misfortune of others.

It was over for his father in less than ten minutes, but the matter being settled in the Criminal Courts Building on Centre Street couldn't be dismissed as easily. Stanford's lawyer, Cornell Nash, arrived while his client's body—now thoughtfully covered by a cashmere blanket—was still at the foot of the stairs. The older man, an intelligent attorney with a good courtroom technique who was, unfortunately, not at all suited to this case, started visibly at the sight that greeted him, but recoverd quickly.

"If the jury's come in with a guilty verdict, do I have to bury my father in the Sing-Sing cemetery?" were the first words Sin addressed to him.

"No, *no*—absolutely not!" the attorney replied,

deeply shocked. "Everything is now null and void. I'll call the judge and the district attorney immediately. . . . " His voice trailed off as he regarded the inert, covered form on the floor, luridly fascinated that such a dreadful thing had happened. "Sinclair, I'm so terribly sorry—"

"Thank you, Cornell, I know you are—and you're probably one of the few who will say it and actually mean it." Sinclair shivered, suddenly cold, and turned his attention to Haskell, the butler who had refused to leave and had determinedly taken over most of the household duties. "Has Dr. Carlyle finished calling the undertaker?" he inquired grimly.

"Yes, and they've asked us not to move the . . . to leave Mr. Poole. They'll handle everything."

"I'm sure they will, and spread the word of my father's. . . ." Sin's voice broke off; he was unable to bring the sentence to its natural conclusion.

"Be that as it may, Mr. Sinclair, we still have to follow their instructions," Haskell said with the gentle firmness that only an old family retainer could have and use. "What shall I do now, sir?"

"First of all, please show Mr. Nash to the library so he can make all the necessary calls, and then come back here. I hate to ask you to do this, but I don't want my father to be left here all alone while I'm gone."

"Sinclair, where are you going?"

"Don't look so alarmed, Cornell, I'm only going to the office. I want to tell Martin Lyle myself—he deserves that, and I want to make sure that I have all the papers about the Great Northwest Lumber

Company that the district attorney's office didn't take," Sin said as he began to leave the vast reception hall that looked wintertime grim even on this warm and sunny spring day. "Will I be needed in court?"

'No, I can take care of that, but you'll have to give the police a statement."

"I won't be long, but don't let them take my. . . . take my father away until I get back," he said, his voice growing stronger as he began to know exactly what he had to do.

Outside on Fifth Avenue, Sin hailed a hansom cab and instantly won the driver's loyalty by handing him a twenty-dollar bill. For that sum the man would get him downtown to 256 Broadway as fast as the horse could travel, wait for him outside the building, and then take him and whatever papers or packages he had back uptown.

Within a half-hour, he was striding through the lobby of Manhattan's newest skyscraper. Located between Warren and Murray Streets, comfortably close to City Hall, the sixteen-story structure known as the Home Life Insurance Building had become the new offices of Poole Enterprises less than a year earlier, but now the management that had once welcomed them was looking for a way to break the lease. Sin could hear someone—probably the managing agent, he guessed—calling his name, but he ignored the summons, stepped into a waiting elevator, and ordered the reluctant operator to take him to the seventh floor in a voice that no one short of a four-star general would have refused to obey.

"Mr. Poole, I've been trying to reach you for the last hour, but the operator said the line was tied up." Martin Lyle couldn't wait for Sin to close the doors behind him before he started talking. "He pushed past me, called me a useless watchdog, laughed at me—"

The older man's voice bgan to quaver, and Sin put his hands on the man's frail shoulders. "Who did all of this, Martin?" he asked gently, almost sure of the answer.

"It was Mr. Dutton. He's still here, in your father's office, doing heaven only knows what. Your poor father is going to be so dreadfully upset. . . ."

Somehow Sin managed to tell Martin that Stanford Poole had died. The effect on the already upset man was hardly soothing, but Sin managed to calm him down and left him with a snifter of brandy from the supply kept in the closet of the boardroom before he returned to the conference chamber, gloomy with its heavy English furnishings, but with a convenient connecting door to his father's office.

With the greatest of care, he slid back the bolt on the door in the small file room which served as the connecting passage. Through the panel he could hear Avery placing a call, but the secretary's voice was pitched at a purposely low tone, and he couldn't catch the name of the other party. Not even risking a short breath—not that that action would have done anything to slow the pace of his heart, now racing at an almost sickening speed—Sin turned the ornate brass knob and pulled the door open just enough for him to see Avery standing by Stanford's desk, his back to him, and to hear what was being said into the telephone. The office, however, was so large that even with this further advantage he still missed words, but he could make out enough to confirm almost every suspicion that he'd had about the man he held responsible for usurping the place that should have been his.

"No . . . they should bring in the verdict today— tomorrow at the latest . . . the judge. . . .sentence . . . not our responsibility . . . we can consider this matter closed and go on to other things. . . ."

Avery's laugh grated on Sin's already strained nerves, but he forced himself to remain still and silent. If his nemesis was about to make a mistake, give himself away, he wanted to be the silent observer who heard it all.

"Yes, sir, I won't forget about the letter—it's what binds us together. I trust you entirely, and certainly wouldn't presume to. . . . " Suddenly, almost as if he smelled danger, Avery swung around. At the sight of Sin, his face filled with unspoken loathing. Avery hung up the phone, breaking the connection without another word.

Sin advanced into the room, his footsteps sinking silently into the red, gold, and green Tabriz carpet, glad that the long walk from doorway to desk was giving him time to regain control over his temper and to plot a plan of action.

"You're fired." If nothing else, Sin noted, his direct delivery served to throw Avery off his guard— these words were not the ones he had been expecting. "Get out of here right now, and if you ever set foot in here again, I'll have you arrested for trespassing."

Avery, a few years older than Sin and a few inches shorter, was completely typical of those young men who went to Ivy League universities but never fit in; indeed, a scholarship student from an unknown background frequently found more acceptance among their gilded classmates than these other young men with their nice, refined, uninspired families. True to form, they all seemed to be surrounded by a sort of grayness that sapped whatever vitality or distinctive personality they might posess. And that, Sin realized belatedly, was the secret of their future success. All they needed was one small contact to get them an interview in a good firm and they would take the lowest position available, burrow themselves in the job, make themselves indispensable, and if they had a sneaky turn of mind, work their schemes so that no one knew what they were doing until the poison had been spread.

"I want you to leave now, " he repeated, holding onto his temper. No matter how much he wanted to, smashing his fist into Avery's jaw wouldn't solve his problems—the last thing he needed was to be arrested for assault and battery.

"Your father seems to see things differently," Avery returned, unconcerned. The momentary look of surprise and horror that had appeared on his face and in his eyes only a short time before was now gone. "This is his firm, and despite the unhappy situation he's in now, he makes all the decisions, not you."

"What you say is quite true. Unfortunately," Sin continued slowly, prepared to draw out every word, "The deceased don't make executive decisions."

"De. . . ." The look of panic returned to Avery's eyes. "Are you telling me that Mr. Poole is dead?"

"Less than two hours ago."

Avery blanched. "We never thought . . . suicide. . . ."

"I hate to be the one to disappoint you, but my father didn't kill himself. His poor, suffering heart did. But why are you saying 'we'?" he questioned, his neck rigid with nerves and with the certainty that he had walked into exactly what he had previously only been able to suspect. "Is this connected to your interesting telephone conversation?"

"What telephone conversation?" Avery countered skillfully. "That wasn't anything more than a casual call to an old acquaintance, and if you try to press the matter, it'll be your word against mine."

He's defending something, Sin thought, keeping his expression neutral. Somehow, someway, he's involved in what happened to my father. "I have more important things to do than argue with you," he said at last. "Get out of here."

"I'll just clear out my desk and—"

"No, you won't. When I say I want you out of this office, I mean immediately. I'll send anything that isn't ours to your apartment."

"But I left my billfold in my desk," Avery protested. Even on the edge of down and out, Sinclair Poole was still the same golden boy he'd been at college: in charge and on top of the world. Well, maybe not for much longer, particularly when he learned how many compromises he would have to make just to be considered even on the fringes of social acceptability. "You wouldn't put me out on the street without any money."

"Why not?" Sin sounded almost cheerful. "We're not that far from Wall Street and it's a nice day. You can take a walk down there and palm some money off whomever you were talking to before," he said, placing a hand on his upper arm as he began to steer him toward the door. "And before you leave, I suggest that you apologize to Martin for upsetting him. You've already made an enemy of me, Avery, and I don't think you want another."

In the days that followed, Sin found that while the pain generated by his father's trial was over, another sort of anguish—one that would not easily be healed—began to work its way into his life. Even the matter of a burial service became entwined with the events of the past months.

It wasn't that Reverend Dr. Huntington at Grace Church or Reverend Dr. Morgan at Heavenly Rest or Reverend E. M. Stires at St. Thomas' or Reverend Dr. Parks at St. Bartholomew's refused to bury Stanford Poole. It was all the conditions they put on the service as to when it could take place and what could and couldn't be said. His father hadn't transgressed; instead, he had been transgressed against by men who wanted to ruin him for their own gain. But Sin couldn't say that to four of the most distinguished churchmen in New York any more than he could agree to their wanting to mention

Stanford's "errors" and "follies" during the service. Only the Reverend Dr. George Houghton, the founding rector of the Church of the Transfiguration, offered the comfort and advice Sin needed to hear in his almost overwhelming grief, a grief that was streaked with anger and the need for revenge.

To be sure, there were more curiosity seekers outside the church than there were mourners inside, Sinclair having issued invitations as to who could and couldn't attend. Those few who had continued to believe that his father couldn't be guilty, and even those who had sent a cheering message or telephoned to say a few kind words, were asked. As for the rest of their so-called "close" friends—they no longer existed for him, and he had more important tasks to attend to than to curry favor with them.

Sin made it through the funeral service and internment without a crack in his demeanor, but when he returned to the Fifth Avenue house he was alone, and in the large rooms that seemed to echo with every footstep despite the profusion of rugs and draperies and furniture and paintings, he faced the reality that he now had to settle all the problems left beind and then work on clearing his father's name. He hadn't cried since childhood, but that night he wept for hours, and when he awoke in the morning it was with the certainty that he had two missions to fulfill; but the one to clear his father would have to wait until everyone who had invested in the nonexistent Great Northwest Lumber Company had been paid back in full, even if he had to bankrupt himself to do it.

Divestment came first, he thought as Haskell served him breakfast, placing temptingly filled plates among the paper arranged on the dining room table. He hadn't thought his father had invested so heavily in the lumber company or had attracted so many investors-the list of names went on for pages.

Within two weeks, he'd contacted every person on that list, asked them to come to see him, and told each one the same thing: that as soon as his father's holdings were liquidated, they would be paid in full, and he was giving them a promissory note in the meantime. The only person to refuse the legally binding letter was George Kelly.

"I know that you'll pay me back by and by," he told Sin, "and I'm not in any rush for the money. I have more than enough to live on, and what I invested with your father was my attempt to get rich quick. Now that I've learned my lesson, I can wait to be repaid for my shares until you've cleared your father's name."

For a minute, Sin stared at the former prize-winning boxer. "That's just what I intend to do, but it's not going to be easy."

"True, but as the Bard of Avon once wrote, 'Give sorrow words; the grief that does not speak whispers the o'er fraught heart and bids 't break.' "

"Do you know a lot of Shakespeare?" Sin questioned, distracted for the first time in days from his own difficulties.

"Quite a bit. No matter what the situation, he has a quotation to fit it. I can see you're a man who isn't going to let a series of bad circumstances throw him on the canvas. Would you consider hiring me to be your bodyguard?''

''Do you think I need one?''

''You've been through a difficult time, Mr. Poole, and it's still not over. Notoriety often attracts an assortment of people a gentleman like yourself would not care to know.''

''Let's see. . . .'' Sin smiled, feeling himself relax. '' 'Diseased nature oftentimes breaks forth in strange eruptions.' ''

''I was just about to make the same reference myself,'' George remarked with approval, but the gaze he bestowed on the library was not complimentary at all. ''If you don't mind my saying so, staying on in this house might not be a good idea.''

''You're perfectly right, and since I won't be able to afford to live here much longer, whether I mind or not is a moot point.'' Sin pushed away the stack of papers he was working on. ''And if I want to find the men who destroyed my father, I have to drop out of sight for a few years. Let them think I'm a ruined man babbling on about a frame, and eventually they'll make a mistake.''

''And in the meantime you'll be keeping tabs on your suspects.'' George coughed softly. ''I also do double duty as a private detective, but before I can do anything, it helps to have names.''

''I have one so far—Avery Dutton. If we can keep tabs on him, the others will fall into place,'' he said, and thought for a moment. ''No, I have another name—Davis Moreton.''

''Well, if you have to take on someone, go after

the biggest,'' George replied after Sin finished telling him about his engagement. ''I would say something was definitely brewing there. This won't be quick, you know.''

''I can wait, and while I do that, I'll keep myself busy by continuing with a small sideline of my father's , a firm that imports fine arts from the Orient for antique dealers and auction houses,'' Sin informed George, formulating his plan while he spoke.

''But not from here.''

''My father had a lot of real estate holdings around town, and I'm working on a deal with Elston Harper's people. It would be better if he weren't off on one of his naturalist adventures, but his representatives are honest. I'm keeping one property, though. It's a townhouse on Prince Street off the Bowery.''

''But that's not a gentleman's address!'' George protested.

''And perhaps I'm not much of a gentleman any more. I may even use the first floor as a club for the local businessmen—they probably don't have another meeting place. And since I seem to have hired you as my bodyguard and private detective, would you care to have a look at the floor plans?''

Sin, operating purely on his instinct, which seemed to have sharpened appreciably, knew that George was someone whom he could count on in any situation. A faint sense of unease that the notoriety surrounding the trial might earn him the unwanted attention of those who thought they could better dispense justice than the court system, disappeared back into the woodwork now that he had protection.

As soon as the investors were paid back, his remaining funds were consolidated, and the work for the modernization of the Prince Street house were underway, Sin left New York for a cabin he'd rented in the Adirondacks. Although quite comfortable by nearly anyone's standards, the small structure facing a crystal-clear lake could almost be declared primitive compared with the nearby Poole summer estate that he had had to sell. But the cabin gave him a few months of much-needed peace and quiet. Now there was time to fish and hike and read—and plan his revenge.

Sin went to the mountains before the Fourth of July and returned to the city the week before the leaves began to turn. His nerves were no longer rubbed raw and he didn't regard those who did offer him friendship and support with suspicion. But his determination to clear his father was undimmed.

Under George's supervision, the house was ready for occupancy, and following the instrucitons he'd given, there was a first-class cook in the kitchen and a highly regarded bartender ready to serve beverages to the businessmen who would be having lunch in the new club. Mr. Wong and Vic Sheehan, along with Haskell and Martin Lyle and the indispensable George, quickly formed a tight circle around Sin, providing him with the friendship and support he needed to see him through what was promising to be a rough time ahead. Those five were, in fact, the only individuals he really and truly trusted.

It wouldn't have been hard for him to maintain much of his old social life—provided he was willing to repudiate his father. Several feelers had been put out to him by socially prominent couples saying, in effect, that if he were willing to admit that he knew his father had been guilty all along, the invitations that had stopped when the investigation began would begin to flow again in a steady stream.

It would have been so easy for him to go along, to say what they wanted to hear, to retain a place in the social world that had so quickly cast him out. The temptation was there, but only for a minute—Sin having swiftly reached the conclusion that while he shaved he liked to be able to look at himself in the mirror.

Unhappily, the largely solitary path that stretched ahead of him also meant that he had to cut himself off from those who had also thought the crime his father had been charged with reeked of suspicion and set-up. Newton Phipps and William Seligman and Philip Leslie and Elston Harper and a few others would have been more than willing to help him, and while Sin truly appreciated their words of comfort, this fight was going to be fought by him alone.

Little by little over the next years, going only on his deep distrust and dislike of Avery Dutton and Davis Moreton, plus the scanty details from that overheard telephone conversation, he began to accumulate evidence. There were wrong turns and mistaken leads and incorrect assumptions, but by and large he was succeeding in his task—a job that would be complete when he had the letter. . . .

His import business became a rousing success, his club was welcomed by the local small businessmen, and the few investments he made turned out to be wise ones that would pay extremely handsome dividends for as long as anyone ate cereal or needed film for their box cameras or put glass in their windows, but new dark points appeared in his new world with the natural attrition that occurred among his staff. Neither Martin nor Haskell were young when they'd decided to remain with him, and by the early months of 1900 both had left New York; his secretary had gone to Virginia, and his houseman to California, both places of easier climates and quieter ways of life. He sent off both men with his good wishes and substantial pensions for their many years of devoted service, but they were the last links with his old life, and their departure created more of a sense of loss in his heart than anything else since the death of his father.

It was simply one of those times when nothing seems quite right, and when Vic Sheehan entered Roosevelt Hospital in the late spring of 1900, it was just one more incident during a period when nothing was either very good or very bad. The bartender's surgery was a minor, corrective procedure, but Sin still paid daily visits to the semiprivate room he had made arrangements for (the private pavilion was reserved for those with social standing), and he was therefore rather annoyed when he arrived one afternoon near the end of Vic's stay to find the other bed in the room occupied.

"I took care so that you would have a good room

and some privacy," Sin remarked as he pulled up a chair and sat down. "If you want, I'll go and have a word with the administrator—"

"No, boss, it's all right. They asked me and I told them it was okay to bring him in here. Poor kid. . . ." In a quiet voice, Vic told him about the young man in the other bed, and Sin's original reaction disappeared in a wave of compassion. "I think you should go over and say hello to him, cheer him up, so to speak," the older man finished.

Obligingly—and not without a bit of curiosity—Sin crossed the large, sunny room to the other bed and instantly saw the reason behind Vic's request: the young man, in his early twenties, with one ankle encased in what had to be several pounds of plaster of Paris, looked enough like him to be taken for his younger brother. Gregori Vestovich's hair and eyes were darker, and his cheekbones gave his face a look that went past patrician to aristocratic, but over all he had the same sleek, direct demeanor that was pure Poole.

Quite unexpectedly, Sin's old longing for a younger sibling—particularly a younger brother with whom he could share his interests and offer his advice—surfaced after years of supression. And there was a link between, he was sure of it. Whoever Gregori Vestovich *really* was—and after hearing him talk, he didn't believe for a moment that that was his real name—he had come to New York to escape some disaster in his past, probably involving some woman, and no doubt leaving a furious family behind him.

He offered Gregori the opportunity to be his valet-secretary, and the young man, who only the night before had cried himself to sleep in an agony of loneliness and dispair, accepted not only Sin's job but decided that the quest to prove Stanford Poole innocent was now his also. Ten days later, still in the cast and on crutches, he moved into the house on Prince Street.

For the first time in five years, Sin wasn't the youngest person in the household—the young lord of the manor around which everything revolved. He was unquestioningly the one in charge, but now he had the chance to impart some of the things his father had taught him plus a few of his own theories to Gregori. He taught him how to type, how to read the financial papers, how to read between the lines of annual reports, and the difference between common and preferred stocks.

And now, less than two years later, Gregori was in on every detail that it would take to unmask the men whose greed and love of power had ruined a good and honest man. And for his part, the twenty-one-year-old who had been so rudely wrenched from his family and his priveleged life by a string of circumstances he feared would never be solved had formed a common bond with someone again, was able to feed his own need for a family. There was safety for him in the fine old townhouse, and there was something more: he had an older brother again.

Sin, having reconsolidated his base, forged steadily forward on all fronts. The letter that had first been only a fragment of an overheard conversation, then an elusive object he often thought he'd never hold in his hands, finally became a tangible objective just within reach.

And always just out of his touch.

Sin lay in bed and listened as the sounds of the morning increased. He could hear Gregori coming down the corridor, the sound of his boots making contact with the highly polished wooden floor, and his voice, unusually cheerful, shouting something over the bannister to whomever was in the hall below.

"You've either had a good night or are expecting an even better one," he remarked a minute later as Gregori, dressed in riding clothes, came in carrying his breakfast tray. "You look in very good form."

"So should you." He put the wicker tray with its side pockets holding the *New York Times* and the *New York World* across Sin's lap before going over to the windows to pull back the curtains. "I saw a photograph of Caroline Worth in this week's *Town and Country*."

"So?"

"So if I were you, and last Thursday's lunch was as pleasant as you claim, I'd almost say forget about the letter and concentrate on what may turn out to be more important."

Sin took a bite of toast. "Do you really think I should do that?"

"Remember, I said almost." Gregori closed the

windows. "What suit do you want to wear today? You want to be at your best for Miss Worth."

"Don't you get tired of playing valet? I'm going to make you a rich man and you're still going to carry in my breakfast tray and ask what I want to wear," he said, pouring out his coffee. "How do I get you to stop?"

"Why don't you try getting married? I have far too much discretion to invade the blissful privacy of the newlyweds' bedroom."

"So that's why they say a married man doesn't need a valet. No, not that one, the new pin-stripe. What else is on the agenda for today? I want most of it out of the way before Caroline gets here."

"Not much. The contracts should be arriving for the paper box company in Los Angeles that you're buying. I'll check over the papers and make sure the lawyers didn't slip in any of those little clauses they love."

"If George were here, he'd quote *Henry IV*—'the first thing we do, let's kill all the lawyers.' "

"Well, neither of us are going to do that,"Gregori said when they stopped laughing. "But all of those California investments are going to go very well with your father's shipping line when you have control of it again."

"This morning I think 'if' is more like it. By now, the Consortium must know I'm after them, have been after them all these years, and they've closed ranks to keep me from getting that close again."

"But you've made them good and nervous, and jumpy people don't make rational decisions."

"Let's hope that's just how it goes. Look, enough of that—get out of here and let me get ready. We'll take this up later, and with George's help we'll get back to work on them."

Gregori left, going swiftly down the stairs toward the stables, where the saddle and carriage horses were kept, and Sin began to get ready for the day ahead. Let Monday be blue or dreary to other people. They didn't have Caroline Worth coming to lunch.

But as he bathed and shaved and dressed, his mind began to dwell on the incident with Davis Moreton. He had expected to be closely questioned by the Woodbury police, even to have them bring along an official of the New York City Police Department for added influence, but when Chief Hathaway did arrive on his doorstep—on the day of Christmas Eve, offering the information that he was in town to accompany his wife while she did some last-minute shopping at Lord & Taylor—he was alone and his questions were surprisingly routine. Miss Worth and Drake Sloane had verified his presence on the terrace at the time of Mr. Moreton's demise, he told him. No further statements would be necessary.

But was it murder or was it suicide? he wondered, knotting his tie. And where was the letter Moreton, ill and distraught, had promised to hand over to him? If the Consortium had it again, his quest had been moved back several crucial steps, but if it were some other place that no one except Moreton knew about. . . .

The pain that usually nagged him suddenly intensified, and Sin closed his eyes until it passed. It was a reminder that he had to recover the letter and force the Consortium to make restitution without the luxury of a great deal of time. The longer he took, the greater the risk of incompletion.

Ever since he'd started on his quest, Sin, in his more literary moments, had regarded himself rather like a knight with a special mission. If he failed, nothing would ever be right, but if he won. . . .

The money mattered far less to him than the accomplishment of proving that his father had been the victim of a conspiracy, and he had been able to unmask the guilty parties. His quest—and there really wasn't another appropriate word for what he was doing—was, despite the help of George and Gregori and the very few others whom he trusted, primarily a solitary endeavor. Like the knights in the old stories on whom he had patterned himself, he thought of himself as a single force moving forward against incredible odds. But now, since the night he'd met Caroline Worth, he was thinking beyond the point when the letter would be in his hands. Ever since he learned of its existence, he had been unable to formulate what he wanted to do when he had taken care of the most important details. But with Caro on his mind, he was quite suddenly aware of any number of delightful possibilities.

Except that the nagging pain growing in severity and frequency was there to remind him that he might not have the opportunity to fulfill either desire, or to see which would be paramount over the other. Seeing Caro again, he realized, was at the same time a challenge to his sense of purpose and an unplanned source of potential happiness. Suddenly, without his expecting it at all, his choice as to what was the most important thing in his life might not be the one he'd always thought he would make.

Chapter Twelve

Although nowhere near as scandalous and vice-ridden as the uptown Tenderloin district, the Bowery, which stretched from Chatham Square to Cooper Square, was hardly a neighborhood of propriety and respectability. To be sure, there were any number of small and successful businesses, and a lesser number of homey restaurants catering to the families who had not moved away, and of course there was McSorley's Ale House, where the founder, John McSorley, ruled over his establishment with an iron hand, serving only ale at the tables, allowing clay pipes to be smoked, and discouraging any would-be patrons who might disturb his carefully cultivated workingman's atmosphere; but despite these exceptions, the overall impression of the Bowery with its numerous saloons and other potentially shady dealings was raffish and disreputable.

Still, as far as Caro was concerned, what she saw of the neighborhood between Cooper Square and

Prince Street where her brougham turned off the Bowery, except for the Third Avenue El, wasn't all that terrible or threatening, only rather down-at-heel. But not this part of Prince Street, she was happy to observe, noting the neat rows of red-brick houses with black trim and clean white windowboxes lining either side of the street. It was very quiet, with only one or two horse-drawn vehicles on the street and one rather bulky-looking man waiting on the stoop of the largest house. When the brougham stopped, he ran down the steps with the grace of a much lighter man, crossed the sidewalk, and opened the carriage door.

" 'Welcome hither, as the spring is to the earth,' " he said with a happy smile as soon as he caught sight of her.

"You're George Kelly," Caro said with an equally delighted smile, her apprehension fading. "I've heard so much about you."

"And I'm very happy to return the compliment," George replied, offering a large hand to help her down to the sidewalk, taking approving note of her Lucile coat and black velvet hat trimmed with an oversized oyster-white silk faille bow. "Mr. Poole sent me out to wait for you. He'd have been here himself, except that he's had an unexpected call, long distance from Washington," he finished in a voice that made it clear that such communications were indeed a modern miracle and should be regarded as such. "Now if you'll come right this way—"

The front door, painted a shiny lacquer black, opened into a small square hallway with three closed doors, a highly polished brass umbrella stand, and a vast dark green leather armchair. The white-walled anteroom was warm and protected from the icy chill outside, but it was also bare and rather forbidding, as if it were decorated to give all first-time visitors the signal that this was a house where secrets were closely kept. One of the three doors proved to be a spacious closet outfitted with shelves and the best large wooden hangers suspended from the rack, revealed when George helped her off with her coat and hung it up with great ceremony.

"This would make a wonderful story," Caro remarked as she took off her hat and placed it on a shelf. "One door out of three explained, but the other two are a mystery. "Which one do I go through, George?"

"If you don't mind, Miss Worth, you can wait here while I let Mr. Poole know you've arrived. I'm sure his telephone call must be finished by now," he said with an appreciative look at her Paquin suit of café au lait wool with velvet tabs and a gold silk blouse.

"Well . . . of course, if that's the way Mr. Poole would prefer it—this is his house," Caro replied, too well bred to protest.

" 'Fair lady, by your leave, I come by note to give and receive,' "George said gallantly, waiting until Caro had settled herself in the chair. These were not the instructions that Sinclair Poole had given him regarding the welcome and treatment of Caroline Worth, but despite his very Irish-American genes, George sometimes agreed with the French that every so often things—particularly in situations of the heart—had to be arranged in order that life might be allowed to fall into its most pleasant lines.

" 'Happiness courts thee in her best array,' " George announced a short time later, walking into Sin's second-floor office to find that while his employer was off the phone, his desk was all but hidden under stacks of papers, all of which had been consulted during the course of his long-distance call.

"I never thought I was going to get that dumb bastard off the phone. Rutherford Van Dyne sits in the Treasury Department all day and probably doesn't do anything except figure out new bids for his bridge game, and at night he goes to fashionable parties where he'll tell Washington's elite how crafty I am, but when he needs help, who else but me does he place a long distance call to." Sin spat out savagely, thrusting a stack of files at a very patient Gregori. "Did you say something, George?" he asked, suddenly breaking off to look at his bodyguard with an intensity that could make lesser men quail. "Were you quoting *Romeo and Juliet* to clarify a particular point?"

"You might say that." George paused and looked over at Gregori, and the two men exchanged smiles. "Miss Worth is downstairs."

Sin didn't blink. "Then she's in the club?"

"No, I took her coat and left her in the anteroom."

"And why, may I ask, did you do that?" Sin

inquired with admirable patience. "You could have shown her upstairs."

"That's the duty of a butler, and if you want someone to show your guests around the house, hire one of them," George replied blandly.

Sin opened his mouth, closed it, and satisfied himself with a glare as he pulled his suit jacket off the back of his chair and shrugged into it. "Do you find something amusing in all of this?" he asked Gregori.

"No, Sin, nothing at all," Gregori said as he found something of great interest in one of the files he was holding. "But you really shouldn't keep your guest waiting. I can handle everything up here."

"I just bet you think you can," Sin said bitingly as he swung out the door.

"Well," George said when the door slammed and the two associates were alone.

"Well, indeed." Gregori leaned back against the wall, his arms still full of files, a perplexed look on his face. "Was that whole performance really necessary?"

George looked wounded. "What performance?"

"You know what I mean."

"When you look like that, I can almost believe that you and Mr. Poole are brothers."

"Don't change the subject." Gregori began to smile. "Did you see how he took off out of here?"

"Oh, Sinclair's going down for the third time all right, except that I don't think he realizes it yet. In fact, I wasn't sure myself, which is why I left Miss

Worth—a truly lovely lady, by the way—in the anteroom. I wanted to see his reaction.''

''Well, it was just about worth it,'' Gregori offered. He walked toward the closet where the file cabinets were concealed. ''I suppose you have a quote handy for this situation. All things considered, *Romeo and Juliet* is not the best play to pluck lines from.''

''You're right. *Much Ado About Nothing* really does say it better.''

''Not *A Midsummer's Night Dream?* What about 'let her shine gloriously as the Venus of the sky'?''

''That's an excellent choice, Gregori. But I think that 'Love goes by haps: some Cupid kills with arrows, some with traps,' really fits this particular situation much better.''

Whoever had been in charge of putting together this anteroom, Caro thought, looking at the unadorned, mirrorless walls, definitely didn't think that a woman might have to wait in its confines. This was clearly a masculine preserve; part business, part home, but all male.

As that self-evident thought surfaced, Caro's apprehensions, which had faded at her pleasant welcome, began to spiral upward, and to keep herself from spinning out foolish fantasies, she opened her handbag and took out a gold powder box.

She applied the puff to her face with an experienced touch and thought about Vanessa's carefully phrased advice. Although impressed with her stepdaughter's inventiveness, as well as her having a higher motive in wanting to see Sinclair again than just to find out exactly how he regarded her, she had offered a warning. "You must tell me exactly where you're going, darling, and how long you'll be," she had insisted. "New York can be quite threatening, and it will make me feel better to know your whereabouts."

So Vanessa knew where she was right now, but the only advice she had offered on this matter was to treat this meeting exactly like a business appointment. Which is a perfect way for both of us to save face, Caro thought, snapping her powder box shut and returning it to its place in the fitted moroccan silk interior of her handbag. If he cares for me more than I care for him, or vice versa, if we keep talking about the Orient, neither of us risks being backed into a corner we can't get out of.

It was absolutely sound advice, the only route an honorable woman could take, but as soon as she heard the sound of swiftly moving footsteps on the other side of the door, her heart moved to a faster beat. Instinct announced that Sinclair was on his way to her, and a second later the door was flung open and his presence seemed to fill the anteroom.

"Welcome to my house, and I'm sorry you've been waiting here," he said, crouching in front of her, an appealing smile on his face. "It was George's idea of a joke—on me, of course, not you."

"I want to hear all about it, and I want to tell you right now that I haven't been uncomfortable at all," she responded. Who cared if this was a social

203

lie? Caro thought . . . not when she had Sin on eye level with her and it was taking all her self-control not to reach out and touch his face. "I've kept myself occupied by speculating about what's behind two of the three doors here."

"Sometimes I think it's all a maze. The frontage is only average for New York houses, but it stretches halfway back to Spring Street. Do you care about real estate?"

"I'm intensely interested in it, particularly in apartment buildings," she said, abstractly wondering why her voice suddenly had a slightly breathy tone.

Sin's eyes glowed like amber. "I bet you have an excellent eye for decoration. For instance, how would you improve this anteroom?"

Was he serious or simply teasing her? Caro thought. Well, in either case she didn't see any reason to be coy. "I'd hang a mirror."

Sin looked at the bare walls. "I never thought of a mirror."

"That would be obvious to any woman."

"We'll see about that." Sin flashed a smile that very few people saw any more and stood up straight, holding out his hands to her. "Shall I show you the business side first?"

"That's why I'm here," Caro said, recovering the composure she felt slipping away. "Incidentally, I like George very much, and his command of Shakespeare would probably send most dramatic actors hiding in a closet. Am I going to meet the others who work for you?"

"If I didn't introduce you, they'd all resign by

204

sundown," he assured her, opening the door Caro was facing. "This is the bar and dining room. I suppose you could call it my version of an London clubroom, although as you must know by now, my opinion of private clubs doesn't rank very high."

Still, Caro observed silently, he had obviously taken a leaf from those very clubs he detested when he created this room. She noted with approval the tables that would seat two or four, the crisp white linen tablecloths, the dark-red leather chairs, and the unobtrusive but highly polished mahogany bar. But it was the painting over the bar that caught her attention. Mounted over the mirror, the large canvas depicted a young man rowing a single scull, the oars dipped in the heavy flowing water while the foliage showed that this was the first appearance of autumn.

"You have a Thomas Eakins!" she exclaimed, hurrying across the deeply carpeted floor to stop at the bar, the best spot, as it happened, to observe the painting. "It's simply stunning. I can almost hear the Schuylkill."

"That's exactly what I think," Sin said, coming to stand by her. "This is the only one of my father's collection that I didn't sell. That was about the same time Eakins was having trouble with the Pennsylvania Academy, and the appraiser from the Plaza Art Galleries told me this work probably wouldn't even bring a single bid. Not that I care very much," he added.

"I should hope not. I think the Pennsylvania Academy of Fine Arts must be the biggest bunch of idiots for not appreciating this man's talent."

"He is one of the most remarkable artists of this century, and his insights into his subjects is almost too much to bear."

"You sound as if you know him."

"In a way." Sin looked slightly embarrassed. "I had a fit of vanity last year and decided I wanted my portrait painted. I wrote Eakins, told him about this painting as well as a few other things, and he wrote back that he wanted to paint me."

"May I see your portrait?"

Sin shook his head. "I have it put away. As I said, it was commissioned during a temporary fit of vanity."

There was an undertone in his voice that clearly told Caro this was not a subject to pursue, and the arrival of Vic Sheehan, a tall, compact man with a bright smile on his face, eliminated the need for either to fish around for a topic of conversation that would effectively change the subject. Vic had with him an assortment of bottles from the wine cellar, and after the introductions, he was very eager to tell Caro about Sin's rules for serving liquor.

"There's no beer or ale here, and very little whisky," he offered. "Mr. Poole prefers that the guests who come here to discuss business to have a nice dry martini, and there's a fine supply of good, sound red and white wines."

"What about champagne?"

"It wouldn't be a proper household without champagne," Vic asserted proudly. "And I've already put a very special bottle on ice for you and Mr. Poole."

206

"I'm sure we're going to enjoy it," Caro said, delighted, as Sin, also murmuring his thanks, began to edge her backward.

"I'm sure you'll forgive us for leaving so quickly, Vic," he said. "But there's quite a bit to this house, and I wnat to show it all to Miss Worth and still have time to consult with her about a few things before lunch."

In the butler's pantry, Sin opened the doors to the glass-fronted cabinets and the fitted drawers so that Caro could examine and admire the Lenox china, the Waterford glassware and the Reed & Barton silver which was used for the club's service. He explained that except for the costly gold and silver services which had been sold, there had been so many sets of china, crystal, and silver purchased by his parents that he had no need to buy from the restaurant supply houses, and when that part of the tour was finished, the kitchen and Mr. Wong were next.

In the middle of the thoroughly modernized kitchen, an Oriental man of indeterminate age, wearing the usual chef's garb of white trousers and shirt, was stirring something savory-smelling that was bubbling on one of the six burners of the great black Garland stove. Without missing a beat, he reduced the flame, covered the pot, and turned to be introduced to Caro.

"It is a great honor to have you visit my kitchen, Miss Worth," Mr. Wong said, his English perfect.

"Tao-chia, thank you," Caro replied, and continued in careful Chinese, "I have to tell you that I've

heard nothing but compliments about your cooking.''

''And you have an excellent Peking accent,'' Mr. Wong returned, pleased. ''I was born in Peking and lived there for several years before my parents took me to Shanghai. Most foreigners who attempt our language have a Cantonese pronunciation, which is far less pleasing to the ear.''

''I was very fortunate in my teacher, but I'm afraid my vocabulary isn't very large.''

''It doesn't matter. Mr. Poole has never brought a lady to this house until today, you honor us all with your presence.''

It was a very touching moment for Caro, and she practiced her somewhat rusty Chinese with Mr. Wong until Sin indicated that it was time to move on.

''I don't know how to tell you this, but the Chinese I do speak has a marked Cantonese accent,'' Sin said as they left the kitchen. ''Mr. Wong will never admit it, but I must be rather a trial to him. There are times I think he perfected his English so that he wouldn't have to talk with me in his own tongue.''

''I suppose you think that's funny,'' Caro returned, choking on her laughter as she saw the humor in Sin's eyes.

''I have an idea that this is not one of my better days. Actually, Mr. Wong has always spoken superb English,'' he said, showing her into a room where a fiftyish woman was studiously ironing a fine damask

208

tablecloth. "Mrs. Murphy, I hate to interrupt you, but I'd like to present Miss Caroline Worth."

The woman's handsome face broke into a wide smile. "Ah, and haven't I been wating for this minute for the longest time," she exclaimed in a rich voice through which the lilting beauty of Ireland still flowed. "Mr. Poole's description of you didn't do you an ounce of justice."

It wasn't hard to figure out that a serious matchmaking plot had been hatched below stairs, and Caro knew that her role was to pretend that she didn't notice anything out of the ordinary. The people who worked for Sin must care for him very much if, sight unseen, they had decided to encourage him toward her . . . not that she minded.

"Thank you, Mrs. Murphy, that's very sweet of you. I've been made to feel so welcome here."

"Well, none of us want you to think that even though Mr. Poole doesn't hobnob in society the way he used to, it means this is an unfriendly place."

"Yes, Mrs. Murphy, I'm sure Miss Worth realized that at once," Sin said, blushing. He knew what was going on with his staff—God only knew what Gregori would say when he was introduced to Caro—but despite the devotion that those closest to him gave, he had never in any way sought to suppress their opinions or bend their will to his, and as long as he had never done that, he now had no right to complain. "I've found that she is very *sympathique* to her surroundings. Which brings to mind something you can help us settle," he continued, seeing a graceful way to end this meeting. "When she arrived, Miss Worth made an observation about the anteroom, and I'd like to see if you agree. If you were redecorating, what would you change about it?'

Mrs. Murphy was not a woman used to beating around the bush. "Well, I can't brag as how I know one antique from another, but if I were to make any changes there, the first thing I'd do to that anteroom is to hang a good-sized mirror on the wall!"

"I have two offices," Sin said a short time later as he turned the key in a brass lock of a solid hardwood door. "I handle all my importing business here, and financial transactions are handled on the second floor."

"Do you practice *feng shui* in both places?" Caro asked, seeing the red lacquer wall clock which would keep thieves away.

"Yes, but much more down here than up there," he replied casually. "I take it that you're a firm believer in the art."

"Oh, yes." Caro walked around the spacious office, all tan and blue and red, with fine Oriental furnishings and in one corner a tank in which six black fish swam. "When we first moved into the Osborne, Vanessa and I really didn't have the heart to do any special placement except for the mirrors, but when we found so many of our lost belongings at Fowler's, it was like—and please promise you won't laugh—like a sign."

"I don't think there's anything to make fun of in that. It's one of the most touching things I've heard." Sin sat down behind his desk. "It's why we're here together today," he went on, looking closely at her. "Where's your hat?"

Caro laughed. "I know no lady ever removes her hat indoors unless she's in her own home, but ever since I wore that costume wig, I don't seem to care for anything heavy on my head, so I left it on one of the shelves in your closet," she explained. "It's black velvet and bit much."

"It sounds very attractive, but I prefer the sable toque you had on the other day."

Caro couldn't resist a smile. "So you're an expert on ladies' millinery?"

"It's not as arcane a subject as one might suppose, and I do seem to have the habit of acquiring odd bits of information."

"Isn't that always the case?" Caro examined a handsome tobacco-leaf platter. "And for the record, I prefer the sable toque also."

Sin suppressed the urge to tell her that she was made for the finest and most luxurious of furs; that he wanted to buy her a full-length sable cloak that, in an erotic moment, would cover them both. . . . "Are you familiar with the Japanese expression *sabi*?" he asked, shaking himself free of the dream that suddenly seemed within reach.

"Of course I am. It's the way they describe things that have been made more beautiful through the passage of time. But I prefer another Japanese expression, *mono non aware.*"

"Then you believe that objects take on the patina and the history of the people who own them?"

"Actually, I never thought about it very much," Caro admitted as she sat down in the comfortable chair placed next to the desk. "But when we found so many of our belongings again, I remembered the theory. It does seem nice to think that my father, stepmother, and I made such a strong imprint on what we owned that we had to get back something of what we lost, that it wouldn't willingly go to anyone else."

"Do you care at all for the woodblock landscapes of Hiroshige?" Sin asked, opening a file to withdraw a small stack of papers. "An American dealer in Japan has written offering me a dozen mid-nineteenth-century views of old Edo."

"They're thrilling to look at, but if I owned any, I'd offer them to a museum. Edo is now in Tokyo, and as much as we think of the Orient as unaffected by change, it's nonetheless going to be, and it would be nice to share that period of time with as many people as possible."

"I think that's just what I'm going to do," Sin said. "However, I have to admit that this business about stolen merchandise has made me a bit wary. Are you familiar with Reginald Warren, by any chance?"

He handed her some papers, and Caro looked at the all-too-familiar letterhead engraved on heavy white stationery. "That's an interesting way to put it. A few years ago, Reginald Warren and I were engaged to be married."

"I see."

"Are you upset? These days, most of us have a

212

broken engagement or two to our credit," she said, and then remembered Cynthia Moreton–Chandler. "I'm sorry I said that. . . . you must think any woman who doesn't follow through with her wedding plans to be of pretty dubious character."

"No, Caro; somehow that conclusion never ocurred to me. My father used to say that modern girls acted as if their Tiffany solitaires were made of glass." Sin laughed without any mirth. "And the further I get from the incident, the more I think Cynthia did me the favor of my life when it turned out she didn't care for me any more than I cared for her. But what about you?" he went on, quickly turning the question back to her as if to forestall her asking any questions about Cynthia. "Isn't Reginald Warren a little old for you?"

"How old are you?"

"Thirty-two, but I don't see—"

"I'm twenty-six . . . and Reginald is thirty-four."

"I really thought he was much older. We've never met," Sin admitted, slightly embarrassed at having jumped to the wrong conclusion. "I just assumed—"

"Oh, that's all right. Reggie's really an excellent judge of anything Japanese—so much so that he seems older than he is."

"Is that why you didn't want to marry him?"

"Have you ever heard the expression that there's nothing worse than a convert?"

"Once or twice. Is that what came between the two of you?"

"Reggie adored Japan and all things Japanese.

Everything there was perfect; everything American or even European was sadly lacking. He didn't act like this all the time, of course, or I wouldn't have accepted his proposal in the first place, but as most women know, a man sometimes doesn't reveal his true nature until his engagement.''

"Then count yourself lucky,'' Sin couldn't resist saying. "Think of all the women whose bridegrooms didn't confide their innermost thoughts until after the ceremony.''

"Well, it was you who wanted to discuss this, not me. If you want to know about Reggie and how he conducts his business, I'll be glad to tell you. He's honest and you'd never have to worry about anything he had to offer. But I really don't want to talk about why I became engaged to him, or why I broke it off!''

Caro wasn't proud of the edge that appeared in her voice or of the faint sense of resentment that she felt toward Sin's questions. That nine-month period that had marked the term of her engagement now seemed to be one complete mistake—something that should simply be allowed to fade and not be raked up every so often by a potential suitor suffering a spasm of jealousy.

Potential suitor: her choice of words sent a strange feeling coursing through her veins and abruptly she stood up and walked away from the desk, leaving a nonplussed Sin behind her. She went to one of the uncurtained windows and stood there, looking out at the small, deserted garden at the back of the townhouse.

"I seem to have put my foot right into my mouth," Sin said as he came to stand at her shoulder . . . far too close, yet not near enough, she thought.

"One handmade English shoe, no doubt," she said, not trusting herself to take even a half-step backward.

"It still has a lousy taste. I'm sorry . . . those questions made me sound like a puerile schoolboy."

"You were *never* a schoolboy."

"I'm still sorry I asked you those questions, and the only thing I can say in my defense is that I brought up Warren's name out of the blue, and the answer you gave threw me off completely."

"It's not a crime for a girl to break an engagement, provided it's done for an honorable reason. But is what I did offensive to you, or does it bring back bad memories? Please don't feel angry toward me because of an unfortunate coincidence.

"Don't you know that how I feel about you has absolutely no anger at all attached to it?"

"Yes, but I wanted you to say it first."

"Oh, Caroline, why did I have to meet you now?"

They were in each other's arms, standing in a close embrace, touching but not kissing, and Caro felt a new happiness and contentment welling up in her. She rested her head against his shoulder, and it was so still in the room that she was certain he could hear her heart beating just as she could hear his.

"This is much nicer than the terrace," he murmured at last, his breath soft and warm against her ear.

"There's so much to be said for central heating," Caro heard herself reply, lulled into a condition in which she didn't want to consider any of the possible ramifacations of their embrace.

"I don't recall being particularly cold that night—not after I met you."

"It's taken you long enough to admit it," she couldn't resist saying, and felt Sin's lean, elegant body shake with laughter.

"You have to admit that our first meeting—not to mention our subsequent one—was somewhat unorthodox."

"True, but today's meeting was very properly arranged," she said, sliding her cheek against his as she drew back to look at him.

Sin's eyes turned a deeper shade of amber. "And look where it's gotten us."

Caro felt his hands tighten at her waist, not an impossible sensation since she didn't lace, and instinctively she braced herself against his waist.

"I won't complain if you won't."

"That's a mistake I have no intention of making," he promised, and then forgot everything except how much he wanted to kiss her.

Separately, they had been waiting, quietly longing for this moment to come again since the night at the Linden Trees. Then a gunshot had abruptly put an end to their first interlude, but today there were no interruptions.

With a deep sigh, she placed her hands at the back

of his neck, stroking his silky, carefully barbered hair, letting her delight in the moment and her happiness in anticipation of the future surge through her body, making her doubly aware of the slightest touch from the man she loved.

The kiss was intense and sweet and their arms tightened around each other as their embrace lengthened. Suddenly nothing was very important except the magic they were making together.

This is the beginning of bliss, she thought, and when they broke away for a moment of air, she heard herself gasp, "Don't stop."

"I can't—you can't." Sin's voice sounded unfamiliar even to his own ears. He was rapidly losing himself in the heavy rush of blood flowing through his body, in the scent of Caro's perfume, and in the sweeping sense of passion that reduced everything in his life to the two of them. "We don't want to."

Their lips met again, and with new urgency their kisses resumed. At that moment all they needed was each other, but their embrace wasn't an isolated incident in their lives. It had to lead somewhere to stop completely, and they had reached the crossroads.

Slowly and very reluctantly, a silent signal passed between them and they drew apart. The magical mood enveloping them, although in no way marred, had inevitably lessened as reality took over. They remained facing each other and holding hands, but now their gazes reflected their sensibilities as well as their passion. Neither was about to deny the strong strain of desire that their kisses had uncovered, but their existing responsibilities were still with them.

Sin ended the pregnant silence between them.

"I think I've really done it this time," he said quietly.

"I hope you don't intend to use the word compromise. If you did, I might have to forget I'm a lady and take a swing at you."

"I believe you would—if I were that much of a fool," he told her, raising her hands to his lips. "I thought I was immune to this, but now I have to admit that I never felt like this before."

"I hate to say this," Caro breathed, "but I feel very shaky."

"So do I," Sin admitted, trying to recall the last time his knees had turned to water and not able to remember. "Shall we sit down?"

Together they crossed the floor to the sofa covered in peacock-blue silk. To late, they silently realized as they sat down close together, this was far more dangerous than merely standing by the window.

"Do you know you enhance any room you're in?" His voice was quiet and gentle. "It doesn't matter if it's a ballroom or a church or the inside of a carriage or the corner of a restaurant. I can't wait to see how you look riding in a motorcar."

His fingers moved along her cheekbones as he spoke. She saw herself reflected in the depths of his amber eyes, but somehow there was no surprise that she should look both expectant and happy. It went without saying that they shouldn't be sitting so close to each other. Was the door locked? She didn't know and, for the first time, didn't care.

This wasn't a moment to be rushed, and she

slowly closed her eyes as they moved into a new embrace. Her lips parted, eager for his, and when his mouth touched hers, she tightened her hold on his strong shoulders. For a brief second, both were tentative, all too aware that this kiss might change everything between them.

"What are you thinking?" he asked, his mouth moving close to her ear.

"That we're at another crossroads."

"Every time I see you, there's another set of decisions to make."

Was there a touch of reluctance in his speech? She didn't think so. Was he drawing back from her even while she was locked in his embrace? No, but his life was made up of so many complications she couldn't even begin to guess at that she knew even his most natural impulses were checked and examined.

"Shall we shake hands and go back to the business of Orientalia?" she suggested lightly, letting humor win out over either romance or annoyance. "We do have higher ideals and priorities—"

They drew back slightly from each other, neither saying another word. For a reason he didn't want to consider, Sin was immensely relieved to see his own silent laughter mirrored in Caro's bright eyes.

"My ideals aren't that perfect," he whispered.

"I can't tell you how happy I am to hear that."

"I want to be a gentleman about this."

"There isn't any way you can be anything but a gentleman in any situation."

Their eyes never left each other's faces, and as if mesmerized, they leaned back against the cushions.

Sin felt his side protest this movement, but he had more important things on his mind.

His lips met hers in a kiss so rich and so deep that she felt the small office tucked away in the back of the house transform itself into their own private universe. When his hands moved from the curve of her waist upward to encircle her breasts, she stifled a cry as a new warmth spread through her veins.

She stroked his shoulders and the back of his neck and pulled him even closer to her in this half-sitting, half-reclining position. Each kiss, every touch of his tongue against hers was a new revelation. Had her heart ever beat like this before? Would it ever slow to a normal cadence again? Was this just the prelude to all the love they could share?

The silence in the house was overwhelming. No noise from the street penetrated the thick walls, and not a footstep sounded upstairs, but they were not alone here. And if he wanted to make love to her, it would mean that within a short time everyone here would know their secret.

She did want him, and not out of curiosity, to find out what it was like. But it couldn't be a self-enclosed experience—this one time and never again. And not here in this room—at least not the first time.

A similar thought occured to Sin. His pulse was pounding, but a thin shaft of reality refused to go away. It did more than remind him that this was not a way for a gentleman to behave toward a lady. The women whom he'd seen in the past few years—and they were all in one way or another ladies—held no subtle surprises for him. In each case, both Sin and the woman knew exactly what they wanted from each other beforehand. But Caroline was very different: he couldn't make love to her and then break her heart—which was exactly what he would do if in any way he pledged to her a future that in all probability wasn't there for him.

Now, in addition to all the other burdens of responsibility that he bore, the deepest feelings of his heart and the threat his health made on him were secrets he had to keep.

"No," he said at last, and his voice seemed to come from very far away. "No, I can't do this to you." *Or myself*, he thought.

He pulled gently away and after a minute they both stood up. Confusion and regret and an attempt at understanding were all in the air as they moved away from each other, each waiting until some sense of normality was restored before speaking.

"I take full responsibility for this," he said finally. "I should have thought of what this could mean to both of us, but I've never been so taken by surprise before. I never thought I could care so much."

Caro felt her throat close. "And do you want to?" she asked, feeling as if she were pushing against a brick wall. Here she had discovered something rare and fine, and although it was clear to her that Sin didn't deny that he felt the same way, it was equally obvious that he couldn't accept this new closeness with her same equanimity. "Do you want to sit down at the desk again and discuss Orientalia?"

"I don't think I could get a coherent sentence out."

"If I've disconcerted you so much, I'll leave," Caro responded, meaning every word. "Believe me, not too many women would want to give a man time to think."

Sin began to smile. "I don't want you to leave now. We can go upstairs—"

"Oh?"

"For lunch," he assured her. "We'll be much more comfortable there, and while we eat, we can talk about anything you want."

The second-floor sitting room was a bright, soothing spot. Even the pale winter sun coming through the classic casement windows curtained in a brown-and-cream *toile de Jouy* seemed stronger and warmer. The walls were painted a soft lemon yellow, and a Chinese pictorial rug of yellow, apricot, cream, and dark blue graced the basket-weave parquet floor. Two long sofas were covered in an apricot and cream brocade, numerous chairs were upholstered in contrasting silks, and the fruitwood tables and chest were lovingly polished to a high gleam.

Lunch wasn't quite ready yet, so Sin took her around the room, explaining the provenance of each painting, some of them by the finest post-Revolutionary War artists. With a slight touch of acid in his voice, he told her that most of them were not high-ticket items for the art collector, but museums weren't totally ignorant of the charms and the enduring value of such paintings, and he'd had several offers to buy them.

"Perhaps I will do that," he said a little distractedly as he showed her to the alcove that served as the dining room; a snug little place with a tole chandelier, a large armoire with the top section open, refitted to hold china and glass. Sin held out one of the cane-back chairs with apricot velvet seats. "Let all the robber barons collect Old Masters, I prefer the idea that American museums reflect our history."

"I agree with that," Caro said as she sat down. The circular table was set with a heavy damask tablecloth, Baccarat crystal, and Minton china of such a fine, rare pattern that she doubted the company manufactured it anymore. "But if you don't mind a bit of advice, this is probably something you can put off a few years. I don't think you'd like the bare spots on your walls."

"I know, I'd have to repaint to hide all the discolored squares. Do you like Moët?" he asked, lifting a bottle from the silver wine cooler, putting a napkin over it, and deftly removing the cork.

"I love all champagne, and it's the perfect way to end our morning and begin our afternoon," Caro said as they touched glasses. "Your house is wonderful."

"You haven't seen it all yet."

Caro looked at him over the rim of her glass. "Is this where you offer to show me your etchings?"

"Now that I know you, I'm going to seriously consider buying some."

Before she could think of something appropriate to say, Mr. Wong appeared, carrying a china soup tureen. Caro smiled, exclaiming over the chicken–

caviar soup, and by the time they were alone again, she decided that the best thing to do was simply to ignore their last exchange—at least for now. There were so many other things for them to talk about that it seemed silly to get bogged down on a topic that really had no place in their lives just yet.

Through the soup course, and during the entrée of poached salmon served with a perfect Hollandaise sauce, asparagus, and a cucumber salad, the conversation covered subjects that they hadn't touched on before. They discussed the work of *Weiner Werkstatte* in Vienna, and talked about how Frank Lloyd Wright and his Prairie School of Architects who worked out of Chicago might influence how Americans thought their homes should look. Caro told him about the pineapple plantations and orchid cultivation she had seen in Hawaii, and Sin offered the intriguing tale of an enterprising fellow who, the summer before, had filled a section of Central Park with green rocking chairs, charging a nickel to anyone who cared to sit in them for a short period of time, only to have his scheme fail when a heat wave struck the city and the less fortunate crowded the park and refused either to vacate the rockers or pay for the privilege of sitting in them. He was explaining the salient points of baseball and the importance of the New York Giants when dessert arrived.

"Mr. Wong more than lives up to his reputation," Caro said when they were left with lemon mousse, petits fours and a pot of café filtre. "He must be an absolute master at Peking duck."

"He could give lessons to Escoffier, and probably puts any number of New York chefs to shame."

"I'll forgive your saying that because you've never eaten food prepared by our Mrs. Cavendish," Caro challenged lightly. "Every cook and chef in Hong Kong raises his cleaver to her in honor!"

Sin laughed. "Someday we'll have to play compare and contrast."

"Peking duck versus lemon chicken?"

"That sounds about right."

They became quiet, and the enjoyment of dessert was tempered by the certainty that they had reached a pivotal point. If they didn't start to go beneath the surface of the events that influenced them most, all that they were starting to mean to each other would be lost, because there wouldn't be a strong enough foundation to build on.

"Sin, is the appellation "Consortium" a real one, or just a name you made up that stuck?"

For a long minute his expression didn't change. Finally he sighed and closed his eyes so that she wouldn't see the pain welling in them.

"Unhappily, that name is very real and not one I gave them, even though most people think I did and that the whole thing is a figment of my imagination," he said finally, his eyes calmer even though a troubled expression remained on his face.

"Since you've been investigating it for nearly seven years, I'd think you'd have more people on your side," Caro observed. She wanted Sin to have enough trust in her for a total confidence, but she

225

would rather he told her nothing than feel as if she'd forced him to divulge even a single detail.

"People prefer to believe what they want to believe, and it's simply much more convenient to think that I somehow managed to slip through the net that caught my father."

"How ugly."

"So this whole matter is a clear indication of how greed can warp people."

Caro sipped her café filtre. "How many people does the Consortium involve?"

"Six, now that Davis Moreton's dead," Sin said, and began his tale. "At first I went after Avery Dutton, the man who'd been my father's private secretary. He's a spy and a sneak if there ever was one. The first assignment I gave George was to follow Avery," he went on after telling her about that overheard telephone conversation. "I was convinced he was a homosexual, and that once I had proof of his deviation, I could force him into giving up the names of the men who framed my father." The look on his face was full of irony. "Are you familiar with the expression that experience keeps an expensive school?"

"No wonder you told me not to jump to conclusions about Jay Fowler. I hope you didn't spend too much time on that dead end."

"Long enough. I was so convinced I was right that even when George brought me proof I was wrong, it was weeks before I could fully accept the truth.

"I knew beyond any doubt that there was a letter

that connected all those concerned, and if I found it—well, it would be all the proof I needed."

"How did you get back on the track?" Caro asked, intrigued.

"First I had to force myself to lie low for several months. Avery may be many things, but he isn't stupid, and he must have known I was looking into his past and present activities. When I had to pay back all the investors in the Great Northwest Lumber Company, I sold off nearly all my father's holdings as quickly as possible. It wasn't until I was so stymied as to what to do next that I realized I had no idea who'd bought the shipping line or the railroad or the steel mill or the coal mines, just to name a few. I contacted the bankers who handled the sales and they sent me a complete list."

By mutual agreement, Sin paused in his story so they could move to a more comfortable spot. Carrying their coffee service and the plate of petits fours, they left the dining room alcove for the sitting room, placing everything they carried on a black lacquer and gilt-work Chinese Export tea table before sitting down on one of the sofas.

"Surely the men you were trying to identify weren't so overconfident as to buy your father's companies outright?" she inquired, refilling the delicate bone china cups.

"Oh no, not those fellows. Some of the men I contacted had no ulterior motive—Elston Harper and George Horton, for example—but the real money-making operations had been purchased by a holding company that called itself the Consortium."

"This sounds like the start of an experience in infinity."

"It was that exactly. For over a year, I had to peel away phony companies and figurehead employees to find out who and what the Consortium was. I couldn't have done it without George. He found out information that I might never have discovered on my own. And then, quite inadvertently, there was George Horton, the steel magnate. I had to write him for some details, and out of the clear blue he rings me up to discuss steel, and when we get that out of the way, he goes into a long song-and-dance about how Davis Moreton and Kenneth Chandler had tried to get him to sell my father's steel mill to them."

"And you had your first two names. I take it that Kenneth Chandler is Curtis Chandler's father."

"Like father, like son—and if you meet them, which you probably will, considering your social circles, you'll understand why that cliché rings so true."

"Never mind my social circles," Caro said somewhat more sharply than she intended. In a softer tone, she continued, "Did you suspect Curtis was lurking in the background when you were engaged to Cynthia?"

Sin put his cup and saucer back on the table. "Before I go any further in this tale, I want you to know why I asked Cynthia to marry me," he said, and told her about his father's request and his assurance that there need not be a wedding. "He saw it as a way to stop Davis from trying to worm his way into his investments. He had no way of knowing that in the game that was being played, he definitely didn't hold the trump card.''

I can't ask him about Alix, she thought. Everything she told me about their not contacting each other because they knew they weren't right for each other was true, but it's still only her side of the situation.

Caro found herself at an unexpected loss for words, something that was sure to prove awkward in a situation which called for tact and understanding. If she wanted to suffer some small jealousy, this was neither the time nor the place. Fortunately, her search for the right words was cut off by someone rapping on the door.

''I hate to interrupt,'' Gregori said a moment later as he walked into the room, ''but I thought I'd turn into an old man if I waited for you to introduce Miss Worth to me. All through lunch I had to listen to George and Mr. Wong and Mrs. Murphy rave about you,'' he said to Caro, joining them on the sofa. ''I see they weren't exaggerating.''

''Caro, my upstairs office was going to be the next stop on our tour, but since this gentleman couldn't wait, I'd like to introduce Gregori Vestovich,'' Sin said, his eyes bright with laughter. ''On any given day he's my secretary, valet, right-hand assistant, and kid brother.''

I don't believe that name for a minute, Caro thought, but aloud she said, ''That's rather like being called a jack-of-all trades.''

"Yes, but unlike the rest of the saying, I like to think I've mastered a few of them."

"Mostly on alternate days," Sin added. "But I'm glad to see Greg knows his own value."

"And I think that on those encouraging words, I'll leave," Gregori said, gracefully bending over Caro's hand in an inbred, old world touch that she didn't miss. "There are letters to type and files to arrange, but before I go I want to tell you that your photograph in *Town & Country* didn't do you any justice."

"What interesting words to use," she said when they were alone again. "Justice. It does tie very neatly into what we were talking about. I don't think for a moment that Gregori was listening at the door, but I have the feeling that there's a great deal of brotherly sensitivity between the two of you, that you always understand what the other is talking about. He isn't your half-brother, though."

It was so clearly a statement and not a question that Sin felt a distinct sense of relief at Caro's acceptance of how things were. But then, hadn't part of him always known that she was a woman who didn't require miles of explanation?

"No, Greg isn't, but the resemblance between us is so startling that some people—the same who are always ready, willing, and eager to believe the worst and most sordid in any situation—think that he is. It's one more strike against my father—the false notion of his having an illegitimate son. Of course I'm not really sure which is worse," Sin went on after he told her about his first meeting with Gregori, "those who believe there's a blood relationship between us, or those who know there isn't but are sure we're doing something far more evil . . . or classic, depending on your education and taste."

Caro laughed. "That's a bunch of horsefeathers."

"Among other things," he agreed, and joined in her laughter. "But the more complicated things appear to outsiders, the easier it is for me, although sometimes I wonder when I consider the twists and turns of my life. When I first heard the word *letter* mentioned—"

How did a man bear this for so long? she wondered. How did he keep himself on an even keel, how did he keep the bitterness he must feel from seeping into every part of his life?

"When I finally had all the names, I realized that I could only go after one of them, and he had to be the weakest link. Avery was out because he was already suspicious of me. Cynthia and Curtis presented a closed unit, Benjamin Wyndham was always being called down to Washington to advise President McKinley on the matter of business in America, Adam Marsh was too cautious and moved from too small a base to undermine, and Wendell Simpson was living in Europe. That left Kenneth Chandler and Davis Moreton, and I had to watch them very carefully to see which would begin to weaken first."

"Did you suspect it would be Davis?"

"No, and even after I knew he was starting to come slowly apart at the seams, I couldn't quite believe it was finally happening. His wife died, he had a long bout with pneumonia, and Cynthia wasn't the support and comfort he always thought she'd be.''

"You don't need to be Sherlock Holmes to figure that one out."

Sin's smile didn't reach his eyes. "Davis began to drift, the way so many men just past middle-age do when there are differences between them and their families. Also, he was never really well again, and it was then I began to make contact with him—little meetings about inconsequential things. It took over a year, and then I made my move and asked for the letter."

"You sound so calm about it, almost cold-blooded. Not that I blame you." she amended swiftly. "You've done everything so correctly. Some men with not even half the justification might have turned to violence, but you're so calm and matter-of-fact about it."

Sin absorbed her words with not a little bit of self-searching. He knew he was neither vicious nor cruel, either toward strangers or those he considered his sworn enemies, but his wanting to exact revenge for how his father had been treated was another matter entirely. Of course he was calm about it. If he for one moment let his deepest emotions take charge, he might very well behave in a way that would cause untold, unending problems for him later—and the immediate attention he so sought to avoid. But now for the first time he found his mind spinning out questions, some of which he didn't want to answer.

Being cold-blooded was one thing; being cold-hearted was quite another.

"Do you know what you've just made me do?" he responded as normally as possible. "You've made me ask myself if my quest to clear my father's name has become something else—something I won't like myself for, even when I do succeed."

"You're not doing anything wrong," Caro reassured him, her heart aching at the look of conflict in his eyes. "The last thing you should do is let men like that get off. Suppose they decide to do it agian to someone else?"

"You make me sound so noble." Sin attempted to smile, but to his horror, his eyes burned with tears.

"Oh, my darling, you are noble," Caro said, putting her arms around him. He rested his head against her shoulder, and full of concern and tenderness, she stroked the back of his head and murmured comforting words in his ear. "The only time you'd have to worry is if you never asked yourself this."

"But I never did before, not until just now," he said, his voice heavy with emotion. "I've been so single-minded—"

"I think purposeful and responsible is a better way to put it."

"It does sound better, but it doesn't change the fact that I did a number of things I never asked my self about. But I think George and Greg have begun to speculate about me, wondering if all this has gone on too long, that it might be warping me in some

way I won't even be aware of until it's too late."
He raised his head from her shoulder, and Caro was
relieved to see that his face was calm and composed.
"Do you think that also?"

"I think that you have a very tight hold on yourself, that you know exactly what you do, and the
only thing that you might have to watch out for is
confusing justice and revenge." Caro reached out
and touched his face. "There are times when the
lines can become rather blurred."

"You're very tactful. What you could have said
is that when all this began I had the dumb luck not
to lose my temper and beat Avery to a pulp."

"As long as you don't really want to do it."

"Only on alternate Thursdays." Sin smiled
briefly. "I think it's time for you to leave."

I haven't seen your other office, I haven't seen
the rest of your house, we haven't said half the things
to each other that we should have, Caro protested
silently, but this was Sin's home and the rules were
his.

"If you want me to."

"No, I don't want you to go at all." They rose
and stood close together, not really embracing but
close enough to hear each other's heartbeats. "I simply don't trust myself very much today. If you can
come back Thursday—"

"Then I'm not being banished, forever barred
from coming below Eighth Street?" she asked, and
was rewarded with a wide smile.

"How could I do a thing like that?" Sin asked as
he drew her closer into his arms and their bodies

touched. "We've been brought together by bonds of affinity."

Bonds of affinity: the Buddhist belief that people who on the surface have nothing in common, who are complete and utter strangers, can meet and find a connection, an understanding.

But it was far more complicated than that, Caro knew. All the way back uptown, and even now in the elevator of the Osborne, she turned that expression over in her mind, remembering Sin's face as much as she thought about the kiss that followed. A bond had been formed between them, one that went beyond mere attraction, one that could last when his father's name had been cleared.

It certainly hadn't been like that with Reginald Warren . . . Reginald, so immersed in the complex culture of Japan that he assumed she would be happy to spend her days studying *ikebana* and the Japanese tea ceremony. But she hadn't wanted to do that any more than she'd have wanted a married life in which she wore a kimono and had rice powder on her face, always deferring to her husband. Those expectations of his had at first confused and then rapidly dissolved her affection and regard for Reginald, and giving back the ring and breaking the engagement had filled her with such relief that with the passage of time she knew she had made the right decision.

I could never have been happy married to Reginald, it would be as bad as marrying someone who hated the Orient and everything connected with it,

235

she thought, leaving the elevator car. She exchanged pleasantries with the operator, but by the time she reached the apartment door she was once again lost in her own thoughts.

Caro pressed the doorbell almost absent-mindedly, too involved in reviewing the events of the day to open her handbag and remove her apartment key.

"Oh, Miss Caroline, you're here at last," Cavendish announced in clearly relieved tones when he opened the door. "Madame has been very concerned that you might not be back in time for tea. There is a guest," he continued as Caro stepped into the entry foyer. "This has been very unexpected. . . ."

For a split second, Caro thought that the butler's somewhat agitated condition meant that Reginald was in the drawing room, that he had just arrived in New York with the intent purpose of convincing her to marry him. But that was patently ridiculous, and after a moment Caro was amazed that even her active imagination could come up with such a scenario. She came out of her thoughts to catch the end of whatever it was Cavendish—who had a tendency toward pronouncements—was saying.

". . . .and Mrs. Cavendish is rather upset to have a Secret Service agent sitting in her kitchen."

"Excuse me, Cavendish, did you say a Secret Service agent?" she inquired, hoping she didn't sound as if she hadn't been paying attention.

"Of course, Miss Caroline. It seems that one of those men has to accompany the President wherever he goes—even to tea in a private home."

Chapter Thirteen

Less than a half-hour later, Caro paused at the closed double doors to the drawing room. Unlike far too many women, she had no difficulty making a swift change of clothes if the occasion called for it, but with the President in the drawing room she knew she must not appear in any way to have hurried. In her room, she had taken off her street clothes, washed her face, applied a fresh layer of face powder and lip color, and sprayed on a fresh application of Jicky. Marie, Vanessa's French maid, did her hair, and she chose a Lucile afternoon dress of celadon chiffon cloth with insets of Russian lace and a velvet ribbon belt, deciding that a tea gown would be inappropriate, considering their guest. Quickly she ran her hands over her hair to make sure her hairpins were secure, knocked on the polished wood panel, and opened the doors.

"Darling, I'm so glad you're here!" Vanessa's voice sounded no more concerned than if Caro had spent the day having a fitting—something which they had agreed on. "President Roosevelt is honoring us with his presence at tea."

"Mr. President, we're so pleased to have you visit us," Caro said warmly as she joined them, and shook hands with Theodore Roosevelt, who had risen to his feet. "Has my stepmother given you the grand tour of our new home?" she asked, sitting down on the sofa opposite them.

"Vanessa has been so meticulous and informative that I'm thinking of offering her the position of White House tour guide!" At forty-three, the youngest man ever to occupy the highest office in the land, Theodore Roosevelt was enjoying his position immensely. Born to an old and fine and respected New York family, he was a graduate of Harvard, an author, a rancher, a seasoned politician, and a devoted family man. With some men, one has a sense of wonderment that they could think they were in any way suited for the Presidency; with T. R., it seemed like the most natural progression that he should hold that office. "I'm on my way back to Washington tonight, and I promised Mrs. Roosevelt that I would call and see if both of you were happy and comfortable here at the Osborne."

"And I was very happy to tell him that we're adjusting quite well, and then I insisted that the President have tea with us," Vanessa said from her place behind the silver tea service. Her Worth afternoon dress of pale sage green silk, cut on princess lines, with a lavish yoke of Pointe de Geve lace, gave her skin a luminous quality. She certainly didn't give away for one moment her deep concern that her stepdaughter might not make it back in time from someplace where she shouldn't have been to begin with. "I do wish it could be a bit more lavish, though."

"Well, coming on the spur of the moment, I'm not sure I deserve this much," T. R. offered in genial tones as Cavendish carried a tray laden with covered dishes and small plates.

There were a variety of small sandwiches, tiny triangles of crustless bread filled with pâté and cucumbers and thin slices of smoked salmon. This was followed by scones, hot from the oven and waiting to be topped with sweet butter and strawberry jam, and finally there was an assortment of iced cakes. Vanessa poured cups of Earl Grey tea and led the uncontroversial small talk until everyone was truly relaxed.

Alice Roosevelt's coming-out ball was the most natural topic of conversation. It had taken place on the coldest night Washington had known in years. There had been no cotillions or expensive favors, which were the usual hallmark of the lavish debutante party. The Temperance people had put so much pressure on the White House that only New York State cider was served instead of champagne; and the debate on appropriations of funds for a proper dance floor had gone on so long that when it was finally approved there was no time to install it. Guests had been forced to dance on a floor on which a thick layer of wax had been spread across heavy linen.

"Of course I was upset when Alice told the Marine Band to start playing dance tunes again after dinner," the President said, accepting a second cup of tea. "But about ten bars into the first number, I decided that no harm was being done and the young people certainly were enjoying themselves. Naturally, most of the stories have it that I was absolutely livid, but such are the tales people tell."

"There are certain men and women whose main aim in life seems to be to enjoy the misery of others," Vanessa agreed. "I remember when we were in Tokyo in the summer of 1900. It was during the Boxer Rebellion, and all of us staying at the Imperial Hotel banded together while we waited for the news services to send runners over with the latest bulletins from Peking. There was a Russian there—one of those people who call themselves Baron or Count, but who love to gossip so much that you doubt the veracity of their title—and he would spend hours regaling us with the scandal that had rocked St. Petersburg that past winter."

"Is that the one about the son of the Russian prince who murdered the ballet dancer?"

"But no body was found—at least not when we heard about it," Caro said, correctly guessing that Theodore Roosevelt thought very little about the dissolute nobility of Europe. "That might have changed by now."

"It hasn't," Roosevelt said, his voice a little sad. "The Russian ambassador keeps me apprised of the unhappy situation. No body ever turned up and the young man in question has vanished. They're both

240

probably dead by now. Strange things do happen, though—your missing furniture was found, for example.''

''Yes; but Mr. President, how did you hear about that?'' Vanessa asked, even though she knew about the nonstop gossip that went on in the art-and-antiques world.

''It was Mrs. Roosevelt who heard about it first. Her salesman at the Sloane Galleries in Washington was the source. It was such a fantastic story that I did a bit of discreet checking with Fowler's here in New York, and found it was all true.'' Quite unexpectedly, the President chuckled. ''I have to compliment both of you on your handling of the Fowler family. I know from experience that they can be a very formidable group, but you ladies seem to have held your own with them.''

''Thank you, sir. But to their credit, the Fowlers *do* recognize the truth.''

''And a package of letters hidden in a secret drawer,'' Caro couldn't resist adding.

''Would I be wrong in guessing that they were love letters?''

''Oh, Mr. President, what other sort of letters would be worth putting away in a secret drawer?''

Theodore Roosevelt laughed, but his merriment was quickly replaced by an even more serious mood. ''I have to admit that I was disturbed to hear that Sinclair Poole was somehow involved in it.''

''And that thought distresses you, sir?'' Vanessa asked in her best British accent, giving her stepdaughter a signal that it was better to let her pose the first question.

"Yes, unhappily, it does. At first, I believed that Stanford Poole had swindled his investors with the Great Northwest Lumber Company, but later on I began to have some doubts. By then, too much damage had been done to the reputations of both father and son for anyone to offer to help make things right—or find out the real truth," he said regretfully. "Also—and this I'm ashamed of—I allowed a man I considered a trusted friend tell me not to involve myself, that it would hurt my political career if I didn't distance myself from the situation."

"Mr. President, would it make a difference if my stepmother and I could assure you that Sinclair Poole had nothing whatsoever to do with the theft of our belongings?" Caro asked, sensing that this was the proper moment to ask the question. She knew she was on tricky ground, but this was her chance to do something for Sin, and she had to seize the moment. "It's true he consigned them to Fowler's for auction, but we have substantial proof that what we might as well call the merchandise passed through so many different dealers before Mr. Poole purchased it that he couldn't possibly have known he was dealing with stolen goods."

"That's right," Vanessa said, deciding to go along. "We've asked the Fowlers not to make any trouble for Mr. Poole. Unfortunately, these things do happen, and the main thing is that we got back so many of our precious belongings."

The President's pale-blue eyes behind pince-nez

spectacles gave nothing away. With a wife and two daughters and female relatives almost beyond count, he was long used to feminine wiles, but the Worth women seemed to have integrity. If they believed Sinclair Poole was uninvolved in any wrongdoing. . . .

"Mr. President, I'm certainly not questioning your feelings concerning those in responsible positions who misuse that special trust," Caro began, hoping Theodore Roosevelt wouldn't guess she was making this up even as she spoke. "But if there was clear and unquestionable evidence that Stanford Poole was a victim of a conspiracy to take away all his vast holdings—"

Caro didn't have to go any further.

"If such a despicable thing were true, I wouldn't hesitate to make it known that his son had my full support." T. R. hesitated for a crucial half-second. "If indeed there were any proof that such a thing had taken place."

The brief spurt of hope that had filled Caro began to fade. She didn't doubt the President's integrity for a moment; as far as she was concerned, he was the most honest of men, but his position was such that he could deal with nothing but the hardest and clearest of facts.

"Whenever there are very crafty men going after an objective, you can be sure that at some point they'll make a mistake and leave some proof of their actions behind."

The President put down his teacup. "Are you

suggesting that the trial evidence might have been tampered with?''

''No, sir: I'm saying that all the evidence at Stanford Poole's trial was false, it had been planted over a long period of time, and it was believed because there are always more than enough people who are ready to believe the worst immediately.''

''Unfortunately, what you've just said can be quite true, even when one is speaking in terms of the greatest generalities.'' Roosevelt looked solemn, almost as if he were considering a matter he had ignored for far too long. ''Sinclair Poole has made quite a career out of insisting just that. Tell me, Caroline, why do you believe him when no one else does?'' he questioned, tactfully not asking how she had come to have this information in the first place.

''I'm not a believer in lost causes, Mr. President; but I don't think I'm the only one who believes in what Sinclair does—just the first to say so out loud.''

''Injustice is a horrible thing, Mr. President,'' Vanessa pointed out. ''Indeed, it can be a tragedy if the people involved are poor and disenfranchised, but it is no less easy to take if the person is part of America's aristocracy.''

Theodore Roosevelt looked from Vanessa to Caroline. ''Is there proof—evidence beyond any sort of doubt?''

Caro didn't blink. ''There's a letter, signed by all the men who were involved in Stanford Poole's downfall,'' she said, but didn't elaborate any further—with T. R. there was no need to.

''If Sinclair comes to me with that letter and I see

it with my own eyes, I'll believe it, he said. "Something like that never should have happened, and if he wants me to, I'll be more than happy to counter all the tales that have been spread and try to right some of the grievous wrongs committed."

Chapter Fourteen

"I want you to see this," Sin announced, excited as a boy, as he showed her into his office on Thursday morning. "This was found in a warehouse downtown a few days ago, buried under several packing crates. It must have been lost and neglected for years, but once I brushed off the dust, I knew I'd found a treasure."

Resting on a table in the center of the room was a large rectangular box, which although cleaned up, still showed the effect of many years of neglect.

"The New Canton Trading Company," Caro read, deciphering the tortuous, spidery script; the heavy black ink had survived the years but the penmanship was nearly impossible to read. She ran her fingers over the brown paper label that was in the process of shredding. "Canton to New York, September 1820; contents: silk. Sin, do you mean that no one has seen this silk until now?"

"That's just about it," he said, standing beside

her, breathing in her perfume. "I can't even be sure if a customs inspector saw it back then. But then what I enjoy most about the importing business are all the wonderful and unexpected things there are to discover. Open it."

"Oh, it's simply stunning!" Caro exclaimed. "How could anyone forget about this?"

Inside the box covered by heavy black paper to protect it, was bolt after bolt of fine China silk— black undimmed by the passage of years, white that had turned to a rich cream, as well as sea green, rich plum, several shades of blue, the palest mauve, and a rich pink-and-white stripe that had been much favored during the Regency period.

"It must have been meant for a very special lady," Sin said, fingering one of the lengths of fine silk. "That's why I would like you to have it."

Caro's heart lifted on a wave of tenderness. "Thank you—I'm terribly touched." She turned to face him. "It's one of the loveliest presents I've ever been given."

"I hope your stepmother doesn't belong to the candy-and-flowers school of presents from suitors."

"I wasn't sure about that," she said as her heart-beat made a distinct change.

"What, my gift-giving abilities?"

"No, how you think of yourself in terms of the two of us."

"I'm not a man who uses an inappropriate term because he is unable to come up with a more accurate one."

"That's an excellent way to put it," Caro replied,

covering the silks again. She was tempted to put her arms around Sin and look deep into his eyes, but it would be a useless endeavor to search for hidden meanings from a man who was a master at hiding. "But it's not your intellectualism that I doubt."

It was his turn now, Sin realized as he watched Caro turn away from him and return to his desk, sitting down behind it instead of in her customary chair beside it. She crossed her legs in a rich swish of expensive material that subtly hinted at what was hidden underneath. If only Caro were playing at this, he thought, it would all be so easy, but there was no doubt that she wanted to know what was in his heart now. And the only truly distressing thing was that he wanted to tell her.

"You look better behind my desk than I do," he said finally, frankly admiring how she looked in her Paquin street dress of soft French-blue wool trimmed in black silk braid. "It's a highly persuasive argument for women in business."

Caro smiled. They were both too highly directed to be swayed from an important topic of conversation by small talk, but she had nothing against his compliments *per se*—particularly since they could be a vital ingredient in easing a tense situation. "The silk buyer at Altman's could use your advice, and I'm glad to know that you're a progressive man of the new century."

"Considering my current situation in life, it would be rather hypocritical of me to hold onto all the traditions I was raised with," he told her with not a little irony. "Tell me," he went on, sitting down on the edge of the broad desk, his voice conversational, "what do you do at night?"

Caro knew what was coming. "I go to sleep."

"No, I mean what do you do when you leave here or finish your appointments at Siegel–Cooper's or Lord and Taylor?" he persisted, not wanting to dwell on the delightful thought of Caro at home in bed. "How do you spend your evenings?"

He takes all the newspapers and magazines, Caro thought. He *knows* how I spend my evenings, and we'd better get this out in the open now. "I have invitations to parties, to the theatre and the opera, to balls and receptions—and I accept a fair number of them," she said in a neutral voice. "And if you're going to point out that you're not at any of those functions, I've already noticed that fact."

Sin's eyes narrowed slightly. "You don't bother to put things politely, do you?"

"Not as long as you're ready to make some great and important point about the vast difference between us. . . ." Caro heard the sarcastic note take hold in her voice, and she stopped for a moment— there was no need to go for the jugular over this. "What do you *really* want to tell me?"

He heard the change in her voice, saw her cool jauntiness replaced by a tender expectation, and it struck a responsive chord in him. "I want to be your suitor," he said. "I want to be the man you sit next to at the theatre and be the one you save the supper dance for, but I made another choice a long time ago and I still haven't fulfilled that promise."

"No, you haven't." Caro laced her fingers together and stared down at her lap. "But you certainly haven't thought that what you must do precludes your having a full set of human emotions. This house and the people that surround and care about you prove that," she said at last, looking up to meet his gaze. "And not once since we met did you give any indication that what we seem to have found is. . . . is not what you want also."

"Perhaps we really don't have a choice—the bonds of affinity we spoke about."

"Oh, please! That's a wonderful belief, and I do share it, but I can't run my life by it. This is New York in 1902, not the ancient and mysterious Orient. We have choices to make and decisions to reach and I won't believe we have no control over what we do and don't want."

"And what do you want, Caroline?" he asked, feeling oddly ashamed of himself. He could keep his solitary ways, but hurt them both terribly, or he could open his heart, even if it meant losing some of the fine edge he was so proud of. "Most couples wait a great deal longer before they have this conversation—and some never have it at all—but even I'm willing to admit that we're not like other couples."

"We have to get to know each other better, to trust and confide in each other," Caro said, rising as she spoke and going over to Sin. Directly, but with a depth of feeling that went far beyond flirtation, she placed her hands on his shoulders, drawing in her breath when his hands came to rest at the sides of her waist. "If you don't want to see me

251

again, you had better say so now, Sin, because I do want you to be my suitor."

"If I left you now, I'd probably have more to fear from you than I ever had from the Consortium," Sin said as he drew her closer to him.

Caro laughed and fluttered her mascaraed lashes against his cheeks. "That's the general idea."

"Everyone here missed you on Tuesday and Wednesday—especially me."

"Oh, that's what I want to hear," she said, responding to his caress as he nuzzled at her neck. "But you know that business on the China Trade isn't quickly or easily conducted."

For a few minutes they stayed together in a close embrace, exchanging kisses and whispered endearments, all thoughts of business temporarily suspended as their already rooted affection grew in even richer ground. But there were still unraised topics, foremost among them the promise Caro had extracted from the President, and at this moment there was no way to fit it into the conversation. And with Sin's arms around her and the first set of barriers between them down forever, it seemed like something that could be temporarily postponed.

"We can't stay like this forever." Sin's voice, husky and regretful, sent a shower of sparks through her.

"Awful, isn't it, how responsible we are?"

"If we don't go back to work, I may forget that I still like to consider myself a gentleman."

Caro kissed him under an ear. "You don't have to convince me of that."

For the rest of the morning, the potential lovers became business partners. Sin, like most dealers in the arts of the Orient, was constantly receiving lists and catalogs of merchandise available, and together they pored over these selections. Mainly they were looking for any indication that the still-missing furniture that belonged to the Worths was being offered. Since Caro and Vanessa had their own sources and dealt in small items, the information which Sin received on a regular basis wasn't usually sent to them, and poring over the photographs and detailed descriptions, she looked for something familiar— even the listing of a flaw could be a vital clue.

"I wish I could say I recognized something here," she said at last, closing a thick catalog issued by a noted Hong Kong firm. "I have an idea that we're just going to have to be glad we got back what we did."

"You shouldn't be that easily discouraged," Sin said, putting aside a stack of closely typed pages.

"Yes, but there's no need to be overly greedy, either. What Vanessa and I found—the rug, all the blue-and-white porcelain, the vases, my writing table, and all the rest—may be all we ever find. And by some strange coincidence, it was nearly all the things we cherished and missed most. Besides," she went on in a voice that was practical and amused at the same time, "it's not as if we can't buy furniture. To tell the truth, the apartment is so well decorated at the moment that everything went from Fowler's straight to Manhattan Storage!"

Sin laughed. "I'd love to see where you live."

"That's not impossible," Caro said, her first opening found. "Vanessa and I are giving a theatre party next month. We'd originally planned it for January, but after several intense conversations, my stepmother and Henry Miller decided that February would be better."

"That would be for *D'Arcy of the Guards* at the Savoy Theatre, wouldn't it?" Sin waited a moment. "I still go to the theatre."

"I never doubted you did, and probably with a significant trinket from Tiffany's in the inside pocket of your coat to present after the final curtain to a member of the chorus."

Slowly Sin began to smile. "You're not supposed to know about things like that."

"Sinclair, *all* women know about things like that." Caro tucked a hairpin back into her Gibson knot. "You have figured out by now that we'd like you to come."

"I didn't think you were the sort who gets a thrill from telling some poor man about the grand party she's giving and to which he's not invited. But then, as they say, such is life."

"Well, not mine or yours. I just thought I'd give you advance word about the invitation that'll be turning up in the mail."

"Engraved at Tiffany's?"

"From Dempsey and Carroll's, actually," she replied, noting the teasing look in his eyes.

"Would you like to know my answer in advance?"

"No, I don't think so. A lot can happen between

today and the day it arrives in the mail, and it's quite possible that your answer won't be the same then as it is now. And it's also possible that the night we've chosen will be inconvenient for you. I'm willing to just wait and see.''

"Yes, I think that's the best idea all around," Sin said, feeling not a little bemused. "One thing we can't wait for, however, is lunch, and it's time we went upstairs." Sin took a step back and held his hands out to her. "While we eat, you can tell me all about the plans you and your stepmother have made for a gala night at the theatre."

Like Monday's meal, lunch today was perfectly prepared and served, and the food both complemented and encouraged conversation. It began with clear, hot borscht and was followed by baked potatoes with caviar and sour cream, a mixed green salad, and *oeufs à la neige*. Caro, who loved caviar and hated predictable menus, was so delighted with their lunch that it wasn't until the floating island was served that she noticed Sin wasn't eating very much.

"Are you all right?" she asked, noting that he looked strained and somewhat pale. "You're not eating. . . .''

"I'd rather look at and talk to you," he responded gallantly, but Caro wasn't fooled.

"There's a lot of influenza going around. Let me see if you're feverish—"

Sin remained patient and even managed a slight smile as Caro placed a hand on his forehead. "You are a little warm—and don't put the blame on me. Perhaps I should leave so you can rest. I know a good doctor. . . . ''

I've already seen one, Sin thought, but it was something he couldn't say out loud without leading to a whole other set of questions. "Please don't worry," he told her, holding her hand in his. "It's nothing for you to worry about, I promise, but if I find I can't manage, I'll ring you up."

"And that's the most any woman can hope to hear," she replied, and meant it.

"I expect that if I have to do that, you'll want some extravagant favor in return," he teased as they continued with their dessert.

"Oh, nothing much," Caro said, playing along. "You'll just have to show me the Eakins portrait of yourself that you've hidden away."

"Perhaps that's my version of Oscar Wilde's *Portrait of Dorian Grey*. All of my indiscretions show up on my painting and not on my face."

"Then if you don't mind my pointing it out, I think you should have a word with Mr. Eakins. I seem to see a character line or two."

They were laughing over coffee when the sound of the drawing room door redirected their attention to Gregori as he approached the dining alcove. His purposeful step and the serious expression on his face immediately stilled their merriment.

"What's gone wrong?" Sin asked, able to sense the slightest danger at twenty paces.

"Nothing that terrible," he said swiftly. "But there is something you should have a look at now. I hate to interrupt, but—'' He gave Caro an appealing look, and she returned his smile, ''I promise it won't take long.''

''If it does, I might consider taking it out of the overly generous salary I pay you,'' Sin remarked as he stood up. He hesitated for a moment, as if adjusting to some unexpected pain. ''Will you excuse me?''

When Caro was alone at the table, she found herself considering carrying the coffee service over to the sofa, but decided it was unwise since Sin would be likely to view it as a proprietary move rather than one made by mutual agreement. No, she would stay here at the dining room table until he returned and they picked up the conversation where it had left off.

Now is probably the best time to tell Sin that I discussed him with the President, Caro thought. He won't be very pleased; in fact, I can't be sure what he'll say, but this is no secret to keep. . . .

Caro heard the drawing room door open and then close with the extreme quietness that is desplayed when a man's temper is under the tightest control. Far more curious than anxious, Caro, disregarding all rules of etiquette, placed an elbow on the table and rested her chin on her hand, waiting for Sin to come back to the dining alcove. Wisely she stayed silent, deciding that the first move in this situation was up to him. Sin might be used to keeping his own counsel, but he didn't appear to have any trouble articulating.

''I've seen year-end reports that are smaller,'' he

257

said, placing a large, square, heavy white envelope beside her coffee cup. "Would you care to have a look at this while I pour myself another cup of coffee?"

His voice was calm and polite, but perfectly aware that he really wasn't making a request, Caro turned her attention to the envelope addressed to Sin in the hand of a master of the Palmer method. Its contents, however, were no suprise, since she had received a similiar one in her morning mail, and working with the greatest of care, she removed the enclosures, laying them out as she would a hand of playing cards.

As with all wedding invitations, it was enclosed in two envelopes. The second, with no mucilage on the flap and superscribed "Mr. Sinclair Poole," contained the invitation and the supplementary cards. Engraved in script on heavy white paper with a raised margin was the church invitation.

Mr. and Mrs. Albert Fullerton Hull
request the honour of your presence
at the marriage of their daughter
Nancy Delilah

to

Mr. Drake Sloane
on Saturday the twenty-third of February
at six o'clock
at St. Thomas' Church
in the City of New York

This was followed by the church card of admittance the size of a visiting card, engraved in block letters.

PLEASE PRESENT THIS CARD
AT ST. THOMAS' CHURCH
ON SATURDAY,
THE TWENTY-THIRD OF FEBRUARY

And finally, the same size as the church invitation, was the most coveted of all: the invitation to the reception.

Mr. and Mrs. Albert Fullerton Hull
request the pleasure of
Mr. Sinclair Poole's
company on Saturday the twenty-third of February
at half-past seven o'clock
at Sherry's
R.S.V.P.

"I always thought that the fashionable hour for New York weddings was either noon or four in the afternoon," Sin remarked conversationally, and for a second it was almost as if they were a couple discussing their own invitations.

"Late weddings are all the rage on the West Coast," Caro offered in what she hoped was a similarly pitched voice. "Nancy told me that she didn't want another—and I quote—'dreary noontime or late afternoon wedding.' She's always wanted a candlelight ceremony, and Drake's being from California is just the excuse she needed."

"Well, she's picked the right time of year for candlelight."

"Don't grumble, darling, it's not you."

The words slipped out before Caro could think twice, and for a countless minute there was a silence that simply hung between them. Sin held his coffee cup frozen in his hand halfway from his mouth to the delicate saucer. "What did you say?"

"Don't grumble."

"I thought so," he said, and began to laugh. "I also suspect that you know what I should do with this invitation."

"Some people put their invitations on the mantlepiece."

Sin drained his coffee cup. "That's a lousy bit of decorating."

"I couldn't agree more, so you can simply put the invitation in a convenient desk drawer and mark the date on your appointment calendar."

"Is that what you've done with your invitation?" he inquired, taking it for granted—and quite correctly so—that she had also been invited to the wedding.

"It seemed the best thing to do." Caro gathered up the engraved invitations and pushed them toward him. She wouldn't ask him if he were going to accept, but she still had no clear idea of how he felt about what had so unexpectedly arrived in the mail. "This is quite a surprise for you, isn't it?"

"I think this comes under the heading of the understatement of the year.'' Sin looked faintly non-plussed. ''Drake Sloane did *me* a favor, not the other way around, and he must be nothing short of a con artist if he could convince an entrenched knicker-bocker couple like the Hulls to add me to the guest list.''

''Drake *is* from southern California.''

''That explains a lot.'' Sin smiled. ''I'll send them a Ming vase, and that should make everyone happy.''

''I don't think you were invited because of the quality of wedding present you could provide. Look, Sin, I don't know why you were invited either, and the decision whether to go or not is up to you, but I hope you do give it some thought.''

Sin's hand closed gently over hers. ''I promise to give this wedding invitation the same consideration I'll give the invitation to your stepmother's theatre party. And that, I promise you, is quite an improve-ment over my past reaction to such requests for my company. The few that came my way six years ago were promptly torn up and disposed of. Have you ever noticed how well expensive paper burns?''

''It does have a very satisfying glow,'' Caro said, and hesitated for a moment. ''Were all those invi-tations from curiosity seekers?''

''No, a few of them were probably offered with the best of intentions, but I wasn't ready to accept any of it. Finally, I've begun to realize that things— and people—do change.''

There wasn't anything Caro could say at that mo-ment that wouldn't sound either glib or grasping, and she simply tightened her grip around his hand, letting him know by touch and look that she was there for him. They were still sitting in the silence of the dining alcove, basking in the weak winter sunshine coming through the casement windows, when Gregori came in. He didn't knock this time, and his eyes were wide with surprise, anticipation, and a good deal of uncertainty.

"Sinclair, there's a telephone call," he said without the preamble of greeting. "You have to come at once."

Sin's smile was indulgent. "What happens if I don't?"

"This isn't a joke, Sin. The White House is on the telephone—President Roosevelt wants to talk to you."

It was if an electric jolt had invaded the room's quiet atmosphere, so completely was the mood of solitude and communion shattered with Gregori's announcement. Instantly, Sin let go of Caro's hand and stood up, disbelief written all over his face. Caro also rose, but with no disbelief whatsoever. But spreading through the pit of her stomach was the awful feeling that she had delayed telling Sin about her talk with the President and now it was too late.

"Sin, there's something I haven't had a chance to tell you yet," Caro said. He was already halfway across the room and gave no indication that he heard her. "I saw the President on Monday afternoon."

It was like shouting in the wind, and Caro followed both men out the door and down the corridor toward Sin's upstairs office, where he conducted his financial affairs. Did all men who handled money have offices decorated to look like they had been transported lock, stock, and barrel from London? she wondered a minute later. The desk itself was a masterpiece of workmanship, but it was so out of proportion with the rest of the room, so large that it threw all the other furniture out of balance. She knew it could only have come from Stanford Poole's office.

With a growing feeling of unease, Caro watched Sin approach the telephone, the look on his face so unreadable that it sent a feeling of fear rippling through her veins. Never before in her life had she tried to *help*, to interfere in another person's way of doing things—until now.

Well, I may be the least meddlesome person in the world, she thought, but I certainly know how to make a mess the first time I do meddle. Butterflies took flight in her stomach.

It was then that she noticed Gregori wasn't looking at either of them, but instead had fixed his dark-amber gaze on an English hunting scene that hung on the wall behind the desk.

And I don't blame him one bit, she thought, watching Sin reach for the telephone.

''This is Sinclair Poole,'' he said into the receiver, noting that his voice sounded cool and collected and didn't display any of his inner apprehensions. The miracle of modern communication, he thought as a White House functionary identified himself and then asked him to wait to be connected to the President. What was it that Caro wanted to tell him—had she said something about seeing Roosevelt? He could ask her while he waited, but suddenly the silent line came alive.

"Sinclair, is that you? How are you, my boy?"

"Very well, Mr. President," he replied, accepting the familiar manner of address with a grain of salt. Politics. This call probably had something to do with the information he'd given Rutherford Vance, but then again. . . . "Is there something I can do to help you, sir?"

"No, Sinclair, it's the other way around. I want to assure you that you have my full support. Your effort is a very noble endeavor."

With effort, Sin kept his voice respectful. "Thank you, sir. It's very kind of you to say that, but if you don't mind my asking, how did you find out about this?"

"Why, from your friend, Miss Caroline Worth, of course!" The President's voice boomed bright and genial. "I had tea with her and her stepmother on Monday afternoon, and we were discussing several topics, one of which was the unhappy fate that befell your father. I owe you an apology, Sinclair."

"You don't have to say that, sir," Sin replied, feeling faintly embarrassed. "You shouldn't have to. . . . "

"Being the President, my dear boy, doesn't mean that a mistake I made in the past is erased. I should have paid more attention to the evidence against your father; I should have asked why you didn't come to me for help."

As Sin registered the well-meaning words (and not for one minute did he doubt that Theodore Roosevelt meant every word he said), anger slowly but surely replaced surprise. He couldn't be rude to the President, but. . . . ''

''. . . . when you find the letter Caroline told me you need to prove your father's innocence,'' T.R. was saying, ''I want you to send me a telegram saying 'letter traced,' and then I'll be of any help to you that I can be.''

''I've come this far alone, sir, and—''

''Nonsense! I'm delighted to do whatever I can for you, Sinclair. Absolutely dee-lighted. . . . ''

Caroline heard every word Sinclair said, and her active imagination could supply the other side of the conversation. Sin spoke to the President in the most respectful of voices, but as the conversation came to its conclusion, she was relieved that Roosevelt couldn't see Sin's pale and tightly controlled face. For a fleeting moment it occurred to her that as long as he was engaged on the telephone, she could turn and leave, safely escaping any further explanation; it didn't surprise her at all that this was exactly what Gregori did, murmuring softly to her that if Sin wanted him, he would be waiting in the sitting room. But her situation was entirely different.

For a long minute after Sin hung up the telephone, he sat with his hands covering his face, not moving or saying a word. For Caro it was a frightening sight, and forgetting all caution as well as her decision to let him speak first, she crossed to where he sat behind the desk and put her arms around him.

"How difficult that call must have been for you to go through."

Sin didn't move, gave no indication that he was aware of her touch, but when he spoke his voice struck her with the force of an icy gale. "No more difficult than realizing what lengths you went through to plan this."

"What did you say?" Caro released her hold on Sin and stepped away from him, one hand curling around the edge of the desk, the wood a real and substantial thing when her only overwhelming sensation was that of disbelief. "I tried to tell you that the President had tea with us on Monday."

Sin uncovered his face to reveal features that looked as if they'd been cut from stone. The eyes that burned with amber fire were riveted on her. "And exactly when did you try to tell me this, Caro? Two minutes before I came in here to take the call."

"Why don't you ask me a question you don't know the answer to?" Caro shot back. "I'm perfectly willing to have an intelligent discussion with you about this. I should have told you about the President the minute I walked in here this morning, but what I will not do is let you harangue me. I didn't do anything that terrible."

"That is a topic open for discussion." Sin stood up, a subtle threat implicit in the way he moved.

Caro registered the way he looked, but met his gaze without blinking, although his next words filled her heart to overflowing with hurt.

"Did it ever occur to you that the little discussion

you had over tea was something I wanted kept private?''

''What is it exactly that you think I said?''

''Why don't you tell me?''

Caro did precisely that, simply and directly, not embroidering a single detail, and Sin, for all his simmering anger and resentment, felt a grudging admiration for how she told the story. It was like reading a newspaper account, and he didn't doubt for a minute that she was telling the complete and utter truth. But it didn't mitigate what she had done, and the pain that knifed through his side told him what he had to do.

''How could you do that?'' he asked with an anguish that while real enough was being fueled out of all proportion by another matter entirely. ''How could you tell Roosevelt everything I told you? I spent years building my case, and now, thanks to you, it can collapse like a punctured balloon. Did you consider, even for one moment, that once the President gets wind of corruption it becomes his crusade? As soon as he starts poking around all that I spent years trying to find—'' Sin pushed the papers on his desk, shoving them with a motion that hinted at the anger concealed beneath his cold and controlled exterior.

''I never mentioned a single name,'' Caro protested. ''If the President wanted to, he'd find out who it is you suspect, but I don't think he will, because he knows it might disrupt all you've done.''

''Don't you see that I can't trust anyone with what I'm doing?''

"You trusted me."

"Do you really expect me to say something about that?" he shot back. "I share the deepest secrets of my life with you, and you tell the first person who comes along. If it hadn't been T.R., you would have gossiped to anyone else who sat on your drawing room sofa!"

"That's a beastly thing to say! I spoke to the President because I wanted to help you!"

"Isn't help yourself more like it?" he questioned sharply, taking hold of her wrists. "A wedding invitation here, a theatre party invitation there, and before I know it, I'm back in the social whirl."

"And isn't that simply the most awful thing that could happen to you in your brave and solitary life!" They were shouting at each other now, and as much as Caro hated the sarcastic tone in her voice, there were certain things that had to be said. "Heaven forbid that you compromise your precious ideals for one single evening."

"If you need an escort, Miss Worth, I'm not the man for you. This is the way I lead my life, and I'm not about to change it for you."

Caro pulled her hand free. "I don't want to change you, and I don't want an escort dancing attendance on me—all I want is to help you!"

"Don't cry," he warned her. "I won't be moved by your tears."

"I guess I'm not as lucky as you; my emotions aren't as frozen as yours. I still feel things, see situations in shades of gray as well as black and white," Caro said, the burning in her eyes replaced by a burning around her heart. "All you see is your own personal plan of revenge, and you're so tied up in it that you lose sight of what all this is about."

"What it's all about is finding that letter and clearing my father's name."

"Yes, that may have been your start, but is it your finish? What happens after you get the letter? What revenge are you going to exact, and more important, what are you going to do with your life afterward."

Caro was right; every word she spoke was the truth. These were the words that neither George nor Greg could bring themselves to say to him, and it was the question he wouldn't ask himself because the pain building in him made the answer all too bleak.

"And that's of primary importance to you, isn't it?" he asked at last.

"No, not right now. I don't think I want to care for a man who can't see past a single incident, no matter how important the task is." Her voice was quiet now, full of regret and pain. "That doesn't say much for our future together."

"I didn't ask you for any of the things you said and did. I didn't ask you to love me."

Caro's eyes filled with tears and she blinked them back before her eye black began to run. "If you have to ask for love, then it's not coming from the person it should." She took a deep breath, her temples pounding and a feeling of claustrophobia coming over her. "Good-bye, Sinclair."

"Where are you going?"

Halfway to the door, she spun around to look at

him, and his ashen, strained face tore at her heart. "I'm going home," she said quietly. "You don't want either my love or my help and, unfortunately for you, they do go hand-in-hand. What I did might have been foolish, but I'm not stupid enough to stay here any longer so we can shout at each other."

In her heart of hearts, she wanted him to stop her, but she also knew that his pride was too great to allow him to make this move, and the only option left to her was to get out of here before the solid wall of pain pushing against her chest liquified into tears.

In the anteroom, she put on her coat and hat and gloves, and a minute later let herself out of the house, closing the door quietly behind her. She had to hold onto her dignity and self-possession; when she got home would be soon enough to cry her heart out—which was something she was sure to do whenever she thought about Sinclair, whom she loved dearly and had left standing alone in his office with so much still unsaid between them.

Chapter Fifteen

Breakfast on Friday morning was a morose affair.

Caro had cried herself out the afternoon before and had fallen into an exhausted sleep at night, so that now her headache was gone—except for the sick feeling around her heart and the certainty that she had made a terrible mistake when she walked out on Sin.

"I ended up doing exactly what he wanted me to do," Caro said sadly as she put a spoonful of honey into her cup of English Breakfast tea and stirred it. "I told him he was impossible, and then I left him just as he wanted to be—all alone."

"Unhappily, darling, you may be right." More than anything else, Vanessa wanted to comfort her stepdaughter, but one thing neither of them could stand was a pretty picture frame put around the ugly truth. "His efforts to clear his father's name have been largely solitary, so the very last thing he expected was the sort of help you gave him. Suddenly

Sinclair was faced with an embarrassment of riches, and like most people in similar circumstances, his reaction was to push it all away and say he was better off without it.''

"You make it all sound so logical. And intellectually, I probably knew all of this, and I *still* played right into his hands. I was angry at his stupid reaction, and I didn't see the point of our standing there exchanging insults,'' Caro said, and took a bit of brioche, surprised that she could actually taste the bread and strawberry conserves. "I don't think there was a right thing I could have done. Sin was determined to be furious, and at least I don't have to look back on it and realize I acted like a scared rabbit. I couldn't change what was happening between us, but I didn't have to act like an idiot. For all the good it's going to do me.''

"I know it sounds like cold comfort, but when Sinclair does calm down—and he will eventually—you'll be much better off to have been true to your principles.''

"Yes, though living through the interim is going to be the difficult part,'' Caro observed. "But I refuse to sit around waiting for the telephone to ring.''

"Now that's what I want to hear you say,'' Vanessa said approvingly. "Let's finish breakfast. Then we'll go to the Lenox Library to see the Rembrandt etchings and prints on loan from J.P. Morgan's collection, and after lunch we'll go up to the Metropolitan Museum.''

Caro smiled for the first time that morning. "I'd

feel much better looking at paintings than buying a new hat.''

"Now would I come up with such a jejune suggestion as going shopping?'' Vanessa asked. "We can do that in a day or two, but right now you have to lift your mind to a higher plane and—Yes, Cavendish, is something wrong?'' she asked as their butler entered the dining room.

"I hope not, Madame. There's a gentleman at the door who says he is a friend of Miss Caroline's. He gave his name as Gregori Vestovich.''

Caro's heart, which had leapt at Cavendish's first words, now plunged with disappointment. Was something wrong, or had Gregori come uptown because Sin was driving him crazy and he thought she could smooth things over?

"Is Mr. Vestovich in the library or the drawing room?'' she asked.

Cavendish suddenly looked a trifle apprehensive. "Neither, Miss Caroline. Mr Vestovich is waiting in the hallway. He didn't have a card,'' he explained as both women stared at him, incredulous at his high-handed treatment of a caller.

"Perhaps he was in such a hurry to get here that he forgot his card case,'' Vanessa suggested, her voice too calm.

"I'll bring Gregori in if you'll have another place set,'' Caro said to Vanessa. As she stood, she heard the swishing of the skirt of her Lucile suit of dark green corduroy velvet, trimmed with dark blue braid and gold buttons and worn with a dark blue silk blouse. Caro had no doubt her stepmother would have a few well-placed words to impart to their butler on the proper welcome to anyone who turned up at their door, but for now the important thing was seeing to Gregori.

She found him waiting just outside, seemingly enjoying the quiet of the elevator hall, leaning against a paneled wall, his hat tipped rakishly over his eyes and his expression more amused than hurt or annoyed.

"I'm so sorry," she said, holding out her hand to him. "Our butler is very protective of us."

"It's perfectly all right," Gregori replied, releasing her hand. "I didn't ring up first, and when I went for my card case, I realized I'd left it at home."

"Vanessa said you must have done that," Caro replied, opening the door wide. "Please come in and I'll introduce you to my stepmother before we talk about Sinclair." An apprehensive shiver went through her. "That is why you're here?"

"I'm afraid so."

Cavendish was waiting in the entry foyer. Without any indication that the high-handed treatment he'd received rankled, Gregori handed the older man his hat and gloves and after unbuttoning his black melton overcoat, waited to be helped off with it.

Despite her certainty that whatever Gregori had come uptown to tell her couldn't be good news, Caro was struck by the young man's attitude and gestures. In themselves, they meant nothing—the proper way to act toward a butler was a lesson easily enough learned—but there was something else. . . .

He looks as if he grew up with servants, Caro observed as she showed Gregori down the long, wide hallway toward the dining room, letting him admire the fine watercolors in slim frames hung on the oyster-white lacquered walls. Inside the dining room, she made the proper introductions and decided to let Vanessa take over for the moment.

The charming smile she turned on Gregori was genuine, and without any fuss or bustle she made sure he was settled in his chair before rising and going over to the sideboard where the chafing dishes were set out.

"Nonsense, of course you want something to eat, it's a long trip from Prince Street to the Osborne," she said brightly, filling a plate for him with scrambled eggs and crisp bacon. "Caro, does Gregori have a brioche?"

"Would you care for some orange marmalade?" she asked, handing him the silver bread basket. The marmalade was from Fortnum and Mason and had been ordered by Maison Glass."

"No, thank you, the conserves will be fine," Gregori said, and attempted a smile. If it weren't for the gravity of the reason behind his visit, he would enjoy all this. Even his little set-to with the stuffy Cavendish could be thought of as amusing. The dining room, with its antique Chinese wallpaper, pink-beige silk curtains, and handsome Adam mirror above a beautifully designed sideboard, was a place redolent of good food and conversation. It was also a household with a highly feminine atmosphere, something Gregori didn't mind at all. He sat quite contentedly at the large table set with embroidered placemats and smiled over at Vanessa, an elegant figure in a Paquin tailleur of navy twill worn with a silver-gray silk blouse, before looking at the plate in front of him. "It all looks wonderful, Mrs. Worth. I want you to know how much I appreciate your hospitality."

"I know that already," Vanessa said, reaching for an empty cup and saucer. "We're having tea, but if you prefer coffee—"

"No, thank you; tea will be fine." Gregori began to enjoy the food set in front of him, but after a few bites it became apparent that the news he had come to impart was troubling him.

"Does Sin know you're here?" Caro asked, not able to stand either the suspense or the expression on his face another minute.

"He has no idea where I am, or even if I've left the house. I know I'm saying this badly," he continued, hating the look of alarm that appeared in Caro's eyes as he spoke. "I'm sorry, but this is very difficult. . . . "

"Did something happen after I left yesterday afternoon?" she asked. "If you're trying to put what you have to say in pretty terms for my stepmother and me, I want you to know that it isn't necessary."

"It isn't that exactly," Gregori said. "I'm not here because of what Sinclair said, but rather because of what he didn't tell you—specifically, that he's ill."

Belatedly, Caro recalled Sin's lack of appetite and the strained look on his face that had increased as their argument had gone on. "Then he was trying to push me away," she said, looking across the table at Gregori, who nodded solemnly. "I must sound horribly self-centered, but I haven't been able to stop thinking that he was looking for some sort of ulterior motive, and that the telephone call from the President gave it to him."

"That's entirely possible," Gregori replied, his loyalty toward Sin conflicting with his desire to tell the truth. "Sin hasn't been feeling well for a few months, although he's hidden it so well that George and I could only suspect that something was wrong. But yesterday, after you left, when we confronted him about the things he said to you. . . . " He stopped, unable to continue.

"You heard us," she said; it was a statement, not a question.

Gregori pushed his plate away, his appetite gone. "They could hear the two of you at City Hall. I'm sorry, that was an uncalled for bit of levity. We were so angry at Sin for letting you leave. . . . He said he had to, that he was ill, that it was for the best."

Dread and fear filled Caro to the point of making her feel sick. "What is it?"

"Sin has appendicitis," he told them. "This is exactly what he told us. He was. . . . not well last night, and this morning he showed me some papers he drew up, adjustments to his will." Gregori's voice began to shake, and he had to stop until he felt steady again, but his main concern was Caro, seated across from him, and Vanessa, at his left. Both women had paled and Caro's eyes were full of alarm. "He wanted all of us to be taken care of. . . . and he wants you to have his mother's jewelry.''

"My God." Caro turned whiter than white. "How ill is he?''

"Very. He couldn't get out of bed this morning, and I'm sure he's in pain.''

"Hasn't he seen a doctor?'' Caro asked, amazed that she could talk normally while her heart was pounding.

"Some Fifth Avenue physician—I'm not sure who. . . .''

"I know, one of those fellows who checks to make sure his new patients are in the Social Register, and on a bad day can't tell one end of his stethoscope from the other.''

"I'm sorry,'' Gregori said, looking as if he were on the verge of tears. "I came because I didn't want you to hear about this when. . . . when. . . .''

"Oh, no!'' The look of alarm in Caro's eyes gave way to one of determination. "No, I won't believe that he hasn't a chance, or that he won't fight,'' she said, taking the napkin from her lap and tossing it on the table for added emphasis. "And I'm not going to sit back and do nothing. I'm not ready to mourn him when we have too much to celebrate!''

Vanessa, who had been silent throughout most of the exchange, decided that it was time for her to speak up. It wasn't that she disagreed with Caro, but she wanted to give her another minute to think, to be sure that her head and her heart were working in tandem.

"Caroline, are you sure you can do some good for Sinclair?"

"Mummy, would you have me do nothing—just sit in a corner and cry?"

"No, I agree that you have to seize the moment, but you also have to think clearly when you do it."

"I *am* thinking clearly. The worst thing to do in a situation like this is not to *try.*" She turned to Gregori. "How did you come uptown?"

"By hansom cab."

"Good, that means you can ride with us. Try and finish eating if you can," she went on in a gentle but effective voice. "It will take a little time for Lawton to bring the brougham around, and then you can tell us the rest of it while we all go down to Prince Street together."

The first thing that struck Caro as she entered Sin's house was the unnatural silence.

Where do I remember this kind of quiet from? she thought, and then it came back to her in a rush of memories: it had been like this at their house in Shanghai while her father was dying, and the quiet had been so thick, so intense that it seemed palpable. For a long minute the three were silent. Their conversation in the brougham had hardly covered a pleasant topic. Now Caro saw the look on Vanessa's face and knew her stepmother had also picked up on the atmosphere of the house and had made the same connection. She reached for Vanessa's hand, wanting to tell her that she understood and how much she relied on her love and support, but the door to the clubroom opened before she could say anything.

"Gregori, where have you been—?" George, still poised in the doorway, looked at the tableau in front of him. "I expect I shouldn't be surprised at where you went but this—"

"I'm afraid I don't give up easily, George," Caro responded when the older man hesitated. She introduced her stepmother, and then asked, "Is Sinclair in a lot of pain?"

"It's not very bad, Miss Worth, at least not so far." George's face was tired and strained and more than just a little frightened. "I gave him some of the little pills that the doctor prescribed, and he seems to be fairly comfortable now, but I—"

"I know, George," she responded as calmly as possible, as much to show that she could handle the situation as not to hear the sentence's natural conclusion. "I'm here to see what I can do. Another doctor to begin with," she went on, taking off her coat and hat and leaving them on the wing chair. "Mummy—"

"Oh, don't be concerned about me. I'll be fine as long as one of these kind gentlemen can see to making me a nice hot pot of tea," Vanessa said, smiling as both Gregori and George rushed to help her off with her coat and sable boa, her charm giving them a moment' surcease against the fear pressing down on all of them.

Promising to join her stepmother in the sitting room as soon as she could, Caro left the anteroom and went straight up the narrow stairs, her heart racing. She reached the upstairs hall and stopped. Where was Sin's bedroom?

It shouldn't be too hard to figure out, she decided. The sitting room is first, then the upstairs office, and with any luck, the room after that will be his bedroom. . . .

For a long moment she stood silently in front of the closed door. She knew there was no hope of calming herself down until she walked in and saw Sinclair's condition, but a wave of fear threatened to keep her rooted to this spot. The strong instinct that told her exactly what to do and which had swept aside any hesitation was starting to waiver.

Turning the doorknob as slowly as possible, Caro opened the bedroom door and stepped inside. It took a minute for her eyes to become accustomed to the dimness created by both the cloudy winter day and the curtains drawn at the windows, but gradually she saw the quietly furnished room and the large bed.

Love and fear merged in her as she saw Sin stretched out in the bed, his head propped up by two pillows, his long and elegant body warmly covered by puffed silk comforters. His eyes were closed and his breathing even, but Caro doubted if he were drugged into sleep; a man as determined as Sin might want to take medication that would blunt the pain, but he would never do it to excess.

She sat down at the edge of the bed and took his hand in hers, inordinately relieved to find that it was dry and fairly warm. "Sinclair, it's me, Caroline."

Her voice was low-pitched and free of any panic,

and Sin's eyes opened slowly. For a moment he looked at her as if he thought he were dreaming, or worse, in the throes of a hallucination.

"I didn't want you to come," he said at last, his voice, to Caro's great relief, sounding only somewhat sleepy and not at all drugged. "I didn't want you to know about this—me—until it was over. How—?"

"Gregori came to see us. He's loyal to you, but very distraught, and he thought I would want to know."

"I'm so sorry for everything I said to you," he said, his hold on her hand tightening. "I know that now it's cold comfort, but I didn't mean a word of it."

"I know," she said, close to tears.

"You're the first person who decided I was worth helping and just went ahead and did it. It was so unexpected that my first reaction was anger."

"It's all right," she soothed, "we might have said those things to each other anyway."

"Our first fight," Sin said, trying to smile. "Unhappily, it was probably also our last."

"Sin, are you in pain?" she questioned, the ache in her heart almost unbearable.

"No, it's not too bad right now. The doctor I consulted said there wouldn't be much until it was almost over. This is just an attack. I might even recover from it—until the next one."

With her free hand, Caro brushed back the dark hair that had fallen across his forehead. "Then we have to make sure that there isn't another one."

"I have appendicitis."

"Gregori told us that."

"Us?"

"My stepmother. Right now, Vanessa's in your sitting room with a comforting pot of tea. In a crisis, she turns properly British."

"Speaking of what's proper, you seem to have picked the strangest time to acquire a chaperone."

"Better late than never, as they say. Sin, who is the doctor you consulted about this?"

"Caspar Merrit."

"That society pill-pusher? Why he's just about four steps away from being a patent-medicine hawker!" Caro exclaimed. "How could you go to someone like that?"

"It's a complicated story."

"Does that mean you had something on him? Enough to make sure that after he saw you he wouldn't gossip about your visit to his other patients?"

"Something like that. But it doesn't matter now about which doctor I see, I've just about progressed to the acute stage."

"I'm going to find another doctor for you."

"Caro, darling, just go." Sin's voice was tired, gentle. "I love you, and I don't want to hurt you any more."

"I love you, and I want to help you."

"I almost cleared my father's name," he said as if he hadn't heard her. "If I'd only gotten the letter. My father's name and reputation is still clouded, and everything I worked for not only stops but

283

doesn't count. No matter how long it took, I was succeeding—but now I've failed."

"No, you haven't, and I can't stand to see you reproach yourself. You have to let the medication work until the doctor comes."

"What doctor?"

"The one I'm going to find for you," Caro said, deciding not to mention any names. She noticed a small brown glass bottle on the bedside table and quickly appropriated it, checking both the label and the tiny white pills inside. Thanks to the volunteer work she'd done as a medical assistant in Peking, Caro had some knowledge of pharmacology, and she was relieved to see that the pills weren't opium based and so wouldn't interfere with the effect of the anesthesia. Don't think about that, she warned herself, one step at a time. "Can you try and sleep now?"

"I will if you kiss me."

"I thought you'd never ask," she said as he pulled her gently forward.

"I'm not going to miss out on this," he murmured.

It could almost be called the sort of kiss shared by a loving but sleepy couple, Caro thought, nestling gently against him, careful not to get too close and cause him further pain.

Sin's hands closed slowly around her shoulders, and for a brief moment they looked into each other's eyes before Caro moved her face closer for his kiss. He covered her mouth with his own, his lips reassuringly warm and alive, but there was no immediate move to deepen the kiss. His tongue did touch

284

and then trace the outline of her lower lip, but he went no further, and Caro was torn between longing for more and knowing that any untoward exertion might well cause further complications to his condition. And this was not a farewell kiss. That certainly floated through her and formed a small center of strength that she would be able to draw on.

"Please rest now," she said at last. "I'll be in again soon, almost before you know it, and a little later on, there may be some more encouraging news for you."

In Sin's upstairs office, Caro locked the door behind her before proceeding to his desk. She needed privacy and quiet to think this out, and any interruptions, no matter how well intentioned, were not needed now.

Strange, she thought—it was only yesterday we used this room to say such bitter things to each other, and now it may be the place where I can try to save his life. She looked at the wide expanse of the desk, with its precisely placed and spotless blotter, filled letter box, and neatly arranged files.

The upstairs office bore so much of Sin's personality that for a minute she simply sat there absorbing the quiet atmosphere, letting it help her decide her next move. A doctor, of course, but which one?

She reached for the telephone and lifted the receiver. True to the reputation of New York Telephone, an operator came on the line immediately.

"Number 1259, please," Caro said, and a minute

later, Doris, Alix's maid, answered on the fourth ring.

"I'm so sorry, Miss Worth, but Dr. Turner isn't here. The infirmary needed her unexpectedly today, and I'm not sure when she'll be back."

Doris gave her the number of the Women's Infirmary, and after thanking her, broke the connection and got the operator again.

"Why, hello." Alix's voice sounded bright and cheerful. "You rang up at just the right time. I'm in a lull between patients."

"I'm glad to hear that. Alix, I'm at Sinclair's, and we have a terrible situation here," she said, seeing absolutely no reason to extend their pleasantries.

"I take it you're referring to something medical?" Alix asked, her voice still cordial, but now a highly competent and professional tone overlaid her words. "Has there been an accident?"

"No, Sinclair has appendicitis," Caro responded, and gave Alix a report on his condition.

"When did the last attack begin?"

"Last night, as far as I can tell."

"Is he in a great deal of pain."

"No, he doesn't seem to be, and he is trying to rest now," she said, and told Alix about the pills prescribed by Dr. Merrit. "How long do you think he can stay like this?"

"A lot depends on the condition of the appendix." Alix took a deep breath. "Caro, when we were at Cove House and you told me you'd observed surgical procedures in China, did you mean you really

286

just observed, or did you actually work with the doctors and nurses?''

''I was right there at the table, and helped out whenever I could,'' Caro told her, a cold chill moving down her spine. ''Alix. . . . ''

''I just want to have a contingency plan—all good doctors do. Sinclair is fairly safe as long as his appendix doesn't burst. Are you there alone?''

''No, Vanessa's here with me.''

''Good. Look, I have to stay here for at least another hour, but then I'll come straight down to Prince Street and we'll see how his condition has changed. As long as everyone stays calm—and I know you all will—it'll all work out.''

Caro's heartbeat went back to normal at Alix's quiet, informative voice. ''What else should I do?''

Alix paused. ''Check over the house,'' she said, and Caro could hear the deliberation in her voice. ''If I have to operate when I get there, I'd want to know right off if there's a room with good lighting and a table long enough to hold Sinclair and high enough for me to work on.''

Caro felt her butterflies take flight again, but the feeling of hope that this would work out right for Sin was still there. ''I'll see about those things,'' she promised her friend. ''We'll be waiting for you—it's not as if I expect you to make a decision over the phone.''

''You'd be surprised at the seemingly intelligent people who think otherwise.''

''Never mind. This has to go one step at a time,

and we'll have things ready for you when you get here.''

Alix replaced the receiver and continued to sit at her desk looking at the phone. This was one of those extremely rare times when she hated modern communication. The walls of her small office seemed to be closing in on her, but her mind spun busily on. First of all, she had to call Dorothy Ross, a surgical nurse for whom she had the utmost respect, and then she had to make a list of all the supplies she might need.

Of course it was her fervent hope that when she got to Prince Street, Sin would be in good enough condition to move to Roosevelt Hospital, but she had to be fully prepared in case the reverse were true. Fortunately, unlike many doctors, Alix's vast private income allowed her to be well supplied with the best and latest medical instruments available.

She thought about the supplies she would need in case she had to perform the procedure. Despite some well-meaning attempts at legislation (and these proposed laws were something Alix strongly agreed with), there was very little difficulty in purchasing things like ether over the counter at nearly any pharmacy in New York.

But even as she made her list, other, far more personal thoughts pushed their way to the top of her list of concerns. Sometimes Alix hated the way her wishes were answered: at times it seemed to her as if they were fulfilled with almost startling regularity, but in ways she often found difficult or even frightening. And her every instinct warned her that this was going to be one of those times.

All I wanted to do was see Sinclair again, she thought, her heart heavy. Now it seems I may not only examine him, but perform surgery as well. Why is it that nothing *ever* seems to get any less complicated?

But it wasn't complicated situations that bothered Alix—truth be told, she sometimes thrived on them—it wasn't even the fact that potential male patients during her intern's year had often balked at the idea of having a woman doctor. It was quite simply Sinclair himself.

This isn't how I thought we would see each other after all these years, she thought. I want us to be equals, but instead we're going to be doctor and patient, and the only thing I can hope for is that I don't succeed in one area and fail in another. The next few hours aren't going to be easy; they may require my making the hardest professional decisions I've ever faced, one that may be so difficult that I won't even think about what we might have meant to each other had things turned out another way.

" 'He straight declin'd, droop'd, took it deeply. Fasten'd and fix'd the shame on't in himself, threw off his spirit, his appetite, his sleep, and downright languish'd.' "

Caro stood in the doorway of the sitting room and

listened to George read to her stepmother from *The Winter's Tale*. All things considered, it was a fairly appropriate quote. But it was also apparent that the people who worked for and were closest to Sin were suffering right along with him.

Vanessa patted George's hand and was about to say something comforting when she caught sight of Caro. "How in Sinclair, darling?"

"The medication is relieving the worst of his pain and making him pretty sleepy," she said, joining them on the sofa. "Suddenly I feel as if my legs are going to give out."

"It's a very understandable reaction."

"I know, but I'd better get over it fast." Caro looked from Vanessa to Geroge. "Sin is going to need surgery, and if Alix decides a trip to the hospital is out of the question, the operation will take place here."

For a minute no one said another word. Knowing that a doctor was coming was a source of reassurance, but the specter of an operation being performed in the house was shattering.

"Alix has asked me to look into a few things before she gets here," Caro went on. "The chances are that Sin will be in good enough condition to be taken to Roosevelt Hospital by ambulance, but in case he isn't, there have to be certain preparations made here, such as a room that can be turned into an operating theatre and a table that can be used for surgery."

"Well, that is quite a task," Vanessa said, recovering. "George, how can you help us so we'll have things ready for Dr. Turner when she arrives?"

"There is extra furniture in some rooms on the third floor and in the attic. I'm sure there's something we could use," George said, his temporary shock dispersed by the need for his help. "There's also an empty bedroom on this floor. It's not much, but it's worth a look. Now, what shall I do?"

"I know Dr. Turner is going to bring most of her own supplies, but I think it would be a good idea if you went to the best pharmacy around here and bought some extras—things like gauze bandages and disinfectant soap."

It was mainly an invented errand, since Caro was sure Alix wasn't going to risk arriving without every possible medical item she might need, but this was a good way to make George feel useful and keep him from brooding. Vanessa volunteered to check over the furniture rooms, and Caro went off to find the empty bedroom.

She found a room that was small and bare of all furniture, but it was also, Caro noted with relief, spotlessly clean and had a small bathroom. The overhead light was bright, there were numerous electric sockets, and with some extra lamps to provide additional illumination, it would probably do quite well.

She was standing in the center of the chamber when Vanessa joined her. Like everyone else in the house, she looked pale and subdued, but managed a smile for her stepdaughter.

"It looks like our first problem has been solved," she said, looking around her.

"I thought so too, as soon as I walked in. Did you find a table in the storerooms?"

"Yes, and there's something else I'd like you to see there."

"I want to see Sin. I promised him that I'd be in from time to time."

"And you'll do that, but this is more important."

"If you say so, Mummy," Caro responded as they made their way upstairs. "You've never led me off on a wild goose chase before."

"And I'm not now." Vanessa led her into a large room filled with enough furniture to qualify it as a small store. "Look at this buffet: it must have been made for Diamond Jim Brady," she said, indicating an extra-long, very high cabinet made of the finest redwood mahogany. "I took Alix's height into consideration, and this should do splendidly. Now if George and Vic and Sean—he's George's young cousin who handles their horses—can carry it downstairs, we have that matter taken care of. But this is what I want you to see," Vanessa finished, gesturing at an easel holding a painting covered by a thick white dropcloth.

"Is that the Thomas Eakins protrait of Sin?"

"If you recall, I haven't met your Sinclair yet, but that definitely is an Eakins." Vanessa's look was quizzical. "You *have* seen it?"

"No, only heard about it. Sin said he had it painted in a fit of vanity and then hid it up here."

"I couldn't resist a look."

"I have to see this for myself," Caro said as she carefully lifted the dropcloth, and at her first sight of the painting, she drew in her breath; she was at a loss for words.

The number of corporate barons who had commissioned Thomas Eakins to paint their portraits and upon completion refused to accept the results were supposedly legion. The artist's talent ran hand-in-hand with his depiction of the truth—not a combination made to please millionaire clients in search of an idealized look at themselves.

Not that his portrait of Sinclair Poole showed his subject to be warped in any way. But what it did show riveted Caro's gaze.

Sinclair was painted in a full-dress suit, a perfect study in shades of black and white. Only a fold of the scarlet lining of the opera cape flung casually around his shoulders provided a sharp flash of color. Sin was staring straight ahead, and his glance was burning bright with an emotion that wasn't difficult to guess. Eakins had caught the patrician slant of his cheekbones, the firmness of his mouth, the severity of his chin, and the determined set of his shoulders. But there was something else, a message that was all too clear: it announced to anyone who saw this painting that Sinclair Poole was a man who wouldn't forget and might never forgive those who had used or betrayed him.

"Stunning work, isn't it?" Vanessa asked her quietly.

"No wonder Sin hid it away," Caro said, breaking away from the spell. "Anyone who looks at it

293

will know that he isn't the kind of man you can cross and then escape from. But he chose not to hang it. The only question is, was he afraid to let anyone see it, or is it possible that Eakins captured Sin's innermost thoughts so accurately that it frightened him?''

While Vanessa returned to the sitting room, Caro went in to see Sin. Sin was now awake, his head turned toward the door, and she knew instantly that he had been waiting for her.

"I'm sorry I took so long, darling," she said, closing the door behind her and crossing the room to his bed. "Did you get some sleep?"

"Not too much." Sin smiled. "I've spent quite a few months thinking about this ending one way, and suddenly you've arrived and handed me another possibility."

"I'm very glad to hear that." Caro sat down gently on the edge of the bed, careful not to jar him. "There's something I have to take up with you. Do you have any objection to a woman doctor?"

"None that I know of. But are you referring to one woman doctor in particular?"

"I wouldn't bring in a doctor unless he or she knew the latest techniques, and that's Alix."

"If it didn't hurt, I think I might laugh."

"Sin—"

"No, darling, it's perfectly all right," he said, lifting her hand to his lips. "If her visit doesn't serve one purpose, it will do for another."

Caro caught his allusion instantly, and she stayed

silent even as her heart began to pound again. "The situation isn't that bleak," she said finally. "Didn't your doctor explain about surgery?"

"Only that it was a highly experimental and not usually successful procedure."

"I don't think Dr. Merrit had it exactly right," Caro said carefully. She wasn't about to question Alix's diagnosis, and too much reassurance would be as bad as too much gloom. "But Alix will be here soon, and then the next step is up to her."

"You're not going to let me give up, are you?"

"No, and that's only because you've fought through so much and you're nowhere near ready to let it all go," she said softly, leaning forward to kiss him. "For the time being, just think of this as a slight delay in completing the noble task you undertook."

When Alix arrived at Prince Street, it was well after two in the afternoon. The fact that what should have been a morning's work at the Women's Infirmary had continued well through lunch did not seem on the surface to be a good sign, and she pressed the doorbell with a fresh attack of apprehension at what she would find.

"Yes, miss, may I help you?" The door had opened a crack, and Alix could see a pair of bright blue eyes regarding her with both suspicion and curiosity.

"I'm here at Caroline Worth's request to see Sinclair Poole,'' she said, deciding to get this over with at once. "I'm Dr. Alicia Turner."

"Well now, Miss Worth didn't say. . . . but never mind." The door opened all the way. "I'm Mrs. Murphy, and I do all the laundry."

Alix smiled. "It's very nice to meet you, and I'm sorry the circumstances couldn't be happier," she said, coming into the anteroom. Without wasting a motion, Alix put down her black leather medical bag and Mark Cross purse on the seat of the wing-backed chair. She pulled off her gloves and unbuttoned her Worth coat of black wool with collar and cuffs of kolinsky mink to reveal a Callot Soeurs day dress of rust-colored corduroy fastened down the back with a long row of small bone buttons. "Have things been fairly quiet here for the past few hours?"

"Yes, miss . . . I mean, doctor. I haven't been upstairs, but everything's as quiet as you please. George has gone to the nearest pharmacy with a list of necessities, the ladies are upstairs in the sitting room, Mr. Wong is busy making soup and brewing tea, Vic is polishing the glasses, and Gregori's around somewhere. That young man is in quite a state, and if you want my advice, you'll find something to occupy him before he goes to pieces."

"That sounds like a very good idea."

"Myself, I've been praying ever since Mr. Poole took ill."

"And that certainly won't hurt. Mrs. Murphy, will you ask everyone to come up to the sitting room? I'll know what I have to do after I examine Mr.

Poole, but I want everyone in the household together when I finish.''

Carrying her medical bag stuffed with everything she could possibly need, Alix mounted the stairs and reached the second floor just as Caro was coming down the corridor toward the sitting room.

''Are you as nervous as I am?'' Alix asked as they embraced.

''Yes, and I hope I'll do as well as you to conceal it.''

''You're going to be splendid.'' Alix paused, and both women regarded one another. ''Do you think we've exchanged enough encouragement?''

''This will probably have to do,'' Caro agreed.

''Then I'd better see our patient. Does he know I'm going to be his doctor?''

''Yes, and his reaction wasn't at all biased.''

Alix smiled. ''I'm going to have to take a second look at those pills he took. They must be—Why, hello. It's nice to see you again. How's the ankle?'' she asked Gregori.

Two steps from the top of the stairs, Gregori froze, unable to take his eyes off Alix Turner. The first time he'd seen her she'd been spinning out the remaining days of her intern's year on duty in Roosevelt Hospital's emergency room. He had been brought there following his tumble down the back stairs at the Metropolitan Club. The second time he'd seen her, her discreet summer skirt and blouse topped by a white lab coat had been exchanged for an exquisite Lucile dress and picture hat, and she had come to visit him. In between the two incidents, she had been the attending physician who had diagnosed his broken ankle, had soothed him during the frightening experience of being x-rayed for the first time, and had found a surgeon who was a wizard in the field of orthopedics to set his ankle and take on the case. During her visit she'd told him that her internship was successfully completed, and she was sailing the next day on the *City of Paris* for a summer in Europe. The last thing Alix Turner had done was to sprinkle a good amount of Jicky on a handkerchief and leave it on his pillow.

"The ankle's fine," he said finally. "And I still have your handkerchief."

Alix smiled and held out a hand to Gregori. "Please keep it. Someday, providing you marry the right sort of woman, you can tell your wife about it." She gave him an oblique look. "So you're working for Sinclair now?"

"He hired me about an hour after I last saw you. I'm a valet, secretary, and assistant all in one, but now—" Gregori stopped, unable to continue, but both women knew what was in his heart.

"Now is the time for me to see what I can do so you can go back to your complicated and manifold duties as soon as possible," Alix said with a brightness she didn't feel. "Just wait for me in the sitting room with everyone else, and I'll be in as soon as I can."

Alix hadn't simply been trying to make Caro feel better when she'd disclosed the state of her nerves.

The combination of seeing Sinclair again after all these years and his having a potentially life-threatening ailment was enough to send butterflies through her stomach—to say nothing of the speed of her heartbeat. It was a situation that could render one helpless, except that at some point during her medical training, she'd found that there was a clinical side to her personality that could, for the time she needed it, supersede her other feelings. It was that utterly professional attitude that now allowed her to enter Sin's room with only a brief flurry of trepidation.

Her only problem remained what to say. Oh, she had her bedside manner down pat, and what she would say when the examination was completed would take care of itself. She was sure her opening lines would be her final hurdle, and as she closed the door and began to walk across the floor, the image of her standing dumbstruck at the foot of Sin's bed formed, but that difficulty was taken out of her hands.

"Would you be insulted if I told you how beautiful you look?"

"Not at all. That's the nicest compliment I've had all day." Alix put her bag down on the bedside table. "Some of the things said to women doctors on their professional rounds can't be repeated in polite company."

"Well, since I'm not considered polite company any longer, why don't you tell me some of them?"

Sin smiled at her, and, unable to resist, Alix smiled back. "I may just do that, but not quite yet.

Caro said that you don't object to having me as your doctor."

"No, but I also don't have much choice in the matter." Sin tried to sit up, but he grimaced with pain and returned to the pillows. "Do you like lost causes, Alix?"

"I don't see anything lost about you, Sin . . . I never have."

"I'm sorry, Alix, for the way I treated you. I led you to expect that I was going to ask you to marry me, and the next thing you know, I'm engaged to Cynthia. I didn't even have the decency to stand by you when you needed those who care for you the most. And even after I behaved like a cad, you still had the heart to write to me, and I compounded my idiocy by not answering."

Alix, in the process of reaching for her medical bag, instead put her hands on Sin's shoulders. "You were under a lot of pressure both times. It's true that I wasn't always so understanding about it, but like you I've had a long time to think about certain things. You had your father's expectations to meet, and as much as I might have wanted to, I can't fault you for your love and loyalty toward him."

"Do you know that's the only thing I have any anger at my father for?" Sin asked quietly. The pill was starting to wear off, but he could bear the discomfort as long as he could think and speak clearly. "He wanted me to become engaged to Cynthia because he thought it would keep her father's ambitions at bay. He assured me that it was only a temporary measure, that I could come back to you later. . . . ''

With lightning swiftness, Alix decided not to make any reply. Now was not the time to tell Sin that that brief moment when they had been so young and so in love with each other had been their only opportunity to seize the moment and move on with it together. Instead, they had been removed from each other's company, and the need and the desire to get engaged, to be married, and to build a life together had passed. Even if all the difficulties that later afflicted him hadn't happened, she still wouldn't have taken him back. That reaction was not out of injured pride, but out of the sure knowledge that no matter how much she cared for him, Sinclair Poole wasn't the love of her life.

And there isn't a way for me to tell him that right now, she thought with not a little sadness. But I will have to tell him eventually, or Sin will start to think I haven't married because of him, and that would cause all sorts of complications, considering his feelings for Caro. But all this is just going to have to wait.

"I'm going to examine you now," she said directly, knowing that the silence between them had gone on for too long.

"I won't make a fuss."

"I'm glad to hear that, and I hope it also means you'll go along with whatever I say regarding treatment."

"You and Caro are both such believers in lost

causes that I can almost find it in myself to have a little hope.''

''Me, a believer in lost causes? Never. . . . and not Caro, either. It's just the ones that need a little help that appeal to us,'' Alix said with fresh assurance, and she gently pulled down the bedcovers to begin her examination.

''Alix, I suggest you give us your diagnosis straight out,'' Caro said as the doctor walked into the sitting room.

''I know you all are very concerned, and I would have come to you right from Sin's room, except that I had to call Dorothy Ross, a surgical nurse I know and trust.'' Alix put her bag on the nearest table and surveyed her audience. Eight people—Caro, Vanessa, Gregori, Vic, Sean, George, Mr. Wong, and Mrs. Murphy—were waiting for her to announce her decision, and it was times like these that she was most aware of the responsibilities of a physician. ''He's resting comfortably now and will for several more hours, but by the time his last pill wears off, I hope he'll be safely through surgery.''

''What do you want us to do now?'' Caro had a list of questions, but her first duty was to back up Alix, to show that she believed in her so that the others wouldn't have any doubts about doing the same. ''We've found an empty bedroom and a table in one of the storerooms—both should do very well.''

''I'm glad to hear that. I knew I could count on you, Caro, and now I have to count on all of you,'' she said, her voice clear and compelling. "First of all, the room has to be made as clean as possible."

"I'll scrub it down so clean that you'd be able to serve a banquet off the floor," Mrs. Murphy announced.

"Good, that's just how we'll need it," Alix said, and began to issue her other instructions. "Nurse Ross will bring her own surgical gown, but Caro and I will need something to wear." She studied the chef's clothes. "Mr. Wong, will you let us have some extra shirts and trousers?"

"Yes, Doctor. Will you need me to continue boiling water?"

Within five minutes, Alix was deep into parceling out jobs for everyone—or nearly so. It wasn't until only Caro, Vanessa, and Gregori were left that she allowed herself the luxury of sitting down on a sofa.

"Gregori, do you have steady hands?" she asked quietly.

"Yes, Dr. Turner," he replied, and held out his beautifully made hands. She could see that despite the fact that the underpinnings of his world had suddenly turned very insecure, his reflexes were unimpaired. "I have to tell you that I don't know one surgical instrument from another."

"You don't have to, but I will need you to hand me or Nurse Ross or Caro supplies, to wipe our foreheads if we get overheated, and to administer supplementary ether to Sin, should he need it."

At her last words, Gregori turned pale, but his dark amber eyes showed a new resolve. "I can do anything you ask."

"I'm sure you can, but first you have to take care of yourself. Go downstairs and have Mr. Wong give you some hot food, and then go to your room and rest. Someone will come up and get you when it's time to scrub."

Caro waited until Gregori was safely out of earshot before she spoke to her friend. "Is there no way Sin could make it to the hospital?"

"His appendix hasn't burst, and that's most important for his getting through surgery, but I can't chance moving him out of here. If we were uptown, at the Osborne or even the Dakota, I'd say it was worth the risk to get him to Roosevelt Hospital, but from down here. . . . " Alix shook her head. "Add on the time it would take an ambulance to get here, and then there's the red tape we'd run into at any other hospital. No, we're much better off staying right here."

"Alix, have you done this procedure before?" Vanessa questioned gently.

"I saw quite a bit of this sort of operation while I was an intern. Roosevelt was one of the first hospitals to perfect the removal of the appendix and the recovery of the patient. While I was there, all the brilliant interns were sure this was quack surgery that would only get a doctor into trouble sooner or later, and you couldn't drag most of them to the operating theatre for instruction," Alix recalled with more than a bit of glee. "Thanks to them, I assisted in more surgeries of this sort than I can count."

"And so many doctors are still ill-informed about

it," Caro said, and told them about the comments Sin's physician had made.

"Unhappily, though, he was right about one thing," Alix sighed. "This *is* a dangerous operation, and it depends on so many *ifs: if* the appendix hasn't burst, *if* there's no problem with the ether, *if* the patient doesn't hemorrhage, *if* there's no infection, *then*—providing the patient is basically strong and healthy to begin with—there's a good chance for recovery." She stopped and drew a deep breath. "Are you still in this with me, Caro?"

"I wouldn't back out no matter what the odds. There are many awful things in this world, but one of the worst is not doing anything."

"And that," Vanessa put in, "leads us to what you want me to do, Alix."

"I've thought about this very carefully, and Vanessa, you can help us best by staying right here and serving as an anchor."

"I have done surgical work in China, Alix. We were always willing to help out when we were needed, and except for the Union Medical College and a few other places, most surgeries were hardly up-to-date, and the conditions were far from ideal in any way."

"I know that, but I need you to serve in another capacity. I'm a woman doctor, and I know I don't have to tell you that if something goes wrong with Sin, I could be in a lot of trouble. There's no shortage of people out there who can't wait for a female physician to make a mistake. In case there are. . . . circumstances I can't control, I'd very much like it if you were here, looking just the way you do now, if I have to contact. . . . the people who handle those things,'' Alix concluded.

"And Mummy, you can also be the mainstay for everyone who'll be waiting for the operation to conclude. . . . successfully,'' Caro said, pushing back the fears that Alix's carefully voiced words had reawakened. "We don't know how long the surgery will last, and I don't know anyone who can keep things on an even keel the way you can.''

"Well, you know us British—give us a good pot of tea and we can handle any situation.''

Alix smiled. "This sounds like something my friend Cecily Benjamin might say.''

"Cecily De Noyer, that was? My mother always said she did quite well for an industrial heiress, becoming Countess of Saltlon. Isaac really could have done so much better.''

Caro and Alix traded looks, barely able to suppress their smiles.

"Well, that's that—at least for the time being,'' Alix said. "It's just occurred to me that I didn't have much lunch, and something tells me neither did both of you. Shall we see if Mr. Wong will give us something to eat?''

Gregori had eaten lunch at the kitchen table, barely tasting or even knowing what it was that had traveled from the plate to his mouth. His knowledge and enjoyment of food had deserted him completely and he ate only because he knew that he couldn't function properly or be of help to Alix if he didn't have strength and energy-giving food inside him.

He left Mr. Wong at the stove—the chef was busily occupied with boiling vast pots of water so Mrs. Murphy could scrub down the bedroom and stirring up something tasty so the ladies upstairs could also have their lunch—and went up to his room on the third floor. On the second floor he had his first whiff of the strong disinfectant soap Mrs. Murphy was using while he waited for George and Vic and Sean to carry down the large, heavy table.

"If you're going to get sick, Greg, you'd better do it now," George advised, not unkindly, when they finished their task. "Dr. Turner's a great lady and an understanding one, but she won't hold for being let down when she needs help the most."

"I won't be sick and I'm not going to let anyone down," Greg replied, stung. "We all owe it to Sin to pull our weight and then some."

Gregori continued to the next floor, the scent of the disinfectant making his stomach turn, but George's words had put a new resolve in him, helping him push away the memories of the past twenty-four hours and center his thoughts on what was happening now. Sin had given him so much, and now he had a chance to return that help in a way that was indeed life-saving.

Gregori's room, although not as severely decorated as Sin's, reflected a great deal of masculine luxe. Done in shades of blue and tan, the chamber was dominated by a large, handsome mahogany sleigh bed. His feet sank soundlessly into the thick wool pile of the Oriental carpet, but he neither turned on any of the lamps nor, as Alix had instructed, lay down to rest.

He took off his jacket and hung it carefully away in the closet filled with well-tailored clothes from Brooks Brothers, pulled off his tie, and rolled up the sleeves of his white shirt after depositing his gold Faberge cuff links in a fluted silver dish. He took a tall beeswax taper from the writing table and walked toward his bed, knowing exactly what he had to do.

On the table beside his bed, along with a porcelain-base lamp and the books he was currently reading, was an icon. Without the jeweled riza that had once enclosed it, it was a deceptively simple work of religious art, an icon suitable for a schoolboy. In fact, it had been his first icon, the one that had accompanied him on his peril-filled journey to New York, and although now, after two years, he considered himself permanently lapsed from the Orthodoxy of his family, he turned to this symbol of his past.

Gregori placed the candlestick in front of the icon, lit the taper, and sank to his knees, crossing himself as he did so. Without a second's hesitation, he said all the prayers he knew, the Russian words coming back to him in a steady, unbroken flow, and when they were completed, he began to make other promises that he would fulfill if only Sinclair would make it through this operation and recover from his affliction.

* * *

Much to their own amazement, Caro, Alix, and Vanessa were able to do ample justice to the excellent food Mr. Wong brought up to them. The wonton soup was followed by strips of chicken on a bed of steamed Chinese vegetables and white rice, and by the time they finished the almond cookies and hot tea they had the fresh strength they needed.

They were finishing the last of the pot of tea when Vic escorted Dorothy Ross into the sitting room. The three women had hardly been exchanging light-hearted conversation while they ate, but the arrival of the surgical nurse brought back with full force their common purpose.

"Dorothy, thank you for getting here so quickly," Alix said, rising to her feet to greet the new arrival. "This is Caroline Worth, Mr. Poole's fiancée, and her stepmother, Vanessa Worth."

"It's very nice to meet both of you." Dorothy was appropriately restrained, but her voice was warm. "I'm sorry the circumstances couldn't be better."

"Perhaps they will be by the time we're finished," Caro replied.

"Would you care for a cup of hot tea and an almond cookie?" Vanessa inquired.

"No, thank you, Mrs. Worth. By now, I expect that Dr. Turner has handled all the preliminaries, and I should take this opportunity to check everything over."

"Then let me show you the way, Dorothy," Alix said. "It's time we got started."

* * *

"It's time, isn't it?" Sin asked a short while later as Caro sat down on the chair beside his bed.

"Just about. Alix is taking care of everything," she told him, seeing no reason why she had to go into unnecessary explanations about all the steps involved.

"That mean's there's something I must attend to," Sin said, and began to sit up.

"Sin, please, don't strain yourself!" Caro said, fear flashing through her. "You have to stay as quiet and as still as possible."

"I am, darling, don't worry. But there is something I have to do. Go to the writing table and find my leather portfolio and a fountain pen and bring them here, please. It's very important."

Caro quickly found both items. A series of questions formed in her mind, but she wisely kept them to herself and switched on the bedside lamp.

"Is this enough light for you?"

"Yes, just fine, and this shouldn't take long," he said, opening the portfolio and uncapping his gold pen. Writing quickly, he covered two pages of engraved white stationery with his strong, clear handwriting, signed it, and made a notation at the bottom of the page. "Sign this, please," he asked her quietly. "It's a letter absolving Alix of all responsibility if anything goes wrong. They'll go after her not because of me, but because the idea of going after a woman doctor is too good to resist. Saying that I decided on surgery of my own free will should save her from any problems."

"This is one of the finest things I've ever heard

of," Caro said as she signed her name under the place marked "witnesses." "And it's also one of the most thoughtful."

"It's the least I owe Alix, and I do owe her quite a bit."

As long as it's not your heart, Caro almost said, but this wasn't the time to worry about where Sin's love and loyalty lay. All that mattered now was his life.

"Who else are you going to have sign?" she asked, seizing on a neutral topic.

"George, of course. If there is some sort of inquiry, he'll get on the stand and quote Shakespeare until everyone is dizzy."

"Perhaps you should also ask Dorothy Ross. She's the surgical nurse Alix brought in. One thing, though," Caro added, smiling for the first time since she entered the bedroom. "She thinks we're engaged."

"Oh?" Sin's face didn't give anything away. "And why does she think that?"

"Because when Alix introduced us, she presented me as your fiancée. No matter how you look at it, that was the only way to avoid a lot of needless questions and answers."

Sin's look was reflective. "I'm certain that this is going to end one way, and you're convinced it'll work out fine. It seems that between us we're simply covering all possibilities."

"Let's just say I believe in those famous words in *Twelfth Night*—'Journeys end in lovers' meeting, every wise man's son doth know,' " she said as a brisk knock sounded on the door.

"Mr. Poole, I hope I'm not interrupting, but I'm Nurse Ross, and I have to prepare you for surgery," the older woman said a moment later, her firm but not unkind expression softening when she saw them holding hands.

"That's perfectly all right, Nurse Ross—provided you can give us five minutes more together," Sin said with a smile no woman could resist. "There's something I'd like you to sign, but I'll explain it to you after you give me a chance to kiss my fiancée."

To Caro's surprise, Alix like to talk while she operated.

Most of the doctors she knew in China were quiet to the point of grimness. Outside of issuing orders and instructions, they never spoke to those who worked with them. But Alix had had things under control from the first and saw no reason to make this situation any more tense than it had to be.

Once Sin had been laid on the long buffet table, now padded with towels, and draped in two large, white sheets, ironed until they were almost too hot to touch, the door had been closed, and when she was sure he was calm and comfortable, the procedure began.

Dorothy fitted the wire mask packed with gauze over Sin's nose and mouth, placed a folded towel over his eyes to keep out the fumes, and began to let the ether drip carefully in, having him count backward from one hundred. His voice went from clear to fuzzy, and once he was under, Gregori— who had already been carefully instructed in how to administer additional ether if and when it was necessary—moved to take his place behind Sin's head while the nurse moved to Alix's side.

Nurse Ross wore the clothes she always did, while Alix, Caro, and Gregori wore the white shirts and trousers that Mr. Wong had given them. Surgical caps covered their hair, cotton masks protected their mouths, and thanks to George, who had paid an emergency visit to the nearest shoe store, they all wore tennis shoes whose rubber bottoms had been wiped with a strong disinfectant.

Caro knew Alix regarded Sin in his present condition as not a man but as her patient. As with any other male patient, his anesthesized body, covered by a single sheet, held only medical interest.

And with not a little amazement, Caro found that she was considering him the same way.

From her place at the other side of the table, she could see the rows of shining surgical instruments, the surgical thread, the gauze pads, and the towels, and smell the combination of strong soap and carbolic acid mixing with the scent of ether. In some strange way, she realized, it was if Sin's anesthetized body which now had no secrets from her was such a part of what was going to take place that he had no separateness from the whole of the tableau.

"Is everyone ready?" Alix asked, her voice slightly muffled by the mask, and when they all an-

313

swered in the affirmative, she nodded. "Fine, then; we can't waste any more time."

First there was the swab of iodine, leaving a prominent orange stain where the incision was to be made, and then the scapel flashed silver in Alix's hand. At the first sight of blood, Caro felt a stirring of uncertainty, but it passed quickly and she absorbed herself in the measured pace of a well-conducted operation.

"Have you read anything good lately, Caro?" Alix inquired some time later as they worked, and if it hadn't been for the mask across her mouth, it would have been hardly any different from any other conversation that they might have.

"*The Red House* and *The Last Word* were both good," Caro replied after a second's hesitation. Obviously, this was something Alix did all the time, and if it helped her work, Caro had to keep her end up. "Did you enjoy *Lord Allingham, Bankrupt?*"

"It was fun. Oh, a salesman at Brentano's called me yesterday—Gauze, please, Dorothy—he wanted to let me know that Scribner's is publishing Edith Wharton's first novel next month."

"I loved *The Decoration of Houses.*"

"So did I, and Thea's absolutely mad for it. Mr. Moore told me the novel's called *The Valley of Decision,* and it'll be published in two volumes. I ordered a copy, of course, but don't ask me when I'll have time to read it—or even if it'll be worth it. . . . "

The conversation continued in fits and starts, Alix directing the questions and keeping the pace going, combining them with her medical instructions so that

314

as the operation progressed an odd sense of normality took over. Alix was in charge; it was perfectly clear that Dorothy was nearly her equal in terms of medical skill; Caro was a good and dependable assistant who would never lose her head; and Gregori was the tyro, eager to please but needing encouragement so that when he had to administer extra ether he did it slowly and carefully.

There were no clocks in the room, and in New York in January, late afternoon faded quickly into a long night. There was no way of estimating how long they were taking, but Caro could see that they were working as quickly as possible. Alix didn't want to run the risk of the appendix unexpectedly bursting, and it was certainly safer for Sin if he spent as short a time as possible under the ether.

Caro watched as Alix began to close, taking each stitch with the greatest of care. Finally, the dressing was applied, and the two friends looked at each other across the width of the table.

"You did it, Alix."

"We all did it, and each of you was absolutely splendid," she announced, untying her mask. "Greg, why don't you open the door and get George and Vic and Sean in here so we can get Sin back to his room. The worst part of this job is over, and I'm sure that everyone is anxious to know how all of us came through this."

"First of all, I want to tell all of you the good news," Alix said some twenty minutes later when

315

they had gathered in the sitting room. Exercising the greatest of care, the men had lent their combined strengths to carry the improvised operating table with Sin on it back to his room. "The situation was acute, but the appendix didn't burst, and that's the most important thing. He also took the ether well. Now the complicated part begins."

Sin's staff patiently waited until Alix had taken several sips of the honey-sweetened tea that Vanessa had waiting for them. They were full of questions, but Alix's weariness, Caro's almost numb responses, and Gregori's look of exhaustion deterred them from pressing for details. Only Nurse Ross seemed unaffected by the past hours, but she had gone to Sinclair's room to sit by his bed, watching her patient for any danger signals.

Curled up in a corner of the sofa, sipping hot tea, Caro felt reality begin to pierce through the fatigue that had threatened to overwhelm her. The medical detachment that had served her so well during the operation was now fading swiftly. The body on the makeshift operating table had been Sin's, as had the blood that had stained the instrument and been absorbed by the gauze. She loved him completely, but for the time he had been anesthetized and under the knife, he had been only the person they had to save.

And don't give yourself airs, it's Alix who had to shoulder all the responsibility, she thought, listening to her friend answer all the questions. She'll be the one at risk if something goes wrong now, the letter Sin wrote nonwithstanding. You just handed over the instruments and did what you were told and kept your head.

". . . . But what are Mr. Poole's chances, Doctor?" George was asking.

"I won't lie to you, George, or to anyone else," Alix said, her voice showing the strain she must be feeling. "First he has to get over the aftereffects of the ether, then we have to be concerned about his possibly developing internal bleeding, and lastly there's the danger of infection—that's why I insisted that the room be scrubbed down as much as it was. Anything that can cut down on that danger has to be used. It's the next seventy-two hours that are crucial, but there's every reason to hope that Sin's recovery will be complete."

"And we'll be here until he's out of the ether," Caro added, telling them what she and Alix had decided on while they had scrubbed for surgery. "Is there a room ready where we can lie down?"

George and Vic exchanged glances; both men looked somewhat embarrassed. Instinctively, Caro and Alix knew what was coming, but they waited patiently for one of them to speak first.

"Well, there is a nice back bedroom here on the second floor," George said at last. "It's very nicely furnished, just the way ladies like, and there's a selection of those pretty Japanese kimonos. It's. . . . er. . . . the place Mr. Poole reserves for. . . . "

"We can use our imaginations, George," Caro said, keeping a straight face. "All you have to do is show us the way. Mummy. . . . "

"I've already found a nice guest room on the third

317

floor," Vanessa said as serenely as if she hadn't spent the last few hours soothing the fears of the staff. "But if all of you don't mind a suggestion, I think someone should put this poor young man to bed," she went on, indicating Gregori, who was slumped in an armchair, fast asleep. "I really think his first experience at assisting in surgery has quite done him in!"

Chapter Sixteen

Caro came awake quickly, her heart pounding in long, swift beats. Somewhere in the deepest recess of her mind she had heard someone knocking at the door, and a softly pitched voice summoning Alix.

Sinclair, she thought with a fresh surge of apprehension. He had to be out of the ether, or worse, something had started to go wrong.

Her eyes adjusted to the darkness, and she saw Alix putting a silk kimono over her lacy Lucile lingerie. The cotton kimono she had gone to sleep in was tossed on her side of the large bed; her hair showed signs of having been quickly brushed and tied back with a ribbon.

"Is it Sinclair?" Caro asked. "I'm sure I heard someone calling for you."

"What sharp hearing you have, even in your sleep! Yes, it was Dorothy, and she thinks Sin seems to be coming out of the ether," Alix said smoothly as she wrapped the kimono around her and secured the belt at her waist.

"Did Dorothy say anything about his having any problems?" she asked, her heart in her throat.

"So far, none at all."

"And what do you think?" Caro sat up in bed, pulling her cotton kimono up at one shoulder. "I know you've been holding back on telling us everything."

"Of course. False hope and doom-and-gloom are opposite sides of the same coin. By the way, aren't you going to insist on coming with me?"

"I want to, terribly, but as much as I love Sin, I'd be in the way right now. Also, I don't think my being there when he wakes up will be in his best interests."

"Most women wouldn't feel like that."

"I wouldn't either—if this operation had taken place under normal conditions. He won't mind that I brought you here, or that I assisted during the surgery. We may even laugh about this one day. But seeing him come out of the ether is another matter entirely."

"I couldn't agree more. Doing that would probably injure his pride, or else he'd feel that he lost face or one of those other impossible male things," Alix said, reaching for her medical bag. "One good thing about Sinclair, though, is what I didn't tell everyone a couple of hours ago. When Sin was younger, he was one of those rare fast healers. I remember once, when he was about fourteen, he fell and cut his arm badly. The doctors were very concerned, but as soon as the wound was cleaned up it began to heal, and it closed within a week. Sometimes people grow out of that as they get older, but I'm going to take a chance and say that Sin still has those healing properties inside him and will be better in almost no time.''

Sinclair knew there was something he had to remember. As he came out of a sleep that seemed to have no relation to any other slumber he had ever known, he struggled to clear his mind, to recall what was so important, but all he was aware of was something hot and sticky pressing against he right side.

''Please, Mr. Poole, keep your hands away from the dressing. Doctor. . . . ''

The woman's voice, firm but kind, blew away the cobwebs. It hadn't all been a dream, he thought, all the broken images coming together. The woman's voice belonged to Dorothy Ross, the nurse, and the doctor. . . .

''Alix. . . . '' His voice sounded like a croak.

''Good! Open your eyes, Sin.''

He did so, blinking slightly at the bedside lamp. ''What time is it?''

''Late. Now, how many fingers am I holding up?''

''Two.''

''Now?''

''Four.''

''And now?''

''Five.''

"What's your name?"

"Sinclair Poole," he replied, his voice growing stronger. "And this is my house on Prince Street, and unless I very much miss my guess, Alix, you just saved my life."

"It's nothing any other skilled doctor couldn't have done."

"Where's Caro?"

"Back in one of your guest rooms, but she'll be the one to tell you why I'm making this bedside visit alone."

"Something to look forward to—I hope."

Alix began to laugh, the deep tension of the past hours finally easing. "Go back to sleep, Sin. Caro will be here when you wake up again. And as for getting well. . . . I think that in a short time this is going to be an unpleasant but fading memory."

"I've been lying here thinking about the things we have to talk about," Sin said on Thursday morning, six days after his surgery, when Caro appeared at his bedroom door. He had come out of the ether with few if any problems and showed absolutely no signs of infection; his suture was progressing nicely. "Can you spare a few minutes from running my business to stay here with me?"

"As if you had to ask," Caro responded happily, crossing from the doorway to the chair beside his bed. "I only looked in to see if you were enjoying your mid-morning nap."

"I'd much rather talk to you than take another

nap," he responded. "We can even hold hands while we talk."

"Well, I'm certainly not going to object to that, but just remember that my stepmother is nearby, in case you think this is the right time to suggest something certain people consider improper," Caro said lightly as she sat down, her Lucile day dress of French-blue wool trimmed with red and khaki bands making a nice splash of color in the somber room.

"It's not that the highly pleasant idea hasn't occured to me, but that might require even more of a medical miracle than the one that's already taken place."

"Alix said you have remarkable healing powers."

"That could be debated." Sin laughed. "I'm almost afraid to ask how my business is coming along. You and your stepmother have probably tripled my income in the past week."

"We're trying our best. Vanessa placed an order for a pair of *famille noir* vases and a jade bowl that a Hong Kong dealer has definitely undervalued. And she wants to know what you think about ordering a two-hundred-piece set of Rose Canton china. . . ."

Caro, Alix, and Vanessa had remained at the Prince Street house until late Saturday morning, when it was clear that Sin had successfully come through the operation and the ether and was resting as comfortably as possible. Alix had rung up a physician friend, John Stern, advised him about the case, and secured his promise to come over and keep a close eye on Sin. When they returned on Sunday afternoon, it was to find their patient, although tired and drained from his experience, awake and aware of everything going on; by Monday he was able to sit up in bed.

A swift recovery seemed assured, but now Caro was aware that an artificial barrier had inserted itself between her and Sin.

There had been no repetition of their exchange of love that had taken place during the stressful hours of Friday afternoon. Sin had made no further gesture either in word or deed, and Caro certainly wasn't about to raise the matter at the risk of his thinking her one of those women who liked nothing better than to back a man into a corner and have him make a declaration he wasn't ready for. The high degree of communion they had discovered the night they met, however, remained unimpaired, giving Caro a good measure of comfort.

Reminding herself that she hadn't expected Sin to come out of the ether calling her name, eager to avow his love and to add on a proposal of marriage, Caro recognized that his recovery came before anything else, and after that it was making sure that his businesses ran smoothly. Toward that end, Caro put her expertise and Vanessa's in the world of Oriental art and antiques to good use. Until he was on his feet again, they would handle that end of it, while Gregori occupied himself with directing the Wall Street investments.

Sin had accepted her offer with pleasure, but now, as she sat next to his bed, telling him of the morning's transactions, she speculated on the possibility that they had either moved backward in their relationship or added a whole new aspect to it. The only problem was that she wasn't sure which.

"I'm very glad to know that this part of my business is being run with such skill and care," Sin said finally, "but I want to talk about us. Unless you'd rather not," he added after a moment's hesitation.

Caro's heart skipped a beat. "I don't mind at all," she said, aware that his words could mean anything. "Provided that you're up to the strain, of course. Alix said that you have to be careful about the sutures, and even strong men can get tired, particularly when they've been through an ordeal like yours," she continued, reaching out to take his hand as she sat down on the bed. If he were going to break it off, she decided, there was not reason she should make it easy for him by sitting down in the bergère now semipermanently placed beside the bed. But her heart reminded her that she could no more resist making this gesture toward him than she could stop feeling something warm and wonderful happen to her every time she looked at him or thought of him.

At her spontaneous gesture, Sin felt a great coil of tension unwind inside him. "The only ordeal I'm going through right now is the one I brought on myself by saying how much I love you."

For a moment, the emotions welling up in Caro prevented her from speaking. "I love you, too," she said. "I think I have since the night we met."

"Right there on the terrace with me wearing that blasted mask?"

"Well, I knew right off it couldn't be hiding anything terrible."

"I thought that you might have changed your mind since Friday."

"Never! But I thought for a moment that you. . . ."

"No!" Sin's voice was definite, and he tightened his grasp on her hand. "We said so much to each other before my surgery, and then afterward. . . ."

"I wanted to give you time to recover. And I also wanted to be sure that you didn't think of me as Ariadne."

"I'm afraid my Greek mythology isn't what it used to be," Sin said, mystified at her allegory.

"Ariadne was Minos' daughter, and the myth says that she gave Theseus a ball of twine to guide him out of the labyrinth, fled with him, but was abandoned by him at the first opportunity," she said quietly.

"Then the labyrinth is my illness and the twine is my surgery," Sin hazarded. "I see what you mean, but why would I ever callously leave the woman who saved my life?"

"Alix saved your life."

"Alix performed the surgery, and I'll be forever grateful to her, but she wouldn't have gotten here in the first place if it wasn't for you," he said, seeing the tears in her eyes and feeling his own emotions threaten to overwhelm him. "And I don't love you only because you rescued me from my own stupidity. I knew from that first night at the Linden Trees that I'd never be able to forget you or be able to live in any sort of happiness without you."

Instinctively, they drew closer together, the depth

of their newly revealed feelings shimmering in the air around them. With the greatest of care, Caro leaned into his embrace, her need to be close to him tempered by the awareness that his body was still sensitive to any jolts or jars, even those committed under the happiest of circumstances.

"This was worth waiting for," Sin said as they nestled carefully together. "The last time I kissed you, I thought it might really be the last time."

"Now it seems that we may have all the time we want." Caro pressed a kiss at the hollow of his throat. She could feel the warmth and strength of his body through the fine cotton of his pajamas, and his arms held her close enough so she could feel the strong, steady beat of his heart. "And in a supreme effort to be fair, I'll tell you that this is your last chance to change your mind."

"I'll pass." Sin sounded happy, content, and excited all at the same time. "You've turned my whole world upside down. I can't go back to the way I was, and I won't go forward without you."

"This is everything I ever wanted to hear from you," Caro said, raising her face to look at him. "I love you so much, but I was worried that some small part of you still thought that having that dance with me and then staying on the terrace kept you from finding the letter."

"There was no guarantee that if I'd gone back to the game room when I was supposed to, Davis would have given me the letter," he replied. "And anything I said to the contrary was to try and send you away before we fell any more in love than we were, and you realized what medical condition I was in. I was so tired, and I thought I'd lost everything."

"But you don't think that now."

Sin's embrace tightened. "No, in the past few days I've realized that I may just be lucky enough to have found all that I could ever want."

The kiss they shared this time was full of promise even as it healed the hurts of the past. If all the truly good things they would find together were still ever so slightly out of their grasp, at least the very worst was behind them.

"I suppose I should wait until I can get out of bed again and try to find a more conventional spot, but that doesn't seem to work very well for us," Sin said some time later. "Will you marry me?"

"Is there any other answer but yes?" she asked, full of joy and laughter, kissing him again. "And don't answer that!"

"Believe me, I wouldn't dare," he assured her, his amber eyes full of laughter. "But I do have to say that since we already seem to be engaged as far as everyone else is concerned, I thought it would be wise for me to complete the rest of the equation."

"It's a lucky thing that you're a convalescent in need of tender, loving care, because that's the kind of statement that calls for a whack on the side of the head with a pillow!"

"Think of all the delicately raised European geese who gave up their perfect white feathers to stuff this assortment of pillows," Sin said, pulling her closer. "We can indulge in a pillow fight on our honey-moon."

"At first, I was so angry that I had to be alone nd then I chose to be solitary because the risks wer o great. One wrong word, one conversation in lub overheard by the wrong person, and the Cor ortium might do just about anything."

"They probably would," Cliff agreed. "But yo till have an advantage. They perceive you as havin ut yourself off from your friends, and having r amily. As far as they're concerned, the mone ou've made doesn't count because you have no ba f power from which to harm them." Cliff looke mused. "I'll wager that you made them rather ne ous when you managed to get to Davis Moreto you don't mind my asking, what did happen im that night?"

"He went completely to pieces in front of me, n remembered. "But no matter how many tim go back and review everything that happened, a have is a series of circles that begin and end in th me place."

"Then why don't we talk about something el: a while, and then by and by we'll go back king about the missing letter and Moreton's su e, and his charming group of friends. Who know at new angle might turn up?"

'You sound just like your father. How are you ents? And your brothers? I couldn't believe n Jimmy went off to join the Rough Riders." liff laughed. "He did spendidly down in Texas de lieutenant in about a week, and did his shar ampa, but he was one of the volunteers that ha e left behind when the regular army got into th

Caro slid her arms around his neck. "And when will that be? As long as we're so comfortable here, it seems like a good idea to take care of some of those boring concerns every couple has to contend with."

"Like setting the date?"

"That's the general idea."

"We might wait until I find the letter."

"I know I should say that I'd wait for you forever," Caro said as she rested her head against his shoulder, "and I might actually do that, but I'd rather not put it to the test."

"Don't you think I'm worth it?"

"Oh, definitely. But birth control simply isn't all that reliable!"

"If I laugh," Sin said, speaking very carefully, "I'll split my stitches open, and Alix will be so furious that we'll never get a wedding present out of her."

"You're awful," Caro said, "but I can laugh for both of us."

"And what do you suggest I do?"

"You might think about a February wedding date."

"Is there a reason for that?"

"A very good one." Caro kissed him under an ear. "If we get married in early February, we can go to Nan and Drake's wedding on the twenty-second as a married couple. You'd be surprised how helpful that can be."

"Yes, I'm sure, but. . . . Caro, where are you going?" he asked as she removed herself from his embrace and got off the bed.

"I'd love to stay right here with you, we could even make some preliminary plans for a wedding trip to California," she said, smoothing down the covers, "but you do need your rest, and I'm sure that by now Vanessa is certain we're doing something highly improper—from a medical standpoint, that is."

"And are you going to enlighten her?"

"Possibly." Caro leaned over to kiss him. "Why don't you nap, and if you don't dream of me. . . . no, make that in addition to dreaming of me, you can dwell on all the surprises waiting for you when you wake up again."

Sin was aware that someone else was in his room even before he opened his eyes. At first he was sure it must be Caro, but when he failed to catch the distinctive scent of Jicky, his instinct told him that it wasn't a woman in the chair next to his bed.

"I knew you'd wake up in time for lunch," Clifford Seligman said, putting aside the book he was reading. "I've never known you to miss a meal, and I have no reason to assume that anything's changed."

"When Caro said I was going to have a surprise when I woke up, I didn't quite have you in mind," he told his oldest friend, and both men began to smile. "How are you, Cliff? How's Julie?"

"She's fine. Jonathan was born on December first, and Virginia and Paul are getting to the age that whenever they look at photographs, they want to know who that man is standing with Dadd[y] of the Parthenon."

"So you have that snapshot. I wonde[r] happened to it. Remember the ouzo we dr[

"Amazing we could stand up straight lon[g] to have our picture taken," Cliff said, a[nd] before casually adding, "Feel free to com[e] and see the picture. You're always welcom[e]

"I know." Sin closed his eyes for a ["Have I made a mess out of all this, Cliff[

"In what way? If it were my father, I'[d] do exactly the same thing," Cliff said, his [blue eyes solemn. With his steely self-a[ready wit, and personal charm—not to [family wealth and power that went back t[o] olutionary New York—Sin didn't doubt [ment for a moment. "And you haven't d[all things considered. You've made a nic[e] tune, you have a good home, devoted p[for you in every capacity, and Caro l[o trust you love her."

"Utterly, totally, and passionately."

"I can't tell you how glad I am to he[since you're in that happy state, will [everything you wouldn't almost seven [

Sin's voice was flat. "All that busin[ess] father selling shares in a company th[at] was a set-up."

"I never thought it was anything [

Quietly and without any self-aggra[told Cliff how he had spent the past y[his quest to obtain the crucial letter.

330

331

act and began to muck things up. But Jimmy can tell you all about that himself. Mother and Dad want to see you again. They care very much about you.''

''And I care about them, but the way things were when my father died, I didn't want them to feel I was some special case.''

It was far more complicàted that that, but Cliff decided to accept it at face value. ''There's plenty of time to renew old ties, and you know my parents aren't the sort who need endless explanations. All they want to know now is that you're making a good recovery and what you and Caro have planned.''

''We're talking about getting married in early February,'' Sin said, and began to smile.

''Are you going to let yourself be happy?''

''I don't seem to have a choice about it.''

''That's the way it should be—realizing the alternative is pretty bleak without the woman you love.''

''What's it like, Cliff, being happily married?''

Cliff stretched in his chair and looked both sympathetic and amused. ''Haven't you ever thought what you would do when you found the letter and this quest was over? I can't believe that Cynthia hurt you so badly and left you so disillusioned about women that you wouldn't want to contemplate marriage at some point.''

''I think this is where I'm supposed to hide my face under the pillows,'' Sin said shamefacedly. ''Caro said almost exactly the same thing to me— the first part, that is. She wanted to know if I ever thought about what would happen when I had the letter and all of this was over. She wanted to know

333

what I would do with my revenge. I couldn't tell her that I was working against time, that I never thought there was any way to give me back my health.''

"Well, now you're on the road to recovery—and matrimony.''

Sin laughed. "That isn't quite the fate I envisioned for myself.''

"Speaking from my own experience, the more you think about it, the more appealing the idea becomes. Believe me, Sin, if you can deal with all those cutthroats, you can certainly get married. It's rather nice, being married. You have a pleasant reception, get lots of wedding presents to alternately admire or groan over, and have wonderful things to talk about. And after the honeymoon, you move into your new home, start to entertain, and in a year or so begin your family. But long before then, you'll wonder why you ever wanted to be a bachelor.''

"I bet you think that's funny.''

"On occasion I've been known for my sharply honed wit and powers of observation,'' Cliff stood up. "Caro told me Mr. Wong is doing something special for lunch today and that I'm invited.''

"Well, when you're feasting, think of me up here with my lunch of clear soup.''

"If that's what you're being fed, be doubly glad that both Caro and Alix rang up to tell me all about you. They decided that if left to our own devices, our pride would get in the way of our renewing our friendship. Julie and Mother are in full agreement

334

also, and it's something we should both think about very carefully.''

"I feel very honored. I wasn't expecting both my doctors at once," Sin said as Nurse Ross showed Alix and John into his room on Saturday morning.

"Well, since we've spent the last week alternating our visits, we decided to come in tandem today," Alix said cheerfully as she put down her medical bag. She unbuttoned the jacket to her Paquin suit of deep red wool edged in black satin and draped it carefully over a chair before returning to the bed. "We want to see how you're feeling."

"Alix is very positive about your remarkable healing powers," John said. "It all might make a great article for the *New England Journal of Medicine.*"

"I seem to be any number of things, but a medical astonishment didn't figure to be one of them," he said. "Do you think this examination will show when I can eat something besides fruit and cereal and gelatin desserts?"

"That's entirely possible." Alix smiled. "How are you feeling?"

"Hungry."

Alix threw John an amused look. "I thought you might say engaged to be married."

"So Caro told you?" Sin grinned in delight.

"If you mean the little gathering you're having at noon on Saturday, February 8th, in the Osborne; yes, she told me all about it. No, don't sit up," she

335

instructed, "stretch out, yes, just like that. For a man, you're not a bad patient."

"That's a compliment, Sin," John said as he opened the door for Dorothy and took a metal tray from her, advising her that she should have a cup of tea. "Shall we see about putting this dressing tray to good use?"

Sin tried to relax as both doctors began the examination. The covers were folded down, his pajamas displaced, and, finally, the heavy dressing taken off to reveal the healed incision. He fixed his gaze on the ornamental plaster ceiling.

"Oh, yes."

"Splendid. Really a fine job, Alix."

"I think doing needlepoint helps."

"Emily does petit point."

"That's good for a women's specialist to know."

"Would it be too much to ask what's going on?" Sin asked, exasperated and amused at the same time.

"Not at all. Your stitches are ready to come out."

"So soon?"

"I think you'll enjoy your wedding preparations and the ceremony—to say nothing of your honeymoon—without them," John said, his fine brown eyes alight with silent laughter.

"I won't complain about that."

"Good. Just relax and think about something else."

Sin tried to put himself on another level, but try as he did—and he was quite adept at rising above difficult situations—there was no way he could block out the sound of Alix and John murmuring medical things to each other, the clink of metal instruments against the tray, the snip of scissors, and the pull of the sutures as they were removed. If this was the true confirmation that he was alive and well, it was also in its own way worse than the surgery.

" 'Fair glass of light, I love you, and could still,' " he quoted.

"They say you get a vampire by driving a stake through his heart," Alix said jauntily without missing a beat. "I wonder if that holds true if one does the same with a scapel on an engaged man who quotes *Pericles*."

"Then you want me to be quiet?"

"I think that would be the best idea," Alix said as she continued with her task. "There, all done!"

"What happens now?" Sin asked when everything was back in place and Alix and John returned from the bathroom after washing their hands again.

"Well, I think we should ring for Nurse Ross," John remarked. "Then I'm going back to Stuyvesant Square and have lunch with my wife."

"And I'm going to Thurn's." Alix fastened the cuffs of her black satin blouse. "There's a Paquin model of white chiffon with gold ribbons that I want to order—plus a few other things I'll need for this summer in London."

"That isn't exactly what I meant."

Alix and John looked at each other, and after a moment's silent communication, regarded Sin.

"You might want to get out of bed now," John said. "Just for a moment, of course, so you can get your sea legs again."

"You took your time telling me that."

"It's just a little doctor's humor," Alix said as

she opened the door for Dorothy. "Since you're already sitting up in bed, why don't you swing your legs over the side?"

Sin did so, and with John's help got out of bed and tried to straighten to his full height. "I don't think I can do this. My side feels like it's going to split open."

"No, it's not." John made his voice severe. "You're in perfect condition. Now stand up straight—yes, just like that, do it slowly—and we'll walk to the window and back."

Sin's first steps were shaky, but when he reached the window, the trembling in his legs had ceased, and on retracing his steps to the bed, he was well on his way to regaining his old stride. "Success?" he questioned to applause.

"Absolute success," Alix assured him delightedly. She looked at John. "Why don't you and Dorothy go ahead downstairs? I want to have a word with Sin."

"I think now is as good a time as any to take up the matter we discussed," he agreed. "Sin, before you and Caro get married, I want to see you in my office to make sure everything is all right."

"What was that about?" Sin asked when they were alone. "Don't you want to be my doctor any longer?"

"That does have a funny sound to it." Alix closed the door and crossed the room to sit at the foot of his bed. "From now on, you're John's patient, not mine. Fortunately, the health department being what it is, not to mention official record-keeping, no one is going to ask too many questions. Still, I think it would be best if we both stayed silent about this surgical matter," she pointed out. "But that's only one thing I wanted to take up with you."

"And the other?"

"First, I want to tell you how happy I am about you and Caro."

"I love her very much."

"I know; it shows on your face."

Sin smiled. "I walked out to the Linden Trees terrace to get away from a pitiful scene, and it changed the rest of my life."

"Considering that you came pretty close to screwing it all up, I'd say that all difficulties aside—and I know you still want to find that letter—you made the right move that night."

"You seem to know some very interesting language. Did it come with the job?"

"You'd be surprised where ladies learn the language gentlemen like to think they don't know. Which brings us to the other ideas that gentlemen like to harbor. I'm not in love with you, Sin."

"I'm not quite sure what I should say to that," Sin said without any touch of levity. "You don't suffer fools—or foolish remarks—gladly. And I came pretty close to it with my peerless quote from Shakespeare. I think that from now on I'll leave the Bard of Avon to George."

"I agree with that. And I also want to be sure that you're not in conflict over how we felt about what might have happened between us seven years ago and how we regard each other now."

"Why is it that *you* can say you don't love me and

I'm not at all hurt by the revelation—yet I don't want to say the same thing to you because it seems too cruel?'' Sin held out his hand to her. "I can't say that I don't care for you, Alix.''

"And I can't say that I don't care for you." She held his hand for a long minute before letting go. "When Caro came back to Cove House and told us about meeting you, I knew I had to see you again, and it wasn't to try and find that romantic spark we lost. That's gone, and it may all be for the best, but we had to tie off the past before either of us could have a future that'll be the way we want it to be.''

"And do you think we've accomplished that.''

"I think we started to do that last Friday afternoon. The one thing I don't want you to do—that you absolutely must not do—is *ever* think that you've gone off with Caro to live a splendid life, leaving me in a corner—the poor, proverbial passed-over spinster with no one to love her.''

"Are you trying to be funny, Alix?'' Sin said as he began to laugh. "Unless the entire bachelor population suddenly turns deaf, dumb, and blind, you'll never be in any corner. And as for the 'poor' part—I've made quite a bit of money over the past few years, but you're probably richer than I am.''

Alix laughed. "I think we'll manage to be friends anyway. No lingering doubts or fantasies about my being discarded?''

"None at all.''

"Then I'll leave now. You still need your rest and I have quite a bit of shopping to do,'' Alix said as she got gracefully to her feet.

"Do you sit on the edge of men's beds all the time?" Sin inquired humorously.

"Actually, you're the first, and the next time I take up this particular position, the bed had better belong to the man I'm going to marry." She smiled at him. "Any more questions?"

"No, just one statement," Sin said quietly. "I just want to thank you for saving my life."

"Sin, do you have a middle name?" Caro asked, looking up from the most current list she was compiling. "Isn't it amazing all the odd little things one has to know before getting married?"

"Getting married seems to be an endless round of collecting odd little details no one cared about before and won't afterward." Sin, dressed in trousers and a white shirt open at the neck, and stretched out on one of the sitting room sofas, looked up from his own list. "It's Hamilton."

"That's very nice."

"It was my mother's maiden name. And since I don't want to be one of those bridegrooms to whom the entire wedding is a mystery, may I ask why this bit of trivia is going on the latest list you're making?"

"This is for our wedding announcement. There's no time for Tiffany's to cut a plate for an invitation—since our wedding is going to be small we really don't need them—so everyone is to be invited by letter, and Vanessa will mail out the announcements before we get back from our honeymoon."

"If it takes all this for a small wedding, I'm afraid to think about what a large one would involve," Sin said with a mock shudder as Caro leafed through endless sheets of stationery listing things that had to be done.

It was Monday afternoon, February third, two days after Sin's stitches had come out and five days before their wedding. Preparations for that event were well underway, and the simplicity that both Caro and Sin wanted seemed to have no relation to the amount of work involved in making sure that all ran smoothly. The ceremony would take place in the Osborne, and when the wedding breakfast was over, they would go out to Cove House for a two-week stay. It was all so simple—until it came down to listing every vital ingredient that would make it flow as flawlessly as possible.

"I could always change my mind," Caro said, fluffing out a fold of her Callot Soeurs princess dress of beige broadcloth trimmed with soutache. "Think about June, and envision a full-scale wedding with six bridesmaids and ushers and yards of lace and chiffon."

"On the other hand, none of this looks too excessive."

"Would you like to hear the form for the written invitation?"

"I'd listen to you read the instructions on a Quaker Oats carton."

"That's the nicest compliment I've had all day," Caro said, looking through her papers for the rough draft she'd used as a form for all the subsequent letters, all of which had been delivered by hand that morning.

Dear Esme—(she read)
 Sinclair and I are to be married on Saturday the eighth at noon. Of course we want you and Newton and Mallory to come and wish us luck. The ceremony and the samll breakfast will be at my stepmother's—Vanessa's—apartment at The Osborne.
 With love from us both,
 Affectionately,
 Caroline

"I can't believe this!" Sinclair's voice was outraged. "Esme Phipps is a very intelligent woman, so why is the letter filled with so many useless details—things she and all the other guests already know!" he said, flinging aside the wedding ring quilt to stand up. "I think it was easier when I used to throw all the invitations in the fireplace!"

"Let me take this opportunity to remind you that I'm the one who's going to have writer's cramp," Caro said, also standing up. "And will you please sit down? You're not supposed to be on your feet."

"I walked from the bedroom, so I suppose I can stand up if I want to," Sin said, aware that he was acting very foolishly indeed, but not quite ready to back down from his position of firm indignation.

"Of course you can stand up, if that's really what you want to do," Caro said, reading his mind with the greatest of ease, "provided that you want to kiss

343

me and not display your rempant case of bride-groom's nerves!''

His arms closed around her waist. "Is it so trans-parent?''

She melted against him. "Yes.''

"I take it you don't mind?''

"Not so you'd notice.'' Her arms tightened around his shoulders. "Feeling calmer?''

The look in Sin's eyes was unmistakable. "Not at all.''

Still holding onto each other, Sin and Caro sank down on the sofa, and without needing to exchange a word, stretched out to their full lengths, the quilt pushed aside. They nestled together, kissing and touching and letting the rest of the world go by.

"It's going to be so lovely,'' she whispered in his ear. "Two tall people like us.''

"The possibilities and the delights seem endless, but at the risk of sounding unromantic, I have to remind you that the door is unlocked.''

Caro's heart missed a beat, then raced on. This moment had been coming since they'd met on the terrace. The care and restraint they'd had to prac-tice during his recovery had served its purpose well. While they'd certainly have to be prudent, there was nothing to stop them from their natural inclination.

Sin's voice pierced her reverie. "What are you thinking about?''

Caro placed a kiss at the base of his throat. "Oh, nothing much . . . just that we're alone in the house.''

"Don't you dare joke about anything like that.''

"I'm not joking." Slowly, Caro raised her head from his shoulder, folded her arms on his chest, and looked deep into amber eyes alight with love. "Everyone else is out on one errand or another and won't be back for hours."

"How did you manage that?"

"If I could, I'd take all the credit, but it's just one of those things that happen to couples in love if they're very, very good. And I think we more than qualify."

Sin laughed; it was a joyous, carefree note not often heard even by those close to him. Love and need had suddenly been joined by merriment, and he closed his arms about Caro. "We certainly do, but are you sure?"

"That question covers an awful lot of territory."

"I wasn't referring to our making love—that's a given, the chemistry that happened between us can't be denied even if it can be delayed—I want to know if you're sure about me."

"I have been from the very first, even when all I knew was that you'd crashed a ghastly costume ball. I knew you were my man the moment I saw you, but I couldn't live with myself if you thought that I'd backed you into a corner. . . ."

His kiss effectively cut off the rest of her words, and when their embrace ended and she opened her eyes to look at him again, the deep emotions so clearly written on his face touched a responsive chord in her.

"Until I met you, I'd almost forgotten how to care, and because I was so sure I no longer had a future, I didn't believe that love was for me," he told her, knowing that in order to begin their lives together in the right way he had to bare every secret that was in his heart, and do it now. "But you changed that for me, and if that's being backed into a corner, I don't ever want to leave it. I love you, Caro, and I need you so terribly in every way. . . ."

When they reached his bedroom, Sin took the precaution of locking the door behind them. Being along together in the house was a piece of luck, but there was no reason to push it by asking for an accidental interruption.

"We have to protect our privacy," Caro said after the strong lock clicked into place. "On the other hand, we can always save our reputations by saying that you only brought me in here so I could see about your closet space."

"That sounds entirely plausible."

"Yes, but there is one slight problem," she returned lightly, her back to him as he concentrated on undoing the long row of tiny hooks and eyes that fastened her dress down the back. The sensation of his hands employed at this delicate, intimate, and telling act was making it hard for her to talk. "It's going to sound like a pretty poor explanation if we have to tell it from the middle of your bed!"

While Sin laughed, Caro slowly turned and slipped off her dress. His laughter stilled and the look on his face turned to pure appreciation as she put the dress over the nearest chair and stood in front of him clad only in her expensive, lacy, ribbon-frilled Lucile lingerie.

"I know this may be hard for you to believe, but I haven't really done this before," she said, her heart beating faster.

"I don't care either way, and you don't have to tell me anything you don't want to. I don't care if your close encounter was with Reginald or any other man."

"It was Reginald," Caro said quietly, stepping out of her handmade, honey-toned calf pumps. "But I think Americans and Europeans who live in the Orient often enter into relationships—engagements, marriages and other alliances—because we *are* aliens there, and sometimes it gets to be too much to bear. And I was curious."

"I was waiting for that."

"And you don't have to smile as though you knew all along."

"Considering my present condition, I might want to know my past competition. But why didn't you go through with it? It wasn't because you were afraid."

Caro looked at him through her lashes. "Because the closer we got, the more it was like attending the Grand Kabuki Theatre for the first time—not unpleasant, interesting in its own way, but not generating much warmth. I also have to say that no matter what your present condition is, you don't have much competition."

"I'm fairly sure that I can do better than the Kabuki . . . something along the lines of a musical comedy.''

''I do think Broadway is the best theatre of all,'' Caro said, holding out her arms to him.

They were laughing, delighted with each other and with their love. The anticipation and excitement was building, but it also seemed like the most natural thing in the world that they were together. It would have been right weeks ago, it would have been right if they wanted to wait until their wedding night, but every couple has to determine when the best time is to realize their love, and this was their moment.

The nearness of each other was still intoxicating, and for a long time they stood locked in an embrace. Sin's senses were whirling, and the ache within him had nothing to do with the discomfort and pain of the past weeks. He had been prepared to face this with equanimity, not to expect too much too soon, but his response had been immediate and ardent, leaving him feeling just a little bit uncertain.

''I don't want to frighten or disconcert you,'' he whispered huskily, his hands caressing her back, ''but I've wanted you for so long.''

At his touch, Caro arched closer to him. His cool skin was warming, expanding, and she knew he was ready to love her. ''And I want you, too,'' she said, pulling back just enough so that she could begin to undo the buttons on his shirt.

Sin helped her with the shirt buttons, his own fingers somewhat unsteady. ''I feel as if I were back in college.''

348

"I don't think what you know is described in Columbia's course catalog."

"At college they instill in bright young men a notion that the best experiences are gained outside the classroom." His shirt was on the floor and he bent his head over her camisole, his fingers tangling in the profusion of ribbons and lace. "Since this is about the time when a husband-to-be confesses his past, I have to admit that I've done more than my share of outside study."

"All in very interesting places, I'm sure," Caro said, a wave of excitement filling her. "But we have plenty of time to talk about that later."

Garment by garment, their clothes fell away. "I forget that I'm no mystery to you," he said quietly, his eyes full of love, "but you're the most wonderful surprise to me."

Gently, but with no shyness, her fingers traced the long scar that stretched along his right side. "Does this bother you?"

"No, I think of this as a very necessary cut—and as a reminder of things won and almost lost," he said, taking her into his arms, his mouth claiming hers.

Their breathing changed, becoming fast and hot, and she moved deeper into his embrace. A new wave of passion swept over them as they kissed, and fused together, they fell to the bed. Caro pulled him close, touching every inch of skin that she could reach. He took the pins from her hair, smoothing out each silky brown strand. His tongue met hers with an explorer's touch. This was the first performance in an act that would, with slight variations, always be theirs, and he took his time, letting his hands learn every curve.

Caro moved beneath him, urging him on, caressing his neck and shoulders and back. His mouth moved from her lips to her forehead, to her hair, and finally to the base of her throat. His hands traced a course from her shoulders to her breasts, cupping one heavy globe and then the other, the tips hardening instantly at his touch.

"Oh, Caroline, I love you so much," he murmured as their arms and legs entwined.

She welcomed the more intimate embrace with a renewed burst of joy. His hands slid around and down her back and beneath her hips, lifting her toward him. Eagerly she opened herself for him, calling his name as he rotated and thrust inside her.

"I love you, Sinclair," she whispered over and over as their rhythm increased, pushing them closer and closer to the ultimate crescendo. They reached it together in a sunburst of passion and emotion that promised everything to them. The valley was behind them and they would only have new and greater heights to scale together.

"I have to tell you something," Caro said a long time later as she lay with her head against Sin's shoulder. "I saw your portrait."

"The Eakins?"

"Are you going to tell me there's another one?"

"No, but when you said you had something to

tell me, my male ego got very nervous." His lips brushed against her forehead. "Did you think I could put on white tie and tails in broad daylight to stand motionless for another artist?"

"Men, when they're having a fit of vanity, will do all sorts of things," she returned, and Sin laughed, pulling her closer into his embrace. "And you forgot to include the opera cape you had on."

"That was Eakins' touch. He's a brilliant artist— one who sees just a bit too much."

"After we're married, will you take it out of storage?"

"If we hang it, we'll frighten all our guests."

"No, they'll stand in front of it and be awestruck."

"If I knew I was going to get compliments like this, I'd have proposed to you over lunch at Roversi's," he said, kissing her hair.

"I was referring to Thomas Eakins' talent and skill as an artist," Caro teased, turning over so she could look at his face. "But on second thought, my new lover and husband-to-be does have certain redeeming good looks!"

Laughter bubbled up between them, and then another emotion, another need, came to the surface. For a long minute they looked at each other. By silent agreement, they knew they now had all the time in the world for each other, that now that they knew each other, there was no need to rush.

"I don't want to raise my voice or even say too much," he told her softly.

Caro pulled him to her. "I won't shatter into a million pieces," she promised.

"All I want to do is love you."

"I return that sentiment, and it's one we're never going to get tired of telling each other."

She turned toward him and moved his side of the sheet slowly downward until more of his body was revealed to her gaze. Not even the slashing, puckered scar could mar his perfection.

"John said that eventually some of it will fade out, but that it might take a couple of years," he said quietly, not taking his eyes from her face.

"I don't care," Caro said as one hand trailed downward, "as long as I'm the only woman who'll see it from now on."

"I promise you that," he whispered, his voice growing husky as her hand come to rest on the closed incision.

Her hand between them, she swayed closer to him, gently pressing against him, waiting for him to make the next move. She heard him catch his breath, and then he pulled her effortlessly against him.

Her body fit to his, and their heartbeats matched as they held each other. "I love you," he said, his fingers running through the soft waves of her hair.

With a gentle motion he traced her cheekbones, her lips, and the length of her neck. "I belong only to you," he promised as his hands cupped her breasts. Going from one to the other, he traced their outline, and then in turn captured each taunt tip in his mouth.

A new desire raced through Caro with each touch.

One hand moved lower, and he caressed the soft, sensitive skin where her hips and thighs met. Reacting instantly, her body arched to meet his.

Moving with exquisite grace, she brought both hands up his back and kissed him with a languid sensuality. There was no immediate need to rush; for this moment they could take all the time they wanted to explore and enjoy and excite.

"Oh, Sinclair," she murmured as he gently pressed her back against the pillows.

"Do you want me now, Caroline? I have to know."

"Oh. . . . "

"Tell me now, darling."

"Oh, yes. . . . yes!"

They had climbed the peak of passion slowly, each giving the other time to adjust, but now there were no more plateaus. Ecstasy quivered through her as his hands parted her thighs and his body pressed into hers. There were still undreamed-of heights to be reached, and each strong thrust of his body took her higher. Somewhere in the deepest recesses of her mind it registered that they were like an orchestra of two, each so finely attuned to the other that together—in whatever they chose to do—there was nothing they couldn't accomplish.

"There are a lot of things we have to talk about," Sin said quietly after a while, a serious expression coming over his patrician features as he turned on his side to face her. "Tomorrow at about eleven, a man from Tiffany's will be here so you can pick out your engagement ring."

"Yes, of course. And I want you to know right now that I intend to select something very impressive," Caro said, instantly sure that he was leading up to something important. "Does what you really want to say relate to this somehow?"

"I've been doing a lot of thinking over the past weekend, and I came to a conclusion I honestly thought I'd never reach. Caro, when we get married would you mind if we lived somewhere other than here?"

Of all the serious questions he could have asked her, Caro knew, this was not about to raise any deep conflict in her. But Sin had obviously struggled long and hard with this, and the first thing she had to do was reassure him and back up his choice.

"I wouldn't mind living somewhere else at all. My home is going to be with you," she told him feelingly. "You know I've grown very fond of this house, but I don't have any particular attachment to it. In fact," she continued in a low voice, "I wouldn't be too surprised if you've also been thinking a bit ahead to consider the possibility of our leaving New York when all this is over."

"When all what is over?" Sin asked a little warily as a different light came into his eyes.

"When we find the missing letter and clear your father's name."

Sin sank back against the pillows, momentarily at a loss for words. "I *have* been thinking that we may do just that, whether or not we find that letter—provided it still exists."

"Oh, it still exists. We just have to find it."

"When you put it like that," Sin said slowly, starting to smile as he took her into his arms, "I can actually believe again that we're going to do just that."

"And the rest of it?"

"I think any further discussions and decisions can wait a while longer. It's not as if we have a lot of family to take into consideration."

"Sin, *do* you have any family left?" she questioned, curious. "I meant to ask you earlier while I was busy with my lists, but. . . . "

"But a few things got in the way," Sin finished, kissing her for added emphasis. "And I do have a second cousin who's a rather important business leader in New Orleans. I don't think Stanley would be adverse to claiming me, but his wife's quite another story. If I turned up at the door of her Garden District house, she'd probably call the police. So I guess the answer is no, after all. No family."

He spoke without rancor or regret, but Caro was still compelled to comfort him in the best way she knew. It wasn't that she believed all family had to be endured (if not embraced) no matter what, but she couldn't bear Sin's being made to feel an outcast by one more social climber. Those days were over forever, and she wanted the man she loved to know that she was at his side.

* * *

Surprisingly, it didn't take too long for them to get dressed again, and once the bed was smoothed down, they were ready to return to the sitting room.

"Do you think anyone will suspect what we've been up to?" Caro asked, stepping into her shoes.

Sin rolled back his sleeves. "We look perfectly proper and respectable, which means that they'll guess in about two minutes flat."

"I thought so. . . . not that is matters."

They smiled at each other the secret smile of true lovers.

"I think we still have a few minutes," Sin said, holding out a hand to her. "Will you sit down in that chair by the window? I have something to give you."

She made herself comfortable on the silk-covered bergère and watched while Sin removed a small painting from the wall to reveal a safe. "Somehow I knew you'd have one of those."

"All the best people do," he replied dryly, spinning the lock and pulling the handle. "Here we are. Something that's been a waiting a long time to belong to you," Sin went on, withdrawing a large black leather case from the safe.

It was a jewel box, and when Sin placed it in her lap, she saw the initials L.H.P. stamped in gold in the lower right-hand corner.

"This belonged to your mother," she said feelingly, reaching out to touch Sin's face as he crouched in front of her, just the way he had the first time she came to Prince Street. "I really don't know what to say. . . ."

"All you have to do is open it," he said tenderly, handing her a tiny gold key. "I haven't looked inside for years, so it'll be just as much of a surprise for me as it is for you. Of course, I had to sell some of it, but it was only the larger pieces, the ones for show, not sentiment. The jewelry my mother loved is still here."

Exercising the greatest of care, Caro opened the lock and lifted the lid. The deep case, lined in faded cream silk, was divided by a seemingly endless series of black velvet-padded trays which held Laura Hamilton Poole's collection of jewelry. The first pieces included a quartet of elegant gold bangle bracelets, an enamel butterfly brooch studded with diamonds, pearls, and sapphires, and an old-fashioned chantelain bracelet of gold set with pearls, onyx, pink sapphires, and diamonds. The next level revealed an emerald bead necklace; a Victorian necklace made to encircle the base of the throat and set with rubies, sapphires, and yellow diamonds; a pearl-and-beryl choker; and a gold, diamond, and tourmaline bracelet. The most impressive pieces came last, and in turn Caro lifted out a pink sapphire-and-diamond necklace with matching bracelets; a pearl-and-diamond choker with a diamond baguette center; and a delicately designed diamond tiara.

"This is all so beautiful," she said at last, blinking back tears so her eye black wouldn't run. "I'm so proud to have this."

"And I'm very proud to be able to give it to you," he said in a choked voice, not needing to add that under another set of circumstances, this jewelry would have been her legacy from him. "If it hadn't been for you, I wouldn't—"

"Don't say that, not ever again!" Caro cried. She leaned forward and put her arms around him. "It's all over, and we have too much to do together without bringing up something that didn't happen."

One by one, the black velvet trays slipped from her lap to the floor, but neither of them noticed the array of precious jewels spilling out on the fine Oriental rug. With her arms around his neck, Caro slid off the chair. For a moment they stayed on their knees, holding each other close, reveling in the deep emotions raised by this embrace. Slowly, they sat down with their backs against the *toile de Jouy*-covered wall.

"I think leaving certain parts of the past behind us is the best thing we can do," Sin murmured, his lips against her ear.

"It's the right way to start the sort of marriage we're going to have. If we don't leave the trivial behind us, we won't be able to accomplish the major things," Caro said, stroking the back of his neck. "Is that one of the reasons why you want to move after we're married?"

"When I lived here, it was because I needed a clean break with the past before I could undertake clearing my father's name. I also had to live someplace where I wouldn't be noticed. But now I need another sort of break: new home, furniture I haven't been sitting on and looking at since 1895, even new china and silver and crystal."

"I was wondering how Tiffany's tied into this.

After lunch, we'll ring them up and request additional salesmen for tomorrow.''

"They can keep each other company on the ride from Union Square—and to the bank to deposit their sizable commissions.''

"I just bet they will.'' She kissed him under an ear. "We have to pick up the jewelry.''

"In a minute,'' he said, pulling her closer. "I want to tell you again how much I love you. . . . ''

It was truly a stolen moment, one that would have to last until their wedding night, but it would make their next encounter all the more important. Their love was an affirmation, one made in joy and certainty. The only people they had to please were themselves, and even without putting it into words, they understood that if they failed in finding the missing letter, what they meant to each other would surmount any disappointment and take them on to other triumphs.

Chapter Seventeen

" 'O most corageous day! O most happy hour!" '
George stood by his place, his champagne glass held
high in his hand, twenty-one pairs of eyes fixed on
him as he quoted from *A Midsummer's Night Dream*.
"To our bride and groom, Caroline and Sinclair,
Mr. and Mrs. Poole!"

"Here, here!"

"Best wishes always!"

"To our bride and groom!"

"To Sin and Caro, with all our love!"

The exclamations of congratulations were followed swiftly by the sound's of Baccarat crystal flutes
filled with Moët & Chandon 1897 touched one to
the other along the lavishly set dining room table in
the Worths' apartment.

It was half-past twelve on Saturday afternoon,
February 8th, and just a half-hour before in the
drawing room, Reverend George Houghton, the
rector of the Little Church Around the Corner, had

married Caroline Worth and Sinclair Poole while those closest to them looked on.

The flowers Sin had selected for Caro's bouquet—white perfumer's roses, lilies of the valley, and freesia—were repeated in vast arrangements in Baccarat vases placed around the drawing room and dining room, as well as in the large but low centerpieces on the table. A French Chamber music ensemble had been engaged and was seated between the two rooms. They played Vivaldi's *Four Seasons* to welcome the guests and Mendelssohn's *A Midsummer Night's Dream* just prior to and following the ceremony, and now, as the wedding breakfast was about to start, the selection was Handel's *Water Music*. The table had all the leaves put in it, not so much for the number of guests, but so that no one would feel crowded among all the silver, crystal, and bone china settings that made the table look its most lavish.

"This is the perfect setting for you," Sin whispered in her ear while the toasts continued. "You're a beautiful bride."

"As long as I'm your bride, I wouldn't care what I was getting married in." Caro didn't have either the taste or the inclination for the traditional wedding gown with its accompanying yards of heirloom lace. Since the wedding took place at home and was not very large, Caro decided to take advantage of the leeway permissable under the circumstances. Thurn's, as usual, had come through with exactly the dress for her. From their extensive stock of Paris imports, she had selected a Paquin model of pure ivory satin appliqued in gold satin which, the saleswoman assured her, hadn't been ordered by anyone else because it was too elaborate to be just another afternoon dress and not quite complicated enough for evening wear.

"I think by the time our friends have finished toasting us, this dress will be out of style!" she whispered in Sin's ear.

He swallowed his laughter. "And if not that, we might end up missing our train. But somehow I don't seem to find myself minding it very much," Sin went on, looking at the cheerful group seated around the table.

Vanessa, looking splendid in Paquin's afternoon dress of jade green and royal blue changeable silk, was finishing her toast. ". . . . my darling stepdaughter, Caroline, for not only knowing the right man as soon as she met him, but for sparing all of us the rigors of one of those relentlessly large weddings." She raised her champagne glass. "To Caroline and Sinclair!"

When the table was quiet again, Cliff rose to his feet. "Since we all want to get to the wedding feast that Mrs. Cavendish and Mr. Wong have collaborated on, I'm going to make my toast as short as I can," he said, finishing to shouts of laughter. "I might make some pithy comments about my friend Sinclair, who needed two best men today in order to become a proper married man, but since Greg and I did our job of supporting him through the ceremony, I'll let all of that pass and simply offer my toast that he and Caro know every happiness together."

This time the toast was greeted with a smattering of applause, and Vanessa signaled to Cavendish that it was time to serve the first course in the meal that was a true collaboration between both households, with a little outside help. Gregori and George were both guests with nothing more to do than enjoy themselves on this happy occasion, but Sean was doubling as a footman, Vic was in charge of opening the countless bottles of champagne that had been put on ice, and Mrs. Murphy, who had lovingly ironed all the table linen, was working as the sous-chef to Mrs. Cavendish and Mr. Wong. Alix had provided her Doris, and Megan had volunteered her Martha to help Sean serve the table under Cavendish's watchful eye, but the agreement between the two cooks was worthy of consideration by the Nobel committee.

The caviar canapes had been ordered from Sherry's. Mr. Wong had taken over the preparation of the main course so Mrs. Cavendish could prepare the soup and devote herself to the wedding cake. He also prepared all the miniature petits fours and bonbons and glacéed fruits that would fill the silver baskets and tiered dishes that would be brought out at the end of the celebration.

"Are you looking forward to moving into your new apartment?" Thea asked. Caro's sole attendant was resplendent in a Lucile afternoon dress of pintucked ice-blue watered silk with insets and panels of ivory lace and bands of turquoise velvet. "I love 667 Madison Avenue."

"I couldn't believe it when the real estate agent

told us the building was ready for occupancy," Caro said as Sean, Doris, and Martha moved around the table serving the turtle soup.

"As much as I could tell from the floor plan, it seems to be just perfect for us," Sin added. A small part of him was still regarding the major events of the past weeks with sense of wonderment. He had come through his illness and surgery and now he was sitting here with Caro, celebrating their marriage. A wellspring of happiness bubbled up in him, banishing six years of isolation and estrangement. He was here among people—friends—most of whom he hadn't seen in years, and it was if nothing had changed. "But modern architecture can be very startling, and the rooms are rather large."

"When it's furnished, you'll love it," Caro advised gently.

"I'm sure I will. It's just the idea of change that I have to get used to."

"You'll be amazed how quickly you not only adjust to all the changes, but actually enjoy them," Dick offered wisely.

There was more laughter around the table, and as the soup was replaced by the main course, the conversation turned to all New Yorkers' favorite topic of discussion—real estate. The tender stuffed breast of veal accompanied by *pommes duchesse* and asparagus tips was greatly appreciated and fueled the talk about the city's newest apartment buildings, the elegant townhouses gracing the side streets in the Sixties from Fifth Avenue to Madison Avenue, and the continuing mode for the more showy millionaires to build their Fifth Avenue mansions in the style of Europe's chateaux.

To be sure, this was not the usual wedding breakfast conversation, but this was a highly convivial group with a wide range of interests. The bond of friendship around the table was as strong as the bond of love and flexible enough to include Gregori and George. The rule of the day was to toast the bridal couple with a steady stream of champagne, enjoy the assortment of superbly prepared food, and dissect whatever topics interested them. Since happiness was also of the utmost importance today, politics and any other controversial matters were left untouched in favor of such topics as the current theatre season, the growing importance of the motor car, new restaurants, and the popularity of visiting California.

"I think Caro would like a wedding trip out to the West Coast," Sin said lovingly. "We'll go in a few months when we've settled one or two matters."

It was quite unnecessary for him to say what those matters were. When they returned from Cove House in time to attend Nan and Drake's wedding, there would be the usual invitations extended to all newly married couples. It was expected that those first requests would come mainly from those invited today, but with any luck, those circles—as Caro and Alix had discussed weeks before—would widen into other circles until once again Sinclair Poole was invited everywhere without either question or comment.

"It sounds like a very good idea." Alix was distinctively turned out in a Lucile creation of blue and silver shot-taffeta with a vest and sleeve puffs of blue mousseline de soie. "With the coronation this summer, it's all going to be the biggest crush imaginable."

"Not that that's going to stop us from having a simply wonderful time!" Angela Dalton, her champagne-blonde elegance set off by a Lucile afternoon dress of lavender silk with a belt of dark lavender and violet satin ribbon, exchanged amused and knowing looks with her friend Alix in the understanding of the wide social swath they were planning to cut during London's famous Season.

"I'm very much afraid that young people mean something quite different when they announce they're about to have a simply wonderful time than I used to when I was younger," Evangeline Dalton remarked with a smile that made it quite clear she really wasn't making any objection.

"And, naturally, that expression meant yet another thing from what it did at the time I used to say it," Kathryn Neal put in, her smile holding the same delight as her daughter, Evangeline, and granddaughter, Angela. "This is one of the endless changes that the generations undergo."

"But the one thing that will never change," Adele Seligman said, "is that you never ask what the bride and groom mean when they say they've had a wonderful time!"

Everyone finished eating, and the air of expectancy around the table moved to a higher pitch. It was time for dessert, and that meant it was time to bring in the wedding cake. The entire kitchen staff wheeled it in on a serving cart, and it well deserved the oohs and ahhs its appearance elicited. Four tiers high and richly frosted and decorated, it was the archtypal wedding cake: far too rich, too decorated, too representative of a tradition where form was more important than substance—and Sin and Caro loved it.

"It's almost too pretty to cut," Caro observed as they stood up. "Mrs. Cavendish, you've outdone yourself!"

"We couldn't be more delighted," Sin added, surprising the already delighted Englishwoman by kissing her lightly on the cheek. "Anything this beautiful on the outside has to be equally special inside."

Mrs. Cavendish had been made aware of the strong dislike both Caro and Sin had for any sort of fruitcake, but she staunchly refused to reveal what she would make in its place, informing them that it wouldn't be proper for them to know beforehand. Now, as the silver cake knife they held together cut through the perfect buttercream frosting, a rich white cake with great ribbons of color running through it was revealed.

The cake was served along with vanilla and strawberry ice cream frozen in heart-shaped molds that had been ordered from Dean's, and the fresh supply of champagne assured a new round of toasts. These were delivered with great good nature, love, and wit, leaving everyone at the table laughing.

Finally, the last of the champagne was drunk, the cake and ice cream eaten, and the silver baskets filled with bonbons and brandy-soaked, fondant-frosted petits fours and glacéed fruit emptied. With reluctant sighs, everyone rose from the table.

Joseph Byron, the city's leading photographer, was waiting patiently in the drawing room, his photographic equipment set up to take pictures of the bridal party. With great skill on his part and eagerness on the part of the guests, he photographed everyone in a variety of shots. During the sittings, those who weren't involved took the opportunity to wander over to the library for another look at the wedding presents. Arranged on tables draped in white linen were lavish offerings of china, crystal, and silver, with several paintings displayed on easels.

The photographer's last flash was even more of a signal than the clock, and the newly married couple went off to get ready to leave. Accompanied by every female guest, from Alix's sixteen-year-old cousin, Mallory, to the seventyish (but youthful) Kathryn Neal, Caro returned to her bedroom for the last time on her wedding day.

"I'm glad I don't have too much to change," she said, taking off a rope of pearls and diamonds that had belonged to her mother. She lay them carefully on her dressing table before turning around so her dress could be unhooked. "I love all of you, but I love Sinclair more, and I can't wait for us to be on our way."

"Well, don't think anyone here is going to hold that against you," Vanessa said, and the other women concurred.

Caro sat down on her bed, pulled off her white

satin opera pumps with full Louis heels, and unhooked her white silk-and-lace wedding stockings.
When her flesh-colored silk stockings and high-
heeled black calf pumps were on, she stood up. "Everything seems to take so long," she joked, well
aware that this task had taken almost no time at all.

"I'm sure Sin thinks you've been in here for *ages*
already," Alix said with a wicked gleam in her eye.

"We'll make our train with plenty of time to
spare."

"That's not why he thinks you're taking too
long."

"I know."

Her going-away outfit was a Doucet suit of crim-
son wool trimmed with black silk faille, worn with
an ecru crepe-de-chine blouse with insets of Valen-
ciennes lace. It elicited a number of compliments,
and all that remained for Caro to do was fix her
maquillage, dab on some more Jicky, and put on
her sable toque.

"Adele, we can't thank you and Bill enough for
giving us Cove House for two weeks."

"It's our pleasure. We want you and Sinclair to
start your married life in the best way possible."

One by one, Caro embraced all her friends, and
when they left, she put her arms around Vanessa.
"It seems like we only just moved in here, Mummy,
and now I've married my way out."

"Let's just say this is a marrying apartment,"
Vanessa said, and for a moment her distinctive voice
quavered with emotion. "You're a beautiful bride,

just as I always knew you would be—and this time you picked the right man."

At this subtle reference to her broken engagement, the air of tension between them dissolved. "I thought you'd say something like that."

"It's just a knack I seem to have," Vanessa said with teasing modesty. "But now is not the time for us to chat. You've taken quite long enough, and men simply do not hold up too well on their wedding day."

"Be serious, Mummy."

"Oh, I am. And Sin is still recovering, so he needs a lot of tender care."

"Which is exactly what I intend to give him."

Their luggage had gone out to Long Island the day before, Caro's Louis Vuitton dressing case was already downstairs in the brougham, and all that remained was for her to put on Sin's wedding present to her—a full-length sable cloak. She picked up her handbag and her wedding bouquet.

"White flowers in February," she said, taking a deep breath, savoring their rich fragrance. "We must have driven every florist in New York wild."

"Just about."

"I love you, Mummy."

"I love you, too."

"We're going to find that missing letter," she said, speaking on a wave of certainty. "Sin's going to restore his father's good name and take back the companies that were stolen from him. But even if he doesn't," she went on, "we're still going to be supremely happy together."

"Why, of course you are," Vanessa replied as she opened the bedroom door. "From the moment I saw the two of you together, I never had a doubt that you both could carry off anything you had to."

Getting away from their friends proved to be yet another pleasant experience in the progress of their wedding day. No one wanted to detain them unduly, since there was a train to catch, but there had to be one last round of embraces and congratulations before Caro and Sin were allowed to leave the apartment and enter an elevator car. Alone except for the operator, they progressed to the lobby at a stately pace, while everyone else—depending on age and inclination—came downstairs in the other elevators or took to the stairs. Finally, there was the joyous rush across the mosaic-tiled library and out through the door onto West Fifty-seventh Street.

"Alix, catch!" With an expert toss, Caro flipped her bouquet toward her friend, who caught it with equal expertise.

"What am I supposed to do with this?" she asked as they all gathered on the sidewalk. "It's never done me any good before."

"It will now," Caro said confidently as they stood beside the brougham, and smiling Lawton holding the door open.

"George, we need you to send us off with an appropriate quote," Sin said. "What do you have for a bridal couple?"

"I believe that *A Winter's Tale* said it best," George

372

said as once more all attention—both guests and passers-by were drawn to the scene—was focused on him. " 'When you do dance, I wish you a wave o' the sea, that you might ever do nothing but that.' "

They made the train to Long Island with time to spare. The trip itself was uneventful, and when Sin and Caro stepped down from the parlor car and onto the platform at the Woodbury station, Dugan, the Seligman's country coachman, was waiting for them. Both were too ecstatic, too lost in the joy of being newly married to have minded the long trip or the cold of the country air on a winter night, but they were very appreciative of both the heated brougham and the mink-lined lap robe waiting for them, and, when they arrived at Cove House, by the sight of all the servants lined up to greet them in the entry hall.

"The last time I was here, it was full of scaffolds and construction men and painters and plasterers," Sin said, wonder in his voice as he looked around him. Unlike many other estates, Cove House, although written about, had never had its interior photographed, so his remembrance of it ws fixed at the time of his first and only visit, when it was still under construction. "Cliff dragged me out here to have a look, but I never thought it would look like this," he told Caro. "Do I need a map?"

"Not when you have me," she said, gracefully surrendering her sable to the waiting maid and pulling off her gloves. "Tomorrow we'll take the grand tour, but now—'' She turned to Rogers, elderly but not at all fragile, who waited with calm dignity for both questions and instructions. ''I suppose all sorts of wonderful arrangements have been made for us?''

''I trust both you and Mr. Poole will find them so, Madam. Mr. and Mrs. Clifford spent last week-end here, seeing to everything,'' he told them with great dignity, ushering them from the entry foyer to the main hall. ''Dinner is ready whenever you want it.''

''I think we'd like to wash off some of the Long Island Railroad first,'' Sin smiled. ''If you'll show us upstairs, Rogers, we won't have to keep the kitchen staff stirring and reheating all night.''

With tact and discretion and fully aware of the sensitivities of newlywed couples, Rogers escorted them to the second floor and left them at their door.

''Alone at last,'' he said in an exaggerated stage whisper.

''Almost but not quite,'' she whispered back, standing close to him. ''I have a sneaking suspicion that Rogers is lurking nearby so he can report to the other servants whether or not you carried me over the threshold!''

Sin laughed quietly. ''I wouldn't want to let any-one down.''

''And since I don't want to do that either, I'll let that pun pass,'' she replied, struggling to keep her own merriment under control.

''Well, in that case. . . . ''

The bedroom in which Caro and Sin found them-selves was one of a series of big, beautiful rooms rich with architectural details that were given to the "young marrieds." Large enough to be half sitting-room, half bedroom, the walls and elegant plaster moldings were painted a whipped-cream white that was a perfect foil for the furnishings. Soft Impressionist watercolors in gold-painted frames hung over delicate French Regency chests and Adam sidechairs with pale blue silk seats. A choice collection of delicate Staffordshire figurines were lined up on the marble mantle under a gold-framed mirror, and diamond-cut crystal vases were tightly packed with pink roses and violets.

"From now on," Caro said, "whenever we come to Cove House, this is going to be our room."

"I guess this is another part of what being married is," Sin said, his voice reflective as he sank slowly into a wing chair covered in a delicate dogwood print on one side of the fireplace. "It's like link after link in a never-ending chain of friendship. Caro, am I making any sense, or do I sound as if I'm suffering the aftereffects of all the champagne we drank?"

"No, Sin, as far as I'm concerned, you're making absolutely perfect sense." The look in his amber eyes struck a vital chord in her, and she crossed the room to sit in his lap, winding her arms around his neck and nestling close to him. "I want to be your wife as much as you want to be my husband, and even though the legal act is very simple, it doesn't prevent our collecting a whole new set of responsibilities."

Sin's lips brushed against her ear. "Some of those

responsibilities seem rather nice. . . . particularly the one over there.''

Caro followed his gaze to the other side of the room. The bed was large, piled high with pillows, curtained in the same heavy white silk that surrounded the large windows, and looked very, very inviting. ''I was waiting for you to notice that.''

''Even in my poor befuddled state as a newly married man, the sight of our first bed as husband and wife was bound to register at some point.'' He nuzzled against her neck until she began to laugh. ''I don't suppose. . . . ''

''It's only eight o'clock. Now that's not too early for me, but we can't shock the servants. They want to see some more romance before we go on to. . . . *other things.*''

He kissed her. ''Do you have some suggestions?''

''As a matter of fact, I do,'' she said, and returned his kiss. ''First of all, why don't you light the fire that's already laid, and then you can soak off some of our trip. Your dressing room and bathroom are to the right of the bed, and unless Rogers is slipping up on his duties, your pajamas and dressing gown will be waiting for you. Whoever is ready first will ring for dinner. Agreed?''

It sounded like a fine agreement to Sin, and as he soaked in the deep marble tub, the hot water easing muscles made tense by the train trip and the cold, he began to realize that Caro, without a touch of bossiness, had made the best decision possible for them. A little privacy was just what they needed right now—an interval between the earlier part of the day and their first night together as husband and wife.

When he returned to the bedroom, he found that Caro had already made some subtle but welcome changes. All the lamps were turned on, the fire was burning brightly in the marble fireplace, and their dinner was set out on the low table between the wing chair and the deep-pillowed loveseat covered in white ottoman silk. He waited patiently until Caro ushered Mrs. Rogers out of the room.

"It all looks wonderful."

Caro leaned against the door and smiled. "Why do I have the feeling that you're not referring to either the room or our dinner?"

"I'm not." His pause was meaningful. "You look absolutely beautiful."

"I could get away with wearing white to get married in, but I thought it would be a bit much for tonight," she laughed, spinning around so he could enjoy the full effect of her Lucile nightgown and negligee of pale pink hammered satin edged in dark pink satin ribbon. "It's very simple, so it's all in the fit," Caro said as her final turn ended in Sin's embrace.

"I thought it was something like that," he said, capturing her in his arms. He trailed a row of kisses from the base of her throat to her lips, breathing in the rich scent of Jicky until his senses began to swirl from the combination of her perfume and the feel of her body beneath the layers of satin. "I have something terrible to tell you."

"What?" she asked, gasping a little from the intensity of his embrace and his kisses. "You want to confess you married me for my money?"

"Worse." He kissed her again. "I'm hungry."

Caro hung onto his shoulders while she laughed. "Oh, that's all right—so am I."

"I take it our meal is hot?"

"It certainly is, and the champagne is cold." She nibbled gently on an earlobe. "Are you sure you can wait?"

"Only if I regard anticipation as an additional course."

The two-tiered serving cart and the low table in front of the fireplace were both covered with a variety of serving dishes, utensils, china, silver, and crystal, and a silver ice bucket held two bottles of champagne. The arrangement was undeniably inviting, and Sin sank down in a corner of the loveseat while Caro fussed at the serving cart.

"I don't suppose I can count on being catered to on a regular basis?" he teased.

"Not like this, so if you have any harem fantasies about being waited on by nubile servant girls, this is the closest you're going to get to it," she returned in the same tone of voice.

"I don't have any particular interest in nubile servant girls—not when I have you."

"Now *that's* the right thing to say, and for your first reward, you get to open this," Caro said, seizing a bottle of champagne by its foil-wrapped neck and holding it out to Sin.

The cork slid out under his skillful handling, and in a short time they were settled on the loveseat for the dinner Julie had planned for them. It was perfect for a new couple who were just married and just off a winter train trip. First there was a fruit cup that combined slices of orange, pear, melon, apple and hothouse strawberries; and this was followed by a rich, hot oyster stew. They ate every piece of fruit, scraped the soup tureen for the last drops of stew, demolished the long loaf of warm French bread spread with butter, and finished half a bottle of the Moët.

"Open the other bottle," Caro said as she put two long-stemmed dishes heaped with chocolate mousse and topped with whipped cream in front of them. "It's a surprise from Julie and Cliff."

"How do you know about it if it's supposed to be a surprise?"

"Julie thinks that new husbands can't absorb too many details on their wedding nights."

"She's probably right. Let's see what this is. It's. . . . a bottle of pink champagne." He faced her, bottle in hand. "Do you know about this?" he demanded, barely keeping his laughter in check.

"Of course. Do you have some objection to pink champagne, or is there a risqué memory attached to the last time you drank it?"

Sin laughed. "If this were the last time and you were wearing shoes, I'd have to offer to drink it out of your slipper," he said, throwing a damask napkin over the cork and expertly working it out. "Other than that, a bridegroom has to have a few secrets."

"What is it about chocolate and champagne that make such an irresistible combination?" Caro asked some time later when all the mousse was eaten and they were in each other's arms, stretched out on the loveseat, their long legs balanced on the rolled arm.

"I think it might have to do with the fact that it's a childhood treat and an adult treat combined, and if the occasion happens to be a very special one," he replied as they nestled together, "everything gets better and better."

"From now on, for every anniversary, we're going to lock ourselves in our room with a bottle of pink champagne and a box of expensive chocolates."

"No mousse?"

Caro moved closer against him. "Variety."

"Oh." Sin wove his fingers through Caro's, letting one digit move over the surface of her fourteen-carat emerald-cut diamond engagement ring.

"I couldn't resist it," she murmured. "When I first saw it set out on that black velvet pad, I knew it was the ring for me. I want everyone to know that I have you."

"When Mr. Napier unpacked his treasures and I saw this ring, it was the one I wanted you to have." His free hand moved along her back, molding her to him. "Shall we turn out the light and see if it'll double as a lantern?"

"I thought you were never going to ask," she said, and reached up to turn off the lamp closest to them, the only one in the sitting room area left on, giving Sin an entirely new view of her full, high bosom. "Isn't it a good thing that we put everything back on the serving cart and left it outside?"

"And now we'll just see if I can carry you and pull the bell at the same time."

"Sin, your side. . . . you don't have to carry me."

"Tonight I do." With great tenderness and care he put one arm under her shoulders, the other under her knees, and lifted her into his arms. Pausing only long enough to press the button that would summon a servant to take away the cart in the hallway, he carried her across the room toward to bed.

Caro closed her eyes for a moment as her body was set down on the elaborately made-up bed, and she opened them again to watch as Sin removed his night clothes. His heavy silk dressing gown was followed by his pajamas, and she feasted on the sight of his lithe, powerful body. She held out her arms to him, and the next moment they were together between the handmade sheets.

His arms closed around her, and there was a new feeling of perfection. They fit together in a way that would never change no matter how much everything else did.

"There's not so much to unwrap this time," she whispered as he freed her of her negligee and night-gown.

"But you're still the best present I've ever had, the one I treasure above all." Sin's hands caressed her back and shoulders, gently moving up and down until she felt like purring. His hands moved forward to cup her breasts, swirling invisible patterns on them before he lowered his head to the coral tips that responded instantly to his touch. "You smell so delicious," he whispered at last, and his tongue traced the outline of her lips. "I'm lost in your perfume."

If she turned her head to the side, she could see the window and the snow falling, and it was as if she could identify the pattern of every snowflake as it drifted down to the ground. Her response to him swirled inside her, and she was kissing him, meeting his tongue, pressing herself closer against him. She could feel his desire, the taut control he was keeping over himself.

Again his fingers swept over her breasts, and Caro felt a strong ache inside her. She gasped, then moaned as a honey-sweet warmth spread through her body and relaxed her muscles.

Sin was brushing the hair away from her face and lifting it off her shoulders before he again lowered his mouth to hers. They were trembling in each other's arms, kissing and caressing as the passion rose higher and higher between them.

There was no hurry in their touch; the result would be inevitable but it would happen in its own time.

She was still aware of the snow outside, but this recognition was growing dimmer as her entire being was centered on the sensations roused by his touch, by his body so close to hers. . . . but not quite close enough.

His hands swept from her breast to her waist and back again. She heard her name murmured and she responded in kind, putting her hands on the back of his neck to bring him even closer as her body shuddered.

He entered her swiftly, and she delighted in their completeness. The tension and pressure inside her was sweeter than anything she had ever known. They moved against each other, slowly at first, and then faster, the passion building higher and higher until nothing existed except their need for each other.

The long wave of delight ended on a wave of explosions that seemed to come from a deeper level than either had known before.

Finally, they lay still, exhausted and exhilarated at the same time.

"It looks like a blizzard outside," Caro said hours later from the warm protection of Sin's arms, her hand over his heart. "It's a lucky sign for us."

"Yes," he agreed, kissing her hair as they lay watching the thick white flakes of snow falling past their window. "Nothing can be better for a couple passionately in love than the prospect of being snowed in at a Long Island estate where our every whim is catered to."

Caro turned over and folded her arms on his chest. "You know as well as I do that hovering servants bearing trays of pink champagne aren't as important as our being together."

"Imagine if I'd come here the night we met."

"I hope you don't think we would have played 'English country house weekend'."

"It might have been fun to play 'Find the proper bedroom.' I remember one time in England—"

Caro put a hand over his mouth. "Those bachelor

memories, my darling, are now as passé and forbidden as your little black appointment book, not to mention the charge account you had at that exclusive house on Forty-third Street off Fifth Avenue.''

"I don't even want to ask how you know all this."

"Every woman has her ways."

"I'm sure you do, but tonight we began our future."

"Oh, I have nothing whatsoever against that," she said as his embrace tightened demandingly. "Tonight is for putting the worst of the past behind us."

Chapter Eighteen

Sin and Caro sat close together on the stone bench in the frozen garden at Cove House. The snow that had begun to sift gently down on their wedding night had indeed turned into a full-blown blizzard that, by the time it ended, had left Long Island under some twenty-seven inches of thick white powder. But the conditions outside had very little effect on them.

They reveled in their first great span of time alone together. In the restrained luxury of their bedroom, they concentrated on each other, making love and sharing affection and exchanging promises of devotion. When they ventured downstairs, all of Cove House was at their disposal. While the storm covered the grounds with inch upon inch of whiteness, the Pooles walked through the conservatory, availed themselves of the indoor swimming pool, and took advantage of the Turkish bath, discovering the last two were very private places and excellent spots in which to lose themselves in their acts of rapture. In the evenings, following delicious meals served in the dining room, where the candlelight on the table reflected off the Georgian crystal chandelier and threw patterns on the beige silk Chinoiserie wallpaper, they went first to the billiard room and then to the library. There was something special about popping corn and roasting apples in a country fireplace, particulary when the tactful, well-trained servants made it seem as if they were all alone in the eighty-five-room house.

But no matter how much they talked—exchanging words of love, discussing their new apartment, planning their California honeymoon trip—Caro was instinctively aware that there was one subject Sin hadn't raised. It was more than likely that their being out on Long Island again, where so much had begun and so much else was left incomplete, took one small chink out of their otherwise complete happiness. Wisely, however, Caro said nothing, deciding that this was something Sin had to bring up first.

On Wednesday night, when Sin suggested they spend Thursday outside, walking around the estate, Caro readily agreed. To be sure, they couldn't cover the entire seventy-eight acres on foot, but there were more than enough paths shoveled through the snow to provide them with plenty of walking space. Dressed in clothes that were kept for winter fishing and clamming—heavy outerwear, mufflers, knit hats, rubber boots, and corduroy trousers—they left the house after breakfast. The morning was given over to a tour of the outer buildings—the carriage house, the stable, the dairy, and the greenhouse—

but after a hearty Italian lunch of soup and bread and pasta prepared by Mrs. Bertolucci, the wife of the head gardener, in their neat, warm little house, Sin and Caro continued along their route.

They skirted the deserted tennis and squash courts and then turned back toward the garden. When they saw a bench brushed clear of snow, it was obviously a sign for them to sit down.

"They don't have the letter," Sin said abruptly, swerving away from their previous topic of conversation. "For weeks I was sure the Consortium had it back again, but now I'm sure I was wrong. There's something in the air—and it's not simply being so close to the scene of the crime again."

"I know; I feel it also," Caro said, pressing closer to him. "And we're going to have to do something about it."

"Yes, but if we sit here any longer we'll be too frozen to enjoy the fun of warming up afterward. Let's walk some more and see if we can figure out just what we should do next."

"I've always found that looking at the water is very helpful whenever there's a particularly knotty problem to work out," she said as they stood up. "And lucky for us, the shore isn't too far away."

They walked down the long paths which in summer were bordered by perfectly tended shrubs, but which were now completely covered by drifts of snow. At the edge of Long Island Sound they came to a halt.

"Did Davis show you the letter when you were in the card room together?" Caro asked as they began to walk back and forth along the beach, the water lapping at their feet, secure in rubber boots.

"No, he gave me his word as a gentleman that he brought it with him." Sin's mouth tightened. "Of course, he could have been lying."

"That's entirely possible. If he were coming apart at the seams—"

"Oh, he was doing that, all right."

"Then he must have had it. You told me he was on the verge of hysteria, and—"

"And that condition doesn't promote crafty thinking, so he had to be telling the truth, but—"

"But did he actually have the letter on him, or did he have enough presence of mind left to put it somewhere safe?"

As Caro finished speaking, the winter sunshine that had made the cold day bearable went behind a bank of thick, gray clouds while the wind increased in both chill and intensity. Suddenly, the pristine white snow-covered ground and the unlimited expanse of water seemed not only harsh but threatening. In what was little more than a split second, they had gone from coexisting with nature to being reminded of its potential threat. Whether it was a sudden squall in the winter or an unexpected thunderstorm in the summer, the weather was not an element to ignore.

"Let's go back to the house," Caro suggested, shuddering. "We can finish talking about this over tea."

"I couldn't agree more." Sin's eyes swept over the threatening skyline. "I hate to sound superstitious, but I'm starting to feel something evil in the air."

Caro and Sin returned to Cove House in record time, but the first fat flakes were already falling by the time they reached the upper garden. Avoiding the terrace entrance, they came in from the east wing, through a small door near the conservatory used mainly in summer by servants carrying pitchers of cold drinks to players on the tennis and squash courts.

"Oh, Mr. and Mrs. Poole, we've been so worried about you," Mrs. Rogers said, concern evident in every word as she greeted them just inside the door. "It looks so bad out."

"You're certainly right about that," Sin said. He knelt to pull off Caro's rubber boots before removing his own. "Even city people like us know enough not to stay outside too long on a day like this."

"And do you think we'd run the risk of being late for one of your wonderful teas?" Caro added as they removed hats, gloves, mufflers, and coats.

"Dressed like this, madam?"

"No, I think we have enough time to go upstairs and change first," she responded, not looking at Sin for fear of losing her straight face. "We'll have tea in rose-and-ivory salon."

"Very good, madam. Will an hour from now be all right?"

"Mr. Poole and I will ring when we come downstairs again," Caro informed the older woman, allowing herself to smile. "We promise not to be too long."

389

"Mrs. Rogers is a wonderful woman, but I'm afraid she does have certain standards," Sin said when they were safely in their room again.

"Which we definitely let slide when we went around dressed like a pair of beach scavengers," Caro replied as she pulled off gray wool socks and began to unbutton her blue-plaid flannel shirt. "Of course, you look dashing no matter what you're wearing."

"It's nice to know that if I hadn't been able to make money again, I would have retained a certain Wall Street style in my rags," Sin said, stripping off his shirt and trousers. "Are you wearing Lucile lingerie under all that flannel and corduroy?"

"I think a satin and lace teddy lends a certain necessary touch," she said archly, watching the look in his eyes as he took in the pale-blue creation she'd worn underneath her heavy outerwear. "Wait until you see me in riding clothes."

"A new husband should have only one surprise like this a day. But I trust you'll help me recover from it."

"What else would a good wife do except help soothe the man she loves?" Caro asked, slowly turning and giving him a flirtatious look.

As she intended, he followed her through her dressing room and into the pink-and-silver bathroom carpeted in fur.

"Do you know how cute you look in that awful baggy winter underwear?" she inquired, wrapping her arms around his shoulders. Her body molded itself to his, curves against taut muscles, and with a fresh wave of pleasure she noted that the heavy cotton flannel combinations he wore in no way prohibited her from being aware of his mounting desire. "But right now I really want to see you in nothing at all.'

"Funny, I was just going to say the same thing to you." Sin's hands caressed her back before coming around to cup her breasts through the rich material. It's at times like this," he went on, "that any clothes seem like too many clothes."

Passion flared in his eyes and desire and laughter suffused his features. He had no secrets from her, Caro realized, and she held out her arms to him.

In an instant, they were locked in an embrace, his mouth pressed to hers. There was no need to say a word, and each pulled impatiently at what garments the other still wore.

When his ungainly clothes and her teddy were flung aside, her body followed his to the rug, and he pulled her urgently on top of him. He moaned at the pleasurable contact of the fur beneath and her feminine curves above.

"This is for you," Caro whispered, her heart racing as she positioned herself above his body, her knees on either side of his thighs, her hands stroking the hard, cool expanse of his chest. Not even daring to breathe, she slowly lowered herself onto his fully aroused manhood, absorbing him inch by inch until they were fully merged. Raw pleasure filled her, but this was all for Sinclair.

She moved over him again and again, and with a groan of pleasure he threw an arm over his eyes. A long shudder ran through his damp body, and her own need was erupting faster than she thought possible. But all that mattered was to love him until every cold, dark aspect of his life was pushed so far away that it would never dare return.

The rose-and-ivory salon next to the conservatory was the smallest of the drawing rooms in Cove House. Fortunately it had the rare appeal of being both comfortably cool in summer and welcomingly warm in the winter. The walls were the color of clotted cream, the walls were graced by fine watercolors in simple frames, and an *oeil-de-boeuf* mirror surmounted the fireplace. Placed at right angles to the fireplace were a pair of armchairs upholstered in a deep rosy-red silk with a wide gold-ribbon stripe; elsewhere several other equally comfortable chairs were covered in a simple chintz with a pattern of full-blown roses. An eighteenth-century English lacquer desk and any number of side tables held a variety of ivory figurines and objects, the bookshelves were filled with the latest novels, and a white cotton damask-covered sofa was placed beneath the wide windows.

When Caro and Sin entered the room on the stroke of four, they found a fire glowing behind the highly polished andirons and an embroidered cloth laid over the low lacquer table in front of the sofa. It was time for tea and all that was lacking, the room seemed to say, were the two main participants and the food. But at the moment, neither Caro nor Sin was overly interested in either tea or decor.

"What do you say to our going over to the Linden Trees tomorrow?" Sin asked when they had rung for Rogers and were settled on the sofa.

"I think it's a wonderful idea."

"I should have thought of it beforehand."

"Well, you could say we've had our minds on other things."

"And you may as well add," he said, "that concentrating on each other may have been what finally jarred that idea loose."

"That's even nicer to hear. But going back to the golf club is a little like. . . ." Caro stopped in the middle of her sentence as Rogers, followed by his wife and one of the maids, all carrying laden trays, entered the room. "Oh, Sin, doesn't all of this look scrumptious?"

"I've just realized how hungry I am," Sin said, picking up her cue. "I guess there is something to the benefits of fresh air."

Resting in the center of the table was a sterling silver Queen Anne tea service, surrounded by Ridgway dessert plates and delicate Staffordshire cups and saucers. There were cinammon scones and orange muffins, still warm from the oven and accompanied by curls of sweet butter; a two-tiered silver cake stand held fondant-frosted petits fours and fruit tarts; and a crystal plate displayed a richly frosted chocolate cake.

"And I thought I was going to be above tea today," Sin remarked. "Right now, I feel like an eleven-year-old in a pastry shop. That chocolate cake. . . ."

"We have to make a stab at the scones and muffins before we demolish the cake."

Somehow it never failed that an infusion of hot Earl Grey tea and a sampling of assorted sweets served to restore a sense of serenity. By the time they were ready for the chocolate cake, Caro was curled up in a corner of the sofa, her Lucile tea gown of blue brocade banded in mink falling in graceful folds around her.

"Going back to the Linden Trees is going to be a little like going back to the scene of the crime," Sin said, finally completing her unfinished sentence. "That was what you wanted to say before our afternoon treat arrived, wasn't it?"

"Exactly. Do you realize that we've spent a good part of the afternoon finishing each other's sentences?"

"Let's hope we can work that well together when we get to the Linden Trees tomorrow." For a moment, Caro debated her next move. "Just before we left the Osborne, I told Vanessa that I knew we were going to be very happy together—even if we didn't find the letter. Do you feel the same way?"

"I feel as if you're a good step ahead of me. I have something I want to say now, this minute, because if I wait until tomorrow, no matter what the outcome, it won't mean nearly as much. If the letter is gone, it's gone," Sin said. He wasn't smiling, but the expression on his face and the look of peace in his eyes eased the strain Caro felt for him far more than any smile could have. "If I can't accomplish all my original tasks, it doesn't mean I've failed either to remember my father or honor his memory. Until the night I met you, I was in terrible danger of wanting revenge for the sake of revenge. If I had to lose the letter in order to find you, it was the best trade I ever made in my life—even if I wasn't ready to admit it at first," Sin said as he drew her into his arms. "Having you means more to me than all the other things I thought were so important."

Chapter Nineteen

Even in the cold glint of a sunny winter afternoon, the Linden Trees looked oddly sinister, and Caro and Sin exchanged looks of trepidation as they left the bushes where the horses were tethered and walked toward the large circular driveway.

"Will the horses be all right there?" Caro asked, her riding boots crunching on the thin ice and gravel.

"That's where I kept my carriage—along with Sean and George—last time." Sin looked at the clubhouse and couldn't suppress the shudder that ran through him. "I honestly never thought I'd come back here, but since we have, I think we should retrace my steps that night."

"You never did tell me how you crashed the costume party. Did Davis get you an invitation?"

"He could have. As an officer of the club, all he had to do was give me one of the general invitations so I could get through the front door. He may have been on the edge of destruction," Sin said with slashing bitterness, "but he certainly held onto enough of his personality to make things difficult for me."

"Please don't tell me that that miserable old man made you climb through a window."

"No, not quite that bad. Davis told me he'd wait for me in the club office. It has its own entrance, and when I rapped on the door, he let me in. I hate to say it, but I probably would have climbed through a window."

"I'm glad you feel that way," Caro said with the trace of a smile, "because from the looks of this place, we may end up having to do just that."

The snowfall that had made their retreat from the beach to Cove House necessary had stopped by early evening, and Friday morning dawned clear and crisp and not too cold—a definite sign that they were meant to go to the Linden Trees. Some judicious questioning of the Cove House staff had provided them with the information they needed: the Linden Trees was closed down until April, and the only staff around the place was a caretaker who came out every day from Woodbury to make sure that the pipes hadn't frozen and that everything was secure. On Fridays he left before noon and didn't return until Monday morning.

Even at first glance it was obvious to them that the caretaker was first-rate at his job. The clubhouse was secure for the winter against all intruders, even those who were on a vital mission . . .

"I bet the window sashes are nailed down."

"I wouldn't be at all surprised." Sin looked at

the small side door with great thought. "Did I ever tell you that when I was a boy, I used to practice picking locks?"

"It seems to me that all rich boys have very strange predilections for somewhat felonious hobbies."

"Let me have a hairpin."

"You're not joking."

"Not at all."

Caro watched, lost in admiration, as Sin made good use of the hairpin she'd given him. With one hand he inserted the prongs into the lock while the other hand rested on the knob, turning it at strategic moments until it finally clicked and then opened.

"Success," Caro said.

"So far, so good." Sin stood beside the door. "Shall we?"

"It seems to be the best idea."

Their brief merriment vanished at the first sight of the grim-looking office. The room was small and mean-looking, with hard chairs grouped around a large oak desk. There were also two filing cabinets, and the walls held a series of English hunting prints depicting dead birds. This was not a pleasant room and neither wanted to spend much time in it.

"I know the heat is off, but shall we hope for the best when it comes to the electric?"

"That's about all we can do," Sin said as he reached for the switch on the lamp closest to him. The light came on, and in short order they had the other lamps on as well, but a winter gloom still hung over the room. "You do realize that we're now guilty of breaking and entering."

"It would be pretty meaningless if we ended up getting caught without having looked for the letter."

The desk yielded nothing but stationery engraved with the club's letterhead, and the files offered nothing more incriminating than records of dues payments and the usual schedule of activities.

"This isn't going to work," Sin said at last, his voice tight. "If Davis hid the letter, it wasn't here. There'd be too many chances for someone else to find it."

"Then it's in the card room," Caro said. "I knew we'd have to go in there."

"I'm sure it's been cleaned up, but I really don't want to search it, either. We're a pretty cold-blooded pair, aren't we?" he asked wearily.

"We definitely aren't cut out for a life of crime," she sighed. "Shall we get it over with?"

The card rooms, at the back of the clubhouse, were a series of identical rooms lining one side of the hallway. Every door was closed, creating an atmosphere even more threatening then the view of the Linden Trees from the driveway. As much as she wanted to find the letter, Caro wanted to be out of this place, and she was sure that underneath it all Sin felt exactly the same way.

He hesitated for one moment, and then went to the right door and opened it. He didn't want to think about what had transpired the last time he'd been here, and he certainly didn't want to see any reminder of what had happened after he'd left the room, but it was clear at first glance that the Linden Trees had been its usual efficient self in restoring everything to a pristine condition.

Caro put her arms around Sin, noting without too much surprise that his long, lean body was tight with tension. She felt the same way herself, and for a moment they comforted each other. "This isn't the easy job we thought it was going to be," she murmured.

"I think the fun ended after I picked the lock." Sin looked around the room with the card table in the center, the simple chairs, and the brass wall sconces. "I wonder if there's a secret panel here?"

"So we're back to *Boys' Own Adventure?*"

"That's just about the only way I can stand to be in here again. I keep thinking what might have happened if I'd refused to leave when Davis asked me to, or if I'd left you on the terrace and come back here. It's bad enough imagining what it must have been like, but I came so close to being a part of one man's last desperate act."

Caro knew this wasn't the moment to remind Sin that if he *had* returned to the card room, he might not have had to worry about his appendix destroying his health. He knew as well as she did that the chances had been more than even that Davis would have pointed his gun at the man who'd exposed his secret. But her husband was suffering from pangs of conscience, and truth be told, Caro would rather have had that than the flashes of cold-minded, single-purpose revenge that he'd displayed when she'd first met him.

401

"I'm not being sentimental about Davis," he said after a long time.

"I don't think you are." Caro cupped his face in her hands. "I still think you're the bravest man I've ever known and certainly ever loved, but if you didn't feel the way you do now, I'd be very disappointed, since it would mean that you wanted revenge more than anything else."

"It's almost embarrassing, how well you know me. I can fool everyone I know, but not you. I can't even pretend to be ruthless," he said, kissing her soundly. "Are you wearing face powder and eye black?" he asked, feeling as if he were speaking through a cloud of Jicky.

"Of course. It's a well-known fact that face powder protects the skin in cold weather."

"And the eye black?" he inquired, trying not to laugh as Caro fluttered her mascaraed lashes across his cheeks in butterfly kisses.

"I wear it because I like it."

"And what would you do if I told you that you could leave all your paint off because your wonderful personality and fine intellect don't need gilding?"

"I'd probably stab you between the eyes with my eye-black brush."

"I believe you would," he replied in a measured voice that didn't hide its humor. A moment later they dissolved into laughter, the deep tension of being in the Linden Trees lessening. "Shall we take off our coats and have a look around?"

They were both wearing superbly cut riding clothes. Caro's midnight-blue jacket fell almost to the top of her shining black boots, designed by the tailor at Miller's to disguise the fact she wore riding breeches instead of the skirt that demanded she sit sidesaddle. Because of the cold weather, both wore warm black melton overcoats with deep slits up the back, and these were now taken off and laid across a straight chair, along with their hats and gloves.

Together Caro and Sin checked over every bit of furniture and every inch of the room that might turn out to be a hiding place. Side tables revealed nothing but packs of cards, score pads, and neatly sharpened pencils. All the floorboards were securely in place; prints removed from their wall hooks had backs so firmly fastened that nothing could be slipped in, and the chairs offered not so much as a single hollow leg.

"And there's nothing here either," Sin said from his spot on the floor under the card table. "Davis didn't put it here, and that probably means he was lying to me—he had it on him all along." He sat crosslegged, looking like a disappointed boy. "Well, I guess we've done our best."

"You've done more than your best," Caro said, holding out a hand to him as he got up. "You care with your whole heart, and you believed when almost no one else would. That isn't failing," she finished as they sat down on the padded window seat.

"You may have to keep telling me that a couple of times a day for the next few months. In fact, the best thing we can do is leave for California as soon as possible. I want to go someplace where I don't know anyone—except you."

"We should go to Nan and Drake's wedding first,

and Vanessa would be hurt if we missed her theatre party, but other than that—" Caro rested her head against his shoulder. "California at the end of winter sounds a lot nicer than New York."

Sin's arms tightened around her. "I'm looking forward to seeing you in summer clothes," he said, his lips brushing against the soft skin between the top of her white stock and her ear. "But for right now, I can't tell you how appealing you are in riding trousers."

"They do serve a purpose, even if they do get in the way of any serious romantic encounters."

"They do, but then, I don't want to have as a memory making love to you in the Linden Trees."

"Yes, but a kiss doesn't fall into that category, does it?"

"Never. Kissing you is just about the only way to take away some of the unhappiness of being in this club. Promise that if I ever get the stupid idea that it would be fun to join an expensive, exclusive club, you'll give me a good swift kick."

"I'll say yes only because I'm sure I won't have to. Sin. . . ."

"Is something wrong?" he asked as he tried to find a more comfortable position for both of them on the narrow seat.

"The window seat just moved under us."

"Are you certain?"

"When I'm in your arms, I'll believe in all the marvelous things nature can do, but I won't subscribe to any theory that says inanimate objects can do the same."

The look on Sin's eyes made her heart pound: it combined surprise, hope, and not wanting to allow himself to believe that there was one more chance.

"I never thought. . . . "

"Neither did I."

Their voices trailed off as they stood up. It was impossible to talk as they knelt in front of the window seat, hands searching for the catch, all too aware that this might be one more fleeting hope that would in the end yield nothing.

The stiff catch gave way and the padded seat became a lid that opened on creaking hinges. What could have been Pandora's box was suddenly Aladdin's cave—at least as far as the Pooles were concerned. Resting on the dusty wood floor was a long envelope that had turned cream with age.

Sin reached for it with a hand that had unexpectedly turned stiff. It was going to be another dead end, one more chance come and gone, he thought, blinking as if he expected the envelope to disappear. But it was still there, and he picked it up with care. They sat on the floor with their backs against the window seat, and Sin slowly lifted the flap, withdrew the folded page, and finally, when neither could bear the suspense a moment longer, opened it.

At first, the closely packed typewritten page seemed indecipherable, but slowly and surely each word began to stand out, the sentence began to flow and the meaning became clear.

They had the letter.

It was not so much a letter, they both concurred, as an agreement between parties that their objective was to take over the companies controlled by Stanford Poole, and the first step in this process was to create the Great Northwest Lumber Company. The undersigned (henceforth to be known as the Consortium) would then seek to absorb as many of these companies as possible and run them under one directorship from which the profit would be equally divided.

Everything was as completely delineated as it could be on one page. It gave the date the idea had been formulated and agreed upon, each objective was listed, and it was all signed. Each signature seemed to burn with a life of its own, every name its own study in wrongdoing.

Sin, much to his surprise, felt the tautness vanish and his body began to feel strangely weak. His hands began to tremble and he handed the letter to Caro. "I always knew I'd find this, but this isn't the reaction I expected. I'm shaking like a leaf, and I don't think I can stand up."

"You don't have to. Just hold onto me until you feel better," Caro told him, putting her arms around him and holding him close to her. "I feel a little shaky myself."

He rested his head on her shoulder, held her close enough so they could hear each other's heartbeat through the layers of their clothes, and finally whispered, "We did it."

"We certainly did," she returned, now not being the time to say that he had done most of this alone. There would be more than enough time later to discuss the implications of this discovery. The deep quiet that was Long Island in winter seemed to surround them like a heavy velvet cloak, but all too short a time later, Caro's supersensitive hearing picked up a disturbance in the silent atmosphere. Somewhere, ice and gravel were crunching under the weight of—of what?''

"Sin—" Caro sought to control the note of panic she heard creeping into her voice. "—someone's coming."

Another man might have told her she was hearing things, another man might have told her that the strain of the afternoon was making her nervous, but not Sinclair Poole. He had spent the last seven years looking over his shoulder, bracing to meet whoever might be coming around the next corner, keeping his instincts sharpened. He would no more disbelieve anything Caro said to him than he would ignore his own suspicions.

"What do you say to our leaving here through the window?" Sin asked, folding the letter back into the envelope before tucking this most important missive into the inside pocket of his riding jacket.

"I'd say it adds a certain fillip to the whole adventure," Caro said as they got to their feet.

They put on their hats and coats, put down the padded window seat, and went to push up the window sash. . . . except that it wouldn't move.

"What do you know," Sin remarked after a moment's inspection, "the window *is* nailed down."

Dismay trickled through Caro. "Somehow breaking the glass doesn't seem to be the best way to get out of here."

407

"No, it certainly doesn't. Let's go back to the main hall."

The heels of their boots clicked loudly against the inlaid wood floor, but it didn't drown out the sound of carriage wheels bearing down on the ice and gravel of the driveway. For a minute, the Pooles stood at either side of one of the large windows, surreptitiously watching a shiny black brougham make its approach, but they had to make a move, and soon. Without exchanging a word, both realized they couldn't use the way they'd come in—it would leave them much to far from their horses.

"Upstairs," Sin said tersely. "We'll have a better view of who's in that carriage."

Caro had more than a suspicion of who was paying a visit to the Linden Trees, but this wasn't a time for a discussion, and they went quickly up the stairs. When they reached the second-floor hallway, she tugged him toward the ladies lounge.

"This way."

"I'm glad one of us knows where to go."

"It's just a guess, but I'd say the room with the view of the water belongs to the men's lounge. That's usually the way. Which is another reason to avoid these places."

Caro's guess about the windows turned out to be right. They took their positions at either side of the largest window just as the brougham drew to a stop in front of the clubhouse. Together—not exchanging a word and hardly breathing—they watched as the carriage door opened.

"Curtis Chandler." Caro instantly identified the

408

tall, athletic man who had jumped down and now began to look around him with great impatience.

"I remember him quite well." Sin's voice was tightly controlled. "And the other man is his father, Kenneth Chandler." For a moment they looked down at the older man, a grayer version of his son; and as the third figure descended with far less energy, Sin's features were overlaid with an icy glare before he spat out, "and there's Avery Dutton, bringing up the rear as usual."

Somehow Caro expected Avery Dutton to be a small, furtive man with a face that would be the same at thirty-five as it would be at fifty. But the man she saw taking off his hat seemed to be a perfectly normal figure: well-kept, well-tailored, and just a little nondescript.

And there is the secret of his success, she thought.

"We'll be safe up here," Sin said softly. "Even the most unscrupulous of men seem to draw the line at the ladies' lounge . . . probably because they know anyone they meet there is going to be smarter and tougher than they are."

Caro smiled. "I like the way you put it. But don't you wish we could hear what they're saying?"

"I already have a pretty fair idea of that—and of why they're here," Sin said, not taking his eyes from the window. "What do you think of our timing?"

"It seems made to order, depending on what we plan to do."

"No playing it safe, then?"

"You don't really want to, and if you think I'm

409

going to hide in here while you look for a good spot to eavesdrop from—''

There was no need to finish the sentence. They were in this together, and it went beyond the promise of ''for better or worse.'' As the three men outside began to walk toward the door, Sin and Caro left the relative safety of the lounge for a secluded corner of the upper hall where they had an unobstructed view of the floor below—without being seen.

''It figures that they have a key,'' Sin muttered as the sound of the lock turning vibrated through the house.

''I'd rather break and enter with you than walk through the front door with them.''

The front door was slammed shut with the force used by men who are either showing off their influence or else are extremely annoyed. The valuable Persian rugs had been rolled up and stored for the winter. None of the men lowered their voices, and the hardwood floors provided the Pooles with excellent acoustics.

Curtis was pacing like a cat, draping his coat over the bannister and pitching his hat on a small table. It was clear that he and not his father was in charge of this expedition, and his annoyance at his late father-in-law was explicit. ''That crazy old man probably gave Poole the letter. And if he did that, then his little trick with the gun was the best thing he could do.''

''Then you don't think Poole did it?'' The sly tone in Avery's voice made it clear that his was a question and not a statement.

"It's mighty hard for a man to be in two places at once, and Sinclair was definitely on the terrace. In fact, I don't believe he said anything that goaded my late father-in-law into doing the deed," Curtis went on. "He would probably try to reason with Davis—unlike some people."

"What are you trying to imply, Curtis?"

"Only that some people who saw a man with a gun in his hand, instead of trying reason and compassion, would urge the distraught party to pull the trigger."

"Of all the insinuating—"

"Stop it, both of you!" Kenneth Chandler's voice cracked like a whip. "This is neither the time nor the place for such discussion. In case you've forgotten, we came here for another reason. The sooner we find the letter, the faster we can get out of this place."

"We have a lot of searching to do."

"Exactly, Avery. But all searches have to begin somewhere. Curits, do you have any suggestions?"

"When we arrived that night, Davis went straight to the club office. He might have left it there," Curtis supplied just as a strong gust of wind shook the windows; a door sounded as if it were being pulled off its hinges. "Now what's happened?"

"One of the French doors in the ballroom has come loose. We can close it before we leave," Avery responded after a quick inspection.

"With letter in hand, I hope," Kenneth added.

"I think we can breathe again," Sin said quietly when the last of the footsteps died down.

411

"We should get out of here," Caro replied in an equally soft voice. "The French door that blew open could be the best way."

"The terrace seems to be figuring in our life again—not that I'm complaining. But we have to wait and see what the contingent from the Consortium are going to do next before making our move."

"I wouldn't want them to see us, particularly since I don't think we could convince them we didn't find the letter."

Instinctively, Sin's hand went to his jacket. "And I certainly won't give it to them."

They didn't have long to wait. The trio had obviously reached the same conclusion as the Pooles about the office not being a likely spot to hide anything. The men who returned to the hall were not so much arguing among themselves as discussing heatedly other possible hiding places. Curtis and his father were all for making the card room their next stop, while Avery wanted to search the second floor.

"Davis was in on the planning of this clubhouse. There's probably a wall safe up there, hidden under a picture."

"Aren't you forgetting about the secret panel and the hidden passageway?"

"Fine, Curtis. You check the card room, and I'll come back with the letter."

"One of us had better find it," Kenneth said shortly. "If Sinclair Poole has that letter—"

"But I *do* have the letter," Sin said in low tones, and not even apprehension about their possible discovery could keep the satisfied smile off his face.

"Yes, but do you know if there's a secret passage where we can hide. Even a closet will do," Caro returned.

"I suggest a strategic retreat back to the ladies' lounge. If nothing else, we'll find out if Avery knows enough not to invade a female sanctuary."

They moved cautiously back toward the lounge, just steps ahead of Avery Dutton.

Sin felt as if his emotions had been torn in half. One part of him wanted to avoid coming face-to-face with Avery; the other, thwarted from their last meeting, longed to do what good sense had prevented him from doing on that long-ago morning. *I could probably take him out right here and he'd never know what hit him,* he thought with increasing satisfaction. His reverie didn't end until he felt Caro tug on his sleeve.

"He went the other way, Gentleman Jim," she told him knowingly. "Right now, it's a choice between getting out of here and you trying out your prizefighting technique."

"Not if we walk carefully," he responded, his proper perspective returning. "At least they didn't take up the carpeting from the stairs. How fast do you think you can run?"

"In boots and riding breeches, fast enough. I take it we run when we get to the stairs?"

"That's it." They left the relative safety of the lounge, moving as quietly but as quickly as possible. "We go out through the ballroom, and once we get to the trees—" He let his words trail off. They were almost to the upper hall, which had already proved its worth as an echo chamber. One wrong word now, and they had no chance at all.

Caro had never gone down a flight of stairs so quickly. She wasn't thinking about the danger of falling, or that as soon as their boots made contact with the parquet floor, the sound would be as loud as a rifle shot. Her thoughts were centered on getting out of the clubhouse and across the frozen ground and reaching the safety of the trees. It wasn't being caught that worried either of them, she realized—it was being seen . . . seen and identified.

Sin was beside her, and they reached the last step at the same moment. Knowing it was impossible to prevent the sound their footsteps would make and still maintain her speed, she would just have to hope that Avery on the second floor and Curtis and Kenneth in the card room would each think that it was the other running to join them, letter in hand.

There wasn't any time to think about possible complications as they turned to the left, across a short hallway and through the open doors of the ballroom. The Pooles ran side-by-side, their steps matching, their flat-heeled boots striking against the polished wood floor in unison. It sounded as if a gattling gun was being fired, and the room that had seemed so small and overcrowded the night of the costume ball now seemed longer than the Hall of Mirrors at Versailles.

The panel of the French door that had blown loose was now swinging back and forth in the strong winter wind. Caro ran through it and across the terrace. She hoisted herself up on the balustrade, swung her legs over the side, and dropped to the icy ground below. A second later Sin was beside her and they were running again. They headed for the trees, using the same route he had taken the night of the ball, their coats flying out behind them as they raced along. Caro felt as if she could run and run and never feel tired. She thought she heard someone shouting from the terrace, but this wasn't the time to turn and look.

"Do women have some sort of secret track-and-field society?" Sin inquired when they reached their horses. "You could put the Columbia track team to shame."

"I know this sounds horrible," Caro replied, her heavy heartbeats giving no sign of slowing down, "but this was the perfect way to end our excursion to the Linden Trees. Just walking out wouldn't have done, and it makes finding the letter worth even more."

"Yes, in an odd way it does." Sin's smile was slow, but well worth waiting for.

"Do you think they saw us?" she asked as he helped her up in the saddle and handed her the reins.

"Only from the back, and since we are dressed rather alike—" He swung into the saddle. "If they do decide to follow us, we can go a lot faster on horseback than they can in a carriage."

Despite this certainty they urged their mounts to a swift pace, not stopping again until they were on the private road that led to the driveway of Cove House. The adventure of the last hour still sang in Caro's blood. Her heartbeat hadn't quite returned to normal, and she was increasingly aware that the excitement of finding the letter and then eluding Avery Dutton and the Chandlers had led quite naturally into another sort of excitement. She felt an increasing sense of elation, and when they drew their horses to a halt, she touched her gloved fingers to his face.

"You did it."

"We did it," he said. "You believed all along."

"But you went through the worst of it and never wavered."

"I think," Sin said quietly, "that we can find a much nicer—not to mention more comfortable—spot in which to compliment each other."

"I couldn't agree with you more—provided our next stop is covered in Frette linen."

"If it weren't so cold, I'd want you right here."

She saw the look in his eyes and smiled. "My feelings exactly. It seems that one thrill simply leads to another, and there's no rule that says we can't begin our celebration as soon as we want."

Dinner that night was a feast. Large Wellfleet oysters were presented on a bed of crushed ice, followed by slices of meltingly rich mushroom quiche. The main course represented the height of the cook's art. Caro and Sin offered their admiration and compliments on the superb roast pheasant accompanied by small russet potatoes and creamed spinach, but when Rogers had finished serving, refilled their champagne glasses, and withdrawn, they returned to the main topic of conversation.

"Can you imagine what Rogers and the others would say if we told them about our afternoons adventures?" she whispered.

"They'd probably think we were brave but very foolish. I'm sure they're all gossiping about the letter we had Rogers put in the library safe for us. I didn't want to use the safe in our bedroom," Sin told her. "I'm still not used to having it, and a little distance is probably best."

"Particularly if leaving it in the library is a deterrent to your getting out of bed several times a night to spin the combination and reread the letter."

"I don't think I'd do that."

"The letter simply isn't in its proper perspective yet," she soothed him. "After dinner, we'll go into the library, look at it again, and decide what we're going to do next."

An endive salad followed the pheasant, and then there was dessert. Vanilla ice cream had been flavored with coffee before being heaped in meringue shells and draped in chocolate sauce, and this was presented with a pot of café filtre and a plate of small cookies. There was no undue haste in the completion of their meal, and eventually they rose from the table to the rustling of Caro's Lucile dinner dress of pale pink Liberty satin overlaid with Cluny lace.

As they had most other evenings, they went to the library. A fire glowed in the fireplace, and Rogers was standing patiently by the painting that concealed the wall safe, waiting for instructions.

"Your perception is excellent, as always, Rogers," Sin said as they settled down on the leather chesterfield in front of the fireplace. "Will you open the safe and give us the letter we had you place there earlier?"

"Of course, sir. You do understand that this is the master safe. Mr. Seligman insists that aside from the immediate family, no one except Sackett and myself have access to the combination?"

"That's just as it should be. Thank you, Rogers," Sin said, taking the letter.

"Will you and Mrs. Poole require anything else?"

"Not at this time. We'll ring when it's time to put the letter back," he said, and waited until the butler slid the doors closed behind him. "Shall we have an after-dinner drink?"

"We're going to need one." Caro shifted on the chesterfield so she could watch Sin as he walked toward the table that held a variety of assorted cognacs, aperitifs, and liqueurs. "Not Remy Martin, though. Tonight we should have something different."

"How does Armagnac sound?"

"In Gascony, where they make it, it's called 'dancing fire.' "

"I'll take that to mean yes." Sin took two balloon glasses and filled them from the bottle of Armagnac Saint-Vivant. With a snifter in each hand, he crossed the library to Caro. "What shall we drink to?"

Caro held the snifter in both hands to warm the liquid, and swirled it in the glass, savoring the exotic, faintly plum-scented bouquet. Finally, she touched her glass to his. "To our first—and, I hope, last—excursion into the world of breaking and entering."

Sin smiled. "To our brief career in skirting the law."

"Are you going to send word to the President? He does care, you know."

"I know . . . even when I was furious at his phone call, I knew he didn't want to do anything but help right an old wrong. In the White Plains house, the telegraph blanks were kept in the drawer of the library writing table."

"It's in the same place here. Wouldn't it be easier to stand up and go around to the front of the table?" she inquired, amused, as he put down his glass, rose on his knees, and draped himself across the back of the chesterfield and the writing table that was backed up to it. Swallowing her laughter, she watched as he stretched to open the drawer, the process giving her an excellent view of his posterior, taunt and muscular under the trousers of his dinner suit. Unable to resist, she patted his bottom affectionately. "If you don't sit down again, I won't be held responsible for my actions."

"We do have a few things to take care of before we go back to the celebration we enjoyed earlier," he said, resuming his seat, several Western Union blanks and a gold pencil in his hand. "First of all, what do we say to T.R. ?"

" 'Letter traced?'" she suggested.

"That's good, but the President is the sort who likes—enjoys—a bit of embellishment."

"I agree. What about saying something like 'Valuable letter traced?'"

"It still needs something more." Sin picked up the letter from the table and they studied it together. "Look at all these names. Do you suppose that when they signed it they thought it meant invincibility, that nothing was going to touch them?"

"I wouldn't be at all surprised. Do you know what this looks like?" she said, sipping her drink. "It reminds me of one of those letters signed by the Founding Fathers. An autographed letter."

"A valuable autographed letter," Sin put the letter down and picked up a telegraph blank and the pencil. "To Theodore Roosevelt, President of the United States, The White House, 1600 Pennsylvania Avenue, Washington, D.C.: Valuable autographed letter traced. Signed: S and C Poole."

"I like the sound of that, and the President should have a clear idea of what we mean, even if he is very busy man."

"In other words, this should make him remember us," Sin smiled. "And don't tell me not to be cynical."

"I'm not, but it isn't half as important for T.R. to remember his promises than it is to make some sort of headway in facing down the Consortium."

"First, though, we have to make them wonder . . . wonder if it was us at the club, wonder if we have the letter, wonder what we're going to do."

"The best thing to do is be as visible as we can."

"I take it that means accepting every invitation that comes our way?"

"Unless it's to an evening of Wagnerian opera, yes."

For a few minutes they sat quietly looking into the fireplace, watching the flames dance and flicker. "I thought finding the letter would instantly solve everything," Sin said at last. "Now I realize that it creates a whole new set of complications. I'm glad we're together now."

"We're going to have to figure out a plan."

"Tomorrow," he said. "Tonight is to celebrate our victory."

"Have you realized that our finding the letter means not only being able to clear you father's name, but finally to answer a question?"

"A question about what?"

"About Davis Moreton."

The Pooles regarded each other. The one unanswered question hung between them for a moment, and then they spoke at almost the same time.

"Was it murder. . . . "

". . . . or was it suicide?"

Chapter Twenty

Mrs. Garrison Worth
has the honour to announce
the marriage of her stepdaughter
Caroline
to
Mr. Sinclair Hamilton Poole
on Saturday the eighth of February
One thousand nine hundred and two
in the City of New York

MR. AND MRS. SINCLAIR POOLE
WILL BE AT HOME
AFTER THE FIRST OF MARCH
AT 667 MADISON AVENUE

Both the wedding announcements and the at-home cards had been mailed out while Caro and Sin were still at Cove House, and by the time they returned to New York on Friday, January 21st, their marriage was a topic of extensive discussion. The city's winter season was in full swing, and when it became instantly apparent that the newly married Pooles were quite happy to see and be seen at a variety of social events, the invitations began to pour forth.

Their first appearance together was at the wedding of Nancy Hull and Drake Sloane. St. Thomas' Church was filled for the candlelight ceremony, and Caro and Sin planned to arrive after most of the other guests. The wedding was an important social event, one to which invitations had been eagerly sought, so this was no time for a guest to go unnoticed.

The bridal party was very attractive, the ceremony itself profound and moving, and the recessional carried off with the greatest of dignity. But the mood of gaiety surrounding resumed outside on Fifth Avenue, where the bridal party left for Sherry's in horse-drawn sleighs, with the invited guests following in their own conveyances.

The interlude created by the trip downtown in no way lessened interest in the Pooles. As a couple they detracted nothing from the bride and groom, but once the receiving line was finished and everyone was seated for the wedding dinner, it was no more possible to ignore them than it would have been to decline to partake of the wedding festivities.

Nan and Drake left for their honeymoon in Palm Beach, and Sin and Caro returned to their new apartment at 667 Madison Avenue to take their places as members of the young married set.

Every mail delivery brought a new supply of invitations, both engraved and handwritten, requesting the honor of their company at dinner parties, dinner dances, theatre parties, opera galas, and balls. As Caro had predicted weeks before, one circle began to widen into another. They attended as many functions as possible, but at no time did they lose sight of the fact that there was quite a difference between being feted by their friends and being added to a guest list because a certain hostess had reached a decision that the Pooles were a social asset.

And all this activity assured them of being noticed by the Consortium.

And I never thought wealthy, ruthless men could look so nervous—or so guilty, Caro thought as she removed her key from her smart black calf handbag, inserting it in the lock of the apartment door, touching the brass lion's head knocker for luck.

It was Monday afternoon, March 10th, and as she opened the door and entered the reception room, her thoughts were full of the parties of the past few weeks. *Another month of this,* she thought, *and we'll have the reputation as quite the wrong sort of young married couple.* Their apartment was already attracting more than its share of talk and attention.

The apartment building at 667 Madison Avenue was the most thoroughly modern one in New York. Ten stories high, it had on each floor two identical apartments replete with high ceilings, parquet floors, and carved plasterwork moldings; it was the perfect

425

place for the Pooles. While they were at Cove House, Vanessa had supervised the painters as they carefully covered the walls with layers of ivory lacquer until each room resembled a highly original jewel box.

One wall of the reception room was covered with squares of mirrors: backed up to it was a serpentine commode of satinwood with tulipwood bindings, ebony inset lines, marquetry inlays, and handpainted floral designs. Resting on the top of its elegant surface was a Flora Danica dish with an arrangement of roses, jasmine, narcissus, and iris; and resting next to it was the latest delivery of mail.

Caro removed the sable boa that set off her Paquin daytime suite of black velvet ornamented with gold braid, and placed it alongside her hat and purse. She was leafing through the assortment of envelopes and magazines when Sean walked in.

"Oh, Mrs. Poole, you should have rung the bell," he said, reproachful of the dereliction of her duties as the lady of the house. George's cousin was taking his new role as houseman very seriously indeed. "That's what I'm here for. Suppose you had a package?"

Caro smiled. "Well, you can take my belongings and the mail into the bedroom. Are Mr. Poole and Mr. Vestovich still discussing business?"

"Oh, yes, Mrs. Poole." Sean looked quite a bit happier now that he had something to take care of for her. "They're in the drawing room. Mr. Poole did ask me when you'd be back: he's likely nearly

426

finished with whatever project he and Mr. Vestovich are involved in.''

"Good, then I should have just enough time to see how things are in the kitchen. How was your driving lesson, Sean?"

"Very well, thank you, ma'am. Mr. Pearce says I show definite skill in handling the motorcar."

"We were sure you'd do splendidly," Caro said as they left the reception room.

The next few minutes Caro spent losing herself in the details that made up their well-run household. In the dining room, she paused to admire the delicate Sheraton table and cane-back chairs with ivory-and-rose-striped silk seats. A snowy winter scene painted by the American Impressionist Willard Leroy Metcalf hung over the fine mahogany and satinwood-inlay sideboard, and the entire room projected an atmosphere conducive to fine dining.

Caro's next stop was the butler's pantry, where the shelves of the glassfronted cabinets were filled with their Royal Crown Derby service of white bone china bordered in black and gold and Baccarat's Montaigne Plain glassware. Both had been selected from the samples brought to the Prince Street house by one of the Tiffany salesmen. This was part of the new start they both wanted, but a new cook was out of the question, and Caro entered the spacious, modern kitchen to find Mr. Wong mixing his famous Chinese herb salad dressing, starting the preparations for what would be one of the Pooles rare meals at home.

"Good afternoon, Mr. Wong. It's very quiet here this afternoon. Where's the rest of our household?"

"It seems that they have scattered on the many winds. . . . at least for the moment." The chef permitted himself a small smile. "Mrs. Murphy has gone back downtown, and George is delivering some papers from Mr. Poole to Mr. Seligman. He left with Mr. Pearce, and they were having a discussion about a quote in *Hamlet*."

"As far as I'm concerned, there are very few people who can quote Shakespeare with more accuracy than George."

"But Mr. Pearce does have his opinions as well as his standards. He still hasn't found a family to work for that has a high enough regard for motorcars to suit him."

"Well, according to Sean, he gives excellent driving lessons."

"Is Mr. Gregori staying to dinner?"

"Not tonight. He has an invitation to a debutante ball."

"Mr. Gregori's recent taste in entertainment runs to diversions rather than improvements of the mind," Mr. Wong observed sagely.

There were four bedrooms in the apartment. One was currently being used for storage of all the wedding presents Caro and Sin didn't quite know what to do with yet: another had been decorated as a guest room. So far, the sole occupant of this room was Gregori on the nights when he was out on the town and didn't feel like returning to Prince Street.

A man with good formal clothes and table manners never has to worry about not being invited out, Caro thought as she went toward the master suite. Thanks to his appearance at their wedding, Gregori now had more than his share of invitations, particularly to debutante balls, where extra, presentable young men were highly valued commodities.

In the bedroom Caro took off her suit jacket, re-secured her Gibson Girl coiffeur, dusted some powder on her face, and touched up her lip color.

With Sin's agreement, she had used the color scheme of blue and ivory with touches of gold that had characterized her apartment at the Osborne. A stunning blue and cream Aubusson rug covered the floor, a reproduction of an elegant 18th-century powder-blue French bed was draped in blue silk, and lamps with rock-crystal bases rested on bleached-wood tables and chests. There were only two items from her old bedroom: the Childe Hassam landscape and her large French ebony dressing table.

The maids who came in on a daily basis left the room in perfect order, and after selecting the dinner dress she would change into later, Caro crossed the entry area of the suite and went into the second bedroom. They had turned this into an office for both of them, although Sin seemed to prefer spreading out his work in the drawing room, letting Caro take care of her share of the silk and importing business from the fine antique partners' desk.

Sitting down on the desk and resting her feet on the seat of the chair, Caro reached for the telephone. She gave the operator Thea's Gramercy Park number and waited to be connected. But when the telephone was picked up at the other end, the Harper family butler informed her that Miss Thea wasn't taking any calls.

"I am sorry, Mrs. Poole, but Miss Thea left strict instructions. She had a business meeting here this afternoon, and she has a ball tonight: she didn't want to take any calls. If you want to leave a message—"

"No, that's all right. Just tell her that I called and will ring back tomorrow. It's nothing terribly important," Caro said, smiling at the thought that since she wasn't going to be able to spend several minutes on the telephone, there was no reason she shouldn't put a very pleasant end to Sin's business day.

The combination drawing room and library was a full forty-eight feet long, and furnishing it had been a creative challenge. W & J Sloane's rug buyer had provided them with a modern wool pile Chinese rug in shades of rose, taupe, cream, and navy with a field woven with discs showing some of the One Hundred Precious things, and bordered with shou characters and bats. The Sisley apple orchard painting hung at the far end of the room, and a William Merritt Chase Impressionist view of the Shinnecock landscape dominated the library end. The sofas and chairs on the library side were covered in a rosy-red patterned chintz, while those on the more formal side were covered in a tea-rose hued silk—which was where Sin and Gregori were relaxing, swapping funny financial stories.

"Are you two having fun?" Caro asked, joining Sin on the sofa.

"I'm so glad you're here," Sin said, kissing her. "Greg and I were getting so bored with business that we were about to crumple up pages of the *Wall Street Journal* and toss them around."

"You can do that as long as you remember that anything you drop on the floor, you pick up. The help is very fussy about fraternity-house pranks," she responded as she and Sin looked into each other's eyes, quite forgetting that Greg was in the room with them. "Did you have a busy day?"

"Lots of boring detail work. And you? Did you completely overwhelm the silk buyer at Lord and Taylor with your fabrics?"

"The order he's going to write will keep a good many little silkworms busy and out of trouble," Caro returned, putting a hand on the back of his neck.

They looked at each other, not paying attention to anything else until a self-conscious cough brought them out of their spell. Blinking but not at all embarrassed, they both looked at Gregori, who was in the process of blushing.

"I think I should leave," he said as conversationally as he could. "I have a few letters of agreement to check over before you can sign them, Sin, and—"

"Oh, stay where you are," Sin advised genially. "We don't want to make you uncomfortable."

"And you never have to feel as if you're intruding," Caro added. "When you go to those debutante parties, you shouldn't have to go back down to Prince Street afterward."

"Caro's right. You should be able to sleep off the questionable champagne and creamed chicken you had to eat a lot closer to the place you originally ingested it," Sin said, but cut his wicked repartee short as Sean entered the room.

"Excuse me, sir, but there is a caller," he said, proffering the salver and card. "The gentleman said to tell you that he is from Washington. Colonel Hugh Miles."

"Well, show him in," Sin said expansively. "Do you know a Colonel Miles, darling?" he asked a moment later.

"I'll be sure when I see him. Right now, the only Colonel Miles from Washington that I know has a highly valuable speciality."

"And that is?"

"Military intelligence."

"I see. And you think he's an emissary from the President."

"I wouldn't be at all surprised."

Whatever else he was, Hugh Miles knew enough not to call on a new couple without the robin's-egg-blue box that announced its contents had been selected at Tiffany's. The middle-aged man whose sharp face and intelligent eyes were eased by a kind smile gave the Pooles their latest wedding present and offered his congratulations.

"Do you remember that I met you and Mrs.

Miles in Hong Kong about three or four years ago?" Caro asked as they shook hands.

"I most certainly do. It was at a dinner party given by a Barclay's Bank official at his house on Peak Road. Do you remember that stuffy English butler whose wife was such a superb cook?"

"Of course, and they're over at the Osborne now, working for my stepmother."

The ice was broken, and after Caro opened the gift box to reveal a very pretty silver pitcher, they were ready to get down to business. But there were still a few pleasantries to take care of first.

"Would you care for a drink?" Sin asked, indicating the black-and-gold lacquer Queen Anne cabinet that had been outfitted to serve as a bar. "As they say in Mexico, our house is your house."

"You're an excellent host, Sinclair, but I believe I'll pass on anything alcoholic."

"Tea, then," Caro said, reaching for the bell to summon Sean. "We have much to talk about, and at this time of day it's so much easier with something hot and sweet."

While they waited for refreshments, they discussed life in New York and Washington. Then Sean placed the Chinese Export tea service with the repousse decor on the blue enameled tiger-maple tea table. The pot was filled with hot Earl Grey tea, and a platter held big, lacy cookies—a perfect treat, since no one wanted to be distracted by too much food while they talked.

"I think the moment has come for me to excuse myself," Gregori said quietly, speaking for the first time since the introductions, his dark-amber eyes serious. "I don't think the good colonel is looking for an audience for what he has to say."

It was clear to all concerned that he expected no protests. Soft-spoken and gentle, Gregori Vestovich had more than his share of steel; when he made a statement like this, he meant every word. He accepted a cup of tea, and with that in one hand and a small plate of cookies in the other, he left the room.

"A very impressive young man, your secretary," Colonel Miles said finally. The older man had fixed his attention first on a jadite mountain of the Hsein Fung period, admiring how the very rare apricot color contrasted with the creamy marble of the mantle; and then letting his gaze rest on the handsome *famille noir* vases filled with a lush arrangement of roses, jasmine, and stephanotis. "Does he live here with you?"

"Only on evenings when he's in demand as an extra man at one or another debutante ball," Sin replied. "I think he's a little embarrassed by all of this, so he tries to fade into the woodwork."

"And that isn't the easiest thing in the world," Caro pointed out. "But we are the only family he has."

"Then you are. . . ?" Hugh Miles' piercing gaze fixed itself on Sin.

"More or less." Sin didn't want to start these proceedings off with a lie, yet he didn't feel that the truth added anything to the situation. "I regard Greg as my younger brother, and that should suffice for all concerned—even the President."

"As you're both probably aware, domestic concerns aren't my usual bailiwick," Hugh said. "I had to come to New York on another matter—one of equal importance to the President—and he suggested that when I conclude my first meeting I might want to call on you."

Caro and Sin exchanged glances. This was the first indication that Theodore Roosevelt had had any reaction to their telegram—or had even seen it."

"We appreciate the President's continued interest," Caro said in a neutral voice.

"Caroline's absolutely right, and even though I may have seemed a little distant the day he rang me up, I did appreciate his call," Sin added.

"He felt he owed it to you to apologize for his previous omissions. And so do I. It's always easier to believe the worst, not to have to think beyond the innuendo and the gossip," Hugh said quietly, "but in the end we pay for letting others do our thinking for us. When the President told me about you, I offered to help in any way I could."

"It isn't as if the President can take the Congressional Limited up to New York just to say he's on our side," Sin said understandingly. "And please believe me when I say that if that's all he cares to do, it's fine with us."

"I'm glad you both realize the limited extent of what the President can do in a situation like this. He is very concerned, however, that you might do something rash in your effort to clear your father's name."

"I'm not going to ambush anyone on the floor of

435

the Stock Exchange, if that's what he's worried about," Sin said. "But I can't hold the letter back indefinitely."

"That is a problem."

"For nearly seven years the Consortium has not seen me in any social situations," Sin pointed out. "They were able to tell each other—and anyone else who would listen—that I was some sort of crackpot, that my father's perfidy had unhinged me."

"Obviously not everyone believed them," Hugh said generously. "Your current social activity proves that."

"We have some very good friends," Caro said, "but we also know that some invitations are based on curiosity."

"Fortunately, we see members of the Consortium at most events," Sin added. "Our friends are very good about adding one person or another to their guest lists just so they can be sure to see us, and we take it for granted that we're going to run into Avery Dutton or Kenneth Chandler or one of the others at the parties of those we have less trust for. Our conversations have been quite interesting at times."

"You haven't spoken to them about the letter?" Hugh was aghast. "That would ruin all your plans."

"No, we've been very careful there," Sin assured him quickly. "When I said our conversations were interesting, I meant from the point of view of what *isn't* said."

"I see," Hugh replied, but neither Caro nor Sin was sure he really did.

For his clarification, the Pooles told the good colonel about their adventure at the Linden Trees. "We hoped the President would enjoy hearing exactly how we obtained the letter," Caro finished.

"I'm sure it will raise a smile or two."

"But the letter won't," Sin said. "I've had two expert copies made, and before you leave, I'll give you one to show to the President."

"I'd like that very much. And I won't ask who you got to make those copies."

"Good, because you probably wouldn't like the answer," Sin responded, and smiled. "But if it will set your mind at ease, the man in question doesn't have any interest in duplicating paper currency."

Hugh laughed, although this in its essence was anything but a funny subject. "But that still leaves you with the question of how best to use that piece of paper—the original, that is."

Sin reflected for a moment. "What we need to do," he said with great deliberation, "is to get the Consortium together, all in one room."

"Not in any room in this house," Caro pointed out. "And I wouldn't want to make our closest friends a part of this plan. They've done enough for us already."

"Yes, the rest of this is up to us alone."

"If you don't mind my asking, Sinclair, what is it exactly that you want?" Hugh asked this question with great care and caution. "There's a good deal of power inherent in that letter, but only if it's used properly."

"I don't want to make a scandal," Sin said after a long moment's thought. "I have to admit that in the beginning that's exactly what I did want. At that time—and for a long time afterward—I saw no reason why the Consortium shouldn't have some of the public humiliation that I suffered."

"But now?"

"I simply want my father's name cleared, and I want to regain control of the companies they took from us."

"The latter may be easier than the former, and I wish either the President or I had some words of advice for you in this matter."

"Swindlers need special handling," Caro said. "By nature they're extremely crafty, so we have to be equally crafty. No threats, nothing violent, and no accusations until absolutely necessary."

Sin looked at his wife, his admiration obvious. This sort of conversation could go on indefinitely, yet Caro had the knack of being able to cut through needless talk.

"That's about it, colonel, at least for the time being," Sin said quietly. "No one ever said this was going to be easy. We'll keep you apprised of what we're going to do next, and when. We've already gotten this far, and one way or another we'll finally sort it all out.

"What do you think about our giving a dinner party?" Caro asked a half-hour later as they walked toward their bedroom, having just shown Hugh to the door.

"Judging by the friends we've had for dinner already, I'd say that we seem to have acquired the elusive knack of giving a good party."

"Well, I hope our luck holds with the one I've just thought up."

They stopped in front of the painting of the nine happy Pekingese.

"Don't tell me your idea has something to do with the Consortium?" Sin inquired with a sidelong glance as he leaned against the wall.

"Unhappily, it does. We have to get them all together, and a dinner party—if we can call it that— seems to be the best way."

"It probably is," he admitted, and slowly began to smile. "And the more I think about it, the more I like it. Since we don't want them here, we'll have to take a room in a restaurant—one we don't like very much."

"We're going to have to take a lot of things into consideration before we can even begin to try to work this out. It's not going to be easy to bring nine people together in the same room."

"Nine people?" Sin questioned, doing some quick counting.

"That includes the Consortium, us, and Cynthia Moreton-Chandler."

Sin's smile was perfectly male. "You're not going to tell me that Cynthia's name is on our unwritten guest list because you don't want to be the only woman at the table?"

"Cynthia has every right to be at the dinner party. I can't believe she doesn't care about how her father died."

"You're jealous of her."

"Oh, you don't have to flash that self-satisfied smile! You know how irresistible you are to women."

"Well, I'm an extremely proper and very happily married man now."

"Yes, and you'd better remember that," she said as they began to laugh. "Shall we finish this conversation in the bedroom?"

"I'd have a conversation with you in the linen closet."

"We don't have to be quite *that* secretive. But from the look on your face now, I'd say that this is definitely going to be business before pleasure."

"We can take care of the business part while we change for dinner," Sin said, and pulled her close for a kiss. "I want to have something else to do while we make plans for our little gathering, because if we stay here any longer, I may get angry enough to melt the lacquer off the walls."

"The painters who worked on this apartment would come after you with their brushes. Besides," she went on, touching the frame of the painting, "if our Pekingese could hear what we know about the Consortium, they wouldn't look happy at all."

Chapter Twenty-one

Delmonico's was established in 1828, when brothers John and Peter Delmonico opened an exclusive confectioners' shop on William Street in lower Manhattan. Hot foods were added to the menu a few years later, and the restaurant's always excellent reputation had nowhere to go but up. A series of moves brought the establishment uptown, these changes carefully timed to coincide with New York's inevitable growth. 1876 saw them relocated from Fourteenth Street to the corner of Fifth Avenue and Twenty-sixth Street, where, along with the Brunswick and the Fifth Avenue Hotels, it created a glittering attraction for increasingly demanding New Yorkers who wanted to see and be seen.

This new establishment included private rooms along with the public, albeit very exclusive, dining rooms, and it served to set the stage for the next move. By the early months of 1902, Delmonico's was firmly in command of the corner of Fifth Avenue and Forty-fourth Street, directly opposite from their greatest rival—the establishment founded by Louis Sherry.

Delmonico's had spent so many years as the *ne plus ultra* of American restaurants that it was hard for some to believe that it had slipped slightly from its perch on the pinnacle. There was no fault to be found with the food, and no complaints were voiced against the green-and-yellow dining room decorated in the style of Louis XVI. The Gentlemen's Elizabethan Café, the Ladies' Restaurant, and the Palm Garden rarely saw an empty table; and the private dining banquet rooms, as well as the ballroom and rooftop conservatory, rarely went begging for lack of private parties. But something in the second year of the new century had changed.

Delmonico's had fallen ever so slightly out of fashion.

It was Sherry's, reposing in a twelve-story Stanford White building, that attracted the fashionable. Delmonico's was now the fondly regarded conservative that everyone still loved in his own way, rather like a wonderful old relative . . . which meant it was just the place for Caroline and Sinclair Poole to entertain the Consortium.

Neither really wanted to hold this gathering at a restaurant they didn't like. A poorly prepared and served meal in less than first-class quarters wasn't going to make the night's objective any easier to obtain. Subtlety was the key, they agreed, and that let out places like Rector's and Shanley's and Churchill's, all of which were at the center of the city's "lobster palace" society. The Café des Beaux Arts was too theatrical, and even though the Café Martin on Twenty-sixth Street offered an authentic and sumptuous French atmosphere and truly elegant private dining rooms, it wasn't quite what they wanted.

Which left a choice between a private room at Delmonico's or at Sherry's. Faced with the fact that after dinner they might not want to go into *either* restaurant again for some time, it was decided that they could stand avoiding Delmonico's far better than they could Sherry's.

And when this conclusion was reached, the next step was to reserve a small private dining room at Delmonico's for what they informed the management would be a business dinner at eight o'clock on Monday evening, March 31, 1902.

Cavier canapés with sherry
Consommé
English sole Marinette ornamented with
tomatoes and orange slices
Breast of partridge on slices of pineapple
broiled in macaroon dust
Asparagus
Salade Français
Crêpes soufflés with apricot purée

Caro looked from the neatly printed list to the calligraphy-written menu cards, checking to make sure that all was in order. She smiled at Andre, the assistant banquet manager who was assisting them with all the arrangements, and handed the master list back to him.

"Everything is in excellent order, just as always at Delmonico's."

"We're very pleased to be of service to you and Mr. Poole," Andre returned pleasantly. "Shall I arrange the menu cards on the table?"

"No, thank you. I'll do that when I set out the place cards. Now I already have our original requests about the food service, but please check with my husband one more time before anyone arrives. He should still be with Felix, checking over the wines."

Andre assured her he would do that, and when she was alone again, Caro moved around the table, setting out menu cards and place cards according to the plan she and Sin had worked out beforehand.

When her task was finished, she surveyed the results of the seating plan. Sin would be at the head of the table, she would be at his left, and Cynthia would find her place at her erstwhile fiancé's right. The other guests on the left side of the table would be Adam Marsh, Benjamin Wyndham, and Kenneth Chandler; and Wendell Simpson, Curtis Chandler, and Avery Dutton would occupy the right side of the table. Without a doubt, this was a table that would give those who authored etiquette books a case of the shudders, but this was the only seating plan that would work.

The thought of Cynthia Moreton-Chandler sitting across from her and next to Sin made the muscles at the back of Caro's neck tighten. It was stupid to feel this way, she thought, but no amount of sensible instruction to herself was going to change a thing. Alix, whom Sin could have married at any time, raised no jealousy in her; but Cynthia, the woman Sin had become engaged to because it was an alliance his father desired, raised in her all the detestable emotions. Their one meeting had set off every female warning signal she had. This was one woman she did not want to know any better.

Nonetheless, Caro wasn't about to let anything slip by her, and that included what she wore. Keeping in mind that Cynthia was in mourning for her father—and she didn't doubt for a minute that Mrs. Chandler would wear anything but black—she knew that her own dress had to complement and not contrast. Her selection for tonight was a Lucile evening dress of black net and lace over pale-blue chiffon and satin. Frost-pink beads were embroidered over the bertha and upper portion of the skirt, and around her throat she had clasped the pearl and diamond choker with a diamond baguette center that had belonged to Sin's mother.

"You look beautiful," Gregori said as he came in carrying a stenographer's pad in one hand and several sharpened pencils in the other. "With you here, the Consortium won't know what hit them."

"That's very nice to hear." Caro laughed. "What do you want to bet that if Cynthia doesn't wear all-black, she'll turn up in flaming red chiffon?"

"I wouldn't touch that bet with a barge pole."

"I won't hold it against you." Caro took another

step back from the table. "Did you have a nice dinner in the Gentlemen's Café?"

"I suppose so. I couldn't eat very much."

"Somehow I don't think we're going to eat very much at this table, either," Caro observed. "I have an urge to apologize to you for not being able to seat you at this table, except that you'll probably be better off in the serving pantry, taking notes."

"I knew the shorthand course I took last year would come in handy eventually," Gregori said as Sin walked in.

"I'd suggest that we have a predinner drink so we can toast tonight's enterprise," he said, joining them, "but I don't think we'd get as much as a single sip down."

"My butterflies are having a very busy evening," Caro said, raising her face for his kiss. "Does Delmonico's understand all our instructions? We don't want them accidently barging in here."

"They assured me several times that on rare occasion they've had other guests who prefer having their own servants serve the food. One thing they're not used to, though," he went on with a slight smile, "is having a secretary lurking in the pantry, taking down everything that's said."

"I hope no one offered to bring up brandy and cigars."

"That would be the last thing I'd want to see on this table. I've always hated that custom anyway, and tonight it seems less appropriate than ever."

"We don't have to create any more illusion than necessary for this little group," Caro agreed. "One

446

thing does make me feel a little better—that the men who banded together to ruin your father probably don't have any idea that we have the letter. All they know is that it's missing."

"How can you be so sure?"

"If we'd been seen while we were at the Linden Trees, they wouldn't have accepted our dinner invitation. What better way to set you on edge and wear you down then by staying apart and making you go to each one in turn?"

"To think that for the first time the Consortium is more vulnerable than I am, and they're not even aware of it," Sin mused. "Our one consolation for the evening ahead."

Sin looked around the small dining room. It was all so restrained and elegant that if a stranger wandered in, he could be forgiven for assuming that the people who in a short time would be seated around the finely set table were all friends, he decided. His heart was thudding to a peculiar beat, but he had never felt stronger.

"Sinclair, darling, are you all right?"

Caro's quiet, concerned voice pierced his complicated thoughts. "As long as you're going to be seated next to me, I'm going to be better than ever," he told her, his heart in his eyes.

The small brass carriage clock on the mantle marked the hour with a series of small thumps. It was eight o'clock, the appointed hour, and they all looked at each other.

"I'd better take my place in the pantry," Gregori said as they heard the sound of approaching guests;

no one was going to be fashionably late tonight. "When this is over—*all* over—I have something important to tell both of you. I owe you so much, Sin, and you never asked me a single question, even though I'm sure you wanted to. It's time for me to repay all your trust in me."

As Caro had so accurately predicted, Cynthia did indeed wear black. Her Doucet evening dress was made of richly rustling black taffeta covered by black sequins on black net, trimmed with matching tulle and chiffon ruffles and black sequin butterflies. Wisely, she had not worn any supplementary glitter in the form of precious jewels, allowing that her wedding and engagement rings were more than equal to the task, but the entire effect was not one that could be equated with mourning.

She's kept the form but not the substance, and she's dressed as much for me as I have for her, Caro thought an hour later as they sat opposite each other, the entire table bathed in silence as George and Sean and Vic served the first course.

Dinner at Delmonico's: from now on, Caro knew, whenever she heard that familiar phrase, she would think only of this night. It wasn't what had happened so far, but what might still take place.

It wasn't that any rude words or angry looks had been exchanged. On the contrary, absolutely everyone was on his best behavior, and there was no indication on the part of the Consortium that anyone had any idea that Sin either had the letter or was going to make any demands on them that they would be forced to obey.

So far, if you don't count the champagne, Caro thought, they were all being so dull and respectable and polite that they might as well be a Temperance gathering.

Strange how their guests (and as much as she disliked the term, there wasn't another word that really fit) met the descriptions Sin had given her so many weeks ago, she reflected as, once again, the conversation resumed.

Seated next to her was Adam Marsh, a man who preferred to operate on a small scale, so in no way could he be considered a moving force in the Consortium. He had meticulous manners, and his cultured voice was so measured and careful that Caro imagined he marked off each word with an invisible mental ruler. He set her teeth on edge.

Seated beside him was Benjamin Wyndham, and he truly looked like a man with powerful connections among Washington's Republican elite. A close personal friend of political king-maker Mark Hanna, he bore a passing resemblance to that piggy-looking man. He wasn't fat so much as bulky, and this made his table manners seem less than graceful, while also giving the impression of his eating a great deal, even though he was picking at his food. Although his complexion was pale, his small, mud-colored eyes seemed to dart everywhere; no one was going to catch *him* napping. Caro was glad she didn't have to face him while she ate.

Kenneth Chandler was almost as familiar to her

now as the son who so strongly resembled him. Pure Old New York, both in patrician face and courtly manner, and that demeanor could skillfully cover any sort of defect. Sin had been right to steer clear of him.

Seated across from Kenneth was Avery Dutton. Caro felt her stomach clench as she looked at him. Here was proof positive that a nondescript man could be even more dangerous than a too-handsome one. Pity Sin didn't punch him when he had the chance, she thought; a black eye might have made him more noticeable.

Curtis Chandler, on the other hand, would *never* run the risk of being passed over. His looks were not the sort Caro liked, but he had obviously appealed to Cynthia, and Caro wondered what their marriage might be like. They had a mansion on Fifth Avenue, two children, and a social life that was an object of envy to some, but no matter how hard she tried, she couldn't use the love and happiness she shared with Sin as a basis for how the Chandlers fared together.

Finally, her glance fell on Wendell Simpson, the one member of the Consortium they had thought was beyond their reach because of his long residence in Europe. Tailored in a fashion that would have made a British duke proud, he was regaling the table with tales of his ocean voyage home aboard the *Deutschland*.

"The four-stackers is what the future of ocean travel is all about," he told them with certainty, "and the Hamburg–America Line is doing it better than anyone. They have a superior time-and-safety record, plus cleanliness and efficiency. What else could a traveler ask for?

"Good food and imaginative decor, for one thing," Caro couldn't resist pointing out. "You have to admit, Mr. Simpson, that German ships aren't noted for either."

Wendell heard her out and laughed indulgently. "That sounds like one of the brochures the French Line puts out. Why, half their passengers must be made up of wives who talked their husbands into booking passage on the *La Savoie* or the *Lorraine* because it's supposed to be the chic way to cross," he told them. "When the German liners learn to please the ladies a bit more with the frills they love, mark my word, they'll be the ones ruling the transatlantic crossings."

"Perhaps both the Hamburg–America Line and the North German Lloyd would be wiser simply to make their liners so appealing to the gentlemen traveler that the ladies have no say in the travel arrangements," Avery put in.

"Being a bachelor allows one to make declarations like that, Avery," Sin said, addressing his first full sentence in seven years to the man he considered first among his enemies. "If you ever find it worth your while to leave that status behind, you'll find that you can't make all the decisions on your own and expect someone else to follow behind you like an overeager puppy."

"Are you trying to make a point, Sinclair?" Avery questioned, an edge to his voice.

"Me? Not at all." Sin put down his soup spoon,

looked to see if the others were finished, and signaled that it was time to clear and follow with the fish course. "I was just observing that marriage, like any number of other endeavors, requires more than one person making the decisions. Surely you're familiar with the notion?"

Sin's words, quietly delivered but full of hidden meaning that was clear to everyone else, seemed to vibrate around the table. The thin veil of politeness that had surrounded the dinner party was now rent. If any of the Consortium had thought Sin was still essentially harmless, they did no longer. Tonight was to right all the old wrongs, and only time would tell how he intended to try to achieve this end . . . and how much he knew.

Sin looked straight down the length of the table, past the low silver bowls filled with white chrysanthemums, to the opposite end from where he sat. There was no place set there, all part of the plan, and he couldn't control the chill that moved down his spine. He hadn't intended to make his first move quite so soon, but now there was no going back. For a moment he let his thoughts drift, and his only touch with reality was a woman's hand lightly touching his. Caro, he thought hazily, and stopped himself from returning the warm pressure when he belatedly remembered that it was his right hand that was captured. Caro was at his left.

He looked at Cynthia in disbelief and annoyance, but Caro spoke first.

"Please take your hand off my husband, Cynthia. I don't want to have to ask again."

Her voice was soft and ever so slightly dangerous, but Cynthia smiled at her even as she complied. It was an expression that would have fooled anyone except another woman.

"I only wanted Sinclair to know that no one here holds anything against him."

"Unfortunately, Cynthia, I think you have that the other way around. And you had your chance with Sinclair seven years ago. You didn't want him then, and you can't have him now. Not that he wants you."

"Do you like Caroline's being so possessive about you, Sinclair?" Cynthia questioned him.

"Very much," he said. "And I'm not here to fight with your husband over you."

"And why *did* you and your charming wife invite all of us here tonight, Sinclair?" Curtis asked. While the other men at the table looked suspicious and sullen and nervous, Curtis merely looked amused, and despite himself, Sin felt a small dart of grudging approval for his manner. "I have nothing against coming here and being in your company, but we all know we're not here to listen to another of Wendell's stories about having dinner with the Kaiser. He's been dining out on them since he returned."

"Much to my own amazement, Curtis, it seems we have something to agree about," Sin returned evenly. "I don't want to hear about Germany, either." He paused to let his gaze travel over the table again. "Not when we have so many other interesting things to take up. George, Sean, Vic. . . . the next course, please."

The partridge, Caro reflected a short time later, might as well have been made out of sawdust and library paste for all anyone at the table wanted to eat it. The sense of tension was subtle, but far too strong to be ignored. Sin was holding the cards, but he was playing them so close to his chest that Caro wasn't sure what he was going to do next. After the meal was finished, after they left the table, once tonight was over, there were no other chances. If he couldn't set things right within the next few hours, he would truly feel he'd failed his father, hadn't honored his memory; and it would forever color the life they would lead together.

The conversation continued in its bland way, and there were no further references, hidden or otherwise, to events the Consortium might or might not have been connected with. In deference to the ladies, the older men restrained themselves from discussing the one topic dearest to them—business both American and international.

The theatre was a safe topic, and so was the opera, but such talk was only a temporary filler. No cartel, no matter how closely the members are linked to each other, is strong when things begin to go badly, when the first crack is made in the concrete wall of supposed invincibility.

It's then and only then that the truth starts to come out, Caro thought.

The charade continued through salad and dessert, but when the last plates were removed and the café filtre served, Sin rose slowly and deliberately to his feet. The smile that played about his mouth was part

454

contempt, part amusement, and Caro found that she honestly wasn't sure how he really felt.

"Do you find revenge as interesting a topic as I do?" Sin questioned, standing behind his chair. "Over the past years, I've experienced a variety of feelings on that particular subject."

"Sinclair, what is your point?" Kenneth Chandler asked, his tone of voice same as he might have used to address an eager new employee fresh out of Yale.

"Why, Kenneth, I can't believe you want to rush me," Sin replied calmly. "My father always told me that you above everyone else loved details, the more the better."

"But we're not discussing business now," the older man replied on a slightly defensive note.

"But of course we *are* discussing business."

"Not in front of the ladies." Adam Marsh offered up a protest, and Sin swallowed his laughter.

"Are you really going to sit there, Adam, and tell us that my wife and Mrs. Chandler don't know what we're going to discuss?" Sin inquired, but before any reply could be made, he went on, "As I was saying, revenge is not one feeling, neither does it take one form, and it changes from person to person. It can even be adapted over the years, so that the results desired in the beginning are not the same in the end."

He's started, Caro thought, her heart pounding. Sin won't go back, won't accept anything less than clearing his father's name, but none of this is going to be settled easily.

"And what do you think you're going to get out of any of us, Sinclair?" Wendell Simpson inquired silkily. "We were *all* friends of your father, and if you're in some sort of financial difficulty, I'm sure we can see our way clear to make a loan for you—at a slightly higher rate of interest, of course."

"Considering you wouldn't do anything to help my father, I suppose I should say 'Thank you.' But since all of you know perfectly well that I don't need a loan, you'll forgive me if the words stick in my throat."

"Your diplomat's manner is lost on Sinclair," Avery snarled. "He says 'Thank you' to servants, to waiters, to newsboys on the street corner, but never to his equals."

"I see you're still giving yourself undeserved airs," Sin remarked, ice dripping from every word. "But if by some awful chance you've become what the business world would call my 'equal,' I think I'd rather be selling newspapers on the street corner."

"I don't think your new bride would appreciate the drop in income," Cynthia put in smoothly.

"How much would you appreciate it, Cynthia, if Curtis' income suffered a dramatic change between tonight and tomorrow morning?" Caro spoke quickly, anger filling her words. There was much more she could say, but suddenly she became aware that anything she and Cynthia might say would not only use up precious time but detract from Sin's objective.

"Caroline and I are leaving for California in a few weeks," he continued in a controlled voice, "so you might say that tonight is a sort of *bon voyage* dinner . . . a chance to settle some unfinished matters.''

As he spoke, Sin left his place behing the chair and began to walk toward the foot of the table. Once there, he stopped, and with every eye on him, he ran a hand over the fine damask tablecloth where another place setting normally would have been . . . the place they had decided to leave significantly open.

''I'm sure you've all noticed that our seating plan tonight is hardly what one expects to see at a dinner party,'' he went on conversationally. ''But when Caro and I worked out our plan, we decided not to set a place here, to leave it as a memorial to the two men who aren't here tonight—Stanford Poole and Davis Moreton.''

The silence that fell over the table was broken by Benjamin Wyndham's coughing fit. The terrible hacking sound filled the small dining room, and everyone at the table regarded the white-faced, coughing man with varying degrees of surprise, concern, and revulsion. For a split second Caro wondered if this could be his way of somehow disrupting Sin's plans, but a good look at his contorted face made her revise that opinion, and she signaled Vic.

''Please bring Mr. Wyndham a brandy,'' she instructed softly.

How many minutes it took until all was calm again, Caro realized she would never know. The coughing spasm ended, the brandy was accepted, and when he was able to talk again, Benjamin regarded his fellow conspirators out of bloodshot eyes.

"Are we going to tell him what he wants to know and put an end to this?" he inquired, his voice hoarse.

"And just what is it we're supposed to tell him?" Adam inquired smoothly. He was long adept at covering his tracks, and this turn of events was not about to faze him. "We have nothing new to say to Sinclair. If after all these years he still holds some sort of grudge, that is not our concern."

As Adam finished his little piece, he reminded Caro of the sort of neat, orderly, eye-on-the-bottom-line banker who could turn people out of their homes and into the streets without a flicker of emotion. But it was the evil smile now forming on Avery's face that made her fix her attention on him, to see what he would say and do.

Sin made the next move. With one swift motion, he brought his fist down on the table. The expression on his face and in his eyes immediately wiped out the few self-satisfied smiles that had begun to appear.

"*Thieves*," he shouted when the glasses stopped shaking.

"You apparently are unaware of whom you're calling names," Avery said with contempt.

"*Swindlers*."

"You've become unhinged." Avery's eyes were bright with disdain. "You don't realize how things have changed, and not in your favor—"

"*Murderers!*" Sin felt the rush of adrenaline course through his body. "It wasn't enough to ruin my father, destroy his reputation, take everything from him, you had to *kill him as well!*"

"No!" With great difficulty, Benjamin stood up. 'It wasn't supposed to happen like that—it wasn't supposed to go so far—it all went our of control—"

"Shut up, you stupid old man," Avery growled. "He doesn't know a thing, it's all a bluff."

"Can you be perfectly sure about that?" Curtis asked with not a little bit of malice. "You've spent seven years telling yourself you got the best of Sinclair Poole, and now you've actually begun to believe it."

"Well, if you want to play this like all the other old men—"

"Sometimes it takes an old man to know when to face the truth," Benjamin said heavily, and turned to face Sin. "I'm ill, and as far as I'm concerned, this has gone on long enough. You do have the letter, don't you?"

"Yes, I have the letter," he said, speaking to the older man as if the others weren't at the table.

"Since the night of the costume ball?"

"No, not that long," he replied, his voice almost casual, not wanting to look at Avery, Kenneth, or Curtis because he knew he would laugh in their faces. "Caroline and I found it in the card room at the Linden Trees, the one in which Davis and I had our last meeting. The window seat opens up—rather like a child's playbox—and there it was. They say honeymoons are lucky times, and ours certainly was—" Sin paused for a crucial half-second. "It brought us to the Linden Trees ahead of the search

459

party you organized, Kenneth. As it turned out, the same luck also got us out of there without your seeing us."

Sin felt an almost indecent sense of pleasure as he saw Avery's face blotch with anger. He knows he practically walked right past us, he thought with relish. Right now he's thinking that if only he'd been a little more careful, we wouldn't be sitting here right now.

Deciding that it wouldn't be good form to smile—at least not just yet—he turned his attention from Avery to Benjamin.

"Why did you do this to my father?" Sin said at last.

Looking like anything but a Republican moghul now, Benjamin grew even paler and clutched the back of his chair for support. "You must believe me when I tell you that a trial and the possibility of prison—and certainly your father's death—were not in our plans. In the beginning, all we wanted was to invest in some of his companies—the railroads in Arizona and Colorado, the West Coast shipping line, the steel mill in Pennsylvania, the forest and paper mill in Canada. They were all there, ready to mint money, and Stanford wasn't even using them to their full potential. . . . "

"What you really mean is that my father wasn't rapacious enough for you," Sin said on a fresh wave of anger and bitterness. "He cared enough about the land not to want to destroy it for the richest, quickest profit; and he believed that those who worked for him deserved a decent wage and as safe a place as possible to work in. That really must have made you and your group insane with anger," he went on savagely. "After all, what's the good of making million after million if some of it isn't dripping with the blood of the men who worked for you."

"You sound like a damned Socialist," Kenneth interjected in an attempt to deflect this conversation from the route it was so inevitably following.

"I'll sound like anything I damn please," Sin replied, his voice too calm. "You game is over, Kenneth, and I'm the one holding the winning cards now. Or, to be absolutely correct and specific, the letter."

"Would you find it too vulgar of us if we requested to see the letter?" Curtis asked in a voice that was almost disinterested. "I'm sure that you'll agree that the pig in the poke is no way to go about any business discussion."

"No, not even this one," Sin agreed dryly, removing the letter from the inside pocket of his coat. "And Avery, please don't grab it and rush to the fireplace. This is a copy—an expert one, I'm sure you'll all agree," he went on as it was passed around the table. "The original is in a safety deposit box at a location I'm not about to disclose, and another copy is currently in the hands of the President."

"*Liar*," Avery hissed.

"I think not," Sin returned, and fixed his gaze on Benjamin. "I believe you were about to tell me how all of you came to form the Great Northwest Lumber Company?"

"It wasn't our aim. . . . It took us almost a year after Adam and Kenneth convinced your father to hire Avery as his private secretary instead of you, Sinclair. We had to make Stanford think that it was all legitimate, and Avery played his part to perfection. He kept his employer busy, never let him see too many papers. I can't count the number of times Avery told us how he had to dissuade Stanford from taking a trip to Oregon to see the headquarters."

"The headquarters that didn't exist."

"Yes. We decided that once Stanford had offered shares in the Great Northwest Lumber Company, it would be time to let the newspapers know that this was a dummy corporation, that one of the most respected financial men in America was perpetrating a fraud," Benjamin went on, his voice growing less strong, less sure. "Once the truth was out, we knew Stanford would want to make full restitution to the investors. That would mean the most profitable of his companies would have to go on the block, and we would purchase them. The idea of a trial was the furthest thing from our minds—"

"*But it still happened.*" Sin's voice was icy again. "And when it kept gathering speed, none of you made even the slightest effort to stop it. But then, why should intangibles like *truth* and *honor* and *doing the right thing* count when they will never show up on a balance sheet or in a bank account?"

The only sound in the room was that of Benjamin Wyndham's bulky body as he lowered himself to his chair. It was apparent to everyone that this was an old, ill man, and even Sin, who had long ago hardened his heart against these men, didn't want to have a medical incident on his hands.

Almost as if he'd whispered the words in her ear, Caro knew what Sin was thinking, and she rose from her chair and went over to the older man. She had no more sympathy for him than her husband did, but where Sin couldn't show any sign of personal interest—it would immediately mark him as having a vulnerable streak that the Consortium would be more than happy to exploit—she could.

"Would you like us to call a doctor?" she asked quietly.

"No, Mrs. Poole, I do not. I may be ill, but I am not facing my problems as a weakling. I am not Davis Moreton."

Caro straightened up and looked at Sin. *Was it murder, or was it suicide?* The question they had asked each other at Cove House ran through her mind. So there were going to be two parts to tonight's confrontation after all, she mused. Now they had the admission that there had been a well-organized conspiracy to ruin Stanford Poole; it still remained to be seen if they could also solve the mystery behind Davis Moreton's demise.

"Fortunately, few of us are." Avery's insolent voice instantly turned all attention to him. "Davis had all the success and power a man could want, and at the end all he wanted was to clean the slate like some second-rate bank robber who got religion. You did quite a job on him, Sinclair."

"Contrary to your twisted fantasies, Avery, I didn't do anything to Davis that he didn't do to

463

himself first. I didn't even help him over the edge. But quite possibly you did."

"What do you mean by that?" Avery inquired in a voice that Sin supposed struck fear in the hearts of his underlings, but failed miserably in its attempt to make him retract his words.

Sin continued to observe Avery in neutral silence while the other men stood up. Benjamin's confession was, in its own way, nothing more than confirmation of everything he'd either found out or suspected over the years, but Avery was still his sore point. The instant antipathy that had been struck between them the moment they met had never gone into abeyance on either side. For him, far more than for any of the others, Sin reserved his special sense of anger, resentment, and jealousy that began the day Avery had been made his father's private secretary.

"You have a good idea of what I mean, Avery. You had a great deal of contempt for Davis, and you seem to delight in making your feelings known at every opportunity. Curtis noticed it even before I did. If I remember the conversation I overheard correctly, he said that if you were faced with a distraught man on the edge of suicide, you'd probably urge him to pull the trigger!"

"I never told him to do that, he was ready to do it all by himself!" Avery shouted. The effect of his words was immediate, and Cynthia's strangled cry of surprise drowned out the others' gasps. "You bastard," Avery said, coming for Sin. "You tricked me."

"Still blaming everyone for your problems except

yourself," Sin returned, smiling as he easily ducked the punch Avery threw. Once again, even after all these years, he felt the urge to punch him in the jaw, but this time he grabbed Avery above the elbows and pushed him backward so that he was neatly propelled into George's waiting arms.

"Now, Mr. Dutton," George said all too pleasantly, "wouldn't you like to continue this conversation with Mr. Poole in a more gentlemanly manner?"

"Never without your faithful bodyguard, are you, Sinclair?" he sneered.

"I believe you just proved George more than earns the salary I pay him. But we were discussing Davis, and how you played a part in his suicide." Sin's eyes bore coldly into his. "Somehow you found out that Davis and I had been meeting, and you began to harass him about it, no doubt reminding him that his first loyalty lay with the Consortium. Were you able to. . . . persuade him to tell you about the things we discussed?"

"Yes. I mean, no . . . I don't know. He may have been lying. Davis told me that when you first called him, all you talked about was the Columbia-Yale game—that and baseball."

"As it happens, he was telling the truth. Eventually, however, we began to talk about other things. But you must have bullied Davis into telling you everything we discussed, from the most innocent of topics straight through to the letter—which he was ready to return to me."

"He wouldn't have given it to you." Avery returned smugly. "He had hidden the letter before you met the last time, and if I'd had a few more minutes, I would have convinced him to give it to *me*. . . ."

Very slowly and with great deliberation Sin began to smile. There was no mirth in the expression, there wasn't even evidence that the moment he'd worked for for so long was at hand. It was simply that he was too aware of the monumental event that had just taken place not to have some sort of positive reaction. The night at the Linden Trees that was so fragmented for everyone involved was now, finally, coming together.

"It was you in the card room with Davis after I left," Sin said, and it was a statement and not a question.

"I tried to reason with him that whole day," Avery said, and Sin realized that this man who had caused him so much grief was actually *proud* of his part in this series of events. "We met in that awful little club office before the other guests arrived, but he wouldn't listen, and when he heard you coming, he made me leave . . almost threw me out."

"But you still listened at the door."

Avery's laugh was high and unpleasant. "I even followed the two of you from the office to the card room. You were both so lost in conversation that neither of you noticed. I thought he was going to take care of all his problems in front of you. That would have gotten you into hot water sure enough," he gloated, almost as if it had happened like that. "Instead, you decided to give him time to recover and left him alone. I waited in the card room next door until you were safely out of the way.''

"And when he was alone again, you went back into the room and you murdered him!'' Cynthia said, her voice scaling upward until it reached a shriek. Her face was chalk-white, and Caro thought she must be on the verge of fainting. "I spend years watching you fawn over my father, then mock him behind his back, and finally, when he wasn't of any more service to you, you killed him!''

"No, it wasn't like that. He did do it himself. I tried to stop him—''

"How, Avery, by telling him he'd make a mess of the room?'' Sin asked.

"I tried to tell him how much we'd lose once you had the letter, but all he could say was how much he regretted everything he did. He took out that little gun and began to wave it around, but I wasn't worried—he was old and weak, and I thought I could take it away from him without too much trouble. But Davis was stronger than I expected, and when I tried to get it from him, he pushed me away, and before I could pick myself up and tackle him again, he shot himself.'' Avery took a deep breath. "When I saw he was dead, I went through the window and came back inside the club by the kitchen entrance. Everything was in such an uproar that no one paid any attention to me.''

"But you made sure that everyone heard two people shouting in the room. Cynthia saw me and made the natural assumption that I belonged to the voice overheard. Which is just what you wanted," Sin pressed on.

"Yes, that's exactly what I wanted. When they all started shouting your name, I loved it," Avery shouted, his face contorted with loathing. "The police were on the way, you were going to be found and hauled off, and if I couldn't get you indicted for murder, I figured that with some good theatrics and crocodile tears, you'd be named as an accessory. Except . . . except. . ." His venomous gaze went from Sin to Caro and back again; not another word was necessary.

"Some things, Avery, no matter how carefully you plot and plan, simply aren't meant to work out."

"I hate you, you bastard, you damn rich boy with the silver spoon in his mouth." Avery's loathing seeped from every pore. "I waited seven years for you to get tired of being beyond the pale. But you never had to beg your way back into a social life, did you?"

"Possibly, I never had to really worry about being left out," Sin responded unable to resist twisting the knife just a bit. "Perhaps it's a bit like being born to the British nobility: no matter what you do, you always remain what you were born to."

"Well, that may be how you choose to live, but you're in an ever-increasing minority—the kind who likes to remember that they have a conscience. Davis liked to think of himself as a robber baron, but in the end he turned to a musheating, quivering old heap of bones."

"But you won't?"

"This is a new century, and gentlemen with your particular moral code aren't going to get very far or last very long."

"So you think I'm a dinosaur?"

"One who has scored a temporary victory. My back may be to the wall this time, but it won't always be." A narrow, knowing smile spread across his face. "You have the letter, but I bet you're having second thoughts about using it."

"If I were, your antagonism would take care of it." Sin reclaimed the copy of letter that now lay ignored on the table. He looked at it for a long time before refolding it and placing it back in his inside pocket. "The one good thing I have to tell you," he said, drawing out every word, "is that making this letter public would serve no good reason, and I won't do it as long as you follow my instructions exactly. All of this, all the plots and the conspiracy and dirty work that all of you banded together to do, stays quiet—provided you return to me every company that you stole from my father."

"You can't expect us to do that!" Wendell exclaimed, outraged. "Why, the bookkeeping itself. . . !"

"Newton Phipps, William Seligman, and Philip Leslie have all offered me people from their firms to help with the transfers. Since all of you were smart enough to set the Consortium up as a corporation separate from your other business dealings, it shouldn't be all that difficult. In particular, I'm looking forward to having control of the armaments

469

company that was among your spoils," he told Wendell. "It was small but profitable, and you've made it quite large and successful. But I may have to scale it down, or at least redirect it, since I'm not interested in helping the Kaiser fuel his war machine."

"Is that all you expect of us?" Curtis inquired. Not that he would admit it here, but he considered the Consortium—to say nothing of his father and his friends—to be stodgy, static, and old-fashioned. If Sin wanted it all back again, fine; he had his eyes on the future—motorcars, skyscrapers and, just possibly some day soon, the flying machine. "No other little interests?"

"I don't intend to confuse justice and blackmail. But there is one thing that I insist on. All of you conspired to ruin my father, and now you can help clear him," Sin said, looking at each of them in turn. "You will not only not keep anything, not so much as a single share of stock or a dollar's profit, but starting tomorrow you will start to tell anyone who'll listen—and even those who won't—that you have some accurate inside information that Stanford Poole was framed, that all the evidence against him was lies, and that considering all those disturbing facts you've uncovered, the only right thing to do was return the companies to me."

"You can't mean that." Kenneth rose to his feet, his face a frozen mask of outrage. "Why, we'd be the laughing stock of Wall Street! And who would believe a word of it?"

"Making your stories believable is not my concern," Sin responded coldly. "But when you think about it, I'm sure you'll prefer a bit of disbelief and snickering behind your backs to a far-reaching and long-lasting scandal in the newspapers and the possibility of another trial—with all of you at the defendants' table this time."

"I suppose you expect us to thank you for generosity in this matter," Cynthia said, all her warmth toward Sin now gone.

"No, I'm not doing any of this out of consideration for any of you. If I can avoid it, I don't want to go through another scandal and another trial—particularly when there's no guarantee of conviction. It would just be the luck of the Consortium to get off. Given the choice, I'd rather wash my hands of you right now—provided you carry out my instructions."

"We'll fight this!" Adam swore. "We'll never forgive you. . . . "

"Oh, spare me," Sin snapped. "Forgiveness is exactly what you do want; if not now, then later. Davis begged me to forgive him, the guilt of his complicity was too much to bear, and human nature being what it is—" Sin shrugged and let his voice trail off.

"It was all business," Adam said in his precise voice. "We have nothing to feel guilty about. That's the free enterprise system, and our. . . . agreement with you is just one more business transaction."

"Anything you say, Adam," Sin replied, walking over to where Caro stood beside her chair. As the clock on the mantle once again marked the hour and

Monday became Tuesday, he began to smile. "But just for the record—and for the only way I can think of to end our dinner—I've reached a conclusion." He looked from Caro to the tableau in front of him. "For whatever it's worth—and because I have too many good things to do with my life than be connected with all of you—I've decided to forgive you."

"And am I included in your dispensation of good will?" Avery asked, and Caro couldn't help but think of him as the proverbial snake at the garden party. "Have you decided to forgive me as well?"

His voice was pure challenge, but Sin only laughed. With his arm around Caro's waist, they moved away from the table and toward the door, the host and hostess about to see their guests out.

"Avery, if you think I've decided to forgive *you*, you've picked the right moment for it," Sin told him. "Happy April Fool's Day."

Caro and Sin sat on the floor beneath a window, all alone in the dining room. It was a half-hour later and everyone else had left. The Consortium had departed with automatic good-nights, and the Pooles had sent George and Sean and Vic home—any final accounting of this night's proceedings could wait several hours.

"I think they were all a little disappointed that we didn't want to break out a magnum of champagne and have a rousing celebration," Caro said, eying the once-elegant table, now reduced to overturned demitasse cups, balled-up damask napkins, and chrysanthemums losing their petals. "They did yeoman service, and we have to reward them."

"A late breakfast tomorrow at our apartment should do for a start," Sin said.

"How do scrambled eggs with caviar and raisin pumpernickel bread with lots of sweet butter sound?"

"Like I'm going to plan on being very hungry," he whispered, nuzzling at her neck. One arm went around her waist. "Do you remember the last time we sat like this?"

"At the Linden Trees." Caro hesitated for a moment. "I wanted you to remember first, but it's as if that afternoon was the start of the third act, and tonight was the final curtain. Besides, there's no one I'd rather sit on the floor with than you," she finished, returning his caress.

"There are several differences this time. To begin with, I saved some champagne for us." Sin showed her the bottle of Mumm's that he'd placed on the window ledge. "I decided we deserved something different from what we served tonight. In fact, I thought we might have a celebration, but I don't feel very enthusiastic now."

"You mean you don't want to drink the champagne?"

"Whatever gave you an idea like that?"

They laughed, and Sin deftly worked out the cork. He noted the lack of glasses, regarded the bottle, and then stripped the foil away from the neck before raising it to his mouth and taking a long drink.

"I've always wanted to do that," he said at last.

"I don't believe this. You're not going to tell me that in your varied bachelor days you never drank champagne straight out of the bottle."

"I never did."

"I guess you must have preferred ladies' slippers."

"Shall I get a glass for you?"

"And miss out on all the fun? Hand it over."

They spent the next fifteen minutes passing the champagne bottle back and forth. The lack of proper glasses in no way diminished the enjoyment derived from the stream of golden bubbles. Champagne had sustained them through the ups and downs of the dinner party, and now it helped them through the period when they could not quite believe it was all over.

"Do you have any plans for the Prince Street house?" she asked at last as, full of love and champagne, they cuddled close together. "We don't have to live there again, but I'd hate to see it on the market. Someone might want to buy it who won't appreciate it, but you'll feel honor-bound to accept the offer."

"You're right—I don't want a stranger living there. I've been thinking about offering the house to Vic. That way he can run the club, and he and his family can live upstairs. We'll take the paintings and whatever other pieces we like best and leave the rest."

"What about your Eakins portrait?"

"If and when I have an office, I'll hang it in the reception area to frighten people."

"That sounds fine with me, but where are we going to put everything else we take?"

"That's the kind of question that sounds as if we're leading up to concrete matters."

"You could put it that way. We have all our plans made for San Francisco, but what happens when we get tired of the best suite in the Palace Hotel?"

"Would you mind staying on in California? We'll keep the apartment so we have a place to stop when we come back to shop and go to the theatre and take care of business, but as you so accurately predicted before we got married, I want to try living where I'm not too well known."

"That lets out Nob Hill."

"Please."

"Oh, you don't have to look like that. I don't want to live in San Francisco, either." She kissed him and nestled closer. "Would I be wrong in guessing that you have someplace in mind already?"

"Do you know anything about Montecito, the ocean side of Santa Barbara?"

"Vanessa and I spent a weekend there when we first arrived back in the States from Hawaii. Are we going to talk about building or buying; and if it's buying, have you had an offer, or are we going to have to look?"

Sin laughed. "There's no fooling you. That's why I want you to take charge of all the importing I do. No one would dare to try and sell you phony or stolen goods. But as for our house. . . . I don't suppose that during your weekend visit you met a couple named Garland and Hortense Powers?"

"They were away in San Diego when we were there, but everyone I met seems to love them. They're both about fifty, and have spent the last fifteen or twenty years building homes in various parts of the state. Their grown children and their families live in some of them, and the Powers use the others, or occasionally sell them off," Caro related. "They have three houses in Santa Barbara—two in Montecito, and one near the Santa Ynez Mountains. Which one are we being offered?"

"The letter described it as a Mediterranean-style villa overlooking the Pacific."

"I suppose it will have to do," Caro said with a mock sigh, and they dissolved into laughter.

"I love you so much," Sin said as their merriment faded away. "But do you know how I feel right now?"

"I'd say pretty much the same way you did right after we found the letter at the Linden Trees," she said, putting her arms around him. "And I love you, too. . . . so very, very much."

"That's wonderful to hear. But where is the satisfaction I'm supposed to find in having my revenge?" Sin questioned, resting his head against her shoulder. "The only thing I feel is sick."

"If you didn't feel like this," Caro comforted him, "I would think I'd married the wrong sort of man."

"I made a mistake, going after Davis. I was right that he was the weakest link, but that he was driven to suicide—"

"But that's not your fault, and Davis might have taken his life anyway."

"I know, but I can't help thinking that I should have tried to work with Curtis. You saw how he was tonight. I don't think he gives a Mexican Peso about the Consortium."

"Probably not," she agreed. "But whether or not you have some business dealings with him in the future—and the way things work, you very well may—if you'd teamed up with him now, somehow all that happened tonight would be tainted or made sour. Davis helped you because he wanted forgiveness; Curtis might have been of aid because you were the highest bidder."

"Then the first choice might have been the only one I could make and still win."

"You could have gone further than you did tonight—you could have effectively destroyed them, but all you wanted was what was rightfully yours. You didn't want to clear your father's name by slinging more mud."

"I have to admit that my original plan for revenge was a lot more bloodthirsty. That's one of the reasons why I began to go to the Little Church Around the Corner. I was becoming so transfixed by the anger and hate I felt that I couldn't center on the individuals involved. I had to get my perspective back and then keep it before I could begin to peel away the Consortium layer by layer."

With their arms around each other, they stretched out on the deeply carpeted floor. They still felt drained by the events of the past hours, but the aftereffects were fading fast.

"Do we have this room for the night?" he asked,

smiling as he gently unclasped the necklace from around her neck.

"You know we do. But do you want them to close Delmonico's down for the night around us?" she queried, wanting exactly that as her weariness began to lessen under an entirely new set of feelings.

"It might be interesting to be locked in for the night. We might even earn a mention in *Town Topics*," he said between kisses.

"Now that would be a proper send-off." Caro laughed and pulled open his perfectly tied white tie. "And we may as well find out if Delmonico's prepares breakfast!"

APR 2 1 1988

THE FINEST IN FICTION
FROM ZEBRA BOOKS!

HEART OF THE COUNTRY   (2299, $4.50)
by Greg Matthews
Winner of the 26th annual WESTERN HERITAGE AWARD for
Outstanding Novel of 1986! Critically acclaimed from coast to
coast! A grand and glorious epic saga of the American West that
NEWSWEEK Magazine called, "a stunning mesmerizing perfor-
mance," by the bestselling author of THE FURTHER ADVEN-
TURES OF HUCKLEBERRY FINN!
> "A TRIUMPHANT AND CAPTIVATING NOVEL!"
> — *KANSAS CITY STAR*

CARIBBEE   (2400, $4.50)
by Thomas Hoover
From the author of THE MOGHUL! The flames of revolution
erupt in 17th Century Barbados. A magnificent epic novel of
bold adventure, political intrigue, and passionate romance, in the
blockbuster tradition of James Clavell!
> "ACTION-PACKED . . . A ROUSING READ"
> — *PUBLISHERS WEEKLY*

MACAU   (1940, $4.50)
by Daniel Carney
A breathtaking thriller of epic scope and power set against a
background of Oriental squalor and splendor! A sweeping saga
of passion, power, and betrayal in a dark and deadly Far Eastern
breeding ground of racketeers, pimps, thieves and murderers!
> "A RIP-ROARER"
> — *LOS ANGELES TIMES*

*Available wherever paperbacks are sold, or order direct from the
Publisher. Send cover price plus 50¢ per copy for mailing and
handling to Zebra Books, Dept. 112 , 475 Park Avenue South,
New York, N.Y. 10016. Residents of New York, New Jersey and
Pennsylvania must include sales tax. DO NOT SEND CASH.*